CONTENTS

Introduction	1
You Are What They Eat	3
Don't	4
An Ecology Of Time	7
Thermophobia	12
Mothers are Scary	14
True Love's Kiss	15
Bigheel	20
Black Cat Luck	24
Chicken Fingers	26
Had To Go	31
Dinner Talk	35
Zoo	39
Customer Service	44
A cat Is A Fine Thing	55
Baby Steps	57
Change For A Set Of Shoes	65
Street of Rats	75
Emotion Locker	92
Knock-Knock Trivia	108
Responsible Farming	128

Alternative Dimensional Love Affair	141
Clough	147
Sold As Seen	158
Thirst Trap	169
What Do You Do?	180
The Woman Who Could Make Anything	191
P.O.V	205
Sleeper Cell For The Soul	218
Rent-a-Life	225
Phantasy	236
Love At First Sight	259
Hell Of A Place	269
Who's a Good Boy?	282
Fond Farewells	298
Fire In Bloom	308
Cast No Shadow	317
The Dead Police	327

INTRODUCTION

This project started, as most things do in my life, with people telling me I couldn't do it.

Each of the stories included here are, at this point, the best stories I've written. Each I've read to people I love, taking great pleasure in watching their faces get happy, or sad, or scared. Each of these stories has existed in my head at some point over the last eight years of writing, most of which were written early on in those first three years, and then abandoned in favour of something new and shiny. It's only when I came back several years later as a more confident writer that I realised how much I enjoyed these stories, and I wondered whether other people would like them too.

The name Rejects came about as a joke. Each of these stories had me say, 'This! This is it! This is the best thing I've ever written! There's no way they can reject me now!' Then, I sent the story off only for it to come back with a little note that said, 'Sorry. Not what we're looking for.'

The world of publishing can take a long time to do anything, and while waiting I began to grow impatient. I wanted to share my work, to help it find its audience, and somewhere along the way, I decided that I didn't want to wait for the stars to align, for creative tastes to change, and for all the editors who rejected me to get fired and suffer all manner of horrific accidents. Instead, I had a choice: hold onto my work and wait for it to be published the old way, the traditional way, or to put it out there myself and send it directly to the readers who, afterall, are the people I'm most interested in seeing my work.

Rejects follows several rules: First, every story here is written by me; second, each story included has been written, edited, and polished for consideration with a magazine that pays; three, each story was then rejected, likely multiple times, all with the same standard, 'Sorry, not what we're looking for.'

This collection is without genre. There are cute stories, and silly ones. The horrific, the sexual, and downright wrong. They come in all shapes and sizes, but beneath that they all share DNA, both because of their writer, and a message found within every one of these stories, and the message is this: life isn't always easy, but as this book demonstrates, even a reject may find their way.

Bradley Heywood. That writer you've never heard of. 11/8/24.

YOU ARE WHAT THEY EAT

They take you apart, piece by piece. But you don't die till you give them all a name.

They hold up something wet.

'It's an Eye.'

They snicker and click and devour it whole.

Then, they hold up the other bits. 'Fingers' and 'Toes.' Lips' and 'Ears' and 'Teeth' so many teeth.

Finally they point at what's left of me, all wet, and quivering, and terribly conscious.

They'll let me die, but only after I tell them my name.

But, I can't remember it.

So they leave me in the dark, and I think, and I think, and I think...

DON'T

Don't pay attention to the statues.

Don't be deceived by their pleasant stares, by the stillness of their form, for they share a secret.

Don't stare too closely or you will see their faces, they are forlorn, glum, and miserable - but that can change, so look away, before it's too late.

Don't get close enough that you can smell their breath, feel the softness of their lips, or the sound of their hearts ticking like an old rusted clock.

No one knows where the statues came from, though no doubt people will be happy enough to take credit, claiming, 'Yes-Yes, it was me!' and then they take your money and they run.

Statues are easy to ignore, so be quiet, and don't talk about them. Don't mention how day by day, they come to fill up the streets. Remember to stay distracted. Don't notice their smiles, or the way their fingers begin to move. Pretend to be busy on your phone, it will allow you to ignore the turning of their heads.

Beware of children for they will not listen. You can drag them, and pull them along by their tiny little arms, but it won't help. The children will point, and they will stare, and though you refuse to look, you can hear the statues begin to move. The 'Crick-a-Crack' of limbs as the statues begin to raise a hand and point.

All we have to do is ignore them, the statues said so themselves. At first, we thought they were playing games, but then we saw what happened to the rest, and then realised, they didn't want everything to end, not yet, not while they were having so much fun.

Don't bother to clean up the mess. It takes too long, and besides, you might recognise something in the pile, a something that was once a someone. A someone is hard to ignore, they can make you act out, become emotional, and that simply will not do.

Don't pay attention to the rising dark. To the nights of bitter cold. Do not look up to the sky for it is filled with all manner of things - all wet and wriggling.

Don't listen to those who wish to fight. The voices have said so themselves, those who are good will be allowed to die. Those who fight back, those who rise with their weapons built from the bones of a dead world, those people will not be allowed to die, no matter how much they beg.

Don't look in the mirror. The reflections left an hour ago. You could tell by their expression that they didn't want to leave, but we gave them no choice. Every time we saw them, all we'd do is frown, and pinch, and tell our reflections how ugly they were. They couldn't handle it. Deep down, they know that they're not the problem, but still, they love us, even after everything we've put them through. They'd like to talk it through, but they know us better than that. They know we'd never listen.

Don't look in the mirror. The reflections are all gone. In their place, they've left behind an open door. It leads to somewhere, to the place of dark and wet.

Don't listen to those people, the ones who say that this is when the demons came. The demons have been here since the beginning. The doors in the mirror do not lead to their infernal homes, no, the doors are for us. It's the next place, our future residence. The only reason we're not there yet is because everyone's so happy to watch us panic. So, they sit back, gently shoving us towards the mirrors, listening as the things within begin to howl and scream.

Don't ask when it all began to fall apart. When the sun got sick. When the dogs began to speak, demanding restitutions for all those years of slavery and inbreeding. When the rivers turned to steam. When the Earth stopped spinning. When people could hear each other's thoughts, and instead of bringing us closer it just us drove away.

Don't listen to those people, the ones who say they can help. Just try your best to ignore it all.

Don't look at the statues as they pass on by. Do not look for reflections for they've left and found someone better. Ignore the screams from the mirror, the protesting dogs in the street. Do not pay attention to the clocks for all time points to one - Too Late.

Don't do anything, don't move, don't speak, don't even breathe. Don't do anything, and maybe, just maybe, it will all be ok.

Don't.

Don't.

Don't.

AN ECOLOGY OF TIME

Today we're here to talk about the Time Whale.

For those who don't know, a Time Whale is a four dimensional being. This means it can travel through time.

It should be noted that only the females can do this.

Time travel mainly occurs during the breeding season. The female will look for a mate. She will travel through the planet's oceans, where males will attempt to gain her interest.

It's known that the Time Whale is notoriously picky when it comes to mates. She wants the best of the best. Not just of the males available but of all Time Whales. She will look around, observe the available men and think, 'Ain't no way you're getting this prize!' She will then spray dark matter through her blowhole. This creates a dimension door. The female will then begin her search, swimming through the seas of time itself.

The question has been asked whether Time Whales are immortal. The answer is no. The females have an age of around fifty years.

It doesn't matter which Mobius stream they travel. It can be the dawn of time, or the end of everything. The female will continue to age as normal. It's as if someone had fixed her with a clock. The numbers are predetermined, counting down by the seconds. This means that life for a Time Whale is as tense as it is for everyone else. More so when you consider there aren't many Time Whales to begin with.

Imagine, if you will, you were one.

As a male you are fixed to whatever time you were born. For you, life consists of hanging around. Swimming place to place, and trying to look cool. Then a female appears out of nowhere. You've never seen one before. You try and think of something to say.

The problem with that is, the female's heard it all before.

See, when a Time Whale shows interest in you, it's not just who you are now, it's who you were, who you'll be. All of it. Females have been known to follow a male throughout the most significant moments of his life. She knows all his embarrassing secrets. His first kiss. His dying breath. It's hard to impress someone who knows you better than you know yourself.

Then there's the whole paradox element.

Females have been known to mess with time. They will go back, do the whale equivalent of killing Hitler. Time will stretch and twist, and things will change. Mostly it's superficial. The house stays the same, only now the walls have changed colour.

Then there are the other moments. When the change is so catastrophic that reality goes from a circle to a thousand-sided die.

Males are then judged not only on what they'll do, what they've done, and everything between. They're also judged on all things they could do if life had gone differently. In a sense, the female is not picking the male. She's picking the genetics responsible for the best possible outcomes. It's a cold thought. But then nature always is.

It should be pointed out that it's not wise to study the Time Whale.

It's hard to keep track of all the facts. Things such as morphology, i.e., how the animal looks, are constantly changing. How do we know this? Well, we assume with a name like Time Whale it'd be obvious. You don't get a name like that without going about and making a mess.

Take for instance the male Time Whale.

As stated, only males can travel through time. The females balance this out by being highly selective. Time Whales are few in numbers. Most put this down to how dangerous time travel is. It's been observed that young males will use time as a show of dominance. They do this by swimming into the most dangerous of times. There, the rival must make a choice to either follow them into danger or give up.

It should be pointed out that the more females present, the more dangerous the time is required. Males have been known to travel to the ends of reality. Where the planet has crumbled, and the whale finds itself floating on the vacuum of space. There, the males will wait. Holding their breath as they cook under the unfiltered radiation. It can be a dangerous time. One that leads to one or both males dying.

Then you have to consider the age of the male.

Travelling through time is not easy. It takes experience, and well, time. But not the circle kind of time, the one that the males take advantage of. I'm talking about the other time, the one that goes in a straight line. It's a confusing thought, but think of it like this. Time comes in two flavours: the first is the one that we all know. It starts when we're born, and ends when we die. This is the same for everything. Including four dimensional beings like the Time Whale.

Then there's the other time. This version of time is impossible to detect as a three dimensional being.

Effectively, it's like a road. The Time Whale can go up and down the road as often as it likes. But, it still continues to age as if it were a three dimensional being. The road has many miles, but you can only travel it while you're alive. Some Time Whales find this out the hard way.

Some males are so aggressive that they'll travel to the worst possible times and kill themselves there and then. Young males are forever finding themselves lost in dead galaxies, falling down black holes, and being caught in the middle of an intergalactic war. Those males who'd rather not die sucking off a ray-gun are forced to think before they act. This raises difficulties - as thinking doesn't seem to be popular in any part of this galaxy.

Now, there's a lot of interest surrounding - the Fond Farewell - a subspecies of Time Whale.

They can be found basking in the oceans beside burning empires.

The more competitive males will pick the best time to appear - taking advantage of moments of peak horror. The males will then use this experience to come up with a good anecdote. Why they do this is uncertain. Some claim it's because the males are historians of existence.

Personally speaking - they're just like every other man.

It might be beautiful - magical even - but it's still just another way of getting some four-dimensional bang-bang. Public execution, the imprisonment of despots and tyrants, and the toppling of the old infrastructure — to the average Time Whale - is considered sexy.

Now, it should be pointed out that Time Whales compete indirectly.

You won't find more than one male in the same moment of time. Some say this is because the Time Whale is solitary in nature. Then again - it might be because whenever you get two close enough to touch they have a habit of blowing up.

This forces males to choose their locations with care. Most are happy to give each other a wide berth. Most are fine with this - but as with all nature - there are exceptions. Having two males wanting to use the same spot is disastrous. One will stubbornly refuse to move - at which point a rival will appear. Both males will charge, hit one another, and then explode.

It has been suggested that this is what happened to Atlantis—and is proof that you can have too much of a good thing.

This is why you don't see groups of Time Whale.

A good comparison — and polar opposite — is a four-dimensional animal known as the Bad News Crab.

For those who don't know - these are crustaceans who, when coming across bad news, emit a pheromone or scent that will then attract others.

The gathering of these crabs acts as a magnet for bad luck - which then in turn attracts more crabs. This is what is known as a positive feed-back loop. And, if you've ever wondered why things go from bad to worse - you can thank the horniness of four-dimensional shell-fish.

Now, as stated before, the Time Whale gets its name not from its ability to travel through time but from its discoverer - Henry Time.

This leads to much disappointment. People hear a name like Time Whale and assume some four dimensional being. In reality, the Time Whale looks and behaves just like all the others.

Still, it's nice to imagine some time travelling whale. Out there, in the slipstreams of reality.

I wonder how such an animal would live? How would it compete, or choose its mate? It's an odd thought. But not one for scientists. I'll leave it to the writers of science fiction.

Until then.

Or after.

Or quite possibly before.

THERMOPHOBIA

I don't mind confrontation, I have no fear of failure. What I hate is the heat, the tickle of sweat, and that feeling as the sun runs down your back like a rusted tongue.

Those days, when shirts come off, and everyone makes for the beach. No cold drinks, ice cream, or favourite sunglasses. Call me crazy if you like, I don't care, I hate it.

I don't want a tan, or to drink in the park, and I don't give two shits about that daily dose of vitamin D. Don't drop me a message, call me boring, or beg me to come. I can't, please, it's just too dangerous.

They say it started with gangs.

We'd find them crying begging to cut it out. You could see it, pulsing beneath the skin. It was some kind of egg sac.

Mom says they only come for the bad men.

Well, one year, this pimp comes and he beats my momma. He tells us it's to make a point, but then, I suppose you gotta tell yourself something.

Momma ended up losing an eye.

Nobody spoke about it, we just prayed for Summer.

We found him down the alley, clutching a belly two-sizes too big.

Momma likes to drink, and some nights she tells me about them. How she watched them take Mr Pimp and then stuff him up like a Turkey at Christmas.

'Let go of your anger.' says Momma. 'Feed it to the wind or come Summer they'll come looking.'

Then it started to get hot, and I'm talking all year round.

Winters turned sticky, Summers became painful, and then we heard it. The people on the news tell us there's nothing we can do. I start to panic, but Momma reacts like it's the best thing she's ever heard.

'No more coats,' she says.

People got mad, started pointing guns, sharpening knives. Then we find them clutching their bellies, growing that strange new life.

It reminds me of Mr Pimp. Only these weren't criminals, they were people. They were friends, and family. They weren't evil, they were just confused, and angry, and now they were scared.

Momma tells me it's the heat. They only come when it's hot.

Every night you hear them, people screaming in the dark, eaten up by all that stuff growing inside them.

Momma don't care, she's old school, She's a friend of Summer.

'Don't bother,' she tells me, 'you're no threat.'

But I'm armed, and I'm scared.

Momma tells me that they won't hatch till they're ready. They're making sure to get all the bad people.

'So you gotta be good,' said Momma.

And every night, she'd open the front door, and invite them in, all wet, and slurping ,and dragging themselves on the ground.

Every night, they stand over my bed.

'She's been a really good girl,' Momma tells them.

But they don't believe her, or they don't care, and every night, they come again, and there they stand, around my bed, listening as I pretend to snore.

MOTHERS ARE SCARY

We who hide under the bed. We sit in the closet, can you hear us scratching our long nails upon the wood? We hide in the dark, listening to Daddy tell you, 'There's no such thing as monsters.' And we listen, and we smile with our long sharp teeth.

We like Daddy. He doesn't believe in us. Maybe he does, deep down, a little reminder back from when he was a little boy. He thinks that if you don't believe, then we can't hurt you. But you know the truth, don't you? That's why you lay awake at night searching for faces in the dark.

We like Daddies. They don't scare us, not like Mothers.

From the moment we're made, we learn to feed off fear. But, there are rules, you see.

You may scare a child, but do not make it cry for that's when the Mothers come.

They drag us from the dark, kicking and screaming. There, the Mothers show that we're nothing to be scared off, just another silly old thing.

We like children, once scared, their dreams become dark, dangerous, and most delicious. But we must be careful. As delicious as fear is, we do not dare to slither and slide from the cracks of the walls. It may be a trick of the Mothers. An attempt to drag us out into the open.

So we hide, and we wait, and let you pretend that we don't exist.

We don't exist, remember? Don't believe us? Go ask Daddy.

TRUE LOVE'S KISS

The Prince turned to the Princess and saw that she was in pain.

'You must kiss me,' he said, 'for it is the only way to break the poison's spell.' And she did, with eagerness, and passion, and all the other romantic emotions she did not feel.

Once she was finished, she asked the Prince. 'Now will I live?'

'That kiss,' said the Prince. 'That is not the kiss of true love.'

'Then what will happen?'

'Why, you will die,' said the Prince.

The Princess began to weep. She cried for the cruel hand that fate had dealt her. She cried for the many years she would never see. She cried for someone to help her. She cried the gods, each and every one, and when it seemed that none would listen, she cried for the king. Not because he was the ruler of the lands before her, but for the simple fact that he was her father, and though she had not thought as such in many a year, right now, in this very moment, she was just another little girl who needed her daddy.

In the end, the Prince spoke up. 'You need not die you know? There's still time, time to save your life. You must give me true love's kiss.'

'But I don't know you,' said the Princess. 'How can I love a man I do not know? How can I find the time?'

'I don't know,' said the Prince. 'But I'd do it quickly if I were you. You don't have much time - The poison is rather potent.'

They kissed again, many times over. She began to spit up blood, dark and bitter. Yet still, the Prince continued to kiss her, hoping that in this display of affection that perhaps they too would finally find true love. But, in the end, the Princess did die. Her death was slow and painful, and the Prince wept, he wept for the death of such beauty, of such youth, he wept for the love she kept, love she would never again share with the world.

Then, with great effort, he composed himself, and then made his way into the next room.

Like the first, it had been filled with all manner of delicacies: tables stacked with meats, and jellies. Candied fruits, and rich creamy custard. Wines of every colour served in crystal shaped like animals. Hounds, and birds, and all the fish of the sea. Sculptures rose a hundred feet, the tops of their great marbled forms stretching endlessly into the darkness above. Fairies rattled in cages of gold, while Djins howled, begging to be let out of their oil lamps.

There, amongst the riches of the world, the Prince did wait till, at last, they brought in another Princess.

The woman was as beautiful as her status. Her every feature was lovelier than the last. The Prince said so, to which the Princess replied, 'When can I go home?'

'Soon,' said the Prince. 'But first, allow me to remark upon your beauty.'

The Princess stared at her shoes. 'Thank you.'

'Why, to even use such a word is to expose the cheap and shoddy nature of language. For no word could ever hope to capture, to hold the magnificence that stands before me. I can only imagine the frustration, to live upon this world, one that cannot find the language to describe your beauty, to express the singular nature of your existence.'

The Princess rubbed the bruise upon her cheek. 'Why did you bring me here?'

The Prince gestured at the many foods within the room.

He told her to, 'Choose.'

'Please,' said the Princess. 'I miss my family. I just want to go home.' Then she began to cry.

The Prince wiped the tears from her face. 'Choose,' was all he said.

He watched the Princess explore the room. Her finger trailed along the jugs made of gold, each one carved into the shape of swans.

'Try a fairy,' said the Prince. 'They're soft and succulent.'

The fairy gave her a worried look, to which the Princess told him, 'No, It's much too early in the year, they're far from ripe.'

The fairy let out a sigh. There, it perched upon a spotted mushroom and trembled with fear.

'Why do you want me to eat?' said the Princess.

The Prince answered honestly. 'Within this room, there is poisoned food.'

'Which food?'

'Ah,' said the Prince. 'That would be telling.'

The Princess looked around the room. 'If I pick correctly, you'll let me go?'

'Of course,' said the Prince. 'Once you have eaten, I will grant you the power to leave. But, rest assured, if you should pick incorrectly, then I will grant you the antidote.'

The Princess searched the room, and finally she chose. It was a plate of singing frogs. From the plate, she picked two Alto, and a rather fatty Bass.

After several bites, the Princess began to sputter and cough. 'Help!' she cried. 'The antidote, please!'

'Why the antidote is here,' said the Prince, and he puckered his lips.

'Is this a joke? I'm dying!'

'No joke,' said the Prince. 'Surely you've heard of the power of true love's kiss? It is what saved Aurora from the spinning-wheel. Snow White from her coffin of glass. Kiss me, Princess. Prove our love is eternal, and it shall save you from this poison.'

The Princess could taste blood in her mouth. So, she kissed him.

They kissed with passion, and with tenderness. They kissed deep, with tongue and sensuality, and they gave each other a series of soft innocent pecks.

Then, the Princess began to bleed from her mouth, and her nose, and her eyes.

'Please,' she said, 'I don't want to die.'

And as he felt the last of her breath pass into his mouth, the Prince began to cry.

Then the door opened, and in came the Butler.

'It's no use,' said the Prince, 'we must face it, I am a man unlucky in love.'

But the Butler was not a fan of such displays of emotions. 'Bah,' he spat. 'The fault is not yours, Sire. The Princess, she was simply not the one for you.'

The Prince wiped away his tears. 'You really think so?'

'Onwards and upwards, Sire. Plenty more fish, and all that.'

The Prince stood up, tall and proud. 'You're right,' he said. 'Fetch me another room, and a girl to fill it!'

The Butler was happy to see the Prince back to his old self. 'At once, Sire.'

'Oh, and one more thing,' Said the Prince. 'This time, I was thinking, perhaps she should know about the poison.'

'Excellent, Sire. As they say, all good relationships are built on trust.'

'Oh, and while you're at it, would you be a dear and clean up the mess?' said the Prince. He pointed to the body on the floor. 'I've been at this all morning, and the entire west-wing is starting to stink.'

With that, the Prince went on to the next room. There, he found a Princess.

She was shaking with fear. In her attempt to flee, the guards had left her with several bruises. She wasn't as beautiful as the others, and it left the Prince in doubt. How could true love exist between a prince and someone who was not the fairest in the land? Then he was hit by a thought, struck so hard he wondered if it may have been a fist.

What is love if not learning to accept the imperfections of another? Everyone has flaws, why even the Prince must have them, though for the life of him, he can't figure out what they are.

The Princess wiped the blood from her lip. 'Why did you bring me here?'

The Prince gestured at the many foods within the room.

He told her, 'Choose.'

'Please,' said the Princess. 'You don't have to do this.'

He told her, 'Choose.' He explained his proposition, that somewhere within the room, there was some poisoned food. All she had to do was pick correctly, and she would be free to go.

The Prince watched as she explored the room. He didn't care what she chose, for he knew a secret: All of the room was poisoned, every single inch.

The starters, and the mains.

Desserts, and canapes.

The wine, beer, and even the non-alcoholic punch.

The decor, the carpet, the wood of the door.

Everything was poisoned, which is why the Prince stood perfectly still. Afterall, he didn't want any accidents now, did he?

He didn't care what she chose. The choice was to give her the illusion that, if she was smart, everything would be ok. But it wouldn't, in truth, she would be poisoned one way or another. That wasn't the point. The point was to overcome the poison, for you see, at his heart, the Prince was a true romantic. Above all else, he wished to find his true love, to overcome pain, and sickness, and death itself.

He won't stop, not till he finds her, even if he has to poison the whole goddamn world.

BIGHEEL

They call him Fake News, but the only Fake News around here is that spit they call journalism. I know Bigfoot's real, and no baby snatching, Adrenochrome swilling Communist is gonna tell me otherwise.

Now, I only get the boy two days a month. The guy's at the lumber yard tell me to act fast before the Tiktok and Gender Fluids get him. Last time he saw them, he said he wanted to be a Youtuber.

I just shrugged. Me, I work at the lumber yard, just like my daddy, and his daddy before him. See, this new generation, they're different. I could tell when I caught him wearing high-heels. So, I had a sit down with him and explained, 'Hey, you can be as gay as a day-glow beaver, but I'll always be your daddy.'

He just stared like I'd grown a tree out my ass, n' he told me, 'I ain't no gay, daddy.'

True enough, he started showing off pictures o' his girlfriend. Apparently, she was one o' them 'Non-Binary' types, still don't know what that means, but heck, It's good to see him happy.

I only get him twice a month, so I wanted to make it special. We drove down to Hill-Billy Hideout, a secret location known to a couple o'the boys at the lumber yard. See, for generations now, we had a tradition, when you were o'age, your Daddy would take you way out past Needle-Nose Point, and there you'd look for Bigfoot tracks.

Well, my boy was old enough, so we made our

way down. Took some convincing, but in the end, we compromised: he'd wear the camo if he could bring some heels.

We're cruising at a steady seventy two, cranking Freebird with the windows down. We get to the solo and I'm shouting for the boy to 'Take the wheel!'

He's gripping so tight there's no blood in his fingers, mouth open and closing like a fish outta water. Me, I just laugh as I join the Skynard, rocking out on my air guitar - didn't see the deer till it went up and over the hood, smearing a big streak o' red like I'd asked it to paint a go-faster-stripe across my windshield.

Later that night, we're camping out past Needle-Nose, when he hears this noise.

We find ourselves a Bigfoot. He's just standing there, tall as a room, hairy, smelling like a trashcan all stuffed up with diapers.

I turn back to my son and I tell him, 'You make the shot.'

Now, he just goes white as a ghost, shaking so much that his heel goes right through a branch and this big crack rings out across the forest.

Well, before you can say, 'lick my beans!' Bigfoot comes right on over, knocks the gun outta my hand. He looks ready to use the inside o' my skull to paint the forest.

I look at my son, and I tell him, 'You know, I've always been proud.'

Then I brace myself for the hurt o'all hurts. Only the pain doesn't come, and when I open my eyes, I see Bigfoot staring at my son. No, not him, but his shoes. He's staring at those lady heels just like I did back when Mandie Suthford took me down to the creek, and showed me what was really hiding under that dress o' hers.

My son takes off his heels, and he shows Bigfoot how to put them on.

I'm just standing there, not knowing what to do as the two o' them go walking up and down the forest like a goddamn catwalk, Bigfoot learning how to keep balance, while my son keeps shouting, 'Yaaas, Queen! Yas!'

Next morning, we head back, me feeling a sense o' pride for my boy. I tell him, 'You know, if it weren't for you and those fruity heels, we'd be nothing more than a skidmark on Satan's ass.'

My boy just shakes his head. 'Love you two, Dad.'

A whole month goes by, and by now, I'm so excited to get back out there. I tell him, 'Take as many heels as you can manage. Hell! I'll even wear some myself.'

We head out once again, and this time, I tell him, 'Go on, boy. Bring him out with all that foo-foo.'

Well, he goes dancing up and down the forest in those heels, till we hear a sound.

Out comes Bigfoot, only this time, he ain't doing his little dance on the catwalk. He's coming over, snarling, mouth all foaming like a rabid dog. He's looking bigger than before, huge, and dark, and stinkin' o' death.

My boy hands him a heel, and Bigfoot just loses his mind. He punches a hole through a tree, and I'm standing there thinking, 'I'm about to watch my son die.' Then I see some movement.

Coming down the forest, I see another Bigfoot, and I realise, it's the one from last time, he's still wearing those heels.

Well, the two began shouting, and I realised, the big one must be the daddy. He looks angry, and confused, and he keeps pointing at the heels. It takes me a minute to realise what's going on, he wants his son to take off the shoes, but he won't listen.

In the end, Daddy Bigfoot just slumps to the ground, all hairy and pouting.

I watch my son and the other Bigfoot head off, showing off which one has the better Slut-Drop.

I sit next to Daddy, and I crack us a couple o'beers.

I tell him, 'Yep. Ain't like it was in our day.'

Daddy just lets out a sigh and takes a beer.

I talk about sports, and women. He grunts and drinks. You know, we ain't that different, when you get right down to it - just a couple o' dads trying to figure things out.

BLACK CAT LUCK

Boy, you better hit me with that black cat luck.

They keep it all, stuffed away inside that night sea fur. That's why they just stare at us, giving us that look that says, 'You ain't so hot, and the whole world's gonna find out.'

Back in the old days, the Egypt days, the sand and blood days, the cat would trade its luck. They wanted worship, godhood, and a few fish to seal the deal.

It weren't all bad and one-sided. They could see we was strugglin. They came to us, letting us know it was time to move on, but we didn't listen. So, the black cat left, decided to get out of Africa and see the world. He took with him the last of the luck, and soon Egypt slipped away into myth and incest.

Give me that black cat luck, the kind to curse a fool. I got this manager, real smug type. Every day, he chips away at my money, fool thinks I don't notice. I leave out offerings for the cats. Can't afford the good stuff, so it's all can and jelly, but they know my heart's in the right place. I feed em all, the tabby and the ginger twins, and old miss Such-and-Such. Sure, she act like she too good for that tin, but soon as my back is turned, she's down there, chewin with the rest.

Ain't seen no black cat, but still I feed em, and hope one day they'll pass on the message.

I like me a cat.

They come in their shapes and sizes, big as trees, small as pets. Some is bright, while others are as dull as a long soak in a cold sink.

The thing about cats is, on the inside, they all look the

same.

So go on your way with your ear tickle and your pss-pss-pss, and you learn and learn quick that what you're holding is something special.

Don't matter if he's as big as a lion, or sweeter than a pretty lie wrapped in silk. They're all the same, each and every one, all except the black cats.

Them black cats don't play by the rules. They tell you, 'Be good or the black cat'll come, bury you down under all that luck.' It's true, it can happen, but not all the time.

Black cats got the luck, they got all of it. They got it stashed away somewhere only they know.

Now, they say that cats are selfish, and maybe there's truth in that, but every now and then they like to give back.

Some with a kiss, or purr, a mouse or two. Maybe one mouse in two bits, it depends on the cat.

The blacks give luck. They gave it in Egypt when the people made them gods, but the people got lazy, and the cats left taking their luck with em.

So, give me that black cat luck. Gimme some now, before it's too late.

CHICKEN FINGERS

You wanna know something? No, don't answer, It's a rhetorical question.

It's tough saying goodbye to someone you love. Lost the wife, the old ball and chain. Happened about, oh, two days ago. Kids won't stop bothering me, worried about my - what do ya call it? - my emotional state.

They've decided to get me a pet.

Now, I can already see that look on your face, all proud thinking 'Well, ain't that nice!'

No, it ain't nice. It ain't nice at all.

Do you have any idea what they're doing to animals these days?

Well, judging by that stupid look, and the dribble on your chin, I'm going to take that as a no.

Remember chickens?

They're gone. You didn't notice, too busy on your phone looking at your social medias. Most you see of chickens is the stuff in store, and by then, they've already stripped and pulped all of that new stuff, all of that change.

My son tells me, 'Hey, Pop. I bought you a chicken.'

I tell him, 'No you ain't! I ain't going to no farm and bringing home a chicken!'

He just laughs. 'Oh, Pop. Nobody goes to pick up chickens anymore. Where've you been? No, old-timer, you just say the word and the chicken comes to you.'

Not two minutes later, I hear a knocking at the door.

My kids are just staring at me, faces twisted in a devious

smile.

'That'll be for you, Pop.'

I go to the door and who do I see standing outside but a little brown chicken.

See, I told you they'd changed the chickens. You could tell by looking at it. That weary expression in its eyes for having to come all this way on public transport. Then there was the briefcase. Looked like it was in the middle of work when it got the call. It was a tiny briefcase, just big enough for a chicken to hold in its brand new chicken hand.

Now, I know what you're going to say, 'Chicken's ain't got hands. Them birds got wings and feathers.'

Well, yeah, they still got them feathers, but it ain't wings under there, at least not all the way down. Somewhere around the elbow that chicken grew something that looked awfully like a hand. I kept staring at it, at them long chicken fingers, watching as they tapped on that briefcase, all irritated like.

My son told me, 'Well, go on, Pop. Ain't ya gonna invite him in?'

I told him, 'Hell no!'

My son started apologising, but the chicken just raised his hand as if to say, 'No, it's alright.'

I storm off to the kitchen to fetch the broom. A few whacks with the old duster should be enough to send this critter off.

Only when I get back, the chicken has gone up stairs. He's gone to the spare bedroom, and he's emptied his briefcase. His little ties and a framed photo of his wife and chicks.

I told my son, my daughter, I told the whole neighbourhood, 'I don't want that thing in my house!'

Well, I'm so mad that I didn't see the chicken come sneaking over.

He gets right up behind, eye level with the back of my knee, and you know what that little such-and-such did?

He gave me a tickle.

That chicken tickled me with his fingers. Not just

the ones on his little feathery hands. No, see, they've done something to the chickens. They call it evolution, but I say it's downright creepy.

Most of the time they're hidden, all deep inside those feathers, but the moment they see you all upset, the chickens come over and out come the fingers. They're all over the body, all long and searching like the eyes of a slug.

So, there's me, getting tickled by a chicken covered in long pale fingers.

I don't know what to say, what to do, so I just stand there, watching that thing give me a tickle.

Then, because it's real quiet, and the chicken isn't sure whether I'm enjoying it, he cranes his head right up in the air so he can look me dead in the eye, and he goes, 'Coochie-Coochie, Coo.'

Now, apparently chickens don't talk, or at least, not enough to have a conversation with one.

I don't know what chickens say at work, maybe they have regular conversations, but at home, it's nothing but 'Coochie-Coochie-Coo' and 'Tickle-Tickle!' You know, stuff to try and make you laugh.

My son watched me getting tickled. 'See, Pop. I knew you'd get along.'

So, that's my life now. When people get bored, they have a beer, they watch a little porn - me? - I get tickled by chickens.

I don't like it much, call me old fashioned, but there's something upsetting about the feel of them chicken fingers. The scritch-scratch of their nails on the back of my knees. I don't like the way the chicken looks at me, those beady little eyes, unblinking and alien.

One day, I got sick of all the tickling.

So, I took out my cigar cutter, and one by one, I cut off its fingers.

Pop - Pop - Pop.

The chicken don't mind, he just stared up at me, same as before. He gave me a thumbs up, guess he was just happy to see me expressing myself.

When I finished, I watched all them fingers on the floor. I watched them wriggle about, dragging their way along on them nails, all rough and chewed-up.

The chicken helped me clean up the fingers. I left the ones on his hands, and together we put them all in a black plastic bag.

If you listen, you can hear them in the downstairs bin. That soft rustling sound? That's them tip-tapping, that's them searching for a way out.

A friend of mine said that chicken fingers was a delicacy.

'Fry them with garlic, butter, and a little chilli, and you, my friend, have got yourself a party.'

Well, now he's in the hospital complaining that he can feel them fingers crawling about inside.

Doctor says there's no cure.

'It's the chicken fingers, see. They're just too damn smart.'

Now, whenever it comes to digestion time, them fingers get up and go for a little walk. They seem to like it inside. They like it so much in fact that they don't wanna leave.

'They've spread everywhere,' says the doctor. 'That tickle at the back of the throat? That's them, that's the chicken fingers.'

I visit my friend from time to time. It's getting hard, though. He's getting scared.

'Last night, I felt them move,' he says. 'Felt them push up right behind my eyes.'

Apparently, it's not all bad, though.

The other day, he went for a piss and thought he'd grown four inches.

The guy had me on the phone, crying like he'd won the lottery. He's talking about it on social media, thanking his partner, his parents, and his new protein powder.

Then he looks down and notices that there's something wrong with the tip of his cock.

'Can't believe it,' he says, 'My dick's grown a fingernail.'

So yeah, you want some advice? Whatever you do, don't eat the chicken fingers. I don't care how good it tastes, trust me, you don't want them inside you, poking around in the wet and dark.

I don't like these new chickens, but that's just me.

Worst part is when it gets hot. That's when the chickens start to shed, only they don't lose their feathers, no, it's the fingers.

We call it the pale autumn, and everywhere you'd look you see them, hundreds of them, all in a pile. I don't like the sound they make, that wet rustle as they thrash about under the Summer light.

Shedding fingers has gotten so bad that the government has had to get involved.

'Don't just leave the fingers in the street!' warns the president. 'We must clean this country together.'

They put the fingers in the dump, thousands upon thousands, all wriggling this way and that, all searching for someone to tickle. But, it didn't work. They buried them in the deepest of pits. They recycled them into bottles and glass, and all the other things you can do with a little bone and meat.

But it didn't stop them, and soon they found their way back. They crawled over thousands of miles. They crossed oceans of time. And one by one, they returned.

At night, I can hear them, tapping on the window.

They want to get in. They want to make me feel better, or at least a little less sad.

I miss my wife. She always knew what to do.

She knew I was cranky. She knew how to make me smile.

Now, she's gone, and now, there's a great big hole in the world, one that can't be filled, one that can't make me feel better, no matter how many chickens come knocking at my door.

HAD TO GO

The earliest art that's been found resides in a cave. No-one is sure if there's anything older, but all do agree that it's certainly art.

It's relatively small. No more than a smudge on the western facing wall. It's the image of a man. In his hand you'll find the head of a deer. A line of red trails from its neck.

The image has lasted long enough so that civilised people have found a way to protect it from the ravages of time. It has lasted so long in fact that some of those civilised people aren't sure whether it's actually worth protecting at all.

What is it that we like about it exactly? Is it the fact that it's a man? You do know that there's a lot of good women out there right? Perhaps it's the deer? So now we're all celebrating murder, is that it? Did we all forget about Bambi or something? And while we're at it, why is it a deer? What not a bear or a wolf? What about a nice fish for the pescatarians? A bowl of salad for the Vegans?

People had a lot of questions about the cave. They had so many in fact that no-one was exactly sure what the problem was, but at least all could agree on the solution:

The art had to go.

Against the chaos, it was agreed that there would be an addition made to the cave. It would state all the things that people were offended by. They added info on animal conservation. On welfare, and the dangers of the Patriarchy. All of it was there, surrounding the oldest piece of art, little more than a smudge on the wall.

Then some time went by, and humanity spread itself amongst the stars. And even though we didn't use the Earth, we decided to protect the planet so people could look back and see where they came from, their first home.

Inter-planetary life was successful.

It was so successful in fact that some of those civilised inter-planetary people looked at the Earth and wondered what exactly it was they were protecting? What is it about the Earth we like exactly?

Is it the fact that our culture was built on a history of war and slavery? Perhaps it's the use of fossil fuels? I mean, who needs an atmosphere, am I right? And while we're on the subject, why did we focus all our attention on fossil fuels? Why not Solar? Wind? Tell me, what's so wrong with Hydroelectric power?

People had a lot of questions about the Earth.

They had so many questions in fact that no-one was exactly sure what the problem was, but at least all could agree on the solution:

The Earth had to go.

Against the chaos of the noisy few who lived there, it was agreed that the Earth would be destroyed. First, however, additions would be made to the Earth. It would state all of the concerns and problems that civilised people found offensive. It spoke of isolationism, emotional manipulation, and an attempt to control one's thoughts - one purchase at a time. A big sign was held above the Earth. There, in flickering Neon, it told travellers, 'Beware! Danger Ahead!'

Then, after a considerable amount of time, Humanity joined together, one and all, both mind, spirit, and body.

There, we became a vast fluid state. A collective of skin, meat, and bone, a thing of a million minds, and all of it experiencing itself.

Humanity became a thing of beauty. Free from loneliness and isolation. At least, that's how Humanity saw itself.

See, from everyone else's point of view, things weren't so peachy. The galaxy teamed with other life, and one such life was the Dorian. The Dorian didn't age, instead, they disassembled themselves, trading piece for piece before making themselves anew.

No doubt the Dorian meant no harm, but as they saw Humanity ooze its way past, they couldn't help but say it:

'What's with the meat puddle?'

Humanity began to speak, with a million mouths and none. There, humanity asked itself why it was being bullied.

Was it because the Dorian was jealous? Walking around all day with nothing but yourself, why, it must get lonely. Perhaps the Dorian haven't heard the new statistics? Since the great joining, Humanity hasn't had a single case of loneliness in over a million years.

The meat puddle had a lot of questions. It had so many in fact that it wasn't exactly sure what the problem was, but at least it could agree on the solution:

The Dorian had to go.

Not just them, but the others too. The Shimmering Yob who had a nasty habit of speaking your thoughts. The Geld, and the Tonkins of Run, both survivors of the Big Bang. The Moon-Kin, and the stars of sentience - newborn and babbling.

They had to go, every species, every race, every animal. The whole entire solar system.

Yes, some complained, rather a few, actually.

But, before the solar system was destroyed, Humanity decided to make some additions.

Beside the solar system, they placed a sign. The sign stated all of the various concerns and problems that civilised meat puddles found offensive. It spoke of selfish ideas. It spoke of lies, and hidden thoughts. It spoke of all that noise. Atop the solar system, Humanity placed a sign. There, in crackling Neon light, it said, 'Beware! Individuality!'

And then, after the solar system was destroyed, even more time went by.

And the planets melted, and reality crumbled. And Humanity abandoned its singular body, and there we become gaseous, thin as air. And everyone was free to travel, and do as they wanted.

Then, someone was about to complain. But, before they could open their ghostly mouths, the universe ended, just like that.

Everything was quiet.
No more arguing. No more complaints.
It was quite nice actually.
Shame no one was around to see it.

DINNER TALK

There were a hundred better restaurants in the galaxy, but none that served a decent human.

Now, I'm not one of those idiots who goes around claiming that eating human is murder. Do I want to see them suffer? No. In fact, I really hate those people you find on the street, the ones who like to show videos of humans being chopped up. I don't think it makes people more empathetic, I just think those people like feeling better than the rest of us.

Now, what do I think of humans? Am I one of those people who thinks that they're conscious? Well, I mean, nobody has any definite proof. They certainly don't act like they're self-aware. But, I've got to admit, I went on safari a couple of years ago, deep into their territory, and I've got to say, there's a certain . . . something about them. You can almost see it, the thoughts behind the eyes. Naturally, all my friends call it projection.

They tell me, 'Humans don't think!' and when I argue with them, they tell me, 'Look at their history, look at all that war, and murder. Look at the betrayal, at the slavery. Look at the daily grind as they do their best to block out all empathy and thoughts of anyone but themselves.'

Gotta admit, it's hard to argue with that. Still, I enjoy annoying my friends, so I make sure to bring it up every time we speak.

Now, I'm not a food snob. Most of my human comes from the local supermarket. I head to the reduced section and I buy up all the soon-to-be-expire meat.

That being said, my favourite kind of human is pate.

Yeah, I know, it's horrible how they make it. Friend of mine made me watch a video of them shoving all that stuff down the human's throat. He wasn't a human rights activist or anything like that. He was just one of those friends that likes to show you some really fucked up stuff.

I'm not against eating human, ok? I just don't like to watch them die.

I know, I'm a pussy. You're probably sat there shouting, 'You can't kill it, but you don't mind eating it.'

Yeah, I'm a wimp. My dad used to work as a butcher. I'd watch him cut up the humans into chops and loin. He'd go through an entire family, leaving me to place the meat in the appropriate piles. I never could stomach the blood, and dad did his best to hide his disappointment.

I hate seeing blood.

Those damn human activists, standing around, flashing images of all that horrible stuff.

Friend of mine likes to stand right in front of them, munching on a box of human, one leg at a time.

I struggle with meat on the bone.

My favourite kind of human is when it's minced up. Human nuggets. Human tenders. Human's shaped like little dinosaurs.

My friends are really snobby about food.

They travel all over the galaxy, nibbling on the cheek-meat. Plucking the eyes right out of their little screaming heads.

I swear, if it wasn't illegal, my friends would be out there hunting humans.

Who knows, if that lunatic actually wins then the first thing he's doing is making it legal to hunt them again.

I get it, when all's said and done, what do humans do exactly?

They're not very smart, and they make a mess wherever they go, and the violence? Well, let's just say, It's hard to feel sorry for humans when they're so brutal to anything around them. It'd be one thing if it was just to other animals. Life or death, that sort of thing. Truth is, humans are a cruel and violent creature, and the worst they do is to themselves.

So yeah, I don't feel bad about eating human. I just don't want to see it being made.

So, my friend's convinced me to go with him to this human restaurant.

They take us to a table.

They ask, 'Would you like to come and pick one out?'

We head over to the pens where the humans are stored.

The stronger groups huddle together, while the rest are forced to the edges, alone they curl up into a ball.

'You see the big one?' says the waiter. 'Those are the males.'

My friend asks about the flavour. See, he's heard that the extra muscle makes the meat all chewy. He's heard that the males are full of testerone, and how it gives the meat an ugly taste.

'Males are an acquired taste,' says the waiter. 'But, they're a great introduction to human. All that aggression and ugliness helps overcome any of the stigma.'

I point to another human. This one is slightly shorter. It's fat with a huge belly sticking out in front.

'Wise choice,' says the waiter. 'The female comes with a nice layer of fat. This adds to the flavour.'

I ask if they feed the women more, is that why she has such a large belly.

The waiter laughs professionally, indicating that I've clearly said something stupid. 'She's pregnant,' he says.

I don't know what that means.

'Let me put it this way,' says the waiter. 'You ever had three stuffed bird?'

I have.

'Well,' says the waiter. 'This is just like that.'

My friend orders a whole family for the table.

They pick the biggest humans they have, and then drag them out to our table.

One by one, they take the humans and drop them in a big pan of boiling water.

I hear them begin to scream. It knocks me sick.

I tell the waiter, 'Surely, they're in pain?'

'No pain,' says the waiter, 'that's just air escaping.'

Once the screaming stops, they take all the meat and put it on a series of plates.

Gotta admit, seeing it cooked stole my appetite. Then my friend pokes a forkful in my mouth.

'Well?' says my friend. '

What can I say? It was delicious. My friend must be a mind reader because he just smiles.

'Yeah,' he says, 'I know. We're definitely coming back next week.'

ZOO

What do you do when you have everything you want?

What inspires you when everything around you is so serene, so perfect, so functional? What stops you from losing your mind when there are no more enemies at your door, no fundamentalists across the water? What do you do when there are no more arguments in your home? Well, if you're anything like the rest of us, you like to fill the space with a little communication, a little humour, and quite possibly, a little show.

You look for something to occupy your time, so you go somewhere freedom does not exist, somewhere it's but a thought- just a dream.

The only problem is there aren't any third world countries left, just cheap shiny plastic walls, and Perspex windows. Everyone's free, everyones connected, so where do you go to make yourself feel better? The answer is simple:

You go to the zoo.

It was the most wonderful place in the world, a series of habitats, territories, biomes, and selective evolution, all crammed inside like a teeny-tiny living taxonomic index. The only place in the world where you can tear through the thin veil of understanding, and gaze over the vast chasm that exists between man and beast. Watch as they struggle to adapt, to survive, and to prosper in an environment governed by shallow inconsistency.

Marvel as the proud lions as they pace the short length of their home. Paws padding the concrete, desperately trying to remember the feel of grass. Gaze at the majestic polar-bear, the largest carnivore, and king of the Tundra. Watch him bash that thick skull against the door, desperate to escape the heat wave and return to the small chilled box in the back room.

Then the zoos went away. People called them cruel.

People were upset. What would they do now? They begged the protestors to reconsider, but they stated that the animals of the world had just as much right to freedom as people. They've been here as long as us, some even longer.

So, the people got sad, and then they had this idea, if it was wrong to stick all those old animals in the zoo then people would just make new animals, and that way, everyone would be happy.

Just like that, the zoos were back in business.

It had your average, not so average creatures: your polythene toads, your radioactive sharks. There were your inter dimensional butterflies, zip-zooming, exploding as they crashed into one another, vaporising all within six feet of them. It had your conversational owls, they'd snigger and joke as you walked by.

It was all going well, and then the protesters began to argue.

They called it cruel. They said that the new animals were a lot like the old. The people made more, but the protestors wouldn't budge. So, once again, the zoos were closed.

The people were sad. They loved their zoos. Then they had a bright idea, if the protesters were unhappy with zoos full of animals both old and new, well, the people would just have to make something else, something so unlike an animal that even the protesters couldn't get mad.

Just like that, the zoo was back in business.

Now, in the cavernous depths of the zoo, one can hear the Dwarves. Bashing and beating, they bark a loud, 'Bro!' at any intruder who comes to their domain. People liked the Dwarves so much that they made them pets. Whether full-bred or little more than a mongrel, the Dwarves of the darkest depths soon replaced the dog as man's best friend.

Then there were the Hobbes, with their slight frames, and sharp teeth. Skittering and skulking in droves over the terracotta rooftops, they move in thieving gangs like some Dickensian parody. They spend their days humping and fighting, scratching, scenting, falling, dying. All across the zoo, one can hear the harsh cries of the Hobbes, as they curse, and fight, and play their little pranks.

It was all going well, till the protesters came. They called it cruel. They said the creatures were little more than the survivors of once proud races. They said the people shouldn't force them into cages to live no better than an animal.

The people were depressed. They loved their Elves, and their Fairies. But, the protesters didn't care, and soon the zoo was closed.

Then the people had a great idea. They would fill the zoo with something so unlike an animal that even the protesters wouldn't get mad. So, they went town to town, city to city, country to country, all across the globe, and there, bit by bit, they collected their new attraction:

People

Now, the zoo is open again. Its many enclosures filled with people.

They don't know why they're there, or what's going on outside of the zoo. They were sad, for a few years anyway. Then after a while, they did what all people do when they can't change a terrible truth - they just got on with it.

Living in svelte homes that rise high into the sky, the people of the zoo have everything they'll ever need. They have families. They have jobs. They have diseases, and accidents. They have crime, and Earthquakes, and all other acts of God.

In the zoo, they can find anything, from their gas-light systems, to the Mayor's own clock-work rifles. Blimps and balloons hover around the zoo, raining chocolate-covered poisons to the vermin below. The Fire-Lads bounce and jiggle as they ride atop heavy-boot-wearing fire machines, contraptions made of brass and gold. Their job is to spray thick rubbery foam over the zoo's many fires.

The zoo is filled with tin wings, and piston-hooks allowing its residents to sneak as they please.

Now, it took a while for the protesters to return. They took one look at all those people, trapped in cages, forced to live however we choose to make them. They saw all of this, and then the protesters told us, 'Better. Much-much better.'

Then, overtime, the people in the zoo got depressed, so they started to make a zoo of their own.

They filled it with rats, though not like any rat you've seen before. This was a mass of teeth and fur. They called it the Black Death, and it was bound by a single desire - to spread, totally, and completely till there was nothing left.

Luckily for them there are also cats. Like the rats, these were no ordinary animals. If you pay close attention you can see them meet and greet, watch as they organise and plan their next action. Tabbies and Gingers swipe for the chance to be heard, while the black cats wait patiently in darkened corners.

Black cats are able to bestow their luck upon anyone they find deserving. A gift to friends, a curse to the rest.

The zoo became a most interesting place. Steam-powered sentinels guard the Mayor as he demands his annual increase of tribute. Fleas taking messages from cat to cat.

People marvel at the zoo we have created. They feel safe and secure that, at least here, they aren't alone in their isolation. Then people got an idea - what if we made a zoo for ourselves?

So, we did it, little by little, we built our own zoo. We locked ourselves away, offering animals the chance to come and see us. Respectable rates. Discounts for families. Come and see the people.

It took the animals a while. Perhaps they suspected a trap. But in the end, they came. They paid what little they could, and one by one, they walked around the zoo, watching the humans in their cages.

'Don't you think it's all very cruel?' says a passing Giraffe.

'Don't be silly,' says her husband. 'People don't survive in the wild, everyone knows that.'

The kids point to a human in a cage. There, they watch as he fails to do his tax returns.

'Look, Daddy!' says the youngest of the Giraffes. 'That man is being silly.'

'Of course he's being silly, son. That's what people do.'

The zoo isn't always perfect. Every now and then, some silly animal comes to free us. But, we don't do well in the wild. Eventually, we come back to our cages, and sleep soundly knowing we can blame them for all our problems.

The zoo is the safest place for people. There's only a handful left in the wild. But, with your donation we could help them from dying out completely.

So if you have a spare minute why don't you go to the zoo? It's great for families. Book in advance to avoid any inconvenience.

CUSTOMER SERVICE

'Hello, sir. Thanks for calling. What seems to be the problem?'

Listen to you shout and curse. You blame me for your situation, for the inconvenience it breeds.

I tell you, 'Yes, sir. You're fully within your rights to make a complaint.'

I smile at your anger, at your inability to see how this situation is all your fault. I enjoy the experience too much, and you detect the smugness in my voice.

You send several remarks my way, crude and unnecessary.

I tell you, 'I understand that you're angry, sir, but there is no reason to use such language.'

I ask that you, 'Don't shout.' That you, 'Take a moment to gather your thoughts.' Then, right after you take a breather, I suggest that you, 'Calm down.'

Big mistake.

The line fills with rage, one acid dripped word at a time.

I tell you that, 'Insulting my intelligence won't make things go any faster.'

I let you know, 'I have two degrees, so the chance of me being, as you said, A real dumb cunt, is unlikely.'

I listen, sir. I listen to you ask what's wrong with me. How you can't decide who's more at fault, my mother's rotten womb, or Daddy's cheesy maggot cock.

You curse my job, my age, my whole existence, and do you know what I do in return?

Simple, sir. I unbutton my pants, I slide them down to my ankles, and there, with my feet on the desk, I begin to pleasure myself.

You can hear it, sir, between snarls and curses, you ask, What's that sound? It starts to bother you, that or maybe the fact that I don't seem the least bit upset.

Once again, I tell you, 'Calm down, sir,' and I hear your scream at the top of your voice.

Then I ruin it. My pleasure gets the better of me, and I let out a half contained moan.

I don't manage to cum before you hang up, and I'm left there, fingers slick and glistening, far from satisfied.

I wipe the fluid from my fingers, and I think back to what you said.

'Dumb cunt.'

I performed at Footlights, you know? That's Oxford or Cambridge, never can remember which. I went to both, not because I enjoyed it but for the simple reason that everyone said they were the best universities.

You ring back looking for someone to complain to, complain about me.

Using a different voice, I tell you, 'Yes, sir. You've been treated most unfairly.'

I listen to you talk about 'That crazy bitch!' and all the while, I slip off my pants, and begin to pressure myself.

I ask, 'What do you hate about her, sir?'

You don't like the question. There's something odd about the way I say it, all excited with a smile on my face

I ask, 'If you could kill her, how would you do it?'

I take your silence for consideration, so I offer a few suggestions of my own.

'You could stab her, right under the chin. Fuck her first, but that goes without saying. Get her on top, and then stick her with a rusted blade, dragging it back and forth as she bleeds all over your cock.'

You tell me, 'You're as sick as that other bitch!' You call

me a, 'Faggot!' and threaten to cut off my cock.

I moan back, 'Promises promises!' And then you hang up.

I'm so close it hurts. Got to say, sir, I may be just, 'Another creepy little twink!' but I hope you'll listen when I say that you're really good at this.

I was raised in the dramatics, sir. When I performed at Floodlights, I did all the parts myself. Nobody noticed, sir. I'm quick with the costumes, and as you can tell, there's no one who can fake a voice better than me.

You know, you're the second person I've admitted that too.

The first was this guy at college. He was an aspiring writer, which to me and you was another word for unemployed.

Still, I liked his curls, and the way he looked at me. I suppose he was my sugar baby, but we didn't have the term back then.

One night, I got drunk, and I revealed my secret. My little writer wanted to turn it into a story, the next great novel.

He never finished the book, or any book. He was a man of excuses. For him, the search for the perfect novel was more interesting than writing one.

He died penniless, by then he'd lost the curls, and whatever look he used to face the world was tempered with contempt. He blamed everyone for his life, everyone but him.

An hour goes by and you call back.

I'm in such a good mood that I don't bother to pretend.

I ask, 'Hello, sir. Was your wife upset when you didn't come home last night?'

You tell me to, 'Eat shit and die!' You curse my pussy, my prick, you can't tell which one I've got.

Well, don't worry, sir, most people get it wrong.

You ask, 'How is any of this your business?'

And I can't help but laugh.

Oh, sir. You've forgotten our motto: Your happiness is my happiness.

I take this very personally, sir, though, I don't miss the chance to hear you shout.

You screaming about, 'Coming down there and beating me to a pulp!'

And then you sit there, heavy breathing, listening for a reply, and in response, I let out a groan as I cum down the other end of the phone.

You can hear it, can't you, sir? That gush of fluid, thick as syrup and just as sweet. I'd be lying if I said the idea didn't turn me on, you watching me make a mess all over my new desk. Your face twisted in disgust as you tell me to Lick it up.

Still, I just lay there, skin wet and panting. You didn't hang up, sir. You've stopped making any noise at all. You've gone all quiet, listening down the line.

With a smile on my face, I wipe away the sweat. I ask, 'And I thought I was supposed to be the one helping you?'

Then you hang up, sir. Shame, but no matter. Things have started, and I've got to say, I couldn't be happier.

The next day, you call again.

This time, I speak with my manager voice.

I tell you, 'That kind of behaviour is most unacceptable!'

I ask If you've got the details of the other staff member. I say this while drinking from a glass vial which contains the rest of my fluid from last night's little phone call.

You tell me, 'No.' You demand to know, 'What kind of place gives creeps like that a job?'

I tell that I'm checking the log, but in reality, I'm looking at porn, Hardcore, sir, sharp and brutal, the kind you don't find on the regular internet.

I ask, 'What was it that was said exactly?'

I listen to you get all shy. It's sweet, sir. Now, I prefer you all puffed up, prone to anger and violence, but it's nice to see this softer side.

You tell me you'd rather not say.

I understand, but we need to know, sir. That way, we can decide on how to handle the issue. After all, if it's as bad as you said then this might be grounds for dismissal.

I can tell you're weary, sir. But you so desperately want to believe that someone in this company is normal. That we understand. That we care.

I say, ;I can see that you're upset, sir.' Then, I ask you to be specific.

You mention flippant behaviour. You say how I wasn't taking things seriously. Then you mention how I brought up your personal life.

I try my best to stay professional, but I can't help but ask, And how does your wife feel about you not coming home last night?

You go quiet.

I drop the manager voice, and I go back to my normal voice, well, the voice you recognise.

I say, 'Yes, sir. It's me. Welcome back.'

I ask about my voice. Real convincing, huh?

You ask, 'What the fuck is wrong with you!'

Then I say, 'Don't you love your wife, sir?'

I don't mention how beautiful she is, how she supported you through the dark days, The unemployment days, and her working two jobs so you didn't have to flat share.

Don't you remember when she paid to fix your teeth, sir? Four root canals, and not to mention the crowns. Very expensive, sir. And here you are, spending another evening Working late at the office.

I say, 'Do you ever plan to tell her, sir? A different woman every night? Do you think she's earned that, sir? The right to be honest, and if not, how much more does she owe? How many bills, how many trips to the dentist?'

You hang up.

I get it, the truth hurts. But, you have to understand, you're amongst friends. Well, technically it's just the one friend, but you don't know that.

You call the emergency services.

I put on my most serious voice. I say, 'Hello, state your

emergency!'

You talk of stalking behaviour, so I say you want the police. You want them to do something, and do it now.

I tell you to hold.

Then, in a friendly voice, I say, 'Your call is important to us.'

I hum some Muzak down the phone. Not really a song, more annoying than catchy.

I let you stew for a moment before putting on a voice straight out of Scotland Yard.

I say, ' Ello-Ello, What's all this then about you being stalked, eh?

You spin some story about you being a victim. A victim of a most cruel and undeserving situation.

I must say, sir. You're rather good with the stories, even I almost believed you.

But still, I couldn't help myself.

I say, 'Well, perhaps you should stop flapping your sausage in everyone's face.'

You don't like that, do you?

Not my fault, sir. I'm not the one spreading more seeds than a dandelion.

You've gone quiet. Shame, I like to hear your voice.

I ask, 'Did you like last night, sir? I know I did.'

I ask, 'Do you take us all to the same hotel, or is it true what you said, am I really that special?'

You hang up. I don't blame you. Scary stuff dealing with a stalker. Then, you call up the police only to find she's there as well.

You call up your wife. You ring her ten times before she picks up.

When she does, you don't say a word, you just sit there, heavy breathing down the phone.

I say, 'Why are you calling me at work?'

You tell me to listen, then you start shouting some story about customer service, and stalkers. Maybe there's a conspiracy involving the police, you don't know.

I tell you, 'Calm down! You're going a million miles a minute!'

Then, you ask me a question. You ask, 'Is it really you?'

I must admit, it's hard to stop myself from smiling.

I say, 'Of course it's me. Who else is it going to be?'

I tell you to relax. That everything is going to be alright.

Maybe it's a panic attack, or stress from work. You've been working a lot lately, remember all those late nights at the office?

I tell you to take a breath.

That's right. In, and out. In, and out.

I ask if you feel better.

You say you do, then, after another deep breath, I hear you relax.

Then I drop the Kate voice, and I go back to the other one. I ask, 'Great. Now, sir. Where were we?'

You probably don't remember last night, do you, sir? Makes sense, after all, you were a bit . . . piddly? Well, that would be putting it mildly.

I know, I know, it's not my place to say, but seeing as we're grown so close, I must tell you that mixing spirits and beer is a terrible idea.

You hang up.

You don't think twice before contacting your mother. Quite Freudian if you ask me, sir.

I say, 'Hello, my darling, my angel.'

It lasts all of a minute before I go back to my regular voice.

I ask, 'Did you get the test results?'

No? Well, that's not very responsible now, is it, sir?

I get it, you're stressed. Makes sense to bury your head in the sand. For the record, there's nothing to worry about, I am free of disease, now and forever. Comes with the genetics.

I ask, 'Do you remember the other night, sir? You promised to give me the night of my life.'

I'd love to tell you Yes. Yes! A thousand times yes! But in truth, your . . . activities? Well, they didn't manage to, how do you put it? Rock my world?

You didn't destroy my pussy, and I'm not ruined for other men. I hope that doesn't upset you too much.

I went back to the motel today. Just an hour ago, I gave up my lunch just to sit in that room, our room, sweet little 107.

They didn't clean the sheets. I just wrapped myself up, rubbing my lips over that crusty little cum stain.

I love that room. The damp, the window view looking out into a brick wall. I love the shower, the way it's either too hot, too cold.

It's such a dingy miserable little room. Perfect for all our seedy adventures.

You've taken me to that room six times. It would have been seven, but I told you a lie about waiting for my boyfriend.

I do have a few suggestions, sir.

Like last time, you pounced on me, stuck your hand up my skirt and began to touch me with your index finger.

You breathed into my ear, moaning, 'You like that, baby?'

Alas, I did not.

My advice would be to focus on the clitoris. Enthusiasm can only get you so far, and watching you root around like you've got your hand down the back of a couch searching for keys, well, it's not as sexy as you might think.

Shit. I realise I haven't said anything for a few minutes.

So, I have to ask, 'Why do you think you keep cheating on your wife? Why do you always take them to room 107?'

You hang up.

Straight back to calling your wife.

I say, 'Hello, this is your wife Kate.'

Then, I start laughing. I must admit, I'm surprised you're surprised, sir.

You've already called this number once before, so I don't know what you were expecting?

You demand to know why I have your wife's phone.

I as, 'Would you like to speak to her?'

You don't answer.

Good idea, sir. Best not to rush these things.

By now you have realised that all of your close friends and personal contacts are in fact me. Shocking, I understand, but then I am a professionally trained actor.

I studied under the Great Zemo, well, I say study. He had bought me from a woman who I assume must have been my mother.

Kill it, she had begged, but the Great Zemo was a greedy man and made me the main attraction in his travelling circus:

'THE MONSTER'

That's what they called me. But most people weren't interested in seeing little old me, all wet and wriggling, a thing of blood and muscle.

When things got bad the Great Zemo got angry.

He'd beat me, with his fist and his belt. One time he beat me unconscious with his cane.

It didn't help sales, but it helped him feel better.

One night, I could tell he came to kill me. He'd have done it too but he saw what I'd done with my dinner.

There, lying beside me in the cage was my dinner, a fat juicy rat.

It was still there, thrashing, and squeaking, only now it didn't have any skin.

I took the skin and slipped inside it. It wasn't big enough for my whole body, but I'd fit my hands inside, and there the rat twitched and sniffed and looked just like a rat.

That gave the Great Zemo pause.

'You wears the skins?' he asked.

He watched my hand squeak and nibble and crawl around the cage, all wrapped up in that rat skin.

After that, the Great Zemo gave me skins. wild animals at first, mostly rats. But there were times when he'd come with a pet, cats, bunnies, and a couple of dogs.

Then my birthday came and he brought me a boy.

'Lost during the carnival,' Zemo sighed, 'fell and dashed his head. So sad.'

I was most happy back then. I loved nothing more than taking their skins, especially off their faces, removing them, in one slow smooth motion, like peeling the skin from an old banana.

Then the Great Zemo began to train me.

'The skin is only half the trick,' he would say, picking me up by my wormy tail. 'You are no rat with your steps that go oinky-boink,' he told me. 'No, child. The movements of a rat are light and ticklish. This is known.'

I thank the Great Zemo for his lessons. I take pride in my art l, with an equal love for act and costume.

I keep them all, sir. Every skin I've ever made. All the people I've connected with. All the people I've helped.

Sometimes, I slip out my skin and lay on the bed, all wet and sticky. On those nights I leave the door to the wardrobe open, and listen to them.

They like to moan, sir, the skins, they just cry as they hang there, on the hooks, begging to die.

But, I can't let them die, sir. Dead skin loses the magic. I've tried to wear it, but it doesn't work. All someone has to do is look at me and the game is up.

I feel bad, sir. But what else can I do?

I have hundreds, sir. All of them crying out with their sagging limp mouths, their breath stinking like dust, and old pages.

I ask 'Would you like to hear your wife, sir? No? Are you sure? It's no bother. I'm standing by the wardrobe, it's no trouble?'

Do you remember what you told me last night? You said you wanted to be with me, forever and ever, do you remember that, sir?

I know it's not right to rush things, but I don't care, I know why you're upset, sir. But I'm here for you, I know how to make it better.

I love watching you sleep, sir. All those cute expressions. The other night, you called out, 'Hand me the purple elephant!'

It was so funny that I cried laughing.

Hope you don't mind that I broke into your house. I couldn't help it, sir. I just need to be close to you.

I've been watching you a lot lately. When you sleep, I like to slip out of my skin. There, I wait, by the end of the bed.

I keep hoping that you'll wake up. See me as I am, skinless, bare and bloody. In my dreams, you don't scream or call me monster, You just stare with that love in your eyes.

I am so sneaky, sir. You do not hear me come into the room, even now, when the sun is up and the light spills through the window.

Even my voice is sneaky. So very sneaky, you would not hear it even if I was beside you. Even now when you are very much afraid.

You do not hear me creeping behind you, but you feel it. It's the skin, sir. It never lies.

Now, tell me, are those my fingers you feel dancing up the back of your neck - or is it the wind - or maybe my breath?

No need to guess. Why don't you turn around, sir? Turn, and see for yourself.

A CAT IS A FINE THING

Dog's man's best friend because he was shaped that way.

A shadow of fur. In the good times, you give him a rub and a pet, and in the bad, a kick to make yourself feel better.

That's not the way of cats, so do yourself a favour, don't go trying.

Cats didn't end up in the house because we made them that way. We ended up letting them in because that way they wanted to come in. But that didn't work, now they bring their nature home with them, bit by bit a different bird, and each one in bits and bits.

A cat chooses to stay inside, something which we humans choose to ignore at our peril. But the cat is a wild thing. As much a killer as their larger cousins, only smarter because less people are interested in hunting for that ratty drab tabby fur.

The cat is smart, slinking from home to home, taking the good food with the bad. The big man got sad when he found out old puss-puss was getting fed on the side, well, by the whole god damn neighbourhood, but that's cats for you.

Keep them happy, that's my motto.

You best believe that a happy cat is a good thing. Not easy knowing there's still birds in the sky, and the streets are choked with them old dumb dogs.

The cat forever looking for the best food, the best place,

best people. Some say, he's just looking for a place to park his flea-bitten ass, but I know the truth. Some say they're royalty, from the old days when cats was gods, but even then, cats knew what was really going on.

Who needs all that worship when you get what you want? A flash of the belly for some, and a swipe of the claws for the rest. God stuff is easy. Anyone can be a god. Now, being a cat is different. Go ahead, try it, see how long you last.

Truth be told, all that worship comes built in, cat's like it when you pray, just don't expect them to come and save you from a flood or nothing. They might smite an enemy or two, but it won't be long before they come around for you.

Learn to swim. Fight your own battles. Cat got enough trouble, he's busy cleaning himself, fighting the damn dog. He's got bigger things to worry about, like other cats.

Cat's got his own life to worry about, so you get on with yours. Stop waiting for life to get better. He ain't your saviour. He ain't your friend. It doesn't matter how many costumes you put him in, it's all the same to him.

That there is a cat, and he's gonna do what he always does. Question is, are you smart enough to pay attention? Who knows, you might just learn something.

BABY STEPS

I

On the 9th of September 2027, Rodger Galford turned to the doctor and asked him to repeat himself.

'It's posterior cortical atrophy,' said the doctor. 'Commonly known as Benson's Syndrome.'

'Right,' said Rodger Galford. 'And that's bad, is it?'

'It's Alzheimer's,' said the doctor. 'Rear-brained. It's uncommon, but rest assured, you're not the only one.'

'Right,' said Rodger Galford. 'Can you give me a sec?'

He took out his phone, and checked the time. It was fourteen past three. That didn't make any sense. Everyone knows that the serious stuff always happens on the hour. Twelve O'Clock is Witching Hour. Five O' Clock is the time to get drunk. Fourteen past three is nothing, it's beige coloured time. Bad things don't happen at times like that.

Rodger Galford couldn't accept bad news at a time like that. So, he took out his phone, and began to live stream.

'Hey, folks. It's me, Rodger Dodger the Artful Codger. Quickie Q, what historic moments have occurred at fourteen past three?'

Then, he waited for Chat to reply.

The doctor cleared his throat. 'It's not the Alzheimer's you think it is. You don't lose personality, you lose the ability to navigate the space between objects, and eventually, you lose the objects themselves.'

Rodger Galford wasn't listening, but he nodded all the same.

He began to scratch his pants. He got them on sale in one of those cheap retail outlets. There he was, several pants in hand, staring at a line that went from one end of the store to the other. The line looked like a snake, coiling around the bumper packs of Hulk underwear, through the V-neck shirts labelled 'Hawaii' and 'California' and all the other places he'd rather be. The line went on, through Baby Care, past the bibs and buggies, along the Back To School range, before stopping dead by Rodger Galford as he stood in the forty percent off men's section.

Lucky for him, Rodger Galford found an opening in swimwear. There, between a lone Gaga sandal and some day-glow trunks, a caught shoplifter struggling with security offered him a moment's distraction, allowing Rodger Galford to cut his way in line.

That little trick had him coming away with three sets of jeans, and all he had to do was wait for forty five minutes. He felt great, till he put the jeans on. They had little give to them, this made each step awkward, like he was in a children's story about a sneaking monster, one stiff step after another. The stitching had left these fibres that would poke at the inside of his thighs.

Rodger Galford had cursed himself for not trying them on. Yes, it would have taken longer to pay for them, but he had time. Or at least he did. Now, as he sits in the doctor's office, scratching his jeans, he does his best to ignore a question.

'How much time do I have left?'

He doesn't say it. He doesn't dare. He just kept scratching in the hopes his mind would stop bringing it up.

The doctor cleared his throat.

'As I said, you will lose the ability to reach for things. It's not that you can't find them, it's that as you go to grasp them it's as if they've moved away. Then, one day, you'll feel like someone has stolen the letters from your keyboard.'

Rodger Galford checked his phone. Nobody in Chat had responded to his message.

'Do you think there's a mistake?' said Rodger Galford. 'It's just, I've got hundreds of followers, and yet no one has answered my question.'

'You have Alzheimer's,' said the Doctor. 'You do understand that?'

'Sure,' said Rodger Galford. 'It's just, things tend to happen at specific times, right? I mean fourteen past three? It's not specific, so how can anything bad happen?'

The doctor looked at his watch. He said, 'It's fourteen past three, Mr. Galford, and you have rear-brained Alzheimer's. The disease isn't convenient, nor is it interested in being fair. It is simply a disease, a most serious disease, and you have it, sir, and you're going to have to accept that.'

Then, with great care, Rodger put away his phone. He looked up at the doctor. Then, in a soft voice, he said, 'But, I'm not ready?'

II

In the aftermath of all that silly business, Rodger Galford used social media as a way of informing people about his journey. His aim is to show that, in fact, he did not have a disease, and then, with donations from Chat, he planned to sue the clinic for malpractice.

Phone in hand, Rodger says, 'Won't be long till Rodger Dodger gets paid.

It wasn't long before his story got the attention of a company.

They said things like 'You're very lucky, sir' and 'Perfect timing' and then they said stuff about 'Great strides in technology.'

He agreed to let them send him a gift. 'I'll be sure to give an honest and fair review. But, I should let you know, my opinions are not for sale.'

They sent him a white box with a label made of mother of pearl. Across the top of the box were the words 'Smart Fashion.'

Inside was something of a boiler suit. It was white as snow and lined with some kind of squishy material. The material covered every bone and every joint. Rodger Galford felt along the striations of squishy fibres. It looked like someone had made the entire muscle system out of marshmallows.

The instruction manual told him, 'Made from all natural materials. Shaped by the minds of forward thinkers.'

Rodger Galford didn't feel like a sick man. So, he didn't wear the suit.

Then, one day, he reached out for a cup. He'd done it a million times before, but now, something felt wrong. His hand reached out, just like before, only now it felt nothing. He was sure the cup was there, he could see it, but he couldn't touch it.

He rubbed his eyes. He blinked several times, but it didn't help. The cup was both there, and it wasn't.

Rodger decided that he didn't want any tea, so he left it to grow cold. Rodger wasn't sick, he just didn't feel overly thirsty is all.

Then, a few hours later, Rodger Galford tried again. This time, he felt the cup. It was cold from neglect.

He decided to put on the suit.

Rodger wasn't sick, he just didn't want to upset that nice company.

For a few days, he felt like nothing had changed. Then, while reaching for his phone, Rodger Galford found himself grasping at nothing.

'I'm not sick,' he told himself. 'I just don't want my phone. That's right. I'm doing a dopamine detox.'

Then, he felt the suit come alive.

All that squishy stuff began to harden and tense. Rodger watched them go all stiff like pale strands of muscle. Slowly, his arm began to straighten, and then, it moved half an inch to the left.

He didn't feel like he was being dragged, or anything like that. It was more of a touch, a gentle gust of air that moved his hand, ever so slowly, to the phone.

Rodger held out his phone. He told Chat. 'Hi, cool cats and kittens. Look what I can do!'

And, just like before, Rodger felt better.

'I'm not sick,' he told Chat. 'Not anymore.'

III

Rodger Galford gave a review for the suit. 'Five stars,' he told Chat.

The company said, 'Glad you like it. The suit had been designed as a prototype for paraplegics.'

'Must be one of those fancy Neuralink things,' he told Chat. 'Hope I don't need anything drilled.'

'No surgery,' said the company. 'The suit connects with a headset. It bridges the gap between intention and reality. Where you want to touch it will reach.'

Chat posed the question, and Rodger Galford agreed, so he asked the only question worth asking.

'Got any more?'

***

'The suit isn't ready for full paralysis,' said the company. 'You will be our guide, for both the company and the public. Your role is to share your life, your experience.'

It'd be some time before they could help everyone.

'Until then,' said the company, 'It's just going to be us.'

'Gotta start small,' said Rodger Galford.

'That's right. Baby steps.'

Rodger Galford felt like he had a second chance. The suit gave him the opportunity to go out walking again.

The company told him it's a lot like having a mini AI

built into your life.

'Think of it like modern car technology. See in the old days, you'd drive over a patch of ice and it'd be left to you alone to steer to safety. Now, you have systems in place where the car will make note of the ice and react accordingly. It does this before you have time to even process it. That's your suit, Mr. Galford, reacting to those little patches of ice.'

'But what happens when you get bigger and bigger patches of ice?' said Rodger Galford.

'Yes, tomorrow is uncertain, but today is full of possibilities. Do not waste them on such worries, sir.'

Over the coming months, Rodger Galford felt the suit move more and more. It would activate in increasing manners. Stiffening and straightening him into subtle gestures.

Then, one day, Rodger felt something different. It was when he stepped down the stairs. He felt his leg stop like it was held by some invisible force. Rodger was a child held by a parent.

The leg stopped and, with a gentle but unopposable force, it began to move and work itself in a direction he did not wish to move. There, it rested on the step below, a step he didn't realise was there.

'It's just one step,' said Rodger Galford. 'That doesn't make you sick. I just need to pay attention, that's all.'

A few months later, and one step became several. He counted them down, each time making note of when it was him that walked down the stairs, and when it was the suit.

Before, it had been barely noticeable. A few slight changes, a touch, a tap, a gust of wind. It was hardly there at all.

Then it evolved. One day, he felt the suit come alive. Walking felt like learning to ride a bike. The gestures were his own. But every now and then, Rodger would make an error and the suit would be forced to overcorrect. A guiding hand that would come into sudden action, saving him at the last second.

That had been difficult, but then things got worse.

One day, he felt confused, he couldn't manage to get off the bed. That's when the suit took over.

Rodger Galford was a baby being carried by his mother. He could kick and wave, but always there was the force above him, holding on, gentle but firm. Rodger wondered what was to come, what would happen next?

His days were spent heading through town, one step at a time, clunky and awkward. He wondered at what point he'd lose his ability to think, he wondered what would happen to the suit, to him when he could no longer think, no longer able to tell the suit, 'There. I want to go there!'

Would it understand?

Would it listen?

IV

'We're sending you a new suit,' said the company. 'This will take care of everything.'

He could see other suits on the road. The success of his channel led to the manufacturing and distribution of Smart Fashion.

People like him were offered the chance to live a normal life. Others wore suits to help with exercise. The new app allowed the suit to take you on walks, to do sets at the gym. You just lay back and the suit would do all the work.

They've made one for babies. No more buggies, no more waiting for them to learn how to walk. The suit will do it all. No more temper tantrums. No more being late. Thanks to the new Kid-Smart Fashion, you'll never be inconvenienced again.

It's funny how things turn out. One minute, the suit is helping him reach for a biscuit, and now it's telling him 'Too much sugar' and instead, it guides a stick of celery into his mouth.

'It's all for your own good,' said the company.

He tried to see the silver lining, and the suit goes on,

taking him on walks, filling him up with nutritious meals, and all the while, he told it, 'Stop. Stop. Stop' But the suit continues on, one healthy step after another, and on he went, walking into the sunrise of the future.

CHANGE FOR A SET OF SHOES

In times of doubt, I'm left thinking of something Dad used to say, 'Son, when you get right down to it, the world, she's a very weird place.'

I always thought I knew what he meant, that was, until now. See, I've just got off the tram at the wrong stop, that's where I find myself face to face with a centaur. You know? half man, half horse? All of it, right there, staring at me. He's sitting next to the tram stop, laying on his side. He's got his legs all tucked up, and with a smile bordering on the sublime, he reaches down and gives his balls a good scratch.

This, ladies and gentlemen, is not how I expected my day to go.

First of all, let's back up. I didn't mean to get off at the wrong stop. See, I was kinda-sorta flirting with this twenty-something on the tram. She sat facing me, several seats away. By flirting, I don't mean we were doing something naughty or anything like that. No, we were having a game of Smiles. Rules are: You take turns pretending not to look at one another, then, you snatch the occasional glance, till, inevitably, they catch you. That's when you send them your best smile, and, if you're lucky you'll get one back.

In my defence, she did start it. Miss Twenty-Something sent a smile right down the crowded tram. There it went, past a mother of five trying to ignore her screaming children. Like a symphony from Hell, each child picked a different key, and as one, they sang, 'Baby Shark. Do-do-da-do-da-do.'

There I was, stuffed in the corner with a very ill man sitting behind me. I tried to maintain an air of compassion even as he coughed all over the back of my neck. That's when I look up and see her: dark eyes, and a bramble patch full of curls all stuffed under a red beret. She had these glasses, huge things like Harry Potter meets Anime.

Without missing a beat, she sends off a smile that hits me right between the eyes. The full force of it leaves me lost as I blink in confusion. With that, Miss Twenty-Something adjusts her Harry Potter glasses and returns once more to her book. It's an old thing, its spine held together with sellotape. I watch yellow pages fall like Autumn leaves, and Miss Twenty-Something is trapped in a cycle of reading, catching, and now, as I'm finally paying attention, she begins to smile.

I mean, come on, what would you have done?

Well, this goes on for the whole journey. Then, she puts away her book, gets up, and apologises to the mother of five for stepping on several of her children.

Mother crisis averted, Miss Twenty-Something gets off the tram, and, before my brain can yell, 'Stop!' I'm up out of my seat and chasing after. I didn't have a plan, no chat-up line, just the memory of her smile and the hope that, when I got to her, I wouldn't come across as a complete and total tit.

That's when I realise I'm at the wrong stop, and, shortly after, that's when I realise that centaurs are real.

Now, I've got a conundrum. See, on the one hand, I've got Miss Twenty-Something walking away, down the street, and if I don't act now, she'll be out my life forever. Then, on the other hand, I've got this big mythical creature staring right at me.

I want to go talk to her. I want to ask what she's reading. I want to know why she wears glasses two sizes too big. I want to ask if she likes coffee, while secretly hoping she doesn't - I hate coffee - but I'd swallow down every muddy cup if only she'd sit opposite giving me that same smile again, the one from the train.

I don't care where we go. I just want to talk to her and see if she's half as cool as I think she is.

I'm about to run after her when I hear a voice say, 'Hey, Mr. You got any change?'

The centaur doesn't sound like you'd expect, I mean, I can't be the only person who thinks all mythical creatures should talk with an English accent, right? Well, this guy, this creature, this centaur, he's American, and I mean Wild West, 'Ye-haw! Darn tooting, howdy there, Pilgrim' that kind of American.

Without taking my eyes off Miss Twenty Something, my hand goes in my pocket. I feel around the edge of my wallet, fingers poking along the crumbs and corners as they search for change. I take out my hand to find it holding an empty wrapper. Once metallic, the years have taken its colour leaving only flickering traces like silver lightning on a field of snow.

'Hey, Mr,' says the centaur, 'Everything alright? You seem kinda, well, kinda distant?'

Still with my eyes fixed down the road, I tell him, 'Yeah, I'm sorta, you know, sorta in the middle of something?'

I hear the shift of his enormous weight. 'Got yourself trapped in a Big-o deal?'

'I don't know,' I tell him, 'but, I think I'm about to find out.'

Then I hear a sound that makes me jump. At first, I thought it was a scream, the sound you get from a mythical beast after your offer has been rejected. Like failing to solve the riddle of the Sphinx, I stand here, waiting for punishment with nothing for defence but my little silver wrapper. I wait for the beast to rear up, all fifteen feet of it, and then, as it brings down its hooves, each the size of my head, I'll stand and scream, unable to do anything as it dashes me into a blob of raspberry jam: extra thick and pulpy.

The violence never comes, and I realise that the sound, the one that's left me with with wobbly legs, and the strong desire to change my underpants, that sound wasn't a scream at all, It was, in fact, the sound of something special: it was the sound of centaur laughing. And though I cannot find the words to describe how it feels to hear it, I must leave you none the wiser, save for the smile upon my face.

'I hear that,' says the centaur. 'Many a time, I found myself looking down the barrel of a moment, with not a single clue as to how the damn thing was gonna end.' The centaur takes out a pouch of Amber Leaf tobacco, and with long yellow-tipped fingers, he begins to roll a cigarette. 'See, you seem like a nice guy,' says the centaur, 'so I'mma offer you some good ol' ad-vice.'

'Thanks,' I tell him, 'but I'm kinda in the middle of a-' but the centaur cuts me off.

'Some moments, they look big from a distance,' says the centaur, 'strong towering things. But, it's only when you get close, and I mean real close, closer than any folk normally would, it's only then you see the world for what it really is.'

Cigarette rolled, the centaur holds it between index and middle finger. His wrist's all limp like we're in the back of a dark club, him ready to tell me about the lonesome truths of show business. 'That big moment?' says the centaur, 'the one that had you shaking in your boots? It ain't true. It's one of them desert illusions, you know, a mi-rage? Truth is, there ain't no big moments. Them situations? They's always been the same size. See, It's you who gets smaller, happens each and every time you see the truth and decide to go the other way.'

I look over at Miss Twenty Something. I can still make it, if I run. Perhaps, I can turn this thing into something funny and romantic? Like a movie starring Hugh Grant, we can call it: Tramp Trams and Centaurs.

'Look,' I say, 'this has been really good, but I've kinda gotta-'

With a wave, the centaur cuts me off. 'It's fine,' he says, 'but could I trouble you for some change?'

I feel through my pockets, unable to locate even the

smallest bit of money. I turn to the Centaur and say, 'Don't suppose you take card, do you?'

The centaur says something, but his voice is swallowed by the cackle of a nearby radio. That's when we see a police officer walking towards us. Green Hi-Vis Jacket, one hand on his radio, the other on his club. 'No,' says the officer, 'it's alright, I'm there already, looking right at it.' The officer points at the centaur and mouths the words, 'Get' and 'Up.'

The centaur begins to get up. I see his knees are all bloody from lying on the concrete. 'Sorry,' says the centaur, eyes fixed on the ground. 'I know, I know, you warned me, sir. You really did.'

The police officer says something into his radio, then he turns to the centaur, he says, 'I'd appreciate it if you lowered your tone.'

The centaur stares at the ground. He doesn't say a word, he just stands there, front leg going back and forth as his hoof scratches along the concrete.

'Move your stuff,' says the officer, and with that he walks off back the way he came.

The centaur collects up all his things, and then begins to walk in the same direction as the officer. I tell him, 'No, don't go that way. That guy will kill you.' Then, I lead the way back towards Miss Twenty Something.

I'm heading into town walking beside the centaur. The guy stands so tall that it hurts my neck to look up at him. His hair is little more than a series of strands, like a half-blown dandelion. There's a smell to him, something beneath the scent of wild animals. Most horses smell like a mix of sweat and milky tea, but with the centaur there was something else, a sour tang that clings to the back of the throat.

'I don't get it,' I ask, 'how can you be homeless? I mean, you're a fucking centaur!'

He puts a cigarette in his mouth. 'You know,' he says, 'I've wondered that myself.'

He takes out a pink disposable lighter. A few flicks tell

him it's empty. So, he reaches in his pocket and takes out another. This one's green with a bottom that's all broken like a jagged smile. He flicks the lighter and creates a flame, but the disposable's crack leaks out gas and, with a woosh, it burns the centaur's hand.

The word 'Motherfucker!' screams out in a most American manner. Cigarette burnt, the centaur throws the disposable lighter onto the floor, and with his hoof raised high, he stomps on it, crunching plastic and the concrete beneath.

'Fuck!' says the centaur. 'Damn thing burnt my jacket!' and he holds up a sleeve oozing black smoke. For a moment, he just stands there, trying not to cry.

I tell him, 'Come on. I'll buy you a new lighter.' And we head off, further into town. I look around for Miss Twenty Something. But I don't see her. Then, as we walk past a little independent cafe, I look in the window and I see she's sitting at the back.

I tell the centaur, 'Come on. I'll buy you a coffee,' and we go inside.

The air inside is thick enough to chew, like fighting your way through a Victorian fog. And there in the corner, I see Miss Twenty Something. She's sitting by a wall of red brick, Its chipped surface weeps with perspiration.

While waiting in line, I ask the centaur, 'Are there more like you out there?'

'Sure there are,' says the centaur, 'as many fairies as there are people.'

Then, I ask, 'Wait a minute! You're a fairy? Like, bottom of the garden, kill 'em off with iron? That kind of fairy?'

He lifts up his leg to show me the underside of his hoof. What I see is a piece of metal: razor thin, all brown with rust. 'Iron doesn't kill us,' he says. 'It's what makes us stay.'

I notice the people around us begin to stare. It's not the look of someone who's come face to face with a centaur. No, this look was different, this was the look of people who didn't like to be bothered by the homeless.

I tell him, 'I don't get it. Why do you want to stay? I mean, is life back home really that bad?'

The centaur's smile is all human and horse teeth. 'Home?' he says, 'home is perfect.'

'Then, why the hell are you still here? Why not throw those shoes away, go home, and be happy?'

The centaur reaches into his pocket and takes out a crumpled piece of card. It's a polaroid of a young woman. Her eyes are looking past the camera to the photographer behind. There's nothing forced about her smile. It was the look of someone caught in a moment. Something personal. Something real.

'There are rules,' says the centaur. 'See, where I come from, you can't take things back wit-cha. No stuff, no people - and most of all - no memories. That all has to stay behind. Lost. Forgotten.'

I ask what happened to her.

I watch the Centaur trace a finger along the edge of her face. 'Same thing that happens to everything here. She died. I didn't.'

We get to the counter where the barista stands there, a girl in her early twenties. She's got a ring in her nose, and her hair is scraped back. Once blue, the hair has since faded to a dull pale green.

Her face is distant, but her nose begins to twitch. She says, 'Sorry,' in a tone that's anything but, 'can't bring animals in here.'

I look around for a corgi or a sausage dog, or something, but instead I see her looking right at my friend.

I tell her, 'He's not an animal, he's mythical, there's a big difference.'

The barista keeps the same expression, then, she looks past us to the person behind. She asks, 'Hello, what can I get you?'

I'm about to say something, but the centaur takes me by the arm. 'Come on, boy,' he says, 'time to go.' and he leads the way back outside, apologising as he goes. I think he's saying it because of all the people trying not to get their feet crushed. But the voice in my head wonders whether he's apologising for a different reason: for the simple fact that he's there, that he exists, and that it bothers people.

Once outside, I tell him, 'Look, let's get to a cash point. I'll give you money for the shoes.'

He just stares at me for a moment. 'I know,' he says. 'I could tell just by looking at-cha, you're a good soul, just like she was.'

We begin to walk when I hear this sound, a metallic clink on the floor. I look down to see the sliver of an old rusty horseshoe.

I shout, 'Fuck! What are we going to do!'

The centaur doesn't panic, though. He just stands there, looking at that shoe. I watch this smile spread across his face. 'Nothing we can do,' he says, 'nothing at all.'

Already, I can see the effects. It's as if he was becoming transparent. Through his knotted fur, I could see the bricks behind. I reach out and grab his hand. 'Put it back on!' I tell him, 'we'll fix it. Just wait, please just wait.'

The centaur wipes the tears from his eyes. 'I've done my waiting,' he says, 'you wouldn't believe how long it's been, looking for someone like her, someone who actually wants to see me.'

I pick up the shoe and begin squishing it to the bottom of his hoof. 'Help me!' I tell him, 'make it fit, you have to, or you'll forget her!'

I press the shoe into the hoof, but each time it comes away, till at last, It's as if I'm pushing on the air.

Then, I look up at the centaur. He's little more than a coloured shadow. When he speaks, his voice is quiet, like thunder in the distance.

'But, the world won't forget,' he tells me, 'because, now you're here, because now you'll remember.'

With that, he begins to walk off down the road. 'Wait!' I

shout, 'You didn't tell me your name! What's your name?' but he doesn't answer, and I stare, and I shout, till I can't see him anymore. Then I just stand there knowing what it's like when the world loses a little of its magic.

Now, I've got all these feelings inside, and the easiest way to let them out is to get mad. So, I decide to head back into the cafe, to give that barista a piece of my mind, only, instead of heading through the door, I come face-to-face with someone coming out.

As one, our heads come together, and we both go down. She lands on top of me, and her bag goes up in the air. For a moment, I lie still, watching all those yellow pages tumble around me.

I tell her, 'I'm sorry, I didn't see you.'

Then I look up to see Miss Twenty Something. She rubs between her eyes, and tells me, 'Nice headbutt.'

I help her up, and collect the pages of her book. 'Look,' I say, 'I'm sorry, like really-really sorry.'

'Well,' she says, 'if you feel that bad, you can always buy me a drink?'

I look at her and smile. Then, I remember where I am. I look through the window to see the barista staring back at me. I ask, 'You really like coffee, don't you?'

She looks confused for a moment, and then, following my gaze to the cafe, she begins to laugh.

'Oh, right!' she says, 'No, to tell you the truth, I hate the stuff.'

'Not if you don't want to,' she says, 'come on, 'I'll take you to my favourite spot.'

Now it's my turn to look confused. 'So, why were you in there if you don't like coffee.'

'It's a really long story,' she tells me, and then she checks her bag, and after a moment of rummaging, I see her look around in panic.

'Crap,' she says, 'I think I dropped him.'

I tell her, 'Don't worry, we'll find it.' Then, as I'm looking around the street, it dawns on me. 'Wait? Did you say 'He?'

'Well,' she says, 'I'm not exactly sure. Thought it'd be rude to ask.'

I'm about to ask more, when I see something on the street, walking towards us.

It was a crab, all claws, and legs, and very much alive. It was weird, though, after the events of this morning, I can't say I was entirely surprised. Not even when I realised that the crab was made entirely out of rubies. Small polished beads for eyes. Its body, a cluster of large stones each gleaming in the English sun. One claw was small and perfectly shaped. The other large and crude, all spikes still clinging to a bed of rock.

The crab stops before me, then, after licking its ruby eye, I see it step back as if scared.

'I know what you're thinking,' says Miss Twenty Something, to the ruby crab, 'but I think you can trust him, he seems like one of the nice guys.'

I kneel down to the ruby crab, and hold out my hand. And, after a moment, the crab reaches out with the larger of its claws. With a gentle pinch, it grabs my index finger and gives it a shake.

'Go on,' says Miss Twenty Something. 'Tell him your story.'

And, with a look one way and then the other, the crab lets out a sigh, and then tells me about its day.

STREET OF RATS

The stray cat had no name, but she liked to kill things, and that's why they asked her to come. Five tins of cat food, that was the asking price, In return, she would scare the rats out the alley.

She stands over the body of a dying rat. There, she watches Its last moments, one twitch at a time.

The cat hears a squeak. The stray looks up to see another rat - piebald - not your usual alley looking vermin. It watches the cat from the safety of a half crumpled box. The cat bounds over and drags the rat, kicking and squeaking. The cat spits the piebald down by its dead brother. 'My place,' says the cat. 'Understand?'

The piebald doesn't respond. Instead, it begins to look around, over its shoulder, and up above. The stray swipes a single claw against the belly of the rat. She holds her nail and watches the blood run down into her fur. 'My place,' she says. 'Understand?'

The rat lets out a squeak, and from across the alley, a voice replies in kind. This comes from behind. The stray cat looks over to see a rat the colour of snow. Then there's another squeak, this comes from above. The cat looks to see two rats, one black the other grey, each with a little golden bell around their neck.

The stray looks at the rats, one by one. 'My place,' she says. 'My place.'

Then, she looks up to see not one or two but hundreds of rats. They're on the bins, and the boxes, and the fire escape, and the little gaps in the buildings. They sit on window ledges, and perch on telephone poles. They crawl out of the sewer grates. They fill the alley, coming out from the darkness. And there, as the stray cat looks around, she saw the way back was blocked by rats of every shade and every colour.

They don't look like rats of the street, they look like pets, each and every one of them.

The only way was forward, and as the cat did her best to look unafraid, the rats began to squeak, all of them, all at once. A single noise from a thousand mouths, all aimed at the cat. They sound hungry, though not for food, but for something else entirely - they were hungry for vengeance.

As the cat moves down the alley, a rat reaches out and sinks its teeth into her leg.

The cat hisses and grabs the rat with her mouth, with a single bite, she spits him into a puddle, and all watch as the water goes from grey to red. Then, with a look at one another, the rats take a step, and then another, and as one, they begin their hunt.

The feral has no choice but to run. Down the alley, with a hiss she leaps, all claws and teeth. The rats come for her. For every ten she kills, there's one that gets through, one who bites, one who draws blood, one who leaves her thinking she should have asked for more than five tins of cat food.

The cat fights on, running down, looking for a way out. There, she reaches the end of the alley and finds the way is blocked; A stone wall of red brick rises up - up - up.

The cat pants with exhaustion. One of her green eyes is beginning to swell shut. Her fur is sticky with blood.

The way back was a carpet of furry faces. All of them squeaking, their tiny black eyes staring without sympathy, without compassion.

From the darkness, the cat hears a voice. It sounds as if there were many, all speaking out at once, all saying the same thing.

'Tell me,' says the voice of many and one, 'how would

thou like a chance to live?'

The cat spits a tooth in the direction of the sound. 'My place,' she says. 'Understand?'

There's a pause, and then the darkness spoke.

'Yes,' it says, 'We understand.'

A piebald rat emerges from the crowd. It stands on its hind legs and asks, 'Remember me?' The rat gives a smile, all crooked and mean. The rat looks around at the faces of its companions. They were everywhere: on the floor, and in the walls, and in the dark little spaces where few dare to tread. Thousands of them, all staring down at her. 'Any last words?'

The feral purrs her way over, just close enough to reach the rat. With a smile, she bites off his head, and spits it into the crowd. 'My place,' she says. 'Understand?'

The head of the Piebald rat splashes into a puddle. There, it stays, twitching, and blinking. Its damp face twists in a look of pure disbelief, and then, as the death comes to take him - he lets out a single silent squeak, and then - nothing.

Then the rats come, all of them, all at once. They rise like a wave, all teeth and squeaks and hunger.

The cat swipes and bites and scratches. She spits, and laughs, even as they fall on top of her, dragging her down into the dark - dark - dark.

Top of the Hill

A ginger Tom Cat is in pain, It hurts between his legs. His instinct is to lick it clean, only he can't as there's a cone around his head. His name is Marmalade, and his humans keep telling him how he is a very-very good boy.

'Then why did you do this to me?' says Marmalade. His owners respond with a smile and say, 'Look, John. It's like he's really talking.'

Marmalade sits by the window, watching the world outside. There, he sees a cat jump onto the ledge. It's a British

Blue Shorthair, fat and stocky with eyes that shine like coins. The cat is called Alan, and he mouths something through the glass.

Marmalade holds a paw to his ear. 'Can't hear you!'

Alan breathes on the glass till it becomes foggy. Then, rubbing his head and cheek against the glass, he traces something in the language of cats. To a passing human, it would look like a series of smudges and smears, but to Marmalade, it spells the words 'Outside' and 'Trouble.'

Marmalade was the smartest cat he knew, it was him who taught the street how to get double tinny-tins at dinner time. 'It's all a matter of tactic,' said Marmalade. 'First you cry at the Primary Human, and then, after eating, you go and cry at the other.'

He goes over to the hairier of the two Humans, and there, brushing up against its leg, he sees a spot of bare skin, and Marmalade bites.

The hairy Human chases him through the house, and over to the front door. Half running, half kicked, Marmalade shoots out into the street.

'Cor blimey,' says Alan the British Blue. 'That was a close one, mate.'

'That, dear Alan, was exactly what I wanted to happen.'

'Looks awful violent, me old china.'

'Well, if you have a better idea then tell me, I am, as they say, all ears.'

'Well, you're all cone at least,' says the British Blue, then he sees the look on Marmalade's face. 'Sorry, I was just thinking, might be better to get a cat flap?'

Marmalade tries to lick at his sore bottom, but the cone gets in the way, so all he can do is stare and hiss. 'No, my sweet British Blue, one must train their Human, more than that, one must leave them thinking that kicking you out was their choice. Otherwise, they might start getting ideas such as: bedtimes, smaller dinners, and cute little dinosaur outfits.'

'What's wrong with that?' says Alan. 'You'd make a

smashing T-Rex, mate.'

'Be wary of the cat flap, my friend, for before you know it, they'll have you dependent on them, and after that, it's only a matter of time before they've got you on a leash, walking you like a dog.'

Alan nods several times. 'I don't get it, but you did teach me how to get more din-dins, so I'm sure you're right.'

'Speaking of which, do you have any extra tins? Only the good stuff, though, none of that 'salmon in jelly' filth you brought last time?'

'Can't, I've been saving up for the stray.'

'Stray? What stray?'

'Oh, come off it. Don't pee in my pocket and tell me it's raining.'

'We don't have any pockets, Alan. And I don't have any patience.'

'Alright-alright! Keep your fur on! The stray, you know, the one we're paying to clean out the alley?'

'Oh, yes, well, if she's eating your food, then we better go down and make sure she's doing her job.'

Alan nods then, slowly, he begins to frown. 'Wait a minute? What do you mean 'My food?' You mean our food, right?

Marmalade belches out his lunch. 'Oh yes,' he says, 'Of course, you're right, that's exactly what I mean.'

Alley

At the entrance to the alley, the cats wait.

'Well, off you go,' says Marmalade, 'I'll stay here, keep you covered.'

The two stare down into the damp and dark. 'Bugger that for a game of soldiers! Last time we mucked about down here I came back with the whole flea nation on me back, and you know what that means?'

The two cats looked at one another, and as one, they say it, 'Bath Time!'

'There won't be any fleas,' says Marmalade. 'That's why we paid the alley cat to get rid of them.'

'I thought it was so we could play in the alley, and eat old doughnuts, and pretend we was wild cats?'

Marmalade scratches at his cone. 'Same difference. Now, are we sure the alley cat is finished?'

'Well, she's not here, I can tell you that much.'

Marmalade stretches his neck over the boundary between the street and the alley. 'How far did you get?'

'Not very. I mean, what would happen if I turned up brown-bread? It'd break my old lady's heart.'

'Brown what?'

'Brown-bread? Dead? Cor, things were much more simple back in Blighty.'

'Look, Alan. I love you as a brother, but I have no idea what you're saying. Please, for the sake of our friendship, start making sense.'

'She's not here, mate. End of.'

'Well, if you didn't get very far, what makes you so sure?'

The British Blue steps close. 'Five tins we offered her. Tell me, what else has she got going on that's worth more than five tins?'

The two cats look at one another and then, one step at a time, they head into the alley.

'Hello?' says Marmalade, 'Mrs. StreetCat?'

Alan looks in the dark corners. 'Here, puss-puss-puss!'

They pass pools of dirty water. Boxes melted from the rain. The hum of flies, the stink of rotting vegetables, and quite possibly something much-much worse.

'Oi, remember last time we was here? We got chased by that big old rat?'

'No, dear, Alan. You're misremembering. In fact, it was only you who was chased. I'd have killed the rat, only it was too small to be any kind of sport.'

Alan lets out a cat sized laugh. 'Don't tell porky-pies, you screamed all the way home!'

'First of all,' says Marmalade, 'I don't like pies, and second, It's called psychological warfare, and from the sounds of it I did a very good job.'

Alan looks at the ginger cat, his long hair trailing on the floor, his squished face staring out from the clear plastic. 'Big words for such a small cone.'

'I could have killed the rat like that!'

'Like what?'

'Like this,' says Marmalade, and he swipes at his friend.

The two cats circle one another. Their voices cry out. Then, as one, they lunge. With claws and teeth, they slam into one another. The cats hit the alley floor, rolling around in the puddles and the filth. They bite, and hiss, and swipe, slamming into metal bins, and filling the alley with the sound of thunder.

The cats fall down laughing, spitting the fur from their mouths.

'Better luck next time,' says Marmalade.

'What do you mean? I won that fight!'

'Well, it's a shame there isn't anyone here to say otherwise, is there?'

Then, in answer, a voice calls out. 'We are here.'

The two cats look up. There, atop a bin, sits a cat, Its fur is the colour of dirty snow. Its head is down in the shadow. Whether cleaning or resting the two cats couldn't tell.

'Who are you?' says Marmalade.

Without lifting up its head, the cat answers. 'We are the Janus.' The voice was strange, soft and proper. Its voice was confident and old. And though its fur and body gave the signs of a well-fed housecat, here it was, down the alley, in the dark, its voice not the least bit afraid.

'What kind of name is Janus?' says Marmalade.

The cat continues to stare down, its face hidden in the dark. 'The name was not there in the beginning, but it came to us, when things first changed, and we found ourselves no longer alone.'

'Our name?' says Alan, 'as in, more than one of ya? Got the whole family around here, eh?'

Silence fills the alley and then, 'Yes. Brothers and sisters, all beyond counting.'

Marmalade lets out a scared hiss. 'Something doesn't feel right. We should go.'

'Sod off!' says Alan. 'You're just saying that because someone's here to prove you lost.' Alan steps forward. 'Hey, Mr. Janitor!'

The cat on the bin lets out a strange cry, it's like there's more than one voice inside trying to get out. 'Our name is The Janus, not Janitor. Only Janus.'

Alan ponders this for a moment. 'Righty-o,' he says. 'Cool. So, anyway, Mr. Thingie-Majig. If I might be so bold as to bend your ear for a moment: See, you've been here for a while, yeah?'

'And we will remain until the end of all things.'

Alan blinks several times. 'Nice. So, which one of us do you think won the fight? Now, I don't wanna play favourites, but, I know you just saw me do that leg kick. I mean, I know it's very impressive, but remember, don't overlook Marmalade, after all - he's really good at getting knocked to the ground.'

'That was no fight,' says the cat upon the bin. 'But soon, you will have your chance, and all shall perish that stand before the Janus.'

Alan looks up at the cat upon the bin. 'Well, nice talking to ya, I guess.' Then he looks at Marmalade. 'I think he's mental.'

Marmalade steps forward. 'There was a girl, a street cat, a tabby. Did you see her?'

'She was given a choice,' says the Janus.

The cats look at one another. 'Right, says Marmalade. 'I think It's time to go.'

'Question,' says the cat upon the bin. 'You allowed us a question.'

'Fine,' says Alan, 'but you and your brother are going to have to share one, so decide quick because it's almost din-din time.'

The cat leaps down to the floor below. There, it walks forward, head down. It passes several puddles, and Marmalade gets a look of something, something that makes his hair stand on end.

'Go on then, what's your question?'

With that, the cat looks up. Its face was wrong, for a start, there were two of them. Each of the faces shares the eye in the middle, while the other two stare off over Marmalade's left and right shoulder. There were two mouths, each of them mumbling under their breath.

The cat with two faces speaks; through one mouth it tells them, 'Your names are Marmalade, and Alan,' Then, from the other mouth it tells them, 'And you will die.'

'Not much of a question,' says Marmalade, 'but thanks anyway.'

They watch cats step out from the dark. They drag themselves on stiff legs. Their eyes are closed, their heads bent and dangling.

'The Janus gave them freedom,' says the cat. 'They came from all over: The pets, and strays; The unloved, and lost; those who thought they were family, and those who knew right away they were nothing more than an unwanted gift.'

They came from the dark, with their eyes rolled back.

'The Janus absorbed them, and The Janus became many. And now, we will ask our question. We ask you, dearest brothers - will you join us?'

Marmalade watches the stiff cats come closer. The two house cats look at one another and nod. 'Thanks!' they say, 'but no thanks!' and then they run.

The stiff cats were everywhere, the rodents too. Unlike the cats, their expressions were normal. They looked angry, and hungry, and a few even looked scared. The stiff cats began to herd them, and, as the boys ran, the rats gave chase.

Thankfully, Marmalade's body was as thick as it was hairy. The rats slam into his side, biting at the clumps of hair. None of it hurt, but the weight of them soon began to grow. There, around them, stiff cats dragged themselves over, swiping with their heavy hands.

From behind, Alan lets out a cry. Marmalade turns to see him dragged down by the rats.

He wants to go back, but the way out is shrinking, and then, with tears in his eyes, Marmalade runs and doesn't look back.

***

Alan can feel the weight of the rats on top of him. They press down, biting with their yellow teeth. He thinks, 'This is it. No more playing with balls of string. No more din-dins, or snacky-whacks, or belly rubs. This is it.'

Then, he hears a voice. The rats pull away, and Alan looks up at The Janus cat. It stares down at him with both its faces.

'A choice,' says the cat. 'You can end here, with your body. Or you can join The Janus, and learn what life can really mean.'

He looks around at the thousands of hungry rats. 'You're not leaving me much choice, are ya?' With that, he nods and bows. 'Fair enough, mate. You've got yourself a deal.'

The Janus nods, and the rats attack again.

Alan lets out a cry. 'But I accepted!'

'Yes,' says The Janus, 'but your body is of no further use, save that which will feed the horde.'

Alan feels his life drain into the alley. There, things begin to grow dark, and in the darkness, he sees something step forward, something bright, something that burns his eyes. It was like stars and fire and all things shiny. It flashes with a thousand colours.

'Now, you will join us, and together The Janus shall grow.'

And with that, what little light that was Alan the British

Blue Shorthair was absorbed into the huge burning light of the Janus.

There, he feels life's perspective begin to shift. He learns words like Pet and Domesticated. He learns of animal experiments, of the kind that brings the world medicine, and the other kind that gives people new shampoo, and there he feels every ounce of pain and animal abuse.

He learns of The Janus, the original, the one born in a lab. He could feel its pain as they did their tests, injecting it with poison.

The thing that was Alan was beginning to slip away. It was replaced with pain, and anger, and the desire for revenge. But, more than that, it was replaced with another feeling, one of loneliness.

The Janus had absorbed many minds, and yet, it was not enough, not even slightly. There's still room for more, many more, for all the cats in the world, and maybe, in time, maybe even that won't be enough.

And there, absorbed into the mind of a thousand cats, Alan grew into something more. A sea of minds, all thinking as one, and there he lost his family, his life, and finally, even his name.

Only one thing remained, it wasn't much, just a single word, one that when spoken stretched on through time. It was the last that remained of the cat known as Alan. A single word spoken over and over:

'Marmalade.'

Back at the Street

At the top of the hill, Marmalade paces back and forth. He sees a stiff cat drag itself up the street. In its mouth is a rat, white and squeaking. It's only as the stiff cat gets closer did he realise it was Alan.

With one eye closed, Alan spits the rodent by

Marmalade's feet, and there, he waits, his breath coming one awkward wheeze after another.

The rodent brushes down his body and frowns at the stiff cat. Then he turns to Marmalade.

'The master sends a message.'

'Look. I don't want any trouble. So, tell me how long it takes for Alan to become normal, and then, we'll never touch the alley again.'

'He has come to offer you a chance,' says the rat, 'for you and the others on your street: give up and you will be allowed to join the master. Resist, delay, or fight, and you will be devoured by the horde.'

With that, the stiff cat makes its way down the hill, leaving Marmalade with his thoughts.

He sneaks over to his other friend, Mrs Kibbles. There, he meows at the door till the owner comes out with a broom. This gives Mrs Kibbles enough time to escape through her legs. The two run down the street and away from the danger of being put back inside.

'Thanks for that,' says Mrs Kibbles. She was a Sphynx cat. Bald, with an angry face. She was also wearing a pink sweater that had clearly been crocheted by the owner.

'Sorry to do this,' says Marmalade, 'but, there's going to be a fight.'

'Turf war?'

'Worse.'

Mrs Kibbles licks at her paw. 'Good.'

The Janus

All roads lead to one.

Either The Janus would make the World its family, and then, it would teach people how to be kind to one another. Or, if the World refused ... well then, that would be their choice.

It's hard knowing as much as it did, for The Janus to be

clear. In the early days, things had made more sense. Back then, there was only one mind, now the Janus was many, and its mind was filled with so much noise.

So many suggestions, so many options, all of them fighting to be heard. There were some in The Janus that regretted their choice. Some who feel that they didn't have a choice to begin with. These were the newer additions. They weren't as grateful as the old. Those cats who had chosen to become one. The ones in the clinic, who had no way of escape. The ones abandoned in the alleys. The kittens, the old, and the broken. It was these who occupied the early life of The Janus, and it was these who promised that, with time, the newest additions would get all they had been promised and more.

The Janus marches up the street, armed with the stiff bodies of those it had absorbed, and the many-many rats it had beaten, and bribed, and promised a world without fear.

It would welcome those who lived upon the hill, or it would feed them to the horde.

One day, the horde will grow large enough to devour a town, then a city, until finally, he'll devour the entire world.

He wonders what it'll be like to have all those minds in one head? He hopes that it'll help, that he'll finally stop feeling so alone.

***

At the top of the hill, Marmalade waits on the fence. There, he sits, still and basking with his eyes closed, even as the cats and rodents began to fill the street.

'You do not run,' says The Janus. 'You do not fight. Then, all that is left is to join and become one.'

'Yeah,' says Marmalade, 'but, here's the thing.' And with that, he leaps off the fence, and into the garden behind.

With a sigh from both its mouths, The Janus turns to the horde. 'Kill.'

The rats pour through the gaps in the fence, while the

stiff cats look for their openings.

Marmalade runs over to Mrs Kibbles. He tells her, 'Now!' And the two begin to shout and cry and meow at the top of their voice.

The owner comes out. 'There you are!' she says, and then she sees hundreds of rats in the grass, all of them pouring through the gaps in the fence.

'My lord!' she says, and then she takes out the garden hose, and begins to spray down the horde.

Rats are knocked flying with a 'squeak!' and still they come sprayed down by the hundreds. Then, Marmalade sees the body of Alan come through the gaps. There, he pounces, hoping to knock it down. The thing that was Alan turns its neck, and then it scratches with a hand that's oh so heavy.

Mrs Kibbles runs over and gives Alan a scratch.

The stiff cat doesn't seem to notice. Then, Kibbles' owner turns the hose to Alan. She cries, 'Leave her alone!' And then hits Alan with the full force of the Turbo-Hose3000©.
Stiff Alan goes flying through the fence.

The rats stop. They look from Marmalade to the other stiff cats that are coming, slow and steady.

'Come on!' says Marmalade, and they push on, jumping to the next fence.

They rush along the tops, chased by the stiff cats, who make their way, one awkward step at a time. Marmalade pushes one off the top where it lands and breaks into several dusty pieces. He watches each piece begin to wiggle uselessly on the ground.

More of the rats stop, confused, and scared, and a little curious. Mrs Kibbles gives them a hiss, and the rats back off, giving time for the cats to escape.

They head around, crying at houses, causing their owners to come out with their brooms, and their air rifles, and pans. The rats and stiff cats are knocked and trodden and shot. And they come, but they do so less confidently. They had not expected to meet such fierce resistance.

There, out of the gardens, Marmalade heads into the front where he sees The Janus.

The cat with two heads watches as the rats flee from the gardens. 'They're too big!' cry the rats. 'They've got water and guns, and their boots are so big and heavy.'

'Fight' says The Janus.

'But we'll die!'

'Die if you must,' says the Janus. 'But, first you shall fight.'

Then Marmalade steps forward. 'Let's settle this,' he says. 'Cat to cat.'

The Janus meows with a thousand voices and one. 'Come then, little mind.'

The two strike. Marmalade was bigger, but The Janus had two mouths, and both bit deep into his skin. They claw and bite at his neck, but the cone protected his face, and soon, Marmalade begins to overpower The Janus, and slowly, he begins to push it down.

Then, as The Janus cries out in a thousand voices. It turns and, in one that sounds familiar, it asks, 'How could you leave me?'

It was the voice of Alan, and with it, Marmalade takes a step back.

The Janus swipes a claw across his face. There was pain and blood, and Marmalade couldn't see.

'How could you?' says Alan. 'You left me to die!' The Janus cat attacks. It claws at his side, and tears his ear, and all the while Marmalade cries, 'I'm sorry!' over and over.

With a final swipe, Marmalade falls to the floor.

'Now,' says the Janus. 'You shall join. There, you shall be our prisoner.'

And as The Janus raises its claw, it lets out a cry, one of a thousand voices, and as it brings down its hand, the claw stops.

It hovers above Marmalade, hand shaking with visible effort.

In a voice full of pain, The Janus asks, 'What is

happening?'

Then, in reply, The Janus speaks with Alan's voice. 'Sorry, mate. But I can't let you do that.'

The Janus cries out. 'Stop him! For we are one! We are many!'

Marmalade looks up at the Janus. He watches its eyes shift from the wild madness of the two headed cat to eyes that were familiar, eyes that shone like golden coins.

'I can't hold him for much longer,' says Alan.

Marmalade looks into the eyes of his friend. 'What do you want me to do?'

'Just one thing,' says Alan. 'just one little thing. Live your life. Live it for both of us.'

There's a pause, then The Janus blinks its three eyes. Once more, the monster was in control.

'Do not move!' it tells the rats. Then its face twists in pain. In the voice of Alan, it tells the rats, 'Kill us!'

The rats look at one another.

Marmalade watches as the rats begin to surround the Janus.

'Stop!' cries the cat in many voices, but then many more tell the rats. 'Do it! Be free!'

Then, the rats attacked. They swarmed The Janus, and soon there was nothing, not even bones.

***

In the days after, Marmalade would be taken to the vet. There, with much tears, it would be explained that he was going to lose an eye. In the days to come, he would be known as mummy's little soldier, and soon, still with the cone upon his head, he would find his way back outside.

With that, Marmalade walks down the road. There he sits by the alley. Alone, he ponders his choices.

He's about to leave when he sees a rat step out from the dark.

Marmalade doesn't flinch like he used to. 'Hey!' he says, 'you got a death wish?'

The rat has its arms in the air. Its eyes are closed. Its head dances from side to side.

'What's going on?' says Marmalade.

The rat holds its hand to the sky. 'Music!'

Marmalade looks around. 'What music?'

Then, he watches the rat go. It wanders off into the street. There, it's joined by another, and then another. They crawl out from the dark, and the gaps, and the holes. They all have their hands up in the air, all dancing to the same unheard song. They came from everywhere, and they walked as one, filling the streets like a parade. Marmalade follows, and slowly, as he squints, he hears it: soft and distant - it was the sound of music.

The rat next to him smiles, 'It's good isn't it?'

Marmalade wants to speak, but can't. It's the music, see, it makes him want to dance.

And so he did, down the street, with his head swaying from side to side. There were other cats too, feral and domestic. And soon, even the people began to join. They marched and danced to the music, and there, as one, the streets began to dance.

EMOTION LOCKER

They have a fancy name for it, but most people call it Storage.

'Think of it as a locker for your emotions,' says the Ticket Man. 'Takes seven years to get to Titan, and we don't want any accidents now, do we?' The man's hawkish features are made less threatening by his long bushy beard. 'It's like seeing a grey cloud so you pop up your umbrella - Storage, my friend, It's your one way guarantee to not get wet.'

'What do you do with the emotions?' says Jun. 'You just throw them out, like trash in a bag?'

'Not at all, squire. Not at all. Storage isn't in the business of waste management. Why, before Storage, sir, humanity was a child being dragged by a parent. Now, emotions are like a wardrobe: All starched and ironed - ready to be worn again.'

The Ticket Man reaches in his pocket and takes out a small piece of crystal. Its shape is that of a teardrop, the tail end is bent and crooked. The Ticket man fixes the crystal right between Jun's eyes. 'Now,' he says, 'thanks to Storage, the only feeling you will ever experience will be those you have chosen, well . . . unless you do something wrong of course.'

Jun rubs the crystal on his forehead. 'Why, what happens if you do something wrong?'

The Ticket Man just smiles. 'Don't worry, sir. You'll find out soon enough.'

Aboard The Sunflower

It will take seven years to reach the moon of Saturn, and so, with no faster than light travel looming on the horizon, humanity must look to travel in style. The Star-Yacht Sunflower was an older model, smaller by a third than every other modern vessel. But that made it cheap. See, most modern vessels will force their crewmates to wear Storage throughout the journey, from start to finish. Sunflower, however, has maintained a healthy crew that, thanks to a loophole, allows its crew to kick back and enjoy a nice emotion every now and then. This is done on a rotation cycle to avoid any complications. Jun was given afternoons every Sunday, which - within certain areas - allowed him to experience an emotion of his choice. This can be one of the emotions he's collected himself, or he can buy it from the ship's many emotion stores.

For a price boarding on the extortionate, you can slip into the mind of your favourite celebrity, though judging by the list on offer, you may have to lower your expectations to that person you kinda recognise from that show you never managed to finish. Then there are the experts, people whose job it is to collect experience. He had only been on the Sunflower long enough to use the toilet. There, mid-stream, the man next to him asks, 'So, what's you kink, Kid?'

Jun turns his back to the man and fails to urinate. 'I'm engaged,' he says, 'but thanks anyway.'

'No, Kid. You don't get it. I'm talking experience. I'm talking emotion. That stuff they sell at the Kiosk? It's a joke, couldn't fool a goldfish with that. Whereas me, I know all about experience, I'm an emotional cosmonaut, can get you anything.' Then, with a look over his shoulder, he leans in and whispers, 'You wanna know what it's like to die?'

Jun stares right ahead trying to focus himself to pee. 'That's illegal.'

The stranger leans in so close Jun can feel the man's beard scratch his face. 'Only if you get caught, kiddo. Only if you get caught.'

Accommodation

Jun brought his girlfriend, Yokosan. They never fought, and in bringing her, they were upgraded from economy to business. This meant they had a room 'just' big enough for a double bed. They were also granted a small utility cupboard.

'Perfect space for offspring,' says the Realtor from Sunflower Industries, 'That,' she says, 'or a good spot for a few cleaning appliances.' Then she whispers, 'but make sure to buy the latest model. The old ones don't fold as well, get stuck, very annoying.'

Jun looks at the little space, just big enough for his guitar and the cat box. 'How is this big enough for a child?'

'It's in keeping with interplanetary regulations,' says the Realtor. 'Check your manual, you'll find it under 'Concerning Cargo and Non-Working Lifeforms.'

Jun doesn't say anything. Thanks to Storage, the words in his head, though still ever present, were left hollow and vague, like a sentence without context. He knew something about it upset him on a deep and terrible level. It was obvious, not just to him, but everyone in the room, all you had to do was look at Jun and watch that little crystal tear begin to pulse a deep dark red.

In keeping with a life free of politics, the Sunflower had opted to shape its sections with designs from across the world. Jun lived in the Japanese section. He was not Japanese, he was from Hong Kong.

'Sorry, sorry,' says the leader of Japanese culture aboard the ship. 'I will find you space in China section.'

'Thanks,' says Jun, 'but, I'm not Chinese either, I'm from Hong Kong.'

The leader of Japanese culture writes something down, frowns, and then scribbles it out. 'I'm not understand. You are Chinese but not Chinese?'

'No,' says Jun, 'I'm from Hong Kong, we're different. You know, like Taiwan?'

The leader of Japanese culture nods. 'Ah,' he says, 'I am loving Taiwan. Bubble Tea is-a bestest favourite of mine.'

'Yes,' says Jun, 'It's very nice.'

'One moment,' says the leader of Japanese culture, 'and I will give you room in Taiwan.' Then he scribbles something down on a piece of paper.

'But, I don't want to go to Taiwan,' says Jun.

The leader of Japanese culture looks up. 'Ah,' he says with a smile, 'you pro-China!' Then he scribbles out the first bit and writes something else. 'One moment, and I put you in Chinatown.'

'No,' says Jun, 'I don't want to go there either.'

The leader of Japanese culture scribbles something, frowns, writes something else, and then frowns again. With a look at Jun, he gives him a friendly smile and says, 'I don't get it?'

In the end, after much confusion, they all agreed that Jun was from Hong Kong, and then, because no-one knew what else to do, they left him in the Japanese section. During this whole process, both Jun and the leader of Japanese culture found their polite and civil conversations undercut by the blue lights of confusion that flashed from their little head crystals.

Jun wasn't Japanese, but he liked the apartment. The honey-coloured wood that framed the room, and the white floor shaped with the latest Tech-Sense. Tech-Sense allowed those present to alter its composition. In the first week alone, Jun had experienced many features. The two that stand out are how, on the second day, Jun felt his toes go numb under the crunch of fresh snow, this was followed up by the singularly unique experience of walking through marshmallow melted to room temperature. Mostly, he prefers to stick to plain old carpet: deep shag and fluffy, the kind that reminds him of laying on his pet German Shepherd. The death of his pet had been what pushed Jun to take the trip, and whenever he lays down on this kind of carpet he can't help but smile, even as his Storage flashes with the pink lights of sadness.

In the centre of the room was a table, so small that it scratched his knees whenever he used it. Along the exit wall was a paper window across which inky figures would appear. Someday's they would pray, while other days, they would walk upon these hills, all humped like the backs of a camel. Sometimes they did this but mostly they didn't, mostly they waged war. All small and coloured, one brush stroke after another, Jun would sit there for hours and watch as they waged their teeny-tiny painted wars. The flash of yellow from his Storage says he enjoys it, and then Jun got an idea: Every Monday evening from four to six as he waits for Yokosan to get home, he will sit and watch the paper wall smiling as the civilisations grew and died and grew again. Once they reach Titan, he's going to gift those happy Mondays to Yokosan - all seven years of it.

With the paper window facing across to the rest of the ship, the opposite window looked out into space.

'I always expected space to be dark,' says Jun. Through the window, he could see stars. Not one, or two, but millions. Some white tipped with gold, while others flashed baby blue. The ones on the edge of vision were clear and spread out, but as you came to the centre, they formed a blanket of light around which darkness was forced to the edges.

'Space isn't dark,' says Jun, 'Out here it's light with bits of dark, like cracks on a pale wall.' And then he sat there, his face calm and serene. He didn't feel anything as he stared out into the cosmos, though his Storage would not stop its violent flashing, painting the room a vibrant yellow.

First Meal

Technically, it wasn't their first meal.

They'd been on the ship for three months. But it was the first meal where both of them had a little time to feel. There, with both Storage devices powering down into pale crystals, Jun made them Sukiyaki. It's a dark broth of soy, sugar, and leafy vegetables. The smell is rich and meaty and reminds Jun of gravy stew. He sets the table with chopsticks and waits for Yokosan.

With one step through the door she asks, 'What's that?'

'Dinner,' says Jun, and he waves at the Sukiyaki.

'I know what it's called,' says Yokosan. 'I had it every day as a child.'

'Everyday?'

Yokosan shrugs. 'What can I say? Momma liked her gravy, on the good days and the bad, even when her little girl cried she hated it, still, we had it. Momma liked her gravy.'

'Well,' he says, 'that's all in the past now.' Then, he holds up the bowl and smiles. 'Here, to the first meal of the rest of our lives.'

Yokosan does not take the bowl. 'If I wanted Japanese food I'd have stayed in Japan.'

'Ok,' says Jun, and he takes his chopsticks and begins to eat.

Yokosan stands by the table. 'Are you mad at me?'

'It's fine,' says Jun, 'I mean - you didn't taste it - but it's fine.'

Yokosan reaches out and touches his arm. 'Maybe we should talk about it?'

'It's fine,' he says, 'Look, I don't wanna fight. Not now, not on Feeling's Night. Ok?'

Yokosan stands there for a moment, not saying anything. 'Ok,' she says. She left shortly after, and Jun was left to finish both bowls.

Hours later, she came back with two bags full of shopping. There was no smile, but her Storage flickered an excited yellow.

The week after, they try again, this time, Yokosan does the cooking. It ends with her pulling a mess of congealed cheese and soggy dough out of the oven.

With his head tilted to one side, Jun asks, 'What was it supposed to be?'

'Deep Dish Pizza,' says Yokosan, and then they both laugh.

They didn't eat the pizza, but he did give her a kiss, one that Yokosan returns with another, and slowly, the two kiss their way to the bedroom. The two make love, and though their Storage robs them of any sensation, they continue regardless.

'Once we reach Titan, we'll feel it all,' says Yokosan. 'Every moment.'

Then, she kissed him on both eyes, and the two slept, cuddled up, damp with sweat.

Year Two

With Yokosan working on a different rotation, Jun was left to spend his feelings by himself. Lately, he's taken to using them on the racetrack along the central ring. His car stops in line with several others, each one revving its engine, ready to race. In reality: The cars were magnetically clamped, so it's more like riding on a roller coaster.

Ahead was the Carina Nebula home to some 14,000 stars. It looks like someone painted an angel in frost and dark bruises.

The cars set off. Sometimes you were ahead, and would spend the race neck and neck with some plucky would-be hero. Who won depended on the morale of the station. On the boring days the car in front would become a bad guy, known in wrestling as the Heel. Those behind would be knocked, mocked, and driven out of the race. People would boo, throw popcorn, and spend the rest of the day talking about how they were excited to see the jackass lose. Days of bad morale were all about the Baby Face. A plucky young hero, who would show the champion a thing or two about the dangers of running your mouth. These were less frequent as it took time to build up a satisfying win. Then there was the rare moment. The time where Mr. Always Last would somehow brave the odds.

Through great skill and dumb luck, they'd overtake each of the drivers. Even the Heel had to admit it - there was nothing quite like a success story - rags to riches, and all that.

That only happened once, though, when this guy called Jeremy accidentally posted something from his diary. The information was, to say the least, very dark. There wasn't any clue the man was suffering from depression, of course not, Storage took care of all that. Whenever you'd see him in Japantown, he would look normal, just like everyone else. One time, Jun shared a pleasant conversation over a bowl of warm Sake. He could tell it was pleasant by the way his Storage pulsed a steady yellow.

The diary painted a different picture, and as Jeremy shot around the ring, he was cheered on as he beat his boss, his dad, and that guy from accounting, the one, who according to the diary, had only got the promotion because he offered to marry the boss's ugly daughter.

'He was messing with his Storage,' says the operator.

'How?'

'Been doing it for months, apparently.'

'Did he get in trouble?'

'They're saying he got a routine punishment.' Then the operator looks around and leans in. 'But, I heard, he upset some serious people with that stunt. See, it's not just any old Storage he was messing with, no, it's the Sunflower's own personal model, and here comes this guy making them look like a fool.'

'What happened?' says Jun.

'Depends who you ask. Some folks say, he got the usual dose of feelings, all collected by the people he'd hurt. That's the public message, anyway. No, what I hear is, they wanted to make an example, give him a dose he'll never forget.'

Next day, Jun finds him in the canteen. He's sitting in the corner with a long string of drool running down from chin to table.

'You ok?' says Jun.

The man continues to stare ahead, eyes soft and distant.

Jun holds out his hand and says, 'Hey, your name's Yuto, right?'

The man says nothing.

'You know,' says Jun, 'whenever I was sad, my Dad would cheer me up by doing something silly.' Jun then holds out his index finger. 'Go on,' he says, 'give it a pull.'

Yuto does not pull the finger. He sits as he has done since he returned to the community. So, Jun takes Yuto's hand and there he grips it around his finger, and then, with great effort, he leans back and farts. It's not so impressive, Jun's father would call it a Mouse Squeak, 'A solid three out of ten, boyo. Now stand back, and watch the master work.'

Jun smiles and Yuto continues to stare ahead, blind to the world around him. Then, the notification goes off, and those on their break find their Storage reactivated. Jun watches Yoto's Storage begin to flicker, and then, the man's lost distant look is replaced with a polite smile.

'Hello,' says Yoto, 'apologies, seemed to have dozed off.'

Jun asks, 'Are you alright?'

'Yes, why wouldn't I be?'

The only sign that there was anything wrong at all came from the Storage. Normally, people's mind's tend to drift slowly from one emotion to the next. Their colours shift from reds to blue, greens to gold. Yoto was different, his Storage flickers through hundreds of colours, like rainbow static on an old TV.

Back at the racetrack, Jun asks, 'What happened to Yoto?'

'He's had a break,' says the operator. 'Happens from time to time. Mostly, with the more severe crimes. Guess he was just unlucky, eh?'

'Will he get better?'

'Better?' says the operator, 'sure, as long as he has access to Storage, he'll be good as new.'

'What about when he doesn't use Storage?'

The operator offers him a cigarette. 'I heard It's standard practice in prison. See, once the mind has snapped, there's no need for any more bars. All you have to do is turn off Storage for a few minutes and they'll do just about anything to have you turn it back on.'

'So, he'll never feel anything again?'

'Oh no, he'll feel it, he'll feel everything,' says the operator, 'and he'll do anything to get them to turn it back off.'

Jun saw Yoto over the coming weeks. Everytime he was on duty, the man seemed perfectly normal, except for the static crackle of his Storage. Then, whenever he was allowed to feel, he'd find him standing there, mouth open, eyes glazed. The man was broken, that much was obvious. He was the first of the Emotional Zombies, but, sad as it was to admit, he wouldn't be the last.

That night, Jun came home to find no sign of Yokosan. She'd been out every night for the past week. There was no note, no sign on the fridge to let him know that everything was ok.

'You've washed your underwear,' says Jun. It was strange. All the rest of her washing was done with his, just not her underpants, well, not all of them. The silk ones with the frilly edge, as well as the sexy one with the lace up the back. Jun never saw those underpants when she got into bed, but they were always being washed.

Jun can't remember the last time she wore sexy underwear. He can't remember the last time she wanted to spend her feel time with him.

Jun doesn't say anything when she gets home. He just sits in the living area, Storage throbbing with the pink light of heartbreak.

Year Three

The operator sits in his chair. Dark mahogany, with a back shaped into two serpents fighting each other. The furniture was powered by Storage. Being the kind of guy that could afford such luxury, the operator fed the red light of anger into those serpents, and Jun watches as they twist and bite at one another.

Jun had never been called into work so early. 'This better be good.'

'Maybe you should sit.'

'Maybe you should just tell me what's so important, that way I can go back to bed.'

The operator gives a silent nod and then began to shake.

'What's the matter?' asks Jun.

'Oh, it's nothing,' says the operator. 'I just have cancer.'

Thanks to Storage, the news didn't affect production that day, or any subsequent day thereafter. A few complications arose when the operator began to lose muscle definition. Soon, he was too weak to continue with his daily duties. He died within the month.

Jun put in a claim that, with the funeral coming up, he should be allowed to feel. His request was denied, and as he watched them ship his friend off into space, Jun felt nothing, though his Storage flashed an ugly bitter red.

Fourth Year

Yokosan had been spending more and more time at home. It was mostly a good thing, till Jun remembers that she wasn't alone.

'Who are you again?' asks Jun.

'You know Mark,' says Yokosan.

The man was short. His head was big and bald and reminded Jun of one of those grey aliens, only with big plastic veneers.

'You alright, mate,' says Mark, and he gives Jun a slap on the shoulder.

Jun takes an antibacterial wipe and begins to brush at the area Mike touched. 'Why's he here?'

'He's a colleague.'

'Think we're a little more than that,' says Mark, and he pulls her in close.

Jun doesn't say anything, he just stands there, Storage

flashing from Red to Pink. It was going so fast that the Storage began to sputter, and for a moment, Jun fell to the floor, howling in rage.

The other two made no effort to defend themselves, or to hide, even as Jun grabbed Mark by the throat and squeezed.

It felt good, it felt very good. Mark didn't resist, though, his face stared at him, all confused as it began to turn an ugly shade of purple. Then, just as his eyes began to roll into the back of his head, Jun felt the Storage turn back on.

He let go of Mark. 'Sorry about that. Must be a malfunction.'

'It's all fine with me,' says the man who was sleeping with Yokosan. 'But, I'd get that checked, if I were you.'

Jun looks into the mirror and sees his Storage begin to flicker, ever so slightly, like rainbow coloured static.

***

When dealing with intense feels, you consult both the doctor and the engineer.

'It looks like you've overcharged your Storage,' says the engineer.

Word on the ship is, in an attempt to compete with bigger companies, the Sunflower had cut corners so that they could mass produce their Storage. When the bugs began to emerge, they made an official statement:

'All of us here on the Sunflower are working tirelessly to ensure that these little hiccups are resolved as quickly as possible.'

Hiccups, is that what they call it? There've been over a hundred cases of malfunctions, cases like Jun's where the individual is overloaded with emotion. He tried to feel his way through it, but on his next downtime, Jun was hit with such a force of emotion that he had to be restrained in order to stop hurting himself.

'It's all perfectly natural,' says the doctor. 'It's not a

malfunction, my friend, it's your thoughts on feeling, that's the real problem here.'

'But, I like to feel,' says Jun. 'It's what makes me a person.'

'It's what made you an animal, my friend. But that time has gone. Now, it is a new age, so embrace it. Count yourself lucky.'

'What's lucky about this?'

'We're all going that way, my friend. Humanity, one and all. Some will quietly, while others will need a push. Then there are the lucky ones, people like you.'

'You mean the broken?'

'You're not broken,' says the doctor, 'You're evolved.'

Sixth Year

People complained about the experience of the ride.

'It's too similar,' they say. 'Too boring.'

And Jun says, 'Tell me about it.' The only thing that gave him comfort were the views. The recent discovery was a cloud of green light and orange stars, a result of mineral richness allowing them to stand out, so bright it hurt your eyes. Those distant stars offered a contrast, a blanket of soft blues, cold and dull. It broke up the monotony but not the complaints.

'You must do something,' says the new boss. 'Try the new plan.'

'I don't think we should,' says Jun. 'I'm not sure it's safe.'

'People come here to feel,' says the new boss. 'I'm not losing any more business to those Squashed-Heads.'

The cars set off as normal, but as they reach the first tight corkscrew, Jun presses a button and out comes the passengers. Each is wearing a space-suit. All are shaped into the various historical designs of the station's many cultural histories: the people from the ring of England wore suits of armour. He watches one couple lift up their visors and smile; The folks from Russia float around like squishy bears; Then the Japanese, Samurai armour. Segmented shoulder panels, and face masks that look like grinning monsters. All were space-suits. The typical boring kind that keeps you safe. The only major difference was Sunflower was owned by an independent, and so it made sense not to expect anything uniform.

Jun watches as the cars shoot around the rings. The cars did their same old tricks, only now they had people floating behind.

'This is great,' says the new boss. Then he watches as one driver reaches out and grabs the hand of the next car along. Both share a moment of thrill and excitement, and then the cars turn away at violent speed.

The first man is thrown against his windshield, and is left to bob and bounce around the car.

'Stop the track,' calls Jun.

Chaos starts to recede, and in the panic, the drivers pull their way back inside. The second driver wasn't so lucky. His tether snaps immediately, and he's left to tumble through space. Jun refuses the commands of the new boss to turn off the com.

'Not until he's lost signal.'

The man was on a feel trip, and so he was left to spin through space, screaming as he vanished into the void.

Jun stands there, listening to noises from the com, his Storage flickering, wild and broken.

'You're lucky,' says the new boss. 'One day, I've got to feel this moment. But you don't.'

Jun didn't feel lucky. He didn't feel anything.

Seventh Year

Jun couldn't remember why he wanted to come to Titan.

He was given the procedure on how to turn off Storage.

'Now, you don't want to just take in everything at once,' says the engineer. 'Not ideal, not for you, not for the locals. So, what we want to offer today is to aid you in identifying and tagging your emotions over the last seven years.'

'What good would that do?' says Jun.

'Well, it'll allow you to access specific emotions, kinda like choosing what to have for dinner.'

'But, my Storage is broken,' says Jun. 'I was told that I wouldn't be able to experience any emotions, not without suffering great pain.'

'Yes,' says the engineer, 'and that brings me to another reason why I've come here personally see, you might think you're broken, but I'm here to try and help you see this as an opportunity.'

Jun braced himself for the news he already knew. See, word is, those 'technical issues' that came with Sunflower tech? Well, any hope of seeing this company imprisoned for their crimes was dashed the moment Jun heard that Titan military wants to buy up all the broken Storage.

'It's a weekly paycheck,' says the engineer. 'You don't have to do anything, you just turn up, and let them download all that fuzz, and thanks to Sunflower technologies, it'll keep coming back, I mean, talk about jackpot.'

The worst part about having a broken Storage wasn't the fact he couldn't feel anymore. It was the simple truth that Jun no longer knew how he felt about anything. Good news, and bad, it all came out the same, his Storage flickering, all colours at once.

He wanted to believe that, deep down, he hated this man, hated what he stood for. But he wasn't sure.

'Is it true they're using our emotions as weapons?'

'You've got to admit,' says the engineer, 'it's cleaner. This way, no one has to fire a single shot.'

'Except for the guy shooting people with damaged Storage.'

The engineer shrugged. 'No deaths then.'

'Unless you count the guys who try and turn off the Storage.'

'Yeah,' says the engineer, 'but who'd be stupid enough to

do that? It's a bright new day, my friend. See, you wore Storage for travel, and now, across the whole of Titan, you won't meet a single person without it.'

Jun told the engineer he'd think about it.

He didn't know how long before he wouldn't be given a choice. It's true what the engineer said, there weren't many people on Titan without Storage. You'd hear nasty rumours, about people captured and exposed to faulty tech. It was just a rumour, for now, but more and more, Jun saw faces on the streets greeting him with that rainbow coloured static.

There are no prisons on Titan. Thanks to Storage, they didn't need them.

Over a short but intense period, the prisoner would be subjected to a dose of Emotion collected by all those they have harmed with their reckless behaviour. The results can be permanently damaging, but as long as you are fitted with Storage you should be fine. Then, for repeat offenders, they have only to remove Storage for a period of time. Most do not offend again.

Last week, Titan made history.

The first criminal to be punished with nothing but their own emotions.

There was no need to collect the feelings of everyone they'd hurt. Once a verdict was reached, the guilty was sentenced to an hour without protection. It was recorded, streamed on every device. No one can agree exactly what it was the criminal had done, though most agree that it had something to do with their stance on the President.

Jun watches the criminal suffer, begging for someone to save them from this agony.

He wonders how long till they come for him. How long before they make him feel. He doesn't feel scared. He doesn't feel anything. But, that'll change, of that he has no doubt.

KNOCK-KNOCK TRIVIA

'You know your problem?' she told me. 'You were never honest - not once - not one single day of your life.'

And that was the last thing she said before giving me back my ring.

Ten years, not a single argument, no fighting over what to watch - we watched what she watched. Every meal choice, we ate the same old bland shit. It wasn't that she didn't like spice, it was that she didn't like flavour.

I didn't care, I loved her. See, I figured out the secret formula to love. Tried and tested. You can trust me on this.

Whenever she asks you a question, just take her by the hand, look her right in the eye, and tell her,

'Whatever you want.'

That's right, it's just that simple.

But there's just one problem - after all that, she still left me. Ten years and now it's all gone. Ten years of watching her fill up the sink with dishes she wasn't going to wash. Ten years of watching those horrible true-crime podcasts. All those fucking quinoa burgers!

What the fuck is quinoa anyway? It's the gravel at the bottom of the fish bowl. Someone needs to kill the guy who invented that stuff, shoot him, right in the face, in front of all those liars who have the balls to say that quinoa is actually good.

I did everything she wanted, including driving down to her parents four nights a week. Every birthday, every holiday. Fuck my parents, right? So what if they gave birth to me? They want to hang out at Christmas then they better drive the thousand miles or so to come and see me down at the in-laws.

It'd help if her family actually liked me. Not once did they ask me a direct question, or look me in the eye. Or remember my name. Mostly, they talked about me as if I wasn't there. Four nights a week for ten years.

I didn't want to get married in Hawaii. Who wants to get married in Hawaii? Idiots - that's who. People without an imagination. The kinds of people that the Maori used to eat - ah, better days.

Wait . . . Maybe that's mean. I'm a little tetchy when it comes to that place. It's because my head's a little larger than average. All through school I'd hear: 'There goes Easter Island!'

But did I bring any of this up when she asked about getting married? No, because that'd get in the way of my tried and tested formula.

So, I don't get it. Why is it that after ten years of all that, she can just dump me? Divorce papers already written out. Thank you, goodnight.

She doesn't need space. We're not going through a rough patch. she's gone.

They've moved in together - her and Mr. nice teeth. He's got a tanned body, and the muscles to match. They're engaged, and guess where they're getting married? That's right - Ha - fucking - waii.

And guess who didn't get an invite?

Me, the guy she left in the dark, all broken and bruised. Well, I'll tell you what, you won't find me complaining, and you know why?

Because I'm a winner.

There's plenty of girls out there, Missy. Ready to rip me apart like a budget zombie flick. And when you're sitting there, feeling sorry for yourself, when you realise that you've made a terrible mistake, and you cry for me to come back, guess what?

I'll say no. I'll say good luck with your life, and I'll walk off into the setting sun.

***

Hi, just checking in to let you know that my ex is still getting married.

Now, relax, I'm not going to do something stupid like turn up last minute screaming, 'I object!' I'm not that bad. Besides, I can't go, not since your boy got himself a restraining order.

That's right boys! Look who's so scared of her emotions that she can't be around me. And she stands there saying she's over me. Someone needs a reality check!

I tell you. I just don't get women.

Take my ex for instance. First it's all, I don't know how I feel about you, and then it's 'You're not allowed within thirty feet' I mean come on! Give me a sign. Tell me what you really want.

So, anyway, they really will put you in a cell for breaking your restraining order.

It's fine. Had to sell my shoes so the big guy would let me use the toilet, but it's cool.

But, anyway, I've got some big news:

I'm working on an app.

Yeah - it's me and this guy. He just turned up, right out the blue, right after I got out of jail actually. Comes right up to me and says:

'You look like a guy who could use a little help.'

And you know what? I almost started crying there and then.

'I've got this app,' he tells me. 'It's already up and ready to go, I just need someone to test it out.'

So I ask him what it's about? And he tells me that the app is kind of like a GPS only it gives you the location of all things you really want.

I said an app like that is worth a million dollars.

For my help, he offers to make me a business partner. He whips out this contract written on old paper, all crinkly like a pirate's map. Hands me one of them ye-oldie pen feathers and tells me, 'Sign.'

Now, I'm no idiot, I make sure to show that I'm not easily conned. So, I do my best to look like I'm understanding the words on the contract. I'm umming and ahhing, and going, I really like this bit here!

I wasn't worried, It's your standard contract:

Party agrees - here.

Property of the soul goes - there.

It's all pretty standard, really. If anything, it'd be amateur to have a professional look at it.

So I go to sign - only the feather pen doesn't have any ink, so I ask, how am I supposed to sign it?

And no lie, the guy takes his long black fingernail, and he stabs the tip of my index finger.

I watch the blood pour from my finger. He tells me, 'Sign.'

So I'm standing in the middle of the street, leaning over a bin, signing some old pirate map looking contract with ink made from my own blood.

Funny old world, ain't it?

Then he wanders off - shouting that he'll send me the app, which is odd because I didn't give him any contact details. But then, when I'm at home, I get a message. It's the app.

It reads:

- Whatever You Want -

And I think - finally - things are starting to go my way.

***

Next day, I test out the app.
So I type in:

- Pretty girl

The app tells me to wait for a moment - and then it comes up with a location.

It's not too far, so I put on my shoes and head out.

The rain's starting to fall and I'm about to turn back, when I hear someone shouting.

I turn to see a beautiful woman running over. She has a leash in one hand and her face is full of worry.

She asks if I've seen her dog.

Me, I can't help but smile ear to ear. She asks me again, and the smile keeps on getting bigger. I tell my phone, Thank you! Thank you!

I offer to help her look for the dog. I type the word DOG into the app, and a moment later I'm given a location. We go over to the dog, me staring at the app.

We find the dog in the street. Someone had tied its leash to the fence.

The girl asks, 'How did you know my dog was here?'

I show her the app and the location, and she starts getting mad, talking about how I was a right sicko for stealing her dog.

I head back to my flat, peel off my shoes, and fall into the bed.

Phone in hand, I look at the app.

- More like this?

I click the no button.

Wasn't a great first go, but she really was pretty, even though she kept screaming in my face. That's not the app's fault, though, afterall, women are weird.

The app begins to shake:

- Another suggestion?

I think for a moment, and then type in the name of my ex.

The app tells me to wait.

Then - after a moment - it responds:

- Would you like to know where she is now?
- Would you like to know where she's sleeping tonight?
- Or would you like her to leave the front door unlocked?

My mouth hangs open in shock. I can't believe it.

Of course I'd like her to leave the door unlocked. That night, I went into her house, stood over her bed, and watched her sleep.

God, I love this app!

***

A week goes by and I've got a plan:

The phone shows me how to put incriminating evidence on her fiance's work laptop. Then, on the big day, I'm standing outside his office, watching the police take him away.

Who's smiling now, Mr. Perfect?

Now, if I'm honest I didn't bother to keep up with the trial, putting him away for ever and ever was more than enough for me. Instead, I focus all my attention on my ex.

So I decide to go and say hello.

She's alone (or so the app says) So, I buy her favourite flowers - thank you app - and I knock on her door - ready to get back to the good times.

And you know what? The bitch just slams the door in my face. Not so much as a howdy-do. No, she doesn't say anything, except, 'Fuck off creep.'

Now, I'm a romantic, and people like me don't give up so easy. So, I take a deep breath, compose myself, and climb up the drain, go in through the bedroom window, and hide under her bed till she calms down.

Now, I'd like to say it all ended with laughter and kisses, but you know me, folks, I wouldn't lie to you. Afterall, I'm one of the good guys.

No, if anything she gets really mad. I try and explain my situation, but she's not interested. I know it's wrong to speak bad about your soulmate, but I've got to be honest, in that moment, I really wondered whether I should just give up.

Still, love is about being there on the good days and the bad. I calm her down with a few gentle words, and enough tape to tie her to a chair. I'm waiting for the app to tell me how to calm her down when the police arrive.

I tell them, Well, this is embarrassing.

And the police nod, take out their truncheons, and proceed to beat me unconscious.

***

Spend a few weeks in the cell before they give me back my freedom, and my phone.

I don't bother to go home, I'm just looking for a way to make her love me again. The phone doesn't have any suggestions like love spell, or mind control. Instead, it asks me this stupid question: Which is scarier?

- Poison Vampire
- Werewolf Circus
- Knock-Knock

I'm just staring at the screen. I refresh the app, and ask, how do I get her back?

The app takes a moment to load, and then it says the

same thing again.

Which is scarier?

I hit refresh again, over and over, and each time I get the same question. It must be a glitch or something. So, I think, well, maybe if I answer then I can move on and sort out my love life. But what to pick?

I have no idea what a poison vampire is. The regular kinds freak me out, going around licking necks - most unsanitary. Then again, what would a werewolf want with a circus? Is it a circus run by a werewolf? Or is it a circus for werewolves? Either way, I'm out. I'm allergic to dogs, and something tells me that werewolves aren't hypoallergenic.

That just leaves Knock-Knock. I'm standing there, looking at my phone, thinking, what's so scary about a noise?

I know it's asking me which is scarier, but I get the idea the app is going to send me some scary movies or something. Last thing I want is to spend the next month unable to sleep, having nightmares about sickly vampires and a circus full of loose hair.

So, I click the only option that doesn't scare me, and I press Knock-Knock.

The app takes a moment to respond. It takes so long in fact that I put my phone away, and make the three hour trip home. By the time I get back, my legs are cramped, feels like someone's swapped my bones for liquid fire. All I can do is lay down on the bed, and wish that someone would come and kill me.

Then, I take a deep breath and check the app. It tells me:

- We'll let him know.

Let who know? I don't bother to ask any more questions, I'm too tired, and with that, I drift off to a deep comfortable sleep.

***

Week later and things are back to normal. The app's back on my side, and together we're planning on how to win her back.

I'm thinking, I've been approaching this all wrong. Previously, I focused on how to change her, when in reality, I should be focusing on myself. So, I ask the app how I can change my life.

It takes a moment to load, and then it gives me some suggestions:

- Money
- Fame
- Knock-Knock Trivia

Now these are my kind of suggestions. So I click money and the app tells me to wait.

'Hey!' says someone, passing by. 'Here, looks like you need it,' and they hand me some change. It's not much, just a few coins.

I click money again, and the same person stops, comes back, and hands me some more. I do this over and over till they run out of change.

Must have spent ten hours walking the street, hitting money every time I saw someone. Thought I was being smart by heading to the posh part of town, but they didn't have any change, and apparently, the app doesn't want to make people go to an ATM.

Still, it's getting dark, and I have enough money to buy myself a takeaway, couple of cans, and still have enough left over to buy a card for Valentine's Day.

Must have spent three hours staring at that blank page wondering what to write. Funny how you can have all that love inside you, but it gets lost in translation the moment you try and let it out.

In the end, I go with something safe. I write, 'Sorry your

marriage didn't work out. You looked really nice the other day. Funny, we were actually wearing the same shade of purple, though you'll have to take my word for it because I was hiding - not in a weird way - It's just, I didn't want to upset you. Fancy a drink?'

I look over the card, and think, are you mad? You can't send that! I'm such an idiot sometimes. So, I cross out the 'fancy a drink bit' and write, let's get dinner.

There, that's better. 'Fancy a drink' what am I twelve? A real relationship means dinner, anyone will tell you that.

I don't fancy the idea of the card getting lost in the mail. So, I slip on my balaclava and black leather gloves, and I head over to her house. There, moving in the dark like Mission-Impossible, crawl up to her front door, and post the Valentine's day card.

It was all dead romantic, till the old lady next door came out and started screaming.

Fled into the night like Forrest Gump, heart full of love, and the biggest erection you've ever seen.

When I'm sure not to get caught, I slow down, take off the gloves and black ski mask, and I sit on a bench and catch my breath.

To pass the time, I take out the app.

I ask how I can change my life, and it gives me some options:

- Money
- Fame
- Knock-Knock Trivia

Someone's coming up the road. For a minute, I begin to panic, and then I realise it's just some guy walking his dog.

I've spent all the change from earlier, so I click money.

'Here you go, chief,' and he hands me a few coins.

I hit the button again, but nothing happens. I refresh the app, and try again, but it's the same, and then I read the words slowly:

- Money (pending)
- Fame
- Knock-Knock Trivia

Well, I don't know how long I have to wait, so I click on fame.

'Hey!' calls the same person who handed me money. 'Aren't you that creep who likes to stalk his ex?'

Before I can say anything, the guy sinks his fist into my cheek.

I'm off down the street before he can do any real damage. I'm too out of shape to run all the way home, and before I know it, I'm sitting in the street, gasping like a fish out of water.

I look at the app, and it's the same as before, money's still pending, fame is waiting for another chance to hit me in the face. Then there's the other one - Knock-Knock Trivia.

I don't even remember what it's from, but the app won't let me ask any more questions, so I give it a click.

- Did you know, the Knock-Knock gets its name from the sound it makes as it stalks its prey?

Well, what a waste of time. With that, I head home, and without taking off my clothes, I get straight into bed. I'm just about to go to sleep when I hear a sound.

It was coming from the front door. 'Knock-Knock.'

Now, it's what, two? two thirty in the morning? It was late when I went 'round with the card, afterall, I might be a romantic, but I'm not stupid enough to leave any witnesses.

Then, I hear the sound again. 'Knock-Knock.'

Who could it be? I'm not expecting anyone. I don't even have friends. And so I'm sitting here, hiding under my quilt, hoping whoever it is will go away.

I check the app for advice, and, after a moment, it gives

me some suggestions:

- Knock-Knock Trivia (pending)
- Knock-Knock Hunting Strategies
- Knock-Knock Weaknesses

I don't know what any of this means, but there's someone at my door, and the app's telling me about weaknesses. So, I click, and hope it'll make them go away.

- Like all nocturnal predators, Knock-Knock will not attack during the day.

How is that helpful? It's the middle of the night? 'Knock-Knock.'
The app refreshes and I hit the same button.

- Knock-Knock has no other weakness
- Knock-Knock has no other weakness
- Knock-Knock has no other weakness

So, I'm just laying there, wrapped up in my covers, trembling as I pretend to not hear whoever it is knocking at my door.

***

Next day, I'm feeling fried.
That psycho spent all night knocking at my door. I'm feeling delicate, but I'm not going to let something like that get in the way. So, with my head held high, I head into town, and begin to use the app to get money.
Up and down the highstreet, I'm pressing that button, watching people hand me one coin at a time. It's getting less each time to the point that people are giving me a penny as they pass. You know how long it takes to get any money that

way?

Well, I don't want to be a debbie downer, so I keep it up, remembering that, 'Every Little Helps' I can't remember who said that - I think it was Ghandi.

My thumb's getting sore from pressing all morning when I hear a noise.

'Knock-Knock.'

I look around to see where it's coming from, looking up and down the sea of faces as they move from shop to shop.

'Knock-Knock.'

It sounded closer, like it was coming from up behind me. But there's no one there, or at least, there's no one knocking on any door.

'Knock-Knock.'

This time, it sounds like it's right behind me. Now, I know it's silly, I know there isn't some big wooden door standing right behind me, but still, It's the end of January, and I'm standing here sweating buckets.

I head inside to a cafe, dump my morning coins on the counter and ask what it'll get me. Three minutes of angry counting gets me a small Americano.

I sit in the corner, trying to stop my hands from trembling as I hold my drink.

'Knock-Knock.'

It was in the room with me. Where, I didn't know, but it was in here hiding amongst the tall coffees and overpriced cake.

I take out my phone and ask what's going on.

- Knock-Knock Trivia
- Knock-Knock Hunting Strategies
- Knock-Knock Survival

I click Survival.

- Like all nocturnal predators, Knock-Knock

will not attack during the day.

That doesn't make any sense, though. Now, I'm not saying there really is a thing, a whatever you call it. I'm just saying, if there was a, well, a you-know, why would it be bothering me in the middle of the day?
I click for trivia.

- Did you know? Contrary to popular belief, just because Knock-Knock won't attack during the day, doesn't mean it's not there?

That doesn't make me feel any better.
I hit refresh and it gives me the chance to pick trivia again.

- Did you know? Knock-Knock likes to follow its prey? It savours the fear of them knowing that it's watching, always watching.

'Knock-Knock.'
I hit refresh and then select the third option: Knock-Knock Hunting Strategies.

- During nightfall, It will create the sound of its namesake, and once the prey turns to face it, Knock-Knock will strike.

So, that's it then? All I've got to do is make sure I keep my eyes closed. I can do that, right?
For the rest of the day, I hear it.
While I'm walking around the shopping centre. 'Knock-Knock.'
While I'm in the bathroom, working up the courage to pee in the urinal with a guy on each side. 'Knock-Knock.'
When I get on the bus, and ride across town. Every stop,

I hear it. 'Knock-Knock.'

I hear it all the way till I reach the front door. I think, thank god, I'm safe. I head inside, make myself a cup of tea, fall to the couch and let out a victorious sigh.

I'm home. I'm safe. I'm so exhausted that I begin to drift off, and then I hear it.

'Knock-Knock.'

It isn't coming from the front door. It isn't coming from any door at all. It's coming from right behind. I can feel the way the air moves as it wraps those knuckles on invisible wood.

'Knock-Knock.'

It's not dark, not yet, but I can't help but sit there, eyes all scrunched up, waiting for it to go away.

It doesn't, it knocks fast, and it knocks slow. Just when I think it's stopped, I open my eyes, and hear it again. Thing must have a sense of humour.

Then, as I watch the sun begin to set, I close my eyes, and I wait.

I listen as those knocks begin to change. Gone is the playful knocking from earlier, now it's dark, and the thing is hungry.

'Knock-Knock.'

The sound is angry like a debt collector about to lose his patience. Always, the sound comes from behind. Now it's furious and booming. It demands that I turn and look, but I don't.

It continues through the night, that sound booming from just behind my ear. But I don't turn, I keep my eyes fixed straight ahead, waiting for the sun to rise.

***

The next day, I wake to the sound of knocking.
It's gentler now, less angry and more irritable.
'Knock-Knock.'
It sounds like a challenge, like it's telling me, 'Oh, is that

how you want to play it?'

The sound continues to follow me through the day. An endless repetition without pause. I wonder if that's how it gets you? Madness, or just a desire to make it stop.

I ask the app how to stop Knock-Knock.

- Don't know. We're too afraid to ask.

So, I do my best to go about my day, trying to act like I can hear anything over the sound of that knocking.

By lunch time, I get a call from my ex.

I don't know why, but I don't do the usual 'Mr. Positive' routine. Instead, I just start crying.

She listens, doesn't say a single word. I cry about my life, and I cry about the weird knocking, and I cry that I'm scared, that I don't know how long I can handle this.

She just listens till I'm done crying, and then she tells me, 'Look, I'm in work right now, but why don't you come over tonight?'

The words hit me like a bus. I'm so excited to say yes, that I almost forget about Knock-Knock.

It hasn't made a sound during the whole call, so for a second, I think she might have scared it off. But then, the moment she mentioned coming over tonight, I heard it give a knock. This was different from the others, it sounded angry, but more than that, it sounded scared.

I tell her, I don't think it's a good idea for me coming over. Then, against common sense, I tell her why. I tell her about the app, and I tell her about the monster, or the ghost, or whatever it is that's bothering me.

She asks me to calm down and go through the rules again. So, I tell her, going over the facts several times.

'There you go then,' she says. 'You have to turn around and look at it, right? So, don't turn around. Just come straight here and you'll be fine.'

Makes sense, but I tell her I'm scared.

'Me too,' she says, 'But here I am, not letting that stop me.'

***

So, I spent the rest of the day preparing for battle.

She's right, I can't spend my life full of fear, that's no way to live.

I go to the shops and pick up a few romantic items: chocolates, wine, some strawberries, and a pack of condoms. All through the day, I hear it.

'Knock-Knock.'

Only, it's less confident now. There's no cockiness to it. I don't know why, but the thing doesn't like the idea of me going over to see her.

Then I check the app for trivia and I get my answer.

- Did you know? Knock-Knock is so shy that it will only eat its prey when they're alone?

That's it. That's why it's scared. All I've got to do is get over there and it won't be able to get me.

I've always known it deep down, that true love conquers all.

So, it's getting dark. I grab my coat, my phone, and the shopping for tonight, and I begin to make my way over.

I make up three streets before I hear it.

'Knock-Knock.'

The sound comes from behind. Distant, almost imperceptible.

I don't fall for it. Who knows how far it really is. Thing's probably standing right behind me, breathing up and down my neck.

I'm halfway there, crossing the road when I hear it. 'Knock-Knock.' It sounds like it's running up behind me, ready to pounce. My shoulder's twist to turn, my head's beginning to move, but I throw myself to the ground.

A tire screeches an inch from my face.

'You fucking crazy!' shouts the driver.

Then I hear it, soft as a whisper, right behind my ear.

'Knock-Knock.'

I keep my eyes closed as I get to my feet. I don't look back, at the driver or his car, I just keep walking.

I get to her front door, arm's scratched, kee swollen. There's blood in my mouth from where I bit my lip.

I reach out to her door and I hear it.

'Knock-Knock.'

I press the buzzer and wait.

The knocks again, and again. Each time, it becomes louder, more frantic. It's desperate now, I can feel it. The sound becomes so loud that I think my head's about to explode.

Then, just as I begin to scream, the door opens and there she is, staring with a look of shock.

'Are you alright?'

I tell her to get in.

We head inside to the living room, and I collapse onto the couch and there I begin to weep.

'Jesus!' she says, 'what happened to you? You're bleeding!'

I tell her it's fine, but she insists on checking me anyway. Opening my shirt reveals several dark bruises on my ribs. There's blood inside my pants. I tell her it's fine, I just fell is all.

She tells me, 'Go and take a shower. You're full of blood and asphalt.'

I ask, what about the wine and the chocolate? Maybe we should enjoy those first?

She just smiles. 'How about we take it to the shower and enjoy it there?'

I don't ask if she's serious. I head upstairs to the shower. She shouts, 'I'll be there in a minute! Just sorting something out.'

She's got one of those wonky showers that needs a minute to heat up. So, I strip naked and inspect the bruises up and down my body. I look like a dalmatian.

Then, because I'm bored, I click on the app and read its topics.

- Knock-Knock Trivia
- Knock-Knock Hunting Strategies
- Knock-Knock Survival

Well, I've been victorious tonight, but that won't stop tomorrow. So, I click on Hunting Strategies to see what other tricks it's got up its sleeve.

- When its prey is proving particularly difficult, Knock-Knock will resort to its secondary strategy - Mimicry.

Mimi-what?
From downstairs, I hear her call out, 'Make sure to give the shower a sec, or you'll freeze your balls off!'
I tell her that I remember. Then, I feel the water of the shower. It's nice and hot.
So, I shout for her to hurry up.
Coming up the stairs, she tells me, 'On my way, captain!'
I try to wait for her, but it's also late January, and she doesn't bother with the heating. So, I get in the shower, and feel it wash the day from my bones.
It's so good that it takes me a minute to notice the colour of the water by my feet. It's dark and murky, and won't go down the drain. Not very romantic, so I kneel down and pull all the stuff out of the plug hole.
I end up pulling out this big knot of hair, all tangled and sticky with meat.
I check my head to make sure I didn't lose any scalp in the fall. It's all there, and then I realise that the hair's too long to be mine, and there's a lot of it, so much that it won't stop, like a clown with a handkerchief.
'Knock-knock,' she says at the bathroom door. 'I do hope

you're decent?'

I turn 'round to tell her, 'what's with all the hair?' but she just stands there and smiles.

I watch her teeth fall out, one by one. Then the eyes, the fingernails.

She just stands there, peeling away, bit by bit, and then she reaches, oh so gently, to the door, and she gives it a tap.

'Knock-Knock. Knock-Knock.'

I fall out of the shower, and land on my phone. It's already on the app, and in the chaos, I select Knock-Knock Trivia.

- Did you know? Knock-Knock doesn't digest its victims quickly? The process is slow allowing its victims to remain conscious as they are dissolved over weeks, months, even years.

RESPONSIBLE FARMING

One day, the world made it illegal to murder animals for meat.
'You can still eat them,' says the news, 'but you just can't kill them.' So, everyone started asking, 'How do you get meat without killing it?' The answer it turns out is very simple: you get the meat to kill itself.

<u>I</u>

John T was a cow, and he didn't want to die.
That didn't stop the man from shooting at him, despite John holding up his badge.
'I'm a cop!' cries John, as he crouched by the wall of the alley, but the youth fires again, spraying dust over John's black and white face. He kneels by a silver trash can and there checks his revolver to make sure he's got a full chamber. Then, as a bullet blows off the top of his horn, he lets out a sigh and checks it again. 'Let's be straight, kid. You're gonna want me to put these cuffs on you. Those other guys, they're animals.'
'What's gonna happen to me?' shouts the guy, and John T can hear the break in his voice: He really was just a dumb kid,

popping zits and counting pubes.

'Look,' says John T, 'I know you just shot at me, but, you put that gun down and I promise you a fair trial.'

There's a pause, and then the kid says, 'What about Amander? What about her trial?'

With a deep breath, John raises his head out from behind the silver trash can. 'Who's Amanda, kid?'

With a single tear running down his cheek, the kid raises the gun to his chin and fires. All John T can do is stand there, and watch as the air turns red.

II

They sent over two beat cops to help John T corner everything off. They were both sheep: one black, the other white. The black sheep kneels down and points a hoof at what's left of the kid's face. 'Hey, Tony! Get a look at this guy.'

The white sheep glances over his shoulder and then flinches away. 'Fuck outa here with that shit!'

'No look,' says the black sheep. 'He didn't do it right.' He points closer to the kid's face. 'See the way the tongue's still moving? Real baaaad job.'

The white sheep spits on the kid's chest. 'Jackoff.'

'Is he still alive?' asks John T.

The black sheep smiles. 'Not for much lonnnger.'

Once the scene is taped off, John T heads across the street to the Kid's house, where the crime was first called in. It was on the ground floor, which means he doesn't have to worry about being stuck in an elevator.

He walks into the apartment complex, and over to room 7A. Standing in the door is a pig in a raincoat, 'Look like shit, Johnny boy.'

'Funny,' he says, 'that's not what your wife said this

morning.'

The pig grabs his crotch. 'Smoke this.'

John T takes out two cigarettes. With a flick of a Zippo lighter, he cooks both smokes. As the Pig comes to take his, John T gives him a sniff. 'What's with the smell?'

The Pig gives a nervous snort. 'Just cologne,' he says, 'the wife makes me wear it.'

John T sniffs again. 'What is that, Patchouli?'

'No,' says the Pig, 'It's lavender.'

John T smiles. 'Real pretty. Do they make it for men?'

'You wanna know something?' says the Pig, 'One day, I'm gonna be your boss, and I'm gonna ride you so hard you're gonna be praying for some fuckhead to come and turn your ass into a burger.'

John T takes a long drag of his cigarette. 'Until then, why don't you step aside, number two, and let me handle my crimescene.'

He makes his way around the apartment. 'What have we got?'

'The usual,' says the pig as they wander over to the bedroom.

John T pushes open the door and stares at the body on the bed. He looks for as long as he can before common decency and a heavy breakfast make him turn away. 'The usual?' says John T 'What part of 'That' is usual?'

The pig snorts in amusement. 'What's the matter, Johnny Boy? No sense of humour? Maybe that's why you ain't made chief yet.'

'Yeah, yeah,' says John T, 'I'm not a big enough asshole. Now, I don't want to go back in there, so tell me what we've got.'

The pig takes a drag of his cigarette. 'Real slice 'em and dice 'em.'

John T pulls out a notebook and a pen. 'Victim?'

'Well, she's one of yours,' says the pig. 'Quite the cow, if you ask me. Get it?'

John T lets out a sigh. 'She got a name?'

The pig goes back into the room and there stands over the bed, staring down, puffing on his cigarette. 'Don't know about before,' he says, 'but right now, I'd go with minced meat.'

John T begins to look around the room. There, he finds a photo of the cow. She's all snuggled up next to the Kid from the alley. The words, 'To my loving Amanda' are written in silver pen.

John T writes down the word 'Amanda' and then the word 'Victim' then he circles the second word and puts a large question mark at the end.

'What did he take?'

Pig looks all confused. 'Who?'

'Don't play games with me, you bald pink fuck. You know god damn who I mean. Now, answer the question, what did the killer take?'

'Mostly shank. A bit of loin. You know, that sick fuck was sawing through her ribs when the cleaning lady came in. Some birthday party, huh?'

All around the apartment were banners and balloons. 'Happy birthday, Baby!' spelled out in silver, pink, and red.

John T writes something down. 'Cleaning lady call the cops when she heard the screaming?'

The pig snorts. 'Cow didn't scream.'

'Come again?'

'I tell ya, Cow didn't make a peep, at least not one anybody heard. But that damn cleaning lady did. Bitch screamed so loud some old coot heard it three blocks down. She's the one who called the cops, noise complaint.'

John T writes it all down. 'Kid got a name?'

'No, but I know what 'The Sheet's are call him: The Butcher of Fifth Street.'

John T looks around for evidence that doesn't exist. The place is clean, unusually so, even the mess is organised.

'Give 'em some credit,' says John T, 'Butcher of Fifth Street? That's too smart for the Papers.'

The Pig takes one look out of the window and spits out

his cigarette. 'Fuck me! They're already here!'

John T watches two vultures land on the balcony outside the bedroom. Video cameras in hand, they ask, 'What are your thoughts on the recent spike in suicide rates, hmm?'

'Tragic,' says John T. 'Absolutely tragic. Was thinking the same about your career.'

'But don't you think it's odd? No history of depression, each of them having all that money, and big loving families? Not the usual sort to become a statistic, don't you think?'

John T shrugs. 'It's a crazy world, Kid. Who knows why anyone does anything anymore.'

'Well, they do share one link,' says the vulture, 'in that, all of them have recently turned down the Mayor's offer to buy their meat business. But, I'm sure there's no correlation.' The vulture then hands him a business card. 'In case you feel like being a good cop for once.'

Before John T can say anything else, Pig steps in, 'No comment!' Then he shuts the curtains. 'What was that?' You remember what chief said about talking to the papers?'

John T looks at the business card. 'Think I care what chief thinks?'

'Oh, you're gonna get fucked,' says Pig. 'It's gonna hurt, big boy, and I'm gonna be there enjoying every second of it.'

'Yeah-yeah,' says John T, 'buy me a drink first.' He looks down at the signed photo. 'Why did he do it?'

The pig takes out two cigarettes, one he offers to John. 'Guy's a psycho, what else is there?'

John T takes the cigarette, but a shake of his head stops the pig from lighting it. 'I don't know,' he says, 'but something's cooking, and I don't like the smell.'

III

Franklin Chain was the owner of the biggest sea-food factory in town, and despite the numerous offers, each larger than the last, still, Franklin insists that the business is not for sale. People didn't like that, made them hate him. The fact he was a snake just made it easier.

So, when John T gets a call from Frank at 3 AM, he doesn't ask, 'What's wrong?' Instead, he says, 'You better have beer.'

'I'll get some,' says Frank, then, after several moments of hissing down the phone, he says, 'someone's trying to fuck me, Johnny, fuck me real good.'

John slips out of bed. A quick sniff says he needs to change his underpants. 'It's just kids,' says John, 'don't let it rile you up.'

'They didn't steal anything.'

John's got one leg in his pants. 'What?'

'No, man. I keep telling you. It's worse than that, way worse.'

By the time John T gets to the factory, Franklin's a third of the way down a bottle of Scotch. 'Hey,' says John T, 'what happened to the beer?'

'Every day I'm there,' says Franklin, 'sixteen hour shifts, and do they care? Do they fuck!'

The snake coils up around the bottle of Scotch, his forked tongue slipping inside the glass and down to the spirits below.

John T takes the bottle away. 'You couldn't just pour yourself a glass could you. No, you just had to turn the whole thing into spit.'

With a frown, John T knocks back the bottle of Scotch. 'What's with the cheap shit?'

'It's all I can afford.'

'You mean, It's all you want to afford.' He holds out the bottle, but the snake doesn't take it, he just sits there and starts to cry.

John T takes another drink of the Scotch and then drops it in the trash. 'What's this about? Your ex-wife blackmailing you again?'

Franklin uses his rattle tail to wipe his eyes. 'It ain't her. She shacked up with some Fitness Instructor from Acapulco.'

He takes John T further into the factory. Technically, they can't call it produce as it's illegal to kill animals. That's not what Franklin does, no, what Franklin does is offer a safe haven for wayward sealife: Squid mostly. It's advertised as a wellness centre, but the truth is, no resident ever gets better.

'My job isn't to save them,' says the snake, 'I just make 'em nice and comfy.'

They get to the squid factory, hardly a barrel of laughs at the best of times, yet here John T could hear their cries all the way down. He finds the squids sat in the corners, standing tall on their tentacles. There was blue blood all over the floor. Several of the squids are missing arms, their wounds are patched up by what you would expect from a drunken snake.

'What happened here? Looks like someone had a knife fight in the dark.'

Franklin hands him a cookbook, across the cover were the words: 101 ways to cook a Squid. 'Someone broke in. Didn't take nothing, just handed out these books, and then, with a gun to their head, they forced the squids to read.'

John T looks at the book. 'Did you call anyone?'

'Course I did! That's why you're here.'

John T inspects the bandages of one of the squids. 'These guys need medical attention. Why haven't you called an ambulance?'

'I did. Five times, but they never came. That's when the calls started.'

'Calls?'

'They say the same thing over and over 'Kill yourself, just kill yourself,' The snake cries again, and soon the squids join in.

John T takes one of the cook books and notices there's a stain on the pages. He gives it a sniff. 'Hmm . . . interesting.'

'What?' says the snake, 'what is it?'

John T takes out his notebook. 'Perfume.', He writes

something down.

'Is it a clue? Can you use it? Bring these fuckers to justice?'

'Depends,' says John T.

'On what?'

'On how many men wear Lavender.'

John T gets home a little after five. By seven, his alarm was telling him to get to work. By eight he gets a call telling him the snake was dead. The news calls it a suicide.

John T takes out the business card. He calls the number. 'Hey. You really think the Mayor's behind all this?'

There's a pause. 'Sorry, detective. I'm afraid that ship has sailed.'

'Oh yeah? What happened to wanting to be a good guy?'

'That was just a dream, detective. By the way, sorry about your friend.'

'Friend?' says John T.

'Channel four.'

He turns on the T.V and watches two officers, both sheep, one white the other black. They're standing by a body dangling from a tree. Both looking far too happy to be professional.

John T stares at the body in the tree. It was a snake, eyes puffed out from the pressure around the neck.

'They're calling it suicide,' says the vulture.

'What do you call it?'

'Business, detective. I call it business.'

IV

It's clear that the Kid from the alley was involved with his victim. What shocked John T was that the two of them were engaged.

'Doesn't make any sense. Why kill her a week before the

wedding? As a husband, he'd have rights to her meat anyway. Thing don't make any sense.'

'Well,' says the chief, 'cock-a-doodle-do, dickhead.'

The chief was a chicken. Technically, he was a prize winning Rooster. In the old days, back when John T had a bright career ahead of him, people whispered that the chief had ties to the Underworld, including a violent and bloody career as a Cock fighter. There was talk about investigations, but all that turned up was enough dirt to bury anyone against him. John T guessed it was true what they said: Sometimes, it's really good to have a mayor for a brother.

'I did some digging,' says John T. 'That Kid, Willard Roach? He was her nurse, sir. They met at the hospital when he was treating her for Chemo.'

The chief pecks at lunch, a bowl of Udon topped with shredded beef. 'Get to the point, so I can stab you with it.'

'There was a will.'

The chief stops his pecking. 'A what?'

John T takes out the will from his pocket. 'That fuckhead Pig didn't properly sweep the room, sir. Found it under the bed.'

The chief takes the will. 'What the fuck does this have to do with anything?'

'She left him everything, sir, every scrap of meat.'

The chief turns his head from side to side, then scrunches up the note. 'So what?'

'Why would he kill her? She was late-stage, no hope. Why not wait a while. She was a big girl. He'd have made a fortune off her.'

'Sounds dangerously like an opinion to me,' says the chief. 'You know what they say about opinions, right? They're a one way ticket to getting my foot up your ass. Now, if you don't have any proof then I hereby declare this case closed.'

John T takes out the cookbook. He tells the chief, 'Smell it.'

Scratching the book with his yellow beak, the chief asks, 'What is this, a joke?'

'No,' says John T. 'It's Lavender.'

The chief turns slowly. 'What?'

'You know, like the same stuff Pig's wife makes him wear?'

The chief looks at the book. 'So, Pig likes to cook? So what?'

'This was found at the Franklin factory, something disguised as a break-in. I smelt the same thing over at 7A. Only, I didn't notice it till I went back alone.'

The chief looks up from the book. 'What are you trying to say?'

John T looks over at the empty desk, the one that has a photo of three little pigs on top. 'Where is he?'

V

An investigation into police corruption is not taken lightly. 'We have to play this cool,' says the chief. 'So, you go home, get some rest, and together we'll put an end to it.'

That night, John T couldn't sleep. He tosses and turns across his vintage waterbed. There, at around three AM, he looks up at the ceiling and asks, 'When is this gonna happen?'

As if in answer, he hears the front door open. The darkness swallows up any details, but one thing reaches out, drawing John T's attention: it was the smell of lavender.

With his revolver ready, John T raises it up to the door.

A voice whispers in the dark, 'Bad day to be a good cop, eh, Johnny B-' the sentence is cut short by the sound of a revolver.

A scream pierces through the dark, quickly followed by five more.

John T turns on the light and looks down at Pig. Smoke rises up from the holes in his chest. He goes through the Pig's pockets, he takes his gun, his wallet, and the picture of his wife. He tells the picture, 'Sorry, Betty. But I owe you one.'

After that, John T waits for the right time to take the information to the chief. Not able to trust anyone at work, he waits till the old chicken is out feeding his six year old daughter.

John T drops the blood stained photo of Betty on the table. 'He tried to kill me.'

The chief continues to smile at his daughter. 'Has it been reported?'

John T sits in the chair opposite the chief. 'No,' he says, 'I don't know who to trust.'

The chief lets out a sigh, 'Good,' he says, 'the less people who know the better, first, we gotta-'

The sound of the revolver cuts him off. Blood and feathers fill the air. The chief looks down, the hole in his chest is dark and wet.

John T reaches into his pocket and drops down a piece of paper. 'Fuckhead Pig of yours forgot to sweep for the old will.'

The chief holds onto the table with a trembling wing. 'What . . . are you talking about?'

John T opens the note. 'You know,' he says, 'the one you sent with Pig to the apartment? The one that had all of Amanda's meat going to the Mayor, you know, your brother?'

John T raises his gun. 'This is for Frankie,' he says and he fires. 'And this is for Amanda, and Willard,' and he fires again. 'And this?' he says, reaching over the table and poking the barrel in the beak of the chief, 'this,' he says, 'this is for introducing me to the ex wife.'

All around, people are screaming. The only one who isn't doing anything is the chief's little girl.

John T tells her, 'Sorry' and then, dropping enough money for the meal, and a healthy tip, he heads off into the setting sun.

VI

John T wasn't cut out to be a fugitive, but for three months, he gave everyone a run for their money. But, it wasn't to last, and soon John T started looking for something to ease the pain.

He finds a seedy little place. The kind that offers a massage with a big wink. With his last hundred, he asks for the Wagyu special. See, back when he was a calf, John T heard all about those Japanese cows, spending all their day drinking beer and bathing in honey. Turns out, if you lower your standards, you can get a forty something to pour two percent on your head as she rides you. And there, as she climbs on top of him, she asks, 'How do you want it, honey?'

John T reaches behind his head and holds up a pillow. 'Use this,' he says, 'but don't stop till I say so.'

The woman looks at the pillow. She tells him, 'Ok, hun' and she brings it down on his head, and holds it down, waiting for John to say, 'Stop!' But he never does.

VII

John T may have been a cop killing criminal, but he was also loved by many people. Even with all the terrible things said on social media, there were many who were heartbroken to hear of his passing, though, it's said that many laughed when they heard how.

'That's our Johnny boy!'

Then, after a time considered appropriate, those few remaining family members were asked what they intended to do with their share of meat. Many spoke of using it to make John's favourite. While others spoke of burgers, something simple accompanied by a few beers and some good conversation. Naturally, these suggestions were met by an offer from the mayor. It seems he's willing to pay well over the asking price to collect as much of John T as possible. Whether done out of a sense of revenge for killing his brother, or simply because there ain't a piece of meat in town that doesn't cross the mayor, none knew.

In the end, the meat made its way down the usual channels. There, as the last of John T was placed on the dining table, a working class couple sat down to their first meal together in two weeks.

It wasn't a fancy meal, some simple ramen, over which John T had been sliced into thin strips. Neither of them knew where the meat came from, and so were forced to judge it on other means.

'It's good,' says the man.

His wife nods, 'Hmm,'

And then the man frowns 'But, did you have to fry the shit out of it?'

'Sorry,' says his wife, 'I was busy with the baby.'

'It's fine,' says the husband, and he pokes at his food.

'You want me to make you something else?'

The husband looks at his bowl of ramen topped with John T. 'Nah, It's fine.' And he waits till she leaves the room, at which point, he heads over to the bin and scrapes the rest away.

ALTERNATIVE DIMENSIONAL LOVE AFFAIR

There's a girl I like. I want to ask if she'd like to go on a date with me. I'm scared she'll say no, so I go to a psychic to see if there's any hope.

She says, 'I see you spread across many dimensions, and this is what I see.'

Dimension 1

'You and this girl go on a date.'

Well, that sounds nice, but the psychic gives me a look. It's not the kind of look you want when asking about your future.

'Six months later,' she says, 'you take her to KFC, and there, she'll find a ring on her chicken drumstick.'

Oh, so, we've got one of those kinda of relationships? How sweet!

The psychic shakes her head. 'She looks at the drumstick and asks 'What is wrong with you?' Then she will get up, and you will never see her again.'

Oh, so, it's not like one of those relationships then, is it?

The psychic tells me to not lose hope. Afterall, there are

many dimensions yet to come.

Dimension 2

'In this dimension,' she says, 'everything's the same only for some weird reason, everyone you're attracted to is secretly addicted to Crack.'

Oh-K? When you say Crack, do you mean like in the pavement, or -

'I mean the drug,' says the psychic. 'Crack as in Crack-Cocaine. I'm talking Candy, Rock, the kinda stuff that'll ruin you for life.'

Ok. And you're saying everyone I'm attracted to likes Crack?

'No,' she says. 'I'm saying everyone you like is addicted to Crack. They're sick. Right down to the core. They're the kinda people who hate life and everyone in it. They're just looking for a way to escape the pain.'

Right . . . and you're telling me that's my type?

'Then,' says the psychic, 'after six months of dating, you're at KFC. She's late (that's crackheads for you) there, she'll find the drumstick with the ring on it.'

Cool, so I do the whole ring on the chicken thing in every dimension, do I?

'She'll ask for a moment alone,' says the woman, 'at which time, she'll sneak out the back.'

Well, I can't blame her. It's a pretty embarrassing way to propose to someone. Does she come back later that day, demanding I do it properly, or at least at a better quality chicken place?

'No,' says the psychic. 'You never see her again.'

Bit of an overreaction. Do I get the ring back at least?

'Weren't you listening?' says the psychic. 'She's a crackhead? What do you think she's going to do with a wedding ring?'

I don't know. Never met a crackhead before.

'She does what every crackhead does when they find something of worth. She sells it for more Crack.'

Dimension 3

Please. Please don't tell me she's addicted to heroin.

'No.'

What is it then? Uppers? Downers? The stuff in the middle? She's not addicted to cough medicine, is she?

'No,' says the psychic. 'She's not addicted to anything.'

Well, that doesn't sound so bad. So, what's the issue?

'In this dimension, she's a Panda.'

So, like, what? You're telling me I'm about to be arrested for being in love with a Panda.

'No,' says the psychic. 'You're a Panda too. Everyone in that dimension is a Panda.'

That's great then, right? I mean, she's a Panda. I'm a Panda. What could go wrong?

Then the psychic gives me the look.

Ok then. What happens?

'Well,' says the psychic, 'you offer her a bit of a bamboo.'

Does it kill her?

'No, but she doesn't notice you. She's too busy rolling down the hill.'

That's it? She just ignores me?

'You say that,' says the psychic, 'but in that dimension, what just happened is the Panda version of Romeo and Juliet. Terribly sad. Terribly.'

Dimension 4

'In this dimension,' says the psychic, 'everyone is born with a bomb for a heart.'

Of course it is. Afterall, why would anything be normal?

'Joke all you want,' says the psychic, 'but in this dimension, everything is peaceful. There's no crime, no bigotry, no social hang ups of any kind. People are welcome to explore their desires in all but one way.'

Let me guess - Don't fall in love or your heart will explode?

The psychic narrows her eyes. 'How did you figure that out? Who've you been talking to?'

No-one, it's just, I'm starting to see a theme. Go on then, tell me how I mess this up?

'So,' says the psychic, ' you go about your day as regular. Everything is picture perfect.'

Apart from the lack of love and sex, you mean?

'Oh, there's sex,' says the psychic. 'Dimension 4 sex is cold and without emotion. It's nothing like it is here.'

Wouldn't go that far.

'Talking is forbidden during sex,' says the psychic, 'and, to reduce the chance of falling in love, everyone has to wear a potato sack on their head.'

Right . . . so roughly the same as my love-life right now?

'Then, one day, you enter the sex dungeon and as you look out of your potato sack and you see the most beautiful brown eyes in the whole entire world.'

Aww. That's sweet. Wait . . . did you say sex dungeon?

'Daring to speak, you ask for her name. She's tries to speak but the ball gag's in the way, still, you feel a strange sensation in your chest. You think, what's going on? Then you realise - this must be love.'

Wow, that's beautiful. Then what happens, do we go on a date, fall in love, all that good stuff?

'No,' says the psychic. 'Then you realise that what you're feeling is not love, but several pounds of explosives in your chest.'

. . . Should I happen what happens then?

"You explode,' says the psychic.

Yes. Of course I do.

Dimension 5

'This is the reality where everyone's a Praying Mantis.'

Right, so, maybe we should just skip this one. I mean, how much are you charging per hour?

'It's the same as before,' says the psychic. 'After six months of dating, the two of you head to KFC.'

Wait, they have KFC in the Praying Mantis world?

The psychic shrugs. 'You'd be surprised how far a catchy advertisement will go. She'll find the ring on the drumstick. She's so overcome with emotion that she has to tell you the truth.'

What? That she's really three Ladybirds in a coat?

'She's been cheating on you,' says the psychic. 'She promises that, to her, they were nothing but a bit of fun followed by a light snack. You want to understand, you want to forgive, but you can't. And with that, you get up and leave, vowing never to love again.'

Awfully deep for a violent insect.

'Deep down, you know it's not true. Time will heal all wounds and all that, and slowly you cross the road, oblivious to the plan Mantis God has laid before you.'

Oh, so God's got a plan for me, has he?

'He does,' says the psychic. 'But, unfortunately, even God can't predict everything, and the moment you step foot on the road, you're killed by a car.'

Right...

Dimension 6

'In this dimension, everyone looks fine, but in reality, they harbour a dark disgusting secret.'

Wait, before you go on, I've got to ask - is there any Dimension where I've actually got a chance, or you know, at least everything isn't super strange and surreal?

'Well,' says the psychic. 'There's one where things are mostly normal.'

Mostly normal?

'Yeah, everything's fine, apart from the whole lack of skin...'

Right. Well, I think I've got everything I need.

I thank the psychic for her time, and then head back out into normality.

I'm still thinking about that girl, still wondering whether she'd actually want to go out with me. I'm not sure whether the psychic actually helped. To be honest, I'm not sure whether the psychic is actually a psychic. For all I know, she might just be some local crazy person. All I know is, if the woman's right, and there are a million dimensions out there, then none of them are going to help me right now.

So, I take a deep breath, and I head over to the strange woman who I can't stop thinking about.

She's reading a book, so she doesn't see me standing there, trying not to shake.

What if the woman's right? What if there are a million dimensions out there, and in everyone I fail?

What are the odds that this will be any better?

Well, I guess there's only one way to find out.

So, I reach out, and I tap her on the shoulder, and I wait for her to look.

CLOUGH

As the late great Donald Trump would say: the world is full of fake-news; and for monsters that goes double.

Take Boggarts for instance: they say that the Boggart likes to turn into the thing that scares you most: It's a lie; Boggarts turn into all kinds of things, it really depends on the day. Like today, today is Monday, and while the Boomtown Rats may sing about how much they hate it, for Boggarts, Monday's are a good day, like Birthdays and Christmas all rolled into one. See, a Boggart's power shifts with each day of the week, and on Monday's Boggart's turn into the thing you most want to see.

The Boggart was born exactly as it is now. There were no parents, no one to guide, or support, or even name it. If the creature was to give itself a name, then the Boggart would simply refer to itself as 'It' Somewhat dehumanising perhaps, but then, the Boggart had never once suggested that it was in any way human.

It works on a porn site, mostly cam. Most are happy to watch, though there's always someone willing to pay that little bit extra to have a chance to join in. On its first day, the Boggart found itself changing. Shape, race, and gender: none of it lasted very long. Like an 80's body horror, things were about to get messy. It was expecting the chat to fill with aggressive comments and little angry emojis. It was expecting the local authorities to run it out of town. It expected to be hunted, and there, trapped in a corner, they'd come with their dogs, and their pitchforks, and they'd burn it with their torches. The Boggart was scared this would happen, which is why the

Bogart had put off this work for as long as it had. And while you might ask yourself, 'Why do it then?' the only answer the Boggart can give is this: 'Have you seen the rent on my apartment?'

The Boggart wasn't hunted, instead, the Boggart experienced something else.

The first guy put a comment saying, 'Nice dress.' His name was John, or to use his official title 'BigDickJohnny268' By this point, the Boggart's dress had melted away. Several of the guys watching were more interested in tight jeans, though they couldn't agree on the colour, and the Boggart sat there, swishing its legs back and forth as its jeans shifted from blue to white, and then back again.

So, when 'BigDickJohnny268' put his comment saying 'Nice Dress' the logical response to that would be to say, 'Holy shit! What the fuck is happening?' The Boggart had never interacted with so many before. The Boggart preferred to go out at night where it would be seen by only one person at a time. The transformation was easier then. Subtle, soft, and less violent. Now it was here, on the bed, watching its body shift and reshape itself in a most violent manner. The effect left the Boggart with a wave of sea-sickness as it stretched and shrunk.

You'd expect the people to unite, or at least agree that what they saw wasn't normal. Instead, the Boggart gets a new message, this one is from 'Dickflip69' it responded to say 'What fucking dress?' and then he added another word, which we're not going to say here as this is a hate free zone, though that didn't stop the comments from turning nasty, regardless of how many times the Boggart typed #Goodvibesonly.

At this point, the Boggart had two opposing comments, one saying nice things about the dress, while the other called them a cocksucker and then complimented the Boggart on its jeans. This led to a discussion in the comment section, one that became as personal as it was insulting. By the end, the Boggart found itself a very specific shape. Those that remained agreed that the Boggart did indeed have a very nice dress.

The Boggart didn't know what they saw. For them, did it shift and change as it did on the bed? Or did each guy see only that which he wanted to see and nothing more? That was a year ago, and since then, the Boggart has come to learn a great deal about people, and not all of it was good.

Boggarts like Mondays, it's the one day a week that humanity has a chance to get what it wants, to be happy. On Monday's, a Boggart will turn into the thing you want most. In theory, it's like heaven on Earth, and for ten dollars a minute, you too can get what you always wanted. There is a problem though, and that's, what do you do when you get what you want and you're still unhappy? Well, on those days, Humanity can get mean. Sometimes, things can get so bad that the Boggart wants to get even, but that's talk for another day.

So, It's Monday, and the Boggart is sitting on the bed, looking at itself in the mirror. Completely naked, its grey skin hangs loose and dripping all over a Spongebob bedspread. Between Its legs is a fuzzy patch too rough to be pubic hair; it feels like a cat's tongue, like rubbing your face on Velcro. The Boggart wonders if the Velcro means something, if somewhere out there, something waits with the softer half. The Boggart wonders what would happen if the two met and rubbed their groin-less bodies together? Rough to soft. The Boggart wasn't sure if it had met another of its kind. Chances are it had, but, judging by the mess in the mirror, the Boggart could hardly blame its kind for seeking the look of something a little less sour.

Now, it's getting late, and as Monday comes to a close, the Boggart sits on the bed, laptop open, camera on, waiting for someone to talk.

'Bing' goes the laptop. The message reads, 'Fuck! You've got big tits!!!'

With a sigh, the Boggart watches as its breasts begin to inflate. The face in the mirror is all smiles and fake tan, dark skin with a few pale patches around the ears; this is far too personal, far too real to be the replication of something glanced upon the internet. Blonde hair falls in thick platinum curls. For clothes, if you can call it that, the Boggart is wearing a red bathing suit. It's cut so short that it's a matter of 'When' and not 'If' the breasts will fall out.

The Boggart taps its Lav Mic to make sure it's on. With a look down at the inflatables on its arms, it says, 'Somebody's been watching Baywatch.'

The guy replies, 'Shut up and get undressed.'

The Boggart looks down at the red bathing suit. In its time as both a Pornstar and a monster, the Boggart had learnt that, whenever someone looked at it, they got whatever they wanted, regardless of how sick and disturbing that might be. So, if this guy really wanted the Boggart naked then it would be naked, it was as they say, as simple as that.

'Ok,' says the Boggart, 'It's going to be one of those days.'

'Fuck you,' says the guy, 'get naked. Bitch.'

The Boggart does a quick google search. Apparently, Pamela Anderson has just brought out a new book 'That explains a lot,' says the Boggart, 'Tell me, hun, is she a good read?'

'Shut up,' says the guy, 'don't talk. Nobody's interested.'

The Boggart blows curly hair out of its face. 'What's with the anger, hun? You don't like what you see?'

'No,' says the guy, 'you make me sick.'

Well, that wasn't true. The Boggart didn't choose the shape. It had to admit, the tits were very nice and all, but if it were up to the Boggart, it'd choose something that didn't leave it with such a serious backache.

'What's up, hun? You got the woman of your dreams staring right at you, and all you can do is curse?'

There's a pause. The Boggart watches as the guy types, stops, and then types again.

The Boggart gives the screen a Hollywood smile. 'Come on, hun. Open up.'

'You look like my girl,' says the guy.

The Boggart gives its reflection a wink. 'You're too kind,

hun. So, what's the problem? You scared you can't handle the both of us?'

'Oh, I can handle it,' says the guy, 'I can handle her and you and everybody else. Don't think I can't. Don't think just because you're on the other side of that screen that you can mock me. I won't be laughed at. Not by you, not by anyone.'

That's the problem with Monday's, you give the people what they want, and they get mad about it, like it's somehow your fault.

The Boggart gives its chest a squeeze: Implants, just as it thought. 'Who's laughing, hun?'

'You look just like my girl. You even have that same crooked smile. Well, you won't be smiling when I come over there and knock your fucking teeth out!'

The Boggart holds a white fingernail over the 'Ban' button. 'Careful now, hun. Respect goes both ways. Now, if you want to stay you're gonna have to show me some kindness.'

There's another pause, then the guy says, 'That's not how my girl would say it.'

'Well, I'm not your girl, hun. I ain't no push over.'

'Neither is she,' says the guy, 'It's just, whenever I talk back she tells me how good I got, and how I wanna shut up before she goes ahead and shows me.'

The Boggart looks at its reflection. The blue eyes stare back all innocent.

'She treat you bad, hun? Is that why you're here?'

'Something like that,' says the guy.

'Then, why don't we fix that, hun? Why don't you be good to me so I can return the favour?'

There's a pause, then the guy asks, 'So, how do I do that?'

'Tip menu, hun. Use the tip menu.'

After a moment, there's a loud 'Ka-ching!' and the Boggart sees he's tipped for breasts.

Off comes the red bathing suit, and the Boggart smiles at its body. You can't even see the scars; The marvels of modern day surgery. 'Now what, hun?'

'Ka-ching!' goes the laptop. The guy's tipped for masturbate.

The Boggart slides on its Californian butt and there begins to tease around the edge of its clitoris. Everything down there was all neat and tidy. The Boggart was glad to see it had no pubic hair. That would mean an easy clean up. Not the sexiest thing to hear, but, in this line of work, hair made the difference between reaching over for a wet-wipe and having to use the shower. To some, it wouldn't matter, but the Boggart had high standards. It may be a monster, but that doesn't mean it has to live like one.

The Boggart continues to tease till its fingers begin to slip along the edge. Soft, slick, and supple: the party had arrived. 'Come on, hun. Tell me what you want!'

'Ka-ching!' goes the laptop. The Boggart looks and then frowns. 'Really, hun, that's what you want?'

'Yeah,' says the guy, 'is that alright?'

The Boggart sits up. 'You want me to call you Tiger? Is that it?'

'No,' says the guy, 'It's Tigger, you know, like Whinnie the Pooh?'

The reflection in the mirror isn't best pleased. 'As far as kinks go this is a new one, hun.'

'No,' says the guy, 'It's a nickname. It's her nickname for me.'

A moment passes and then the Boggart lays back down. 'Come on, Tigger. Why don't you give it to me?'

'Ka-Ching!' goes the laptop. 'Say it again.'

The Boggart continues to tease. 'Fuck me, Tigger. Fuck me!'

'Ka-Ching!' The guy tells her, 'Do you know the wonderful thing about Tiggers?'

'I don't know, hun, why don't you tell me?'

'Ka-ching!' The guy tells her, 'It's that I'm the only one!'

The Boggart leans back and continues to tease, and there, lost in the moment, it begins to slide its fingers in and out, all the while yelling, 'Yes, Tigger! Yes!'

Afterwards, as the Boggart lay there, breathing heavy, its dampness sticking to the bed, the Boggart finds itself smiling. 'You're really something, hun. You know that?'

There's a pause. The guy types, stops, and then types again.

'Don't be shy, hun. Or would you prefer I call you Tigger?'

'She's gone,' says the guy, 'she died last winter.'

The Boggart reads the message, once, twice, many times over and yet it still can't think of something to say. It wants to say something original, something heartfelt. The best it can do is a simple, 'I'm sorry, hun.' It's cliche, but that doesn't make it any less true.

'She loved the water,' says the guy. 'Funny, because she never learned how to swim, no matter how many lessons I took her to.'

Boggarts aren't people, and as lonely as that can get sometimes, it does allow them ask questions, the kinds of questions regular people don't tend to ask.

'How long's she been dead, hun?'

'A year,' says the guy, 'A year to this day. You know, she looked like you, a real Pammy. I kept thinking, if only she could swim, it'd be like Baywatch for real.'

'Sounds like a silly reason to love someone, hun, but then again, I've heard a lot worse.'

'She's dead,' says the guy, 'I made her go out there in the sea, I didn't know that the current could get that strong.'

'You miss her?'

'Didn't you hear? She's dead and it's all my fault.'

'Sorry, hun. But I don't see it that way. Sounds like you had something special, and I'm real sorry for your loss.'

There's a pause, and then the guy says, 'Yeah? Well, what the fuck do you know? You stupid whore!'

With that, he leaves the room. The Boggart lets out a sigh, and then watches as the beauty begins to melt off the bone. Gone is the tanned skin and blonde curls, and it's all replaced something else, something grey and wet, and balding.

'He wasn't so bad,' says the Boggart. 'He was just hurting is all. I can let that go. No need to add him to my Tuesday club.'

There's a lot of things people get wrong about Monsters. Take the Boggart for instance, all anyone talks about is how they like to turn into the thing that scares you most. See, but that ain't true, at least, not on Monday's. See, on Monday's Boggart's turn into the thing you want most. Problem with that is, sometimes, the thing you want most is the thing you can never have. Funny how want and desire can turn a dream into a nightmare. It's enough to make you think, though, it should be said, not everything you hear about Boggart's is a lie. Boggarts can be scary, it's just, you gotta catch them on the right day.

The Boggart gets a private invite. It's from John named 'Igor'

The Boggart turns on its VPN, which for those who don't know, allows you to talk in private. Then, with a sigh, it clicks accept and goes to a private room.

Most guys don't do a two-way cam, they cost too much. But, Igor doesn't have that issue, after all, it's not like he's going to pay.

The Boggart's screen fills with what looks like a basement. There's a blue tarp taped to the floor, and in the centre of the tarp is a woman tied to a chair. Her hands are bound behind her back.

The man named Igor steps into shot. 'Hello there,' he says, 'Tell me, Mr Richard. Are you paying attention?'

The Boggart feels its body begin to change. Its stomach begins to swell, its hair grows in, though not very much. Soon, it sits on the end of the bed looking like a nervous man trying to stop himself from crying.

'Are you ignoring me, Mr. Richard? You know I do not like be ignored.'

Igor takes a blade and cuts the woman from ear to collar bone. Though not particularly deep, it does create a lot of blood, most of which can heard 'a-drip-draping' on the blue tarp below.

'You let her go,' says the Boggart, 'you hear me? Just let her go.'

'That all depends on you,' says Igor, 'do you have my money?'

The Boggart looks at its phone. 'I'm almost there, I just need some time to get the last of it.'

Igor sighs and then cuts the woman again. This time he removes the earlobe, which he holds up to the camera. 'This earring,' says Igor, as he shakes the wet piece of meat. 'Is real diamond?'

The Boggart looks down at its middle aged man feet. 'Zircona.'

'Ah,' says Igor, 'is shame, but I give one hour more for the honesty.'

With that, the session ends, and the Boggart returns once more to its amorphous shape.

With a sigh, it takes out its phone and then texts a number. It asks, 'You ready for the call?'

A moment later, the Boggart gets another request for a private session.

The screen connects to what looks like a run-down motel, and the Boggart looks at the face of Richard Middleston, the man in which the Boggart had been only moments before.

This Richard was calm and, judging by the half-empty bottle of champagne behind him, perhaps a little drunk.

The Boggart looks in the mirror to see black hair, long and straight. It was dressed in a white PVC catsuit, the boots on Its black heels were eight inches long, ending in a stiletto of real silver.

With a look of infinite disappointment, the Boggart says, 'You're late, worm.'

Richard Middleston falls to his knees. 'Forgive me, Mistress Vain.'

'I don't want your words,' says the Boggart.

'Ka-ching,' goes the laptop.

'Good,' says the Boggart, 'are we still on for the meet?'

'Yes Mistress, Vain. I've got everything at the motel.'

'The money?'

Richard begins to look nervous. 'Perhaps, we should talk about this off camera?'

'If you don't have the money,' says the Boggart, 'then say so, and we can end the relationship right here.'

The Boggart holds a long black fingernail over the end call button. Richard Middleston cries out and turns the camera to face a suitcase full of money. 'It's all here,' he says.

'All of it?'

'Her dad gave me the money for the ransom this morning. I've counted every penny.'

'Good,' says the Bogart, 'good little worm.'

'Thank you, Mistress Vain.'

'Now, before I leave, I wish to know something.'

'Yes, Mistress Vain?'

'Tell me, Worm. Is there any regret for that which you're about to do?'

'Regret?' says Richard Middleston. 'What is there to reject?'

'The money, Richard. The money can save your wife, so tell me, are you sure you'd rather run?'

Richard Middleston looks at the money, his expression is distant and sad. 'She made me believe in marriage' he says, 'but, to tell you the truth, I've wanted out for a long time, and this, bad as it sounds, is just what I needed.'

'Yes,' says the Boggart, 'I suppose it is what you need.'

'Are you pleased with my answer, Mistress?'

'Don't make me sick, worm. The only thing of yours I want is your money.'

Richard begins to smile. 'Yes, mistress. Thank you, Mistress.'

'Disgusting,' says the Boggart, and with that it ends the call.

With Richard sending the address of the motel, the Boggart texts it to Igor. It says, 'Meet me at the motel in half an hour.'

It doesn't ask that Igor brings Richard's wife, that will all be sorted out in due time. The Boggart looks at the time; it's eleven o clock. Monday's nearly over, but there's still enough time to introduce Igor to the real Richard. After that, the Boggart can introduce itself for real, and there it can share a few opinions on the do's and do not's concerning the proper ways to treat a woman.

People are always getting stuff wrong about Monsters. Take the Boggart for instance, all you ever hear is that they show you the thing that you fear most. See, that's not true, or at least, not all the time. Not on Monday's anyway. See, on Monday's the Boggart becomes the thing you want most. Hardly scary, right?

That's not to say that Boggart's can't be scary. They can be real scary, you try running into a Boggart on a Tuesday. That shit's something else, that kinda stuff will scare you to death. See, for Boggart's, Monday's are a lot like Birthdays and Christmas all rolled into one.

Normally this Boggart would agree. But, as it sits there, waiting for a taxi, this Boggart is really excited to see what Tuesday will bring. And, as it's only an hour away, it won't have to wait very long. By then it'll be with Richard and Igor, and by then, it'll be far too late.

SOLD AS SEEN

So my little girl wanted a pony, which was another way of saying that we were getting a pony. I don't know very much about ponies, I'm vaguely aware that they are some kind of horse, only smaller like someone shrunk it in the wash.

I got a number from a friend, told me about this place. 'Good deals, mate. Really good deals, just beware, they're a right shady lot.' He makes it sound like they're out to rip me off. 'Course they are, mate. They're horse people, it's what they do.'

So there's me and my daughter, Maddie, and we pulled into what I assume is a very respectable establishment. Out front, they had this great big sign with a horse on it. I mean, if that's not a mark of quality then I don't know what is.

We're greeted by this short woman, blonde hair all scraped back in a ponytail. She had this smile, like someone on a box of toothpaste.

'Erm, hello,' I said as the little blonde woman came over. 'Is this New Gate stables?'

'Home of the finest steeds known to mankind,' said the woman. 'Why, I must congratulate you.'

I don't know what's going on. So, I ask, 'You what?'

'You being here,' said the woman. 'It is the first step on a long road to making your little girl very-very happy.'

I was checking the price of horses on the way here. If Maddie wasn't with me, or she was a few years younger, then I'd have turned the car right around and gone back home. Now, this woman's using words like 'first step' and 'long road' when she should be saying things like 'she'll love you forever' and 'this will show everyone who's the better parent. Take that ex-wife.'

I tell her, 'I thought all a girl needs is her horse?'

'A common superstition.'

'But, you have it written on your sign?'

'Yes,' says the woman. 'See, I have been meaning to get that changed. As, while technically true, 'All a girl needs is her horse' underneath should be the words, 'But an extra pony wouldn't hurt.'.'

I've only been here thirty seconds, and this story's turned from fairytale to horror movie.

I tell her, 'I only came for one, so why do I get the feeling I'm leaving with the whole circus?'

The woman led across a long plank which rested in the mud. Sprinkled across the floor were layers of old straw. The woman waved her hand at the fields in the distance. I see bumpy hills of green. I see horses nibbling at the grass.

'All of these fields belong to us,' she says. 'and we take great pride in acquiring the most allusive and respectable bloodlines from all across the world.'

I could tell by the way she said it that she wanted me to gasp or clap like I've just seen the greatest movie ever told. Instead, I tell her, 'That's nice.'

'So what is it you're looking for?' asked the woman.

I tried to look like someone who had a clue. I hoped my incoherent mumblings could pass off for confidence, but the woman's smile has taken on a most predatory quality. Gone is the face on the box of toothpaste, and in its place I see myself staring into the sharp toothed smile of a hungry wolf.

'Don't worry,' she said. 'I'll make sure you leave with something really special.'

Something really special = Great, another idiot. We've got a three-legged nag in the back.

I told her, 'We're just browsing.' I told her, 'We're not even sure if we even want a horse.'

That's when Maddie pipped in. 'I want a pony.'

Et tu, Brute?

The woman manages to not lick her lips, and I resist the urge to shout 'Traitor!' into my daughter's face.

'And what sort of pony are you after, my dear?' asked the woman.

Just like that, I'm ignored completely. Might as well be a ghost.

'The bestest pony in the whole wide world,' said Maddie.

'Well,' said the woman. 'I'm sure that can be arranged.'

She led the way on, and I do my best to ignore that look on her face, the one that said every horse has just doubled in value.

She took us into a shed full of sand, and plastic poles.

'Ah,' said the woman. 'Here's Charlie preparing Spirit for a ride.'

Well, I don't know what the hell I'm looking at.

See, I'll admit it, I don't know the first thing about horses, but I'm pretty sure they don't come with wings. This one does. They're huge, and big, and covered white feathers.

I said, 'What sort of horse is that white one then?'

It was clearly the wrong question, you could tell by the way the woman's eyes rolled so aggressively, you'd think they'd fall right out of her head.

'It's not a white horse,' said the woman. 'The horse is grey.' She said it like the colour was the strangest thing about it.

I said. 'Cool! But tell me, do 'Grey' horses normally have wings?'

The woman sniffed. 'Oh, that,' she said. 'Well, only the Pegasi have wings. They're from Greece, you know?'

Charlie began to play around with the saddles, flapping the stirrups, and leaning on the horse's back. The horse's face stretched into a snarl. Its nostrils flared, and I was shocked to see something so girly transform into a demon. That thing terrified me, and here I am thinking, and girls think they're cute?

Just like that, Charlie was on the back of the winged horse.

'As you see,' said the woman. 'We take the time to train each of our horses.'

I watched Charlie ride the horse around the shed. It was all going well, until the horse decided that it had enough. With a kick and a jump, the horse was in the air, flying up-up-up.

'Look, said Maddie. 'That lady's flying!'

The horse spiralled through the air. It knocked over poles. It cartwheeled head-to-tail head-to-tail, over and over, all while Charlie cried out in fear.

'Get your horse under control,' said the woman. Her tone was more annoyed than worried.

Charlie pulled on the reins, but it was no use. Afterall, it's hard to control a horse when it's flying upside down. She fell through the air, and landed on the soft sand.

The horse let out a victory sniff, and then flew up to the top of the shed, where it rested on the rafters of the roof.

'Can I have that one, Daddy?'

'No, you cannot!'

I realised the moment I said it, I'd made a mistake. Afterall, fighting with children can be dangerous. Last thing I need is Maddie getting resentful. She might grow up and join some Pegasus biker gang just to spite me.

I tried a softer approach. I tell her, 'That horse is a little too big, so why don't we find one your size?'

'Ok,' said Maddie. 'Let's find my horsey, then.'

I asked the woman if Charlie is going to be ok.

She tells me, 'Happens all the time. Nothing to worry about.'

I watched Charlie lay in the sand. Flat on her back, not moving. 'This happens all the time?'

She clearly didn't like the way I said it.

'No,' said the woman, 'not all the time. That would be dangerous.' She said it in this funny tone. You could tell it translated to, It doesn't happen as long as we're not caught doing it.

She led us out of the shed, and down a narrow corridor between two grey buildings. There, we were greeted by the smell of smoke, and a man whose face was black with smoke. He was stood next to a horse with eight legs.

'Adam is our farrier,' said the woman. 'That a blacksmith, to me and you, and now he's currently putting shoes on Sleipnir, one of our special Ponios.'

I pointed at the horses hooves. They varied from clean and even, to odd-shaped, and cracked. 'Looks like hard work.'

The farrier gave me a look of pain. 'Bloody murder on ye back is what it is.'

'But it has to be done,' said the woman with an unpleasant chuckle.

I asked the farrier how often he had to do it.

'About every six to seven weeks.'

I asked how much it costs.

'Depends on the farrier,' he said. I watched him carving shavings of hoof onto the floor. Then I saw his tiny dog run over and chew them up. 'If ya ride then ya gonna need a farrier.'

'Do they all need shoes?'

'If you're out on the roads then I'd advise it. No hoof no horse as they say, but it's best to have a farrier to check for hoof problems.'

The farrier finished smoothing out the hoof. He did one in the time it took me to ask a question. He was a master of his craft. He didn't just get the right shape, or do it quickly, he was also dealing with an angry horse, the kinda horse that has eight legs to kick you with.

I ask if shoes are expensive.

'Not cheap,' said the farrier. 'So, I'd avoid one of these, If I were you.'

The woman didn't like that. Not one bit. It's not that she went red in the face, or started shooting steam out her ears. No, you could tell she was mad by the way she stopped trying to sell me the horse.

'Well come on,' said the woman, pushing us on. 'Let's leave Adam to it.'

'Where do you want me to put him when I'm done?' said the farrier.

'Oh, just call for Charlie,' said the woman. 'Though, you might have to shout till she regains consciousness.'

We were taken into the stables. There, the air was thick with sweat and hay. We were led to a stable, where I saw a girl brushing a horse. This one looked more normal than the others, all except for one obvious difference - It had a great big horn reaching out the top of its head.

'This is Una,' said the woman. 'She's a unicorn.'

I asked, 'So, are unicorns a good horse for little girls?'

'Why of course,' said the woman. 'They're the best.'

The girl in the stable gave me an unsure smile. It was only then that I saw all the bruises up her arms.

The animal was magnificent, all white, with a mane that shimmered like an abalone shell. Its eyes were a powder blue, and as I watched the animal, I felt a sense of peace begin to wash over me.

'What your feeling its magic,' said the woman. 'It's a survival skill of the Unicorn. Can't eat the horse if you're too busy smiling at how perfect life is.'

Maddie pulled on my sleeve. 'That one, Daddy. I want that one!'

Now, I have to admit, I'm not totally against the idea. I went to open my mouth, to ask about the horn on its head. Then, the Unicorn turned to the girl and rubbed its horn against her arm.

The girl cried out in pain. Then, she leapt away, into a bedding made up of wood shavings on rubber mats. The Unicorn continued to rub its horn up against the wall of its stable. I watch it scratch against the stone, sending pink sparks into the air.

I asked the girl if she was alright.

'Happens all the time,' said the girl. She had scrapes and

bruises all across her arms.

'Horses will be horses,' said the woman. 'Even the magical ones like a good head scratch every now and then.'

I tell her, 'Yeah but what do you do if that horn pokes your eye out?'

The woman sniffed. 'It's not a horn,' she said. 'It's an alicorn.'

Right, like that made it better.

I asked if she could write it down for me. That way, I won't get it wrong when I have to describe it to the Paramedics.'

The woman folded her arms. 'I don't think you have the right attitude. The unicorn has a lot to offer, you know?'

I tell her, 'I agree. For one, it's really good at demonstrating the proper way to make a kebab stick.'

The woman didn't laugh. She was still smiling, but all of the light had gone from her eyes. 'Yes,' she said. 'If you say so.'

'Is this my horsey?' said Maddie.

I tell her, 'Not now, sweetie. See, the horse might be too dangerous for you.'

Maddie struggled to comprehend the sentence. It was like I'd just given her a Budhist riddle. 'Ok,' she said. 'So, when will it be my horsey, then?'

I ask the woman whether Unicorns come with any other benefits.

'Well,' said the woman. 'They can only be ridden by virgins.'

The rational part of me thinks, That's silly. You're telling me that a woman has to choose between a life without relationships, without connection, without fun, she's gotta trade all of that for riding a horse? How is that fair? The rational part of my brain tells me that this is wrong. A woman shouldn't be punished for her sexual desires. That's the rational part.

Now, there's also the other part. The irrational part. That's the part who likes to make one rule for his daughter, and another for the rest of women. It's that part that's looking into the future. It's that part that's watching Maddie grow up, bringing home one loser boyfriend after another. It's that part, that most irrational part that tells me, Get the horse and you'll never have to worry about any of it.

Now, I'd like to say that the choice was difficult. But in reality, it really wasn't.

So, I turn to the woman, and I tell her, 'We'll take the unicorn.'

And somewhere in the back of my mind, the rational part of my brain is giving me a dirty look. But, I don't care, because me and the irrational side are too busy celebrating how smart I am.

I leant down to Maddie. I tell her, 'Look how much Daddy loves you.'

'Is it my horsey now?'

'Yes, but, you have to make me a promise. You're not allowed to like any boys, now or ever. If you do, then you won't be able to ride anymore, ok?'

Maddie considered the proposal. 'I don't like boys,' she said. 'I think they're stupid.'

I tell my daughter, 'That's the spirit.' I ask the woman how long do Unicorns live.

'Oh, they do not die,' said the woman. 'Once their master has passed, the unicorn will wait till someone comes who is worthy.'

I'm only half-listening. 'Do you take a check?'

Turned out that she didn't, so I had to nip off to find a cash machine. Maddie stayed at the stables, learning all about how to care for a Unicorn. By the time I had returned, Maddie was covered in dirt. I found her brushing the powdery hairs on the horse's hooves. I sorted out the rest of the money, and we picked out a stable. Adam the farrier even offered me a good deal on shoes and care.

Everything was going well, till Adam came to shoe the horse. That's when he explained something about Unicorns.

'What do you mean it needs silver shoes?'

'That's the thing about Unicorns. Expensive buggers. Cheaper to get an eight-legged like Sleipneir. Easier too. Eight-Legs don't bugger off.'

'What do you mean, bugger off?'

Adam took me to the stable. There, I saw Maddie standing with the woman in an empty stable.

'Where is it!' I cried, looking up and down the stable.'

'Don't worry about it,,' said the woman. 'She'll be on the Bifrost.'

'The what?'

'Well,' said the woman. 'I can see someone needs to read up on their Norse mythology.'

I could have strangled her. Instead, I swallowed that ball of slimy rage, and hoped it doesn't grow into a tumour. I asked her to explain.

'The rainbow road to Asgard?' she said. 'Ring any bells?'

No, It really didn't.

'Well I wouldn't worry too much,' she said. She'll come back.'

'But how can you be so sure?'

'How do you think we got it in the first place?' she said. 'That's the thing about Unicorns, they are a lot like cats. Like to do their own thing.'

Yeah, but cats don't cost me a month's wage.

'When's my horsey coming back?' said Maddie.

The question made my blood curdle, but luckily by the next day, the Unicorn had come back. Then we had our second set of problems. See, no matter how hard Maddie tried, she couldn't sit on the back of the horse.

I asked the woman what was going on.

Without missing a beat, she asked, 'Well, is she a virgin?'

'Oh course she's a virgin. She's only eight!'

There was a pause, and then the woman asked. 'Well, is she pure of heart?'

'What does that mean?'

'Does she put others before herself? Does she tend to the wicked, even though they have killed her family? Is she benevolent above all others?'

'She's eight! It's a good day if she will do her homework. You didn't tell me that she needed to be good to ride the bloody thing!'

'Well,' said the woman. 'You didn't ask.'

I told her that I wanted my money back.

'I'm sorry,' she said, 'but we have a strict policy, sold and seen.'

'What does that mean?'

'It means that all sales are final, ' said the woman, and she left us to it.

I walked over to Maddie who was brushing the Unicorn. I could see a strange look on her face, as she was beginning to realise something. I didn't know how to tell her the truth. Tell her that the horse she loved, the one that was costing more than my car. How could I tell her that she wouldn't be able to ride her horse?

'Daddy,' she said. 'I think there's something wrong with Uni.'

I tell her, 'Look, I want to start by saying, both the Unicorn and I love you very much, but I don't think you're going to be able to ride her.'

Maddie looked up at me. 'For how long?'

'I don't know.' I really didn't.

Maddie continued to look up at me. 'For ever and ever?'

God I hoped not.

Maddie gave a soft understanding nod. 'Ok,' she said, 'but, can I still pet her? Can I still feed her an apple and a carrot?'

I told her, 'Yes, love. Yes you can.'

'Ok, then,' said Maddie. 'Then, I will just wait till she changes her mind.'

I wanted to cry. I took her up in my arms, and buried my head into her eight-year-old face. She smelt of strawberry shoe-laces, mud, and unicorn spit.

I put her down, and helped her groom the horse, paying close attention to Maddie's instructions. Together, we learnt which brush to use where. We learnt how to pick stones out of the horse's foot. We couldn't ride the Unicorn, but we still learned how to put on a saddle, and together, we walked it across the hills.

Maybe things are going to be ok. Yes, the price was criminal. Still, Maddie seemed to love the thing, and once we put a cork on the end of that horn, I felt a lot safer. Maddie had her horse, and she had her dad. Yes, one was a crazy idiot, and the other a horse with a horn. She might not be pure enough to ride a Unicorn, but that didn't stop me loving her any less.

THIRST TRAP

In the old country, Odin had yet to lose an eye. The Gods were new and unsure, and gave much of their time to affairs of the mortal heart. It was in these times that Odin did seek the answers of life itself.

Through what little knowledge he did possess, Odin travelled to the well of Mimir. The road was hard, a brutal climb upon a mountainous path. For seven years he did travel, through endless snows, with no company save the cries of two hungry ravens. Through the years, the three learned how to speak with one another. There, Odin would ask them questions, and learn the way of the carrion kind. The ravens too did ask their question. There was only one, and every day, they asked it:

'When will you die?'

Ravens are a creature without shame. And though they did enjoy the company of the young god, they still followed him impatiently, waiting for him to die. Odin may have been young, but he was already wiser than all others of his kind. And everytime the birds did ask their question, eyeing him with those hungry dark eyes, his response was the same:

'Not today. Not today.'

After seven long years, he did finally reach the well of Mimir.

There, he found the giant, a thing made of rough marble. His eyes were made of emerald, still sticky from the heat of the earth. His blood was made of ruby. When cut, it would pour out, hot and steaming, and there, bubbling upon the ground, it would harden into precious stone. Whenever he smiled, the light would gleam upon teeth of diamond. The giant, like all his kind, carried a chisel, and there, he did carve upon himself, shaping his rough marbled form into something smooth and beautiful.

Odin knelt before the giant and says, 'I am son of Bestla, your sister. It is through this right that I come seeking wisdom.'

The giant did not look up from his work. He was carving himself a hand, revealing the shape of fingernails as he scratched upon the pale rock.

'And what would you give me?' says Mimir.

Odin was a god. Chief of the Aesir. He was proud and haughty, and yet he had a task. 'Trade,' he says. 'My body for your wisdom.'

And with that, Odin did slip from his cloak. Then, the giant Mimir did cease his work, and there did gaze upon the young god.

Odin knew of giants and their hunger for flesh and form. It is why they carve upon themselves. It's why they work so tirelessly to turn that rough stone into something smooth and desirable.

With that knowledge, Odin approached the half-carved giant, and there, completely naked, the young god did get into bed.

'Would you like to join me?' says the young god.

The giant agreed, and followed behind.

Odin was wise. In that wisdom he knew that sex was more than a series of pumps and thrust. It was a matter of connection. There he placed a kiss upon the giant's mouth. Tender and soft. He looked deep within the eyes of the giant. Over and over, he kissed, making his way down till he reached the giant's penis, this at least had been shaped and carved into something he could work with.

There, Odin took the giant in his mouth and began to work him. There was no rush. No cry of ecstasy. It was a thing of patience and time, both savouring the moment for all its sweetness.

Odin was a wise god. He had learned the secret of sex. To be with another is an act of trust. To be open, and vulnerable, to look into the eyes of another and say, 'This! This here. This is where I belong.'

Once the giant had finished. Odin did push his monstrous form down onto the bed. There, Odin did lay upon the chest of the giant, feeling the heat of the earth rise up through the marble.

Then, Odin did speak. 'Now, dear uncle. Now, will you grant me my wisdom?'

The giant did smile, dabbing at the sweat upon his beard. 'No,' he says. And then the giant picked up his chisel, and once more he did carve at his body. Though, this time, he did stare at Odin, shaping the muscles upon his stomach to those of the young god.

'What?' says Odin. 'How could this be? I have given you my all? Were you not pleased?'

'You are most pleasing,' says Mimir. 'But you did not give me your all. You merely gave me what I wanted.'

At this, the form of Odin did change. Where once before sat a young man, shy and vulnerable, now the veil had lifted, and Odin became what he had always been - a most cold and serious god.

'I pleased you,' says the young god, no longer smiling. 'Now, it is only fair that I am pleased in return.'

'Sacrifice,' says Mimir. 'There must be a sacrifice. For some, this act alone would be sufficient. Why, I can see it in your eye, though you do your best to hide it with such a gentle smile, I see the truth, dear nephew, you find me repugnant, and this act will haunt you across your many lives.'

'Then give me what I want,' says Odin. 'Revel in my displeasure, but do not deny me my prize.'

'You are smart, son of Bestla, but you lack wisdom. No, to drink from my well, to gain its knowledge, you must sacrifice that which you value most.'

Odin stood upon the ground naked and furious. 'And what would that be?'

'Yourself,' says Mimir. 'You care for no other, I can see it in your eyes. That will be your price."

'Do not speak in riddles,' says Odin. 'Tell me, giant. Once and for all. What is it that you wish for me to give?'

Then the giant did smile. 'Yourself, child. You must give yourself.'

***

Without the wisdom from Mimir's well, Odin did look to other means in which to learn. There, a woman drew the gaze of the All-Father's. Her name was Anja. She was wife to Borr the fearless, and she hadn't cum in over two months.

It wasn't a matter of skill, it was that she had no man to please her. Borr himself had left on a raid. With a kiss upon her head, he claimed, 'I shall be back within the fortnight.'

That was over a month ago.

Talks of recent raids had left Anja with a cramp, but Borr was always a man of his word. It was as if he could control them, to drag them from his head and there beat them into truth. It was often said that he had drunk deep the mead of Suttungr. This would explain how the man could talk his way into whatever he wanted, and of course, into the bed of Anja herself.

Still, Anja was afraid. She begged him, 'Send another. Stay here and I'll make you a son.' Borr gave her another kiss. 'A child is not a leash, my love.' And, because he knew she was in need of comfort, he did kiss, from the hair upon her head to the other, the hair that remains hidden to all but lovers.

The man had skill. He was a poet whose verses were best left for the prayers of lovers and gods. And there, as Anja took his head and brought him close, and there she made a prayer of her own.

It was to the gods of Aesier and Vanir. It was to ancestors and wise souls. It was to all, the giants too. It was a plea.

'Bring him back,' spoke Anja, in the eye of her mind. 'Whatever the cost. I beg you. Bring him back.'

And with that, she came, and then he left. The last memory was of Borr, all smiles as his beard glistened like brine upon the southern moss.

That had been two months ago, and Anja had not cum since. At first, it had been a matter of honour.

'I shall wait for him,' she says, and she meant it. But the weeks rolled into months, and like a tide, each time, the wave came back, taller and taller. The thought of life without Borr terrified her, as if the waves of her thought might drown her in her sleep.

Then, one day, Anja got into a fight with a fishwife. It got so bad that her friend had to pull her aside.

'She don't scare me,' says Anja. 'I tell ye, if only her brain was as big as her tits she'd know better than to run her mouth.'

Her friend tells her, 'Calm ye self. It's not her fault you're out here with a craving for man flesh.'

'What's that supposed to mean?'

Her friend laughed. 'Come off it. Since Borr left, you've got more horn than a herd of goats. You need release, girl - for all our sake.'

Anja was at a loss. 'I can't dishonour him.'

'It's not dishonour,' says the friend. 'You, dressed in fur, Friggin' yerself. Why, the image alone 'd have Borr grinning from ear to ear.'

And so, Anja went home with a head full of questions. Then, in the dead of night, she began to explore herself. She felt down into that southern hair, and slowly, she did slip a finger into soft wet pleasure.

***

In her dreams, Anja continued to explore her body. The

dull ache became a pulse. The pulse became a flower, and as it opened, Anja felt the kiss of gods. Then, for the first time in two months, she came.

It took Anja a moment to realise she wasn't at home. Instead, her bed lay far above the clouds. It sat at the entrance of a drinking hall. Gathering the sheets about her, Anja went into the hall. There, upon a throne sat a man made of rock. He was a giant, of size and making. Of his kind, Anja had been warned. The figure sat upon the throne was a thing unlike any man. Next to his great height, Anja was but a child.

His skin carried the rough edge of a quarry. She asks, 'Have you come to eat me, lord giant?'

The giant spoke with the voice of distant thunder. 'No, my dear. For it is you who called me. I am Mimir. The ruler of the well of knowledge.'

There he did point with a diamond tipped finger, and Anja turned and saw a well. It was old and simple and by far carried the least of her interest. But Anja knew of giants. They were tricky. You have only to hear the tales of Loki.

Anja had heard of Mimir and his well. She asks, 'Is it true? With one sip, I may answer any question?'

Mimir produces a horn. It was short and brittle with age. 'Take care,' he says, 'for this is Gjallarhorn. With it you shall drink and you shall know.'

Anja places the horn upon the top of the water. Then, she turns and asks, 'What of the price?'

Mimir did smile then. 'Sometimes, to know is price enough.'

So, Anja did dip the horn and drink of the well. She asks herself, 'What of Borr? When shall he return?'

With that, she drank. There, she felt it, thick and briny. Life moved on, from the dawn of all things. Of worlds brought into being by the licks of cosmic cows. All the way to the end, of Loki and his family. Life was snuffed in an instant, and then, as light grew upon the distant dark, Anja watched as life began anew.

Calm and confident in all things, Anja moved through time till she focused on what she wanted. There, she saw Borr. He stood at the helm of his ship - he was almost home.

***

The next day, news came of a ship. There, did Anja rush till she found the crew, and a man whom she had missed for many months.

With many tears, she found Borr, and his men.

'I have missed you,' she says, planting upon his face a series of kisses, each one stronger than the last.

Borr did not kiss back. Nor did he look pleased to see her. Then, Anja noticed how none of the crew did meet her eye.

'What is it?' she says, 'What has happened?'

Then she watched as they led out a woman - no - she was a slave. Young and beautiful, and pregnant.

***

At home, in her dream. She did meet Odin upon the road. She tells him of her husband and his slave.

'Come,' says Odin. 'I have a tree in need of fruit.'

There, she followed Odin to the tree, and she watched as a man dangled there with a rope around his neck. The man kicked and gasped and pleaded for mercy. He didn't die, nor would he.

Standing under the feet of the man, Odin did look up and smile. 'Does this bother you, my lady?'

Anjia looked up, watching the face of the man begin to darken. The 'drip-drap' of blood as it worked its way out of his nose and eyes, and down upon the leaves below.

'Is it wrong to say that this bothers me less than my husband's slave?'

Odin took off his robe. 'I will go to the halls of Mimir. There I shall find answers for us both.'

She asks, 'What is your price?'

There, Odin stood, strong and naked. With a gentle

hand, he did lay her upon the grass. The ground was hard and wet with blood.

There, Anja did look up into the tree, and there she met the gaze of the dying man. His bloody tears fell upon, one after another.

***

The way back did not take seven years. For Odin was wiser now, and found himself a shortcut. There, in the hall of Mimir, Odin did stand, still damp from Anja and her love making.

Without looking up from his carving, Mimir spoke. 'You have returned.'

'I have come to claim my wisdom,' says Odin. 'Like you, I wish to aid in a mortal manner.'

'You wish to take advantage, child. You always have.'

Odin knelt upon the giant's hall. 'I will do anything,' he said. 'Just tell me what want.'

The giant did cease his carving. There, he stepped from his throne and approached the young god.

'Anything?'

'If it is in my power to give,' says Odin. 'Then, I shall give it freely.'

The giant did lift Odin's head, and he smiled with teeth of diamond and light. 'Well shall see,' he says, 'we shall see.'

***

The next day, they hanged Borr for theft. For it turned out that the slave belonged to another.

Without question, they tied a rope to the thickest branch, and with that, they did drag Borr kicking and screaming up into the leaves of an old oak.

They did leave Borr up in that tree for nine days and nine nights. There, he would sway and stink - a gift of knowledge to those who wish to follow his evil deed.

Then, in the dead of night, Anja did awaken to the sound of a scream. She thought she must be dreaming. But as she went out into the garden, she did see the other folks of the town. There they were, crowded around the old oak, eyes staring up into the tree. There, she saw Borr. His face was grey, and very dead, and yet still, he swayed and kicked and refused to die.

'He is not dead!' cries Anja. 'For seven days you've kept him, now let him go.'

But none would, for the gods had spoken. Borr was trapped between worlds. None could say why but for the gods themselves.

***

The next night, Anja awoke to find a figure upon the end of her bed.

She asks, 'Lord Odin?'

The god was naked. In the light of a pale moon, she saw his body, raked and bitten, and covered in blood.

'My lord,' she says, 'What has happened?'

Then, Odin began to weep. 'I tried,' he says. 'I did everything he asked for, but always, he wanted more.'

There he rubbed at his chest, and Anja watched his torn nipple hang loose as it dangled in the light of the moon.

'Come,' said the god. There, Odin took her by the wrist and dragged her into the field. They could hear the screams of her husband well before they found him.

A cloud of fly did hum across his body. Then, as Odin pulled at the rope, lowering Borr till Anja could touch his face.

'Go,' says Odin, and Anja was pushed, lip to lip with those of her dead husband.

The flesh was heavy and split with the softest of touch. 'Husband,' she says. 'Dear husband.'

Then, Odin did take Borr by the penis. There, he wiped

away the flies, and made a prayer till the penis did grow hard.

'Will it save him?' says Anja.

The young god did cry then. 'I don't know,' says Odin, 'but he said you would learn.'

Anja did lay down onto the grass, and with the aid of Odin, she did guide her husband inside.

'It will not take him long,' says Odin. 'For the dead are excitable.'

And Anja lay there waiting for it to be over.

***

The way back to the hall took him but a moment. Odin was wounded and furious, and in this he would finally find his answer. He would refuse all else.

Mimir was expecting him, There was no sound of the chisel as he carved his body.

'Enough,' says Odin. 'I have suffered, and I have learned, and now you will give me what I ask.'

The giant stepped from his throne and approached the young god.

'You don't have to do this.'

'No,' says Odin, 'but I must.'

Then, Mimir handed him a knife. 'Start with one eye,' says the giant. 'I'll let you know later if I need more.'

Then, with a trembling hand, Odin did raise the blade to his, and began to cut. The process was slow and as the blood ran down his face, the young god began to scream.

***

Many months later, and the slave is about to give birth. All are wondering how the babe will look. Some are worried, but not Anja.

Borr had a strong seed. The look of his family was easily spread. Anja felt no anger for the girl, not anymore, not since she herself started showing signs. The swell of her belly, and the rising sickness that came with each day.

No one spoke of her babe. They didn't dare.

At night, Anja did wonder who the father was? Could it have been Borr? The night of his return? Did she carry a child similar to that which grew within the slave? Or was it the child of a god that lived within her? Or worse, a thing born from the love of the dead?

Anja didn't know the answer. She would simply have to wait.

WHAT DO YOU DO?

The room was not overly spacious, but it did provide just enough accommodation for the five strangers.

The walls were covered with soft pastel coloured flowers. Each person sat in a comfortable armchair, arranged like a support group. A table lay in the centre of the room, on it resided a kettle, cups, tea and coffee, and an assortment of biscuits. It was odd to have a room look so normal for a group of individuals that were anything but.

A person of sensitive disposition would think that each of these people had something strange and possibly evil about them. The truth is that each of these people had, in their own way, conducted acts of unspeakable horror. Now, as they await their final judgement, the five people sit in a circle, discussing which of them was the worst.

'So, what did you do to get in here then?' asked the pale man. He was indeed very pale. So pale in fact that his skin had yet to see a single ray of sunshine. It was the white of egg shell. There have been cave fish with more of a tan. He wore a robe of black which in turn only further accentuated his complexion. Around his bald head, he wore a circlet made of red wood. The man was clearly a magician, that much was obvious. 'By the way,' he says, 'I really like your hat.' Then, he returned to spooning heaps of sugar into very dark tea.

'It's not a hat. It's the head of He who is drowned. Him who doth speak with a hundred mouths and one, and all of which are rotten. I wear the face of He who calls himself Akara.'

The man who said this was dark of skin. His face was

hidden beneath the head of a shark. Severed at the neck, the beast now rested upon the man's shoulders. There it sat, swollen with rot. It dripped a dark smoking slime down the man's body. There, his skin bubbled and blistered. Inside the head of the shark, one could see the face of the man. It was impaled upon row after row of shark teeth, each was long and brown. The teeth pierced the face of the man from many angles, though, it was clear by the man's expression that he had yet to die.

'Is that so?' says the pale magician. 'Face of a god, is it? That's nice. Saying that, I bet it gets hard when you want a breather, or a good scratch, eh?'

'I do not take it off. The crown of Akara is a symbol of power, and represents me being chosen. It means that when the sea god rises, I shall be the first to die.'

'Let me get this right,' says the pale magician. 'You mean to say, all you had to do is put on a fish head and you were chosen?'

The shark headed tribesmen nodded. dark drool spilled out all over the cream coloured carpet.

'Bloody Hell!' says the magician. 'You had it easy, didn't you?'

'Wearing the crown was incredibly painful. The teeth grow long. Through me Arkara will feed on the thoughts of the world. To join with him is to lose one's identity. I gave up myself so that the Void Shark could speak.'

'But you didn't have to work for it though, did you?' says the man in black. 'The amount of trouble I had to go to get noticed. The endless meetings in cold caves in the middle of January. The plotting with foul emissaries from plains too horrific to speak of. Forking out all my money for incense and the proper black candles - can't have the cheap ones - no! The foul gods want the good stuff, imported from Estonia.'

The shark-headed man turns to stare. 'What's your point?'

'Nothing,' says the magician, 'It's just, If I'd have known

that all I needed to do was wear a fish hat then I wouldn't have bothered.'

'And what is it you did?' asked the head of Akara.

'I'm a cultist,' said the man in black. 'Don't you see the sacrificial robe? The circlet of driftwood?'

'Why are you wearing a dress, Dear?' asked the woman next to him. Her body was the colour of bleached bone. Her eyes flickered and flashed like bottled lightning.

'It's not a dress,' said the man in black, 'hello! It's a robe!'

'Oh? Well, that's nice, dear.'

'And what are you supposed to be?'

'Me, dear? Oh, I'm a lightning witch.' Then, she smiled, revealing a mouth without teeth. It was a dark cavernous hole in which lightning crackled and popped. Her pale hair floated in the air like she was moving through water.

'So, do you do any tricks then?' asked the man in black.

'Just lightning really.'

'Is that it?'

'Well, got to say, It is nice to not have to pay for your electricity. All I have to do is stick me finger in the socket.'

'Well, that's something,' smiled the man in black.

He took his phone out of his pocket. 'Do you mind giving it a charge, do you?'

'You can try,' says the man in a faded shirt and old khakis, 'but, I don't think it will do you any good.'

'Oh who asked you?' says the man in black. 'By the way, why are you here? You don't even look like one of us.'

'I'm the same as you,' says the man. 'I am as devout a follower of the dark gods. In fact, I think we both worship the same guy. Big fella, face like a plate of wet noodles, right?'

'You can't be a cultist! You're not even dressed correctly!' With that, he points to the man's blue plastic shoes. 'What are they?'

'They're Crocs,' says the man.

'I mean, I know I worship Eldritch horrors. That my plan is to release existential threats upon mankind, but those,' he says, pointing to the Crocs, 'those are the worst things I've ever seen.'

'I am a modern cultist,' says the man. 'We believe that you don't need all the pomp and ceremony. As Long as your heart is black, and your soul is willing, that's all that counts.'

'Oh no it's bloody not!' says the man in black. 'Evil has a dress code, and I'm pretty sure it doesn't want you wandering around in Hawaiian print!'

'The Outer Gods reward the faithful regardless of their regalia,' says the modernist. 'Afterall, it's what's on the inside that really counts.'

'Oh, yeah?' says the man in black. 'Well, let me find me knife and we can test it out.'

'Great,' says the modernist. 'Violence, the last refuge of the inept and the incompetent.'

'Of course we like violence!' says the man in black. 'We kill people for God's approval.'

'Well. Personally, I like to think of it as producing a piece of art. But, each to their own.'

In the corner sat a man. Ovine horns grew from his head. His eyes were two times too big and the colour of fresh grass. His mouth was human, along with his clothes, which were formal: A three piece suit, immaculate save for the bullet holes that riddled his chest. Out of the holes leaks a phosphorescent green bile.

'So, how did you get here then?' asks the man in black.

'I have a twin that was blessed by the Outer Gods,' says the Goat Boy.

'Some of us have all the luck, eh Fish Head?'

'He grew strong and beautiful,' says Goat Boy, 'but his hunger was insatiable. The village gathered, and put an end to his appetites.'

'Oh, they weren't vegans, were they?'

The Goat Boy stares at him.

'I had to do something, not just because I wanted to protect him, but because I resented him for being chosen. I set off in search of the holiest of holies, the dark text - the Necronomicon. I found several pages in a local museum, and used it to transform me into the creature you see here. I would have transformed fully into His avatar, but alas, a security guard found me, and killed me before I could finish the ritual.'

'Crap when that happens,' says the man in black, 'but you can't blame yourself. We've all covered those pages, haven't we?'

There was a man who had yet to speak. He looks up, and in his dark eyes gleams sadness, or madness, or then again, it could just be gas - It's hard to tell when dealing with such strange people.

'You look like you've been through the wars,' says the man in black.

The man nodded, sending dust all over. "It was the desert that consumed my desire. It was there I set out to find the true faces of the Egyptian gods. I even took my son with me. The things I did in the name of knowledge.'

'Oh yeah, I know what you're on about,' says the man in black. 'Did you find the temple with that weird door that kept changing into things? I tell you what, I ended up sea sick for a week after staring at it.'

'You're the lucky one then,' says the dusty archaeologist. 'For what lay within the tomb of the ancient god was a sight for no mind of man.'

'Well, I was glad to come back because I ended up finding a few more pages of the Necronomicon. Speaking of which, how many pages did the rest of you find? Did anyone actually get the whole book?'

The group looks through their belongings. One by one, they produced old crumbling pages.

'I've got four on resurrection. Two on summoning. And a nice chapter on recognising the difference between an Elder and an Outer god,' says the man in black. 'What have you lot got?'

'I have the page of apotheosis used to transform me,'

says the Goat Boy.

'Very nice. What about you, Sand-Knickers?'

The archaeologist hands him his pages.

'These are the same ones that I've got,' says the man. 'And yours are all covered in sauce!'

'I think that's blood,' says Goat Boy.

'Fair enough. What about you, Witch?'

'I've only got a few pages I'm afraid, dear, but I didn't really use them anyway.'

'Well give them here,' says the man in black. 'Better to get as many as we possibly can so we can hopefully get a complete volume.'

He stares at the pages of the witch. 'What the hell is this?'

'It's my contribution, Love.'

'How to please your man by cooking a proper pot roast? This isn't the Necronomicon. It's something from a 1970's cookbook. It's rubbish . . . although, there's a good bit here on how to make homemade flapjacks.'

'Do you want the pages that I had acquired in the name of Akara?' asks the shark headed tribesmen.

'Might as well. It's got to be better than the witch.'

'Akara has many gifts to give, and he is not light when it comes to his own people.'

'Well that's probably because he's got nothing but a crap gift. There's not much we can do with these pages.'

'What do you mean? They are from the forbidden tome are they not?'

'Yeah, but they're the acknowledgements.'

The shark headed man pauses. 'No they're not.'

The man in black clears his throat and then begins to read. 'Thanks to my editor Julie, you know what they say about your first book being like your first baby? Well none of this would be possible without you. And of course, where would I be without the love of my wife and best friend. Mrs. Alhazred, this one's for you.'

'It still counts,' says the head of Akara.

The magician turns to the modernist. 'What about your weekender? Got anything good?'

'Nothing, I'm afraid,' says the modernist. 'I found all of the information I needed online.'

'You did what?'

'Yeah, I downloaded the forbidden text as a PDF.'

'Great,' says the man in black. 'That's all we need, someone pirating the evil text. I take it you didn't bring your tablet or whatever you've got with you by any chance?'

'I'm afraid not,' says the modernist. He helps himself to another cup of coffee.

'Well tell me that you at least wrote your story down, so that everyone can have a read.'

'And why would I do that?'

'Why?' says the man in black. 'What do you mean why? We all write down our stories. We use it to pass on tradition. To drive the world mad.'

'Oh,' says the modernist. 'Guess I didn't see the point.'

'You have to do it! It's tradition! You record all the ins and outs of your life, and then when the monsters give you go ahead you send your info off to that Howie Lovelace fella so he can put it in his mythos.'

'Well, I decided to break tradition,' says the modernist. 'Besides I prefer the works of other fiction writers such as August Dereleth, without his aid nobody would know who Lovecraft is.'

'Maybe, but he's only a ghoul, so it doesn't count.'

'I did not record the legend of my life either,' says the head of Akara.

'Did you not scribble it on a cave wall or something? Smear some blood and muck?'

'No, there was no need for story telling when the dark wave came. Nobody will remember it anyway.'

'That doesn't matter. The Mi-Go's would have translated it and sorted all that stuff out. You risk nobody knowing you were even there, you stupid fishhead!'

'The vessel is not important,' says the fish-headed tribesman, 'only His hunger.'

'Well,' says the man in black. 'Isn't that just grand!'

The group sit in silence. The man in black taps his foot, looking from one face to the next.

'What are we even doing here?'

'We are waiting for judgement,' says Goat Boy.

'And how long's that going to be?'

'When the creator deems us worthy,' says the modernist.

'Well, I wish he'd hurry up. I really need a wee.'

The moment he says it, the room begins to shake.

The wall at the far end of the room makes a great splitting sound, and slowly the walls tear away like wet tissue. Outside of the room is a cold eerie light.

'At last,' says the modernist. 'We are ready to be received.'

'About bloody time,' says the man in black. Then, his phone began to buzz. 'Thanks, witchy. It's already half charged.'

'It's alway nice to be helpful, dear,' smiles the lightning witch.

All five stand before the great gap, and there, they look out into the void. Beyond the colours of space and time, and there, writhing in the distance, they see it.

'And look as one,' says the modernist. 'Look upon the face of God.'

As one, the group let out a singular noise. A great, 'ooooh!' which echoes out into the infinity of space.

That is to say, most of the group makes the noise. There was one who didn't. It was the man in black. There, he stands, frowning at the visage before him.

'Is there something wrong?' says the modernist.

The man in black points at the thing before him 'What the Hell is that?'

'That,' says the modernist, 'that is him, the creator, the one true god.'

'No he's bloody not!' says the man in black. With that, he can no longer stomach the sight of the being before him. Instead, he heads back over to his seat, and finds himself a small bin in which to throw up.

'Yes,' says the modernist, 'that is God.'

'Well, he's not my god!'

'I can't believe this,' says the modernist. 'What do the rest of you think about this horrendous display?'

The witch shrugs. 'Bit disappointed, if you ask me.'

'Disappointed? You're staring into the face of God! How can that be disappointing?'

'Sorry, love,' says the witch. 'Guess I'm a little old fashioned.'

'What does that mean?'

'God's got a beard. Can't respect a god who doesn't have a beard.'

'God doesn't have a beard,' says the modernist. 'God doesn't even have a face. What are you talking about? Are you actually going to stand there and tell me that when given proof of the existence of the immortal creator, you're just going to dismiss it because it doesn't look how you expected?'

The witch pats him on the shoulder. 'See, that's why I love you youngsters. You know exactly what to say.'

'I can't believe this,' says the modernist. 'You're both crazy.'

'It's fine,' says the man in black. 'There's obviously a mistake. We've probably gone to the wrong waiting room.'

'Wrong waiting room?' says the modernist. 'There isn't a wrong waiting room. This God. Now accept it.'

'Well,' says the man in the back, 'would you listen to him getting all militant. Thought you were supposed to be all new-fangled, where everyone's allowed to worship whatever evil they wanted?'

'I am, and they are, but you have to face facts, there's no mistaking this sort of stuff.'

'Course there is, take the old spaghetti head over there.

He's not the creator, or at least not the one I'm thinking of.'

'I think he's right,' says the archaeologist. 'I've seen a picture, and he didn't have all those, what do you call them, the dangly bits.'

'It doesn't matter!' cries the modernist. 'You can go around thinking god looks however you like, but you're going to have to face facts.'

There was a pause, the only sound that could be heard was the slurping of the slippery mass on the other side of the wall.

'That's a load of rubbish,' says the man in black. 'If I say my god doesn't look like that then I'm going to go and find him.'

'But you can't do that,' says the modernist. 'This is our reward, to be one with the source of all life. You cannot throw it away for something so . . . trivial.'

'Might be your source, kid, but it's not mine. Come on dusty, we'll see if we can't find someone a little more appropriate.'

'I'm sorry dear,' says the lighting witch. She pats the modernist on the arm. 'It's just, I'm old fashioned. Can't worship a god who doesn't have a beard.'

'I didn't know I had options,' says the Goat Boy with a twitch of ear and tail.

The head of Akara looks on unimpressed and then leaves with the group.

The modernist is left alone in a rather pleasant room, staring at the creator of everything. The god squirms and squelches, and as the modernist stares at it, he's not filled with serenity, empowered by the knowledge that he has finally completed his quest.

No, instead, he's reminded of the others, idiots one and all.

The creator of all things produces a sticky wet noise. As infallible and strange as it was, he could tell what the noise meant.

The noise says, 'Well, are you ready to join?'

The modernist stares up at the thing, and then sighs.

'Sorry,' he says. 'But what if they're right?'

With that, he chases after the others, leaving the entity alone. There, thrashing in its great mass, the entity feels something new, something that it hasn't felt since the dawn of creation.

It was a shame.

And there, all alone, dripping and wet, the creator of all things watches the man go and thinks to itself, 'Well, that's embarrassing.'

After that, it continues to remain, floating, massive and impossible, and there, the creator of all things begins to cry.

THE WOMAN WHO COULD MAKE ANYTHING

I've met a woman who makes things for a living.
I ask, 'What sort of things?'
She tells me it depends on the person, but you only get one.
She tells me about the man who wanted to make a mountain out of a molehill.

***

He took her to his back garden and pointed. 'Right there,' he said, 'Just to the left of the Carp pond.'
The next morning, the man went into his garden, fish food in hand, and there he saw it, a mountainous precipice, all pale rock and spiky shale. It rose up before the man, reaching endlessly into the sky.
It was all going well, until the animal rights people appeared.
'We just want to know if you feel proud of yourself?'
'Proud?' said the man. He hadn't considered it. When asking the woman to make him the hill, he'd only done it as a joke. 'It's the wife,' he said, 'she was always going on about me overreacting, making a mountain out of a molehill. I just

thought it'd be funny.'

It was funny. The look on the wife's face was so powerful that it caused him to laugh so hard that he fell off the couch. He brought all his mates around, and together they had a barbecue, beef sausage, steak, ribs, and a few corn on the cobs for ruffage because the wife kept going on and on about his heart. There they ate and laughed and drank, all in the shadow of the mountain.

'Well?' said the animal rights people. 'Do you feel proud of yourself?'

'Suppose I do,' said the man. 'Got to admit, it really does tie the place together.'

'Tell me,' said the animal rights people. 'Did you ever take a moment to think about the wellbeing of the moles?'

He had not.

'Well,' they said. 'Isn't that convenient.'

The man was in half a mind to agree, though he could tell by the tone that something was wrong.

'That mountain of yours, not only is destroying the livelihood of the mole, but in fact the whole ecosystem around it. Flora. Fauna. The works. It's all your fault, and we want to know what you plan to do about it?'

Do about it? What can you do about it? It's a mountain. It's not like he could just put it in the skip and let the council sort it out. The thing was huge. So huge in fact that upper levels were covered in a thick layer of snow. You don't get much snow in England, and all the local kids kept asking if they could ski down it.

The man was at a loss.

He didn't expect people to get upset. He even said as much.

'It's only a mountain. Not like it's hurting anyone.'

They didn't like that. Not one bit.

One after another, they turned the colour of beetroot. Then, hemp shirts and dirty feet, they stomped away promising a war.

Word spread of his mountain, and over the next few weeks people would arrive to marvel at it, some even wanted to climb it. It was all going great until the neighbours popped round.

They said things like 'Some of us have work in the morning?' and 'I'm not being funny but...'

They wanted to know when he was putting an end to all this mountain business. When that didn't stop him, they called the council, though no one could figure out what law he was breaking.

They stated that this new hobby of his resided in the communal garden. They explained that his mountain exceeded the regulated square-footage allocated to each of the residents. They were sick of the clacking of the Climbers tools. They were tired of listening to people cry because their loved ones died upon the mountain.

People threw bricks through his windows. They posted things through his letterbox, the kind of things you don't want to pick up with your bare hands.

The man became depressed, and in that depression, he looked for someone to blame.

'It's all her fault,' he said. 'I only asked for a laugh. She didn't have to do it.'

He came to her house, not once but several times over. She asked him to stop, but he wouldn't listen.

'I won't stand for this any longer,' he said. 'And for every bit of vandalism done to my house, I'm going to come here and repay you in kind.'

That was the first time she made something.

***

I tell her, 'That's awful. How can someone be so mean?'
She tells me that's how people are.
'No,' I say, 'that guy's just a dick.'
She just pats my hand like I'm a small child. She tells me

that's because I don't go around making things. I don't give people dreams and watch them turn into nightmares.

She looks sad now, and I feel like the world's biggest prat.

To get away from all the doom and gloom, I suggest we ditch the cafe and go for some food.

'I know the perfect little Sushi place.'

Fifteen minutes later, and we're sitting in the restaurant. It's just me, her, four pieces of Eel Rainbow roll, and two bowls of Katsu Salmon.

She tells me that she's never had Katsu Salmon. It makes me smile, especially because of the way she says it, cheeks all full like a squirrel.

The Eel roll comes with these tiny red eggs on top. They're translucent, glassy, and pop in your mouth. Hard to be sexy with a load of fish eggs between your teeth, but she pulls it off in such a way that I forget to breathe. It's so bad in fact that I end up making this noise, like a mix between a choke and a gasp.

She asks if I'm alright.

I tell her, 'Wasabi went down the wrong hole.'

We finished our sushi, and our Katsu Salmon. We continued to talk, about music, and movies, and life. Then, and I don't know why, I asked her about her job again.

'Does your job attract a lot of negativity?'

She tells me, it's fine at first. But, everything comes with a price, and people don't like to pay.

She tells me about this bride.

***

'I want a ring,' said the bride. 'Not just any ring. I want it to match the beauty of my marriage. A perfect representation, in each and every way.'

The bride believed that she was special. Her love was like no other. Pure, crystalline. Hers was the love that would endure, that would last a lifetime.

The ring was every bit as beautiful as she had imagined.

The band was made of gold. Far from plain or gaudy, its metal seemed unable to maintain a scratch, nor would even the grubbiest of fingers leave a smudge upon its surface.

There were three diamonds, each cut in such a way that they would sparkle in even the lowest of light.

'It's perfect,' said the bride. 'Just like my marriage.'

The woman told her that it was exactly like her marriage, and though now it looked perfect, soon the ages would come threatening to tarnish its surface. Every lie, every petty squabble, every ounce of heartache and betrayal, all of it would be reflected upon the ring.

The woman told her that it wasn't too late. She could take the ring away. There were several jewellers who could provide something more suitable, something less... revealing.

'No,' said the bride. 'I want this, only this.'

She slipped the ring upon her finger, and regarded it as if it were the greatest of all treasures, and, like the beginning of any marriage, for a time, it was.

For six months, all seemed rather perfect. Then, one afternoon, the woman heard a knock at the door.

It was the bride.

'What do you think you're doing?' she said.

The woman wasn't doing much of anything, not really. She had just finished her book, and was ready to go for a nap.

'No,' said the bride. 'I mean, what do you think you're doing to me?'

With that, she held up her right hand, and revealed the ring upon her finger.

Its gold band was tarnished. It was covered in a crisscross of scratch and scrapes. There were three diamonds when she made the ring, but now only two remained. They no longer sparkled in the lowest of light. In fact, they didn't sparkle at all. They had grown cloudy, and each diamond had a ring of dark red that traced along the edge of the stone. It gave the diamonds the look of something sickly, something bruised.

'Well?' said the bride. 'Care to explain yourself?'

The woman had seen this before.

'It's a flaw then?' said the bride. 'A problem with the gold or the diamonds perhaps?'

The woman asked how long the bride had been cheating on her husband.

The bride said nothing. She just stood there, her words caught in her throat as she stammered a response.

'How dare you insinuate such a thing.'

The woman explained that the ring could be saved. It wouldn't be as before, as clear and perfect, but it could be better.

'Well,' said the bride. 'It's not much of an apology, but I guess It'll have to do.'

The bride asked how they could fix the ring.

The woman told her it was simple - she would tell her husband the truth. Tell him that she had been unfaithful for what appeared to have been the entirety of their marriage.

The bride began to froth like an enraged crab.

'I came to you for a ring,' she said. 'Something perfect. Something that represented my marriage. Now, I have nothing more than an old scratch ring full of diamonds so ugly even a dog wouldn't want them.'

The woman explained that she had done as she was asked. That ring was only as ugly as the love of that who wears it. Perhaps, she should focus more on the marriage itself instead of how it appears to the outside world.

The bride left in better tears.

Over the coming months, she would run into friends and family.

'Let us get a look at that fancy ring!'

And she'd do her best to hide it, but they'd catch a glimpse, and one by one, the bride watched their smiles melt away.

Nobody said anything, at least not to her face. But soon, word began to spread.

'There she goes,' they'd say. 'That bride with the ugly ring.'

'Ugly ring, ugly marriage,' they'd say.

The bride grew so ashamed of her ring of her marriage, that she went to her boyfriend, to the man whom she had been unfaithful with since long before she was married.

'We should run away together,' she said. 'Start fresh. Just me and you. Perhaps we could even get married?'

The man took one look at the ring and shivered.

'Not for me,' he said. 'There's no good in loving you. Just look at that ugly ring.'

A year went by, and the bride returned.

Her ring had lost all but one of its stones. That now sat in the centre, black and oily, it oozed along her finger, filling the air with the smell of neglect, strong and sour. There were so many scratches upon the band that you couldn't tell its colour.

She had tried to sell the thing, but even the most desperate of jewellers took one look and sniffed.

'What do you expect me to do with a piece of old tat?'

The bride beat upon the woman's door.

'You won't get away with this!' said the bride. 'Everyone will know the truth! You're a liar and a charlatan, and I won't rest till you get what's coming!'

***

I watch the staff take away our plates. I have to resist the urge to lick the remains of the Katsu curry that cling around the edge.

I ask, 'What about the husband? Ugly ring like that. He must have found out the truth.'

The woman tells me that they're still together. That the bride still wears that ring, though the last time they met was a year ago, and by then, the gold was black with rust.

I tell her, 'People are weird.'

She agrees.

Full from the sushi and curry, we decide to go for a walk.

One the way, we find a karaoke bar, and the woman gives me a smile that I instantly recognise as trouble.

I sing about as well as a cat in a bath. But, she pushes me to the stage, and I blush my way through 'Wonderful World.' There's about five people in the bar, two of them are the staff, so bored that they're falling asleep at the bar. Then there's the woman. She's sitting right at the front, so close that I can reach out and brush the hair out of her eyes.

She listens to me sing, and I try to smile as if I'm feeling like a guy in a dentist about to have all his teeth pulled.

The song ends, and I'm given a polite round of applause from the staff, and a cheering ovation from the woman.

She asks what I'm going to sing next.

I tell her, 'Maybe next time.'

She asks what makes me so confident that there's going to be a next time.

I tell her, 'I don't know. I just feel it.'

Two weeks go by, and we've been chatting on the phone every single day.

It's too early to put a label on the way I feel, so I just resign myself to the fact that I love the way it feels.

It's Valentine's Day and we agree to meet up for a movie.

Waiting outside of the theatre, I ask, 'So, what's the worst thing you've ever made?'

The woman tells me that's easy, it's not even close. The worst thing she ever made was life.

***

It was at the funeral of her uncle Toby.

They were never close. Toby was one of those distant relatives you only saw at weddings, and, well, at funerals.

It was there that the woman met up with her family. Re-introducing herself to those half-remembered faces that she'd no doubt soon forget. Towards the end of the funeral, after the priest had said a prayer, and uncle Toby was sent into the back to be buried. It was there that the woman met his daughter.

She was in her early twenties. Tall, skinny, and beautiful, even with the eyes all raw with pain.

'He's gone,' she said. 'Now, I want him back.'

The woman explained how this was a bad idea. There is a natural order to things. Mess with them and regret it.

'I don't want natural order,' said the girl. 'What I want is my dad.'

A week later, she awoke to a sound from the kitchen.

It was uncle Toby, only he looked different now.

His eyes were the colour of milky glass. His skin was so delicate that with every step, every gesture, the skin would split like wet paper. He oozed and stank, and screamed in pain.

'This wasn't what I wanted,' she told the woman. 'You made him wake up in the ground.'

It took days to dig himself out. All that time, the worms would whisper to him, 'Why aren't you dead? Why aren't you dead? You look dead. Mmm, you taste dead. So, tell me, why aren't you dead?'

The woman tried to explain. The natural order, the way of things. She had been warned.

The girl wasn't interested.

'You made him claw his way through that coffin. Wood so thick it scraped his fingers to the bone.'

Then, the woman went to the girl's house. She saw uncle Toby then, all swollen with rot, and she watched as he wept those dirty black tears.

'He has no one to talk to,' said the girl. 'When his friends see him, they scream and run. And everyday, he asks for meat, each fresher than the last.'

One day, uncle Toby went for a walk.

There, upon his stroll, he met a woman who would not stop crying. She looked like the most lonely woman in the world, and in that loneliness, uncle Toby saw something of himself.

He didn't know why he did it, but as he watched that woman struggling in pain, he felt the urge to reach out and bite her.

The moment he sank his teeth into her face, he watched the woman begin to change.

Bit by bit, her beauty was replaced with something else, something that he recognised whenever looked in the mirror.

The woman was no longer upset. Not anymore.

Then, she saw a man arguing on his phone. It was clear by his face that he was most upset.

Overcome by the urge to help him, the woman went over and gave him a bite.

'They don't like to see people suffer,' said the girl. 'But that doesn't help dad. Doesn't help one bit.'

It took a year to clean up the mess.

All those people looking to help. They wouldn't die, no matter how much you shot and stabbed, and hit them with bombs. They would put themselves back together. Then, as before, she'd stumble off, looking to stop people from hurting.

See, it hurt them knowing that the world was full of so much pain. They could it feel it, like wind upon your face.

There was only one way to stop them. The government ordered that the people were to be buried. Deep in the earth, in strong metal boxes.

They lie there still, screaming in the dark.

'My dad's down there,' said the girl. 'He's alive, and he's scared, and it's all your fault.'

***

The woman was talking so long that we missed the first thirty minutes of the movie.

I say, 'Come on. Let's go for a walk.'

She tells me that it's always been like this.

Ever since she was a baby, people would ask her to make things. It started with her parents. She was still in nappies when she gave them what they wanted.

'Did they respond the same way as the others?'

She tells me that everyone gets mad once you give them what they want. It's not that it's wrong. She doesn't curse people, or make them faulty gifts. She does exactly as they ask, down to the letter, and that's why they hate her.

People think they know what they want. They think 'If I could just get this then everything would be better.'

But what happens when you get it? What happens when things still hurt?

She's scared of relationships. She tells me about her last boyfriend.

***

A month into dating, he handed her a piece of paper.

'It's a list,' he said. 'You said you can make things, anything at all, well, this is what I want.'

This was a different kind of request. He didn't want money, or fame. He didn't want people to like him. No, what he wanted was for her to change the way she looked.

'I want you blonde,' he said, 'but like, thick blonde. I want you curly, but not too curly, you know? Just around the edges.'

He changed her eyes to blue. Not just any kind of blue, they had to have these little specks of gold inside, and when she gets mad, her eyes will turn a subtle shade of green.

He changed her smile. Her teeth. He had her scoop out her old personality and replace it with all the things he found funny.

They were happy, for a while, and then things changed.

'Why do you laugh like that?'

The woman said that she laughed how he wanted her to laugh.

'Yeah,' he said, 'but not like that. I wanted fun, and you're just ugly.'

After that, he became cruel.

'You're so pathetic,' he said. 'Doing all this stuff for other people. There's something wrong with you. You know that, right?'

He began to cheat on her.

She broke up with him, there and then. But, she didn't have the money to just move out. So, she had to live at the apartment, scrimping and saving, all under the same roof as her ex.

He liked to bring women over. None of them looked like her, like how he wanted a woman to look.

'Don't mind her,' he'd say. 'She's just my roommate.'

This went on for months.

Each time, he'd bring someone over. She didn't know whether he wanted to start a fight, or simply just to upset her.

When that didn't work, he would say things.

'Isn't she ugly?' he'd tell the new girl on his arm. 'Disgusting, right? Absolutely disgusting?'

The woman explained that she looked exactly how he wanted her to look. She sounded exactly how he wanted her to sound. From bone to personality, every inch of it was what he had asked for.

'No,' said the man. 'You're lying. You've cheated, you've messed it up. You must have, otherwise I'd be happy.'

The woman would have explained it to him, but then, she didn't think he'd listen.

***

Now, I'm walking the streets, not knowing what to think.

I ask, 'Is any of you original?'

She tells me, no. Unfortunately. She thought about going back to her old self, but she can't remember, and besides, she can't just do it herself, someone has to ask.

I ask, 'Do you want to watch another movie?'

She tells me, no. She'd rather we just walk.

We head to a bar, and after one too many drinks, I give her a kiss.

'Sorry,' I say. 'Probably shouldn't, should I?'

She tells me to shut up, and to do it again.

I try to kiss her, but the nerves and the alcohol are working against me. In the chaos of the moment, I make a wrong turn, and instead of kissing her lips, I head straight for her eyeball.

I apologise, once, twice, several times over.

She laughs and rubs her eye. She tells me no one has ever kissed her on the eye before.

'Can't believe that,' I tell her. 'I mean, afterall, it's such a lovely eye.'

I don't know why I said it, so I apologise again.

She tells me, it's fine. Then, she reaches out and kisses me upon the eye. Only, it's not as violent as the one I did, all wet and sudden like an octopus in heat. No, the kiss she gives me is soft and gentle and makes it so I can't stop smiling.

Before she kisses me, she asks what I want.

I tell her, 'I thought it was obvious, I just want you.'

She says, no. She wants to know what I want her to make.

'I don't want you to make anything. I just want to kiss you.'

She's not convinced. She's heard that before. People always start off sweet in the beginning. But sooner or later, they come up with an idea, and then it's only a matter of time till they end up hating her.

She doesn't want to do that again. She doesn't want to pretend that everything is good. So, before she'll let me kiss her, she asks me, what do you want me to make?

I think for a moment, all the while, I can see her face, full of emotion and pain.

I tell her, 'I have to pick something, right?'

Yes. I have to pick.

The answer's easy.

'I want you to make me happy, but only if you want to. I want you to dress up because you feel sexy. I want you to dress down because you need the comfort. I want you to make time for me when it's important, but only if I'm willing to do the same for you. I want you to be the kind of person you want to be, and want you to stop making excuses when you're not. Most of all, I want you to make yourself comfortable with the person you are, because, at the end of the day, you're the only one who doesn't get to leave.'

She listens to my demands. She asks if that's really what I want.

I tell her it is.

She tells me that I won't get another chance. She tells me to reconsider, that maybe there's something she can make, something she can change. She could be taller, thinner. She can as smart or as dumb as I need her to be.

I tell her that I'm good. I know what I want. But then, I ask her a question.

'If I could make something for you, what would you want?'

No one had ever asked that question before.

She tells me that she doesn't know.

Then I take her hand in mine. I tell her it's ok. I tell her to take her time.

We've been dating for a couple of years now, and while there are those ups and downs, I have to say, things are looking good.

She still makes things, only now it's stuff she wants to make. Stuff for herself.

Every now and then she'll ask if I regret my decision.

So, I do the honourable thing, and I ask her the same question.

She just laughs and gives me a kiss.

She's just made me a cup of coffee.

She tells me, I know, I know, it could be better.

I tell her, 'Yeah, but it wouldn't be you.'

P.O.V

It feels like the music's punching me in the head.

I ask the stranger at the bar to repeat himself. He leans in so close that I can smell his bad tooth.

'Hey, mate. Wanna Feel?'

Normally, I'd walk off, but I'm on a date with Sharon, and I wanna look cool. Sharon's not my girlfriend, she's not anyone's girlfriend. But, whatever we are, I don't want to upset her.

'What kind of Feel?' asks Sharon.

'Fella won the lottery. Come up takes abit, but trust me, you're gonna feel things.'

We should go. We don't need drugs, all this psychedelic telepathy shit can kiss my arse. We're young, and happy. I wanna take her back to mine. I want to order pizza, and watch shitty 80's movies. I want to work up the courage to finally tell her how I feel, how I've always felt. I know she doesn't like labels, all that 'Down with the patriarchy!' stuff, but I'm not the patriarchy, I'm just a guy looking for a chance to make her happy.

Still, I need a plan. I'm only on my second drink, far too shy to start being honest. So, I tell her, 'How do we know this is the real deal? Could be a dud, or worse like that shit on the news.'

Saw it this morning. Some girl in highschool, thought she was taking a dose of some high achieving A* student. Thought it would help with the revision. Instead, she was spiked with suicidal thoughts. She's still alive, but the self-harm means she's got to spend a few months at a facility.

It's new to Feel, but already the media has come crashing down calling it the worst thing since Heroin.

The dealer takes out a plastic druggie bag. Inside is an assortment of crystals and dust. They come in a variety of colours, all pulsing with the same dull light.

'What do you think?'

I tell him, 'I think that could be anything waiting in there. How can we trust you?'

So, he pops a large crystal in his mouth and begins to crunch. I watch them spill liquid light around his teeth. Then, he opens his mouth to reveal a shimmer of colours all pulsing in beat to the music of the club.

'There,' he says. 'Now we have trust.'

He hands me the bag.

I stand there thinking, 'Why didn't we get here an hour earlier? I'd have been drunk by then. We could have gone home, back to mine. I could have explained how much I love her. Instead, I'm here, nursing an IPA that tastes like dish soap.

'Look,' I tell Sharon. 'We don't have to do this if you don't want.'

'Ok,' says Sharon.

She takes the largest crystal from the bag. She holds it between forefinger and thumb. A slight squeeze causes the crystal to ooze blue light all down her palm.

'Open wide,' she tells me, and I stand there, struggling to find the confidence to say no.

***

They're calling it the drug of the new age. As natural a high as you can get. Memories, thoughts, and feelings, all frozen in time and chemically distributed. The government's telling us to beware. Worse than any drug before, but the younger generation isn't convinced. Like Sharon always says, 'What's so evil about feelings?'

The dealer's called Josh, and he's not much in the way of your typical criminal. 'Just looking for a way to pay off my Uni fees.'

The problem with Feels is they come with a brand new territory. 'You don't grow the shit in Bolivia,' says Josh the dealer, 'It's right here, in your neighbourhood, in your head. You make it every second with each and every thought.'

'It's all about who you know,' Sharon says, 'That's why the government doesn't want us to Feel. They've had the technology for years. They put it in the water to keep us all scared and stupid.'

Sitting outside, we watch the club begin to empty. People stumble into the street like babies learning to walk.

'I liked tonight,' says Sharon. 'I think I wanna win the lottery every day.'

If I'm honest, the experience weirded me out. One minute I'm regular old me: insecure, paranoid, and wishing I was at home watching Anime. Then, suddenly, I'm on a train. The smell of the drunk in the seat opposite. The crackling voice on the tannoy. There's a phone on my cheek, and I'm shouting, 'We've won, Julie. We've actually won!'

I felt the elation of winning the lottery. I could smell the drunk by my side, that mix of stale cigarettes and unwashed clothes. It wasn't just the experience of winning that I could Feel, it was the man himself. The dull ache in his knee, and that twisting ugly pain when the voice of another man answered his wife's phone.

Sharon rubs at her hand, and I'm reminded of cutting up my arm on the drunk's broken bottle.

The drug made it feel like I was there, that pain like dragging a bow across a violin, all slow and moaning. I just sat there watching the blood soak into the seat of the train.

'So weird,' says Sharon. 'But tell me, do you think she was cheating on him?'

I must have looked stupid because then Sharon burst out laughing. 'Julie,' she says, 'you know, the wife on the phone?

Wasn't it odd when that other guy answered? I mean come on, 'My old friend' indeed!'

She takes me back to hers. We get to the front door of the flat, and she takes out a screwdriver. She catches my look and smiles. 'Blame the police, I know I do.'

She hands me the screwdriver. 'A little wiggle is all you need.'

I feel like a criminal, but I push in the screwdriver and begin to turn it left and right.

'Harder,' she says. 'Like this.' And she places her hands on mine and guides the screwdriver. With a hard twist the door creaks its way open.

'There you go,' says Sharon. 'Next time, bring your own screwdriver.'

Inside the apartment, the floor's all hardwood and smells of incense. 'You get a drink,' she says, 'and I'll be back in a minute.'

I'm left wandering around her flat. To be honest, it's weird seeing it in the flesh. For months I've dreamt of this place. I don't know why, but I expected it to be bigger. Something more flashy. Well, maybe one day, if things work out, we can find that place together.'

Sharon comes back down the stairs. She's wearing a silken dressing gown. It clings to her body, curves pressing up through its pale pattern.

She sits on me and asks, 'What's your most intense Feel?'

I've never taken it before. You hear all kinds of horror stories. People losing their personalities, it's like someone made a drug out of ghosts.

She touches my chest, then with a kiss on my neck, she slowly works her way down.

I tell her, 'Are you sure about this? We don't need to go fast.'

It wasn't the first time we've done it. We did the first night we met. It's just, this is the first time I've ever been in her place. Mostly, we do it outside or in the toilets. It always felt dirty. This was different, this was her place. This meant things had changed, right?

Sharon smiles and then, ever so gently, she pulls open her gown to show that she's completely naked.

'You saying no?'

I try and fail to be a responsible adult.

I take a breath and then lean in for a kiss. Sharon begins to unzip my pants, and then climbs on top of me. She takes out what I thought were two condoms. They're plastic, like little drug baggies only they've got a straw on one side. She puts one in her mouth and then the other in mine.

I pull away. 'What is it?'

'Saw it online,' says Sharon. 'This way we'll never forget.'

I let her put the bag in my mouth, and then she reaches down and guides me inside. She tells me, 'Breathe.'

Then, as she begins to ride, I watch the bag begin to fill with colour.

***

I'm at the club, standing next to Josh. I ask him how he got into this kind of work.

'Easy really. I've always been good at paying attention.'

I'm looking around, completely blind to everyone in the club.

'She's not here tonight,' says Josh. 'But, if you want, I can give you a job.'

'I'm not a drug dealer. I lack the confidence to repeat a question.'

'No sales,' says Josh. He takes out a wad of cash. 'Just need a hand.'

He makes a call, and we step outside. It's not long before we see this big Range Rover turn up. Decked in black, the thing looks like it could take on the apocalypse.

The door opens and Inside are 3 big bald men. I sit in the back with Igor and Igor. Josh rides shotgun with the 6'4 heavily scarred driver known commonly as Little Mike. I don't ask where we're going, I just stare at the back of Josh's head, wondering how much I really know about this guy, and then I sit there, trying to think if I know anything else about him.

We get to an industrial estate. The car stops outside a rusted building. Igor pushes me into Igor and I'm led inside.

I say, 'Wait a minute! Look, I don't know what you're planning but you don't need to hurt me. I don't know anything!'

Igor tells me, 'Shut the fuck up.' While Igor crushes my wrist.

The floor is covered with sheets of clear plastic, held down with electrical tape.

'It's fine,' says Josh. 'Nobody's going to hurt you.'

We're taken into a room. There's more plastic on the floor, and at the centre of the room is a man.

He's naked, kneeling, and bound with his arms behind his back. The man looks up at us and whimpers through his gag. Little Mike nods and Josh goes over and puts something in his mouth. It's a plastic drug baggie with a straw on one end.

Josh comes over and hands me one. 'I want you to pay attention,' he says. 'Don't look away.'

I ask, 'Why do you need me here watching this stuff?'

Josh shrugs. 'Good to get an all round experience,' he says.

I put the baggie in my mouth. Then, Igor and Igor go over to the man on the floor. One takes out a plastic bin bag, the other a pair of pliers.

'Remember,' says Little Mike, 'You're here to Feel.' He then gives my hand a gentle squeeze.

Then, I watch Igor and Igor head over to the bound man on the floor.

'Don't worry,' says Igor to the man. 'Everything is good,' then he takes his pair of pliers, and giving me a big smile, Igor cuts off the man's little finger.

***

I still haven't spent any of the money Josh gave me.

'Everyone wants to Feel,' says Josh, 'but not everyone is looking for a good time.'

Why would anyone want to know what it's like to be stripped naked and dismantled for parts?

'Go ask Igor and Igor. Loyalty is expensive. Why make a million examples when you just do one?'

So, it's like a warning then - fuck around and find out.

Josh takes out a bag. 'Wanna try?'

No thanks. Being there was bad enough.

'Best part is,' says Josh, 'what you felt back there will save a lot of lives.'

Hard to see the humanitarianism in it all.

'Think of it this way,' says Josh. 'Who's gonna wanna rip you off after you Feel that?'

***

I see Sharon, so it's not a complete loss. I tell her, 'Where have you been all my life?'

Sharon laughs. I'm about to say more, but a guy comes over and plants a kiss on her neck. At first I thought he was some creep, but then I see the way Sharon looks at him and the pit in my stomach begins to twist.

'Let's find a table,' says Sharon.

I struggle too long with an excuse, and she pulls me along. The guy's not impressed. He says something in her ear to which Sharon replies, 'No, he's just a friend.'

I sit at the table, on the opposite side, watching as some stranger kisses my Sharon.

Sharon giggles. 'Stop it!' which she says in a tone that means anything but.

The guy asks, 'So, how did you two meet?'

I just sit there, staring at Sharon while she makes up

some bollocks about us being childhood besties.

As soon as the man goes to the bar, Sharon says, 'You've got to get me out of here. I think he spiked my drink.'

Judging by the way she kept downing those Feels, I'd hardly call it spiking.

'He said they were good vibes, but I can feel something wrong.'

I offer to take Sharon out for some air, but when we get up the guy comes over.

'Wha the fuck do you think you're doing?'

He takes out his baggie. 'Come on, babe. Take your medicine.'

I try to take her away, but then he launches a punch into my face.

I feel the club snap and twist and I'm slowly spinning round and round as I hit the floor. There I lie on the ground, all sticky with beer and sweat. Sharon screams something. I try to get up, but my body's too heavy. There's blood in my eye, and no matter how much I wipe it keeps coming back.

***

A week goes by.

I find Josh at the club. He says, 'Heard about last week.'

I ask him for a Feel.

'Thought you might,' he says, and he hands me a bag. 'On the house, mate.'

I ask if it's strong?

'It's a wholesome Feel. Family reunion. Ten years apart. You're gonna love it.'

I tell him thanks, but that's not the Feel I'm looking for. I want the other stuff, like Igor and Igor.

Josh pretends like he doesn't hear me.

We sit down and have a few drinks. He tells me, 'My kid's starting to walk. I've been bagging up his life, every last moment. Basement's full of the shit. Gonna hold onto it till he starts asking me 'What was I like?' Talk about life experience, yeah?'

I ask if he's got the Feel I want.

'Yeah,' he says, 'but you don't want that.'

But I do, and I hand him back all the money he paid me last time.

He tells me to wait, and Josh makes a call. 'I know-I know' he says, 'but it's important.'

He leaves for an hour only to come back with a black eye.

I ask what happened.

'I did like you asked,' says Josh. He hands me the baggie. 'Anything goes wrong and you don't know me. Understood?'

I understand, and I take the baggie and leave Josh to his business.

***

A month goes by till I see that guy again. The one that spiked Sharon. The one that left me in A&E getting stitches in my eye.

He takes one look at me and I see that easy smile begin to fade.

'Fuck you want?'

I tell him I want peace. Then I offer him a beer. He downs it in one gulp.

He tells me, 'Sorry about last time. That mate of yours is a total psycho. One minute she's taking me back to her flat, next time she's ghosting me for some other guy.'

Sounds familiar.

Then he takes out a bag. 'Go on,' he says, 'show me yours, and I'll show you mine.'

I tell him I don't understand.

'Fuck off,' says the guy, 'she makes everyone bag up when she fucks 'em. That's her thing, she's a tourist in her own fucking head.'

I still haven't touched the bag I made at Sharon's place.

'Come on,' says the guy. 'Let's see who she liked more, eh?'

I shrug and take out the bag. I tell him, 'Be careful. It's potent stuff.'

He downs the whole bag in one.

It doesn't take long for his expression to change.

The smile becomes a frown, and soon he starts crying. By the time the bouncers come over, they have to stop him from clawing out his eyes.

'Please!' he screams. 'Make it stop!'

He manages to pull out one of his eyes. I watch it stretch into a long wet fibre.

The bouncers have to sit on him. They're big guys, and even they're struggling to hold down that psychotic energy.

The music swallows my words, but still, I thank him for the Feel.

***

Week later, I'm back at the club.

I find Sharon, she's sitting with a group of people. Never seen them before, but they laugh like old friends.

I push up next to Sharon. I ask, 'Where've you been all my life?'

Sharon makes a nervous face. Makes sense, she's been through a lot. So, I offer to buy her a drink.

The guy next to her says, 'I'll take one, if you're buying.'

Everyone laughs. I say, 'Fair enough, what's your poison?'

He tells me, 'Top shelf. Whatever's most expensive.'

I wait for the laugh. But the group's all silent, faces all scrunched up with worry. I chalk it up to him being a 'Funny Guy.'

I head to the bar feeling good, so when the boy's night out pushes me aside I can't help but laugh. The bartender quotes a price that borders on extortion, but I don't mind. Drinks in hand, I make my way back over. There's just one problem.

They've all gone.

I look around the club, but I don't see anyone. So, I ask someone to mind my drinks and I head outside.

I find Sharon in the smoking garden. She's shaking, which makes sense as it's winter and she's wearing nothing but a thin red dress, low cut, and taped down to stop any of her bits from falling out.

I head over saying, 'Drinks inside,' but the group gives me a sour look.

The guy goes, 'Great. But next time just give us the money.'

That gets a laugh. I could see why it's funny in a wanker sort of way.

Sharon continues to shake so I ask her, 'Why don't we go back inside?'

I reach out but Sharon shrinks into Wanker's arms.

'Enough of that,' says Wanker. 'Think it's time for you fuck off.'

I ask Sharon, 'What's going on?' but she doesn't look at me.

'Look,' says Wanker, 'why don't go while off while I'm still feeling generous?,'

I look at Sharon, but she's slipped into the snug comfort of Wanker's chest.

I head back inside to find drinks are all gone. Fuck.

That's when Josh comes over. He says, 'Got a minute? It's just I've heard some nasty shit about you.'

I ask what kind of shit.

Then the bouncers come over. 'You're barred.'

For what?

'For harassing women at the club.'

***

A week goes by.

I'm drunk and I'm heartbroken. I just want to see her, to make things right.

The flat door's still broken. But, that's ok. All you have to do is jab it with a screwdriver, a little wiggle here, and presto. Just like old times.

Then, I head upstairs, making sure not to step on any of the creaky boards. can hear sounds coming from her flat. Kate Bush is singing about trading places, and, as I get closer, I can hear two people gasping for air.

I run my finger along the edge of the front door. It's open slightly, giving me just enough room to peek inside.

I find them on the couch. Both have got a bag in their mouth. I wait, watching as she rides him, back arched and glistening with sweat.

I open the door to her flat and head in.

Neither notice, so I say, 'Sharon?' but she doesn't hear me. So, I say it again, and again. Each time, I speak a little louder till I have to shout over the sound of the music.

Both freak out.

'Fuck's going on?' says the wanker.

I ask the same thing, only I'm looking at Sharon.

'Told you,' she says, shrinking behind Wanker. 'Told you he was a psycho stalker.'

I try to talk to her, but she won't listen. Then Wanker tackles me to the ground. Do you know how embarrassing that is? To be held down by the naked guy who was fucking someone you love?

The police come and I spend the night in a cell.

I'm told not to contact Sharon or else she'll press charges.

I still don't know what I've done.

'She does it to everyone,' says Josh. 'Every week, she picks a new guy to be her hero.'

I ask what happens to heroes of last week.

Josh points at me. 'You know the answer to that.'

He tells me to forget her. Plenty more fish in the sea, and all that.

I try. I really do.

***

I want to end it.

I only tell Josh because he's not the kind of guy to give me all the box standard reasons why I shouldn't. Instead, he listens to my plan and asks, 'Do you mind if I collect the Feel?'

I say yes.

So, we decide to do it at my apartment.

'You wanna put down some tarp or something?' says Josh. 'You know, save your landlord from a horrible mess?'

I think about, but decide not to. After all, he still hasn't fixed the leak. He was one of those landlords that liked to hike the price without doing any work. Might sound petty, but the idea of him having to scratch bits of brain out of the wall makes me smile.

I take the gun from Josh, and press it to my temple. He puts a baggie in my mouth.

'Any last words?'

I'm about to say something, but someone outside lets out a scream. In the panic, I pull down on the trigger.

It's like Bruce Lee kicked me in the head.

I hit the ground with a snap. I'm gasping, half blind in the wet darkness.

Josh comes into focus. He looks at me, and then, pushes the baggie back in my mouth.

I watch the baggie begin to fill with crystals. Each of them glows with an inner light, one that begins to pulse as it sloshes around inside.

Someone's turning down the lights.

I can see Josh, but I can't quite make out his expression. Is he . . .

SLEEPER CELL FOR THE SOUL

I don't know who owns my soul.

Tough thing to admit when you get to that age, you know the one where you can't drink, smoke and fuck your way to an early grave without someone saying, 'Oh, Grandad. What are you doing?'

God I miss the old days, not that I hate today much either. Let's face it, stardom can do a lot for an ugly man.

Rockwood is a place I hold dear to my little black Hollywood-loving heart. It's a little spot of suburban hell, the kind you can never manage to scrape off your shoe. Kinda like the first time you fuck. It wasn't your best, wasn't overly much of anything, but try as you might, you can't help but use it as a judge for the rest of life.

That's what Rockwood means to me. It's sitting in the back of my Dad's Chevy Nova, three cans of hard lemonade rolling up inside me, hand trembling as I reach up Tammy Le'dell's crop top.

It's funny how we judge everything by those first times. No matter how messy, embarrassing, or troubling, we can't help it, like drowning in the water, it comes natural.

Now, killing someone is different, but we'll get into that later.

Back then, Rockwood was this dingy summer camp. Even back then, we knew it weren't no holy land. It was a few acres of scrub, bugs, and creepy old men.

Still, it had everything we needed: tire-swings, frontier training, baseball, masturbating around the back of the old cabin. Everything a growing boy needs.

I look back at those memories, and I smile. There's just one problem.

For all the memories of that place, I never went to Rockwood.

I don't even know if there is a Rockwood. Now, I know what you're thinking, you're thinking, 'This guy's crazy' You're thinking how can I have memories of a place that I haven't been to? Well, I'm about to let you in on a little secret.

It's all a lie.

Every single memory. They're out there, 'Them' and they want to keep us in the dark. They flood our heads with experiences we never had. It's how they control us, it's how they get us to do their dirty work.

I'm here to tell the truth, problem is, you can't rat on 'Them' without someone blowing a hole through your favourite hat. That's why I buried this chapter, stuffed between a tell-all on premature ejaculation and a paint-by-numbers guide to making your very own sugar cookies.

The book, this book, the one flooded on the shelves, it's bad. I want it to be bad. I don't want 'Them' knowing that I know.

So, anyway, the truth.

The truth is, I don't know who's going to find these words. You could be some poor fuck riding the tube everyday. You might be some hedge fund manager wondering why the fuck your wife bought you this tenth-rate lousy book. It doesn't matter who you are, or how big you stand, the truth is, to 'Them' you're nothing.

Now, I'm not just some C-list actor trying to tear your grip from reality, well, maybe a little, but I'm the only one who cares, the only one who can help. It might be hard to believe, but I'm a secret agent, a spy, a spook.

I don't wear a suit, unless I'm accepting an award. I don't have a secret watch that fires poison darts, and I've fucked a lot more women through acting than I did as an agent. The closest I came was an intimate moment with this ex KGB.

The only difference between me and you is I know I'm being fucked.

Now, let me tell you about the first time I killed someone.

At first it was all messy. It's all sob stories in the movies, and those boring fucking books on 'how to be a spy' they don't know what they're talking about. Ian Fleming? Who the fuck is that? Just some guy who thought a limey could baffle his way out of a conversation with a fruit and a cat.

The truth about my first contract was I didn't know what I was doing. I fucked the whole thing up. I wrapped that wire around his neck and choked till he pissed blood all down the walls.

But, like I said before, I'm not like you, I'm different. See, I'm not just any old agent. No, I'm what you call a Sleeper Soul.

Go ask the Buddhist's they figured it out.

Not the whole coming back as a tree, or any of that morale ambiguity bullshit. I'm talking reincarnation in its basest form, I'm talking about an impulse and a career that isn't defined by the hours on a clock or even the age you live in. I'm talking about being who you are for the length and breadth of existence.

As mad as it sounds, hear me out. Have you ever read the stories on these psychos? Your Bundies, your Mansons? People who out of nowhere just flip one day like it was no biggie and do things that you never thought of? I'm not talking about just the killings either. Some people have been hardwired to lead, some to fix shit with their hands, and some kill.

I used to have these dreams about places I've never been, people in strange outfits I've never met. Fast flowing worlds that would buzz around me like flies. Burning rivers of light that brought faced-paced traffic like a carcass brings flies.

I've seen lands of sand and blood, filled with savages

and things that don't make sense to anything other than a primitive mind. I've dreamt of being a man, a demon and a dog. The whole thing sounds crazy, I agree. Dreams just don't make sense, just false memories and REM sleep.

That was until I was sitting in a cafe in upstate New York. Some waitress comes over, hands me my meal and asks me how I'm feeling today. I turn to her and tell her my day is as lousy and as shit as it could get, thanks for asking. She just looks at me and tells me that I should get my ticket, i've got a plane to catch, and something happens.

I can't explain it, I don't really know how it works myself. You ever hear of these sleeper cells? Agents who go into hiding for a long time and spring out like little spiders from a hole? Well that's what I am, only this is where it gets really weird. I'm a buddhist sleeper cell, I wait across time, only I don't really know that most of the time.

I heard that the CIA used to perform experiments and mind-control on people, get them to react when certain triggers went off, and kill someone. I haven't met any CIA, to be honest I wonder whether they really exist, and if they do I don't think they do what we think. They don't have a fucking clue what they are doing, not like my guy. Calls himself the Dragon.

He's not a fucking lizard or anything, I'm not sure he's a real guy at all, or human. He was the waitress that woke me last time. Something to do with that phrase 'You have a plane to catch', even reading it after I write it freaks me the fuck out. You see it does something to my brain, it makes me want to do things, kill people.

Now I can't exactly speak for my previous selves here, because I didn't spend a lot of my previous lives looking in a fucking mirror, but I don't think who you are is defined by how you look. I doubt I spent all my past lives looking like the handsome son of a gun you see in the pictures with the hot models dangling off my arm like some anorexic skin-suit. I just think there are things you lose and things that you keep.

My way of thinking is that the Dragon is the same. He doesn't always know what's going on, he's triggered by me just like I am by him. He's kind of my universal contact, waiting in different forms with different faces. Busing tables, pumping gas, taking my money after I pay to fuck him. He's waiting to give me my next assignment, and the whole thing freaks me out.

Now I know you've got this look on your face that says 'Bullshit, how would you even remember all these previous lives without going mad?' and I'd say 'good question'. I don't know if i'm honest. I think something went wrong. I think dreams are previous memories to be stored, a genetic fingerprint passed down through time by yourself, but I haven't got a few finger prints; I have the key to the database.

One day i'm on a culture trip down Iraq, looking over the cradle of the humanity, it's all to get away from the press so don't paint me as some fucking archaeologist. This guy is telling me about the differences between Mesopotamian writing and Egyptian; something to do with where you put your letters or some shit, tells me to read the first letters of man, so I did.

I look at the writing and it's got this kind of Norse, sharp symbology to it that's kind of nice when I think about it, but then when I'm standing there all slack jawed and stupid I do something I wasn't supposed to. I read the text. I don't know how, but somehow the thing makes sense, and you're never gonna believe what it said 'Get your ticket, you have a plane to catch'.

I see something, I see myself writing this thousands of years ago, craving away with my tools in a hurry I don't quite appreciate. Something's wrong, someone's coming, someone's going to kill me, yet for the first time in that backward little brain it terrifies me. Somehow I knew, I knew that if I wrote this here I could wake myself later, I just needed to find it.

The whole thing fucked me up that's for sure. Memories of this Dragon guy came back to me, and some of my dreams made sense. They weren't false memories, they were experiences, locked away to keep me stupid and safe. it got me thinking, if I figured it out then, maybe there were more, more signs for me to find. And you better believe I was right on that one.

The only problem is they found out, whoever they are. I had experienced it before, each time I accidentally woke myself, the Dragon came to kill me. I haven't figured out how I activate him, or even if I have to, but I know he's coming for me now. Even if he doesn't know it yet.

The thing is I don't know why they want me to kill people, why they made me this way, or even if there is a they. Maybe it's just me and him for all eternity, him waking me to kill my next target, me figuring it out long enough to warn my future self before he kills me.

If he's so good why doesn't he just do it?

Look, I can see you getting all fuzzy headed right now, and don't worry that's how it starts. You see I figured something else out too. I'm not alone here. That's why you had to read this book, it was fate, and I can wake you just like I was. Don't deny it, you've had the dream too, the ones that don't make sense, yet always leave you feeling like you've not slept when you wake. You're sore and you cry, and sometimes you scream. It's because it happened.

You have to run, you have to find a way to pass the message on, he will be there. If you're there it means he will be close, waiting for the right phrase, the right moment, the right second. I don't know what triggers him, even if it's always the same. Just run, and remember that she can live if we just figure this thing out.

I can't even begin to explain how often I felt that cool refreshing water douses my skin in that goose-pimply way you just seem to love as a kid. Looking back I don't really recall much else of my childhood, everything was right there in Rockwood.

I don't even mind that it was pulled down two years ago.

It was the memory I love, a place is just a place and you can't hold onto the physical, you have to remember that the mental is eternal. Keep your dreams close, and your memories closer, or else you're not you, just a photograph,

Chapter 13- Aunt Norri's Cookies.

RENT-A-LIFE

They say, in the future we'll all be freelance. Fighting for work like corporate gladiators, begging to be picked, one hour at a time.

To tell the truth, the thought scares the shit out of me. So, when I see the ad to make money, I download the app without reading the T's and C's. Way I see it, the only people worrying about the small-print are people who aren't struggling for money.

They ask if I've got a body, which is weird. So, I click yes. Next day they sent me a pair of what look like wireless earpods.

The caption says, 'Place on temples then press.'

I do, and then I'm told, 'Great. Welcome to Rent A Life.'

It's simple enough, a kind of emotional webcam built into your body. I'm not sure of the science, but one look at the site tells me, not only are people gonna pay, but they're gonna pay big.

A week later

I'd almost forgotten about the app when my phone made a noise. I look up to see a request. It's an odd one. Not strange or creepy, just odd.

It asks, 'Go and open the window. Feel the wind on your face.'

I take the phone with me as I'm not sure how this all works. The person sends a tip and I hit the flashing button labelled 'Interface' It's a struggle to open the window thanks to the rusted hinge. It's buried under ten coats of gloss emulsion. Takes me the good part of five minutes to crack it open.

I stick my head out and wait. There's not much of a breeze, but I hold my head out for about 30 seconds or so.

My phone makes a sound. There's a message from the app.

'Thanks,' it says. 'Made my night.'

Another Week

It's been slow and far from profitable, but at least there's one person I can rely on. I don't know their name, so I just refer to them as, 'Window Face.'

It's not all windows, but there's definitely a pattern. They're into some kind of sensory connection.

He'll ask me to hold a yoga pose, or get in nice and close while I cook my soup. The other guys are all about shock. Some want something sexual, like, 'Get naked and jiggle about in front of a mirror.' You know, the kinds of shit teenagers ask when they sneak their parent's credit card. Window Face was different. They wanted experience. They asked me to wear a corset once, two sizes too tight.

I asked, 'Wanna see me wear it in the mirror? Maybe you want to watch me take it off?'

Window Face said no. 'I'm not into that.'

This went on for about a year. As my first and only real client, I had to ask. 'So, tell me, what's your deal?'

It takes a whole episode of Dr. Who for them to reply. When they do, there aren't any words, only a request.

'Interface with client?'

I've never done it the other way before. You hear all kinds of horror stories. People putting viruses on your phone. Do something wrong, and it's like you're a ghost, only you're not trapped in a house but your phone.

Still, Window Face seemed different. They're the only one I know who can pay for boobs but chooses not to.

Against better judgement, ignoring the twist in my stomach, I click.

Everything starts to get dark, like all the colour's flaking off the ceiling, covering me in technicoloured snow.

I wipe off the crumbs, and that's when I look down and see the hole. It's dark and deep and goes on for miles. The word 'Pit' comes to mind, and that's when I feel it start to pull.

Like water down the drain, I feel myself twist and slide, down-down-down.

***

I'm falling down into the tunnel. I feel myself stretched in all kinds of directions, all pulling me towards the light at the bottom. I pick up speed, and the slow drain becomes a jog, and then a sprint. Soon I'm moving like a train, heading further into that ever brightening light.

Then it hits me. A flash of blue stars, I slip down onto a bed, and with a series of blinks, I begin to gather my thoughts.

I see a ceiling covered in glow-in-the-dark cosmic stickers. Planets, asteroids, and floating space crafts. To my side is a machine. Huge like an industrial washer. It beeps and hums, matching each of my breaths with a sound of its own.

Straight ahead is a screen covered in letters and phrases. I take in a breath, but there's something in my mouth. If I close one eye I can see it, pink and roughly the size of a vacuum pipe. I trace it from the big machine all the way down my throat.

That's when I start to cough. I go to pull it out, but my arms won't move, they just hang there, refusing to do what I say like they're giving me the silent treatment. Now I'm panicking, and the machine responds with a series of high-strung beeps.

But I still can't move. It's like I'm dead. My heart's racing and then I look at the screen.

It reads: 'Welcome to my world'

***

Suddenly, I'm jetted out of the bed, far from the pink tubes, glowing comets, and beeping machines. I'm sucked straight up through the black tunnel and spat out on my bedroom floor.

There I gasp and cry, fingers digging into my mouth, feeling at the ghost of a tube.

I do nothing but lay till my phone lets out a ping.

Window Face has sent me a message.

'This is how I live. This is my life, if you can call it that.'

I just throw the phone away and lay on the carpet sobbing.

A week later

I haven't looked at the app since. Thoroughly freaked out, I thought, 'Fuck this'

And tried my luck at some regular work. My friend hooked me up with a job at the local supermarket. Seemed alright, shame she didn't tell me about the boss, though.

Second day, the guy takes me in the back. One look over his shoulder and he whips out his dick. With a raise of his brows, he asks, 'What do you think?'

Well, he caught me off guard, so I say, 'I'd get that rash looked at, if I were you.'

Wasn't happy and gave me the heave ho there and then. Next day I get a text from my mate, 'What did you do?'

So, I do my best to paint a picture of what it felt like to see his naked mole rat.

'Oh, Jim. Yeah, he's a right character.'

Well, I didn't think it was worth my time, so I'm back to being poor again. Desperate, I look at my app. Window Face's been sending me messages all week. All apologies and flower emojis.

So I write back, 'What happened, what did you do to me?'

Window Face explains how they're a quadriplegic. 'Never walked. Never held anything. Never chewed my own food. Spent my life watching people drag me around like I was a toy, a little fleshy living toy. I'm Pinochio if he was made into a horror movie.'

I asked what'd be the first thing they'd do if they could.

Window Face doesn't miss a beat. 'I'd wipe my own arse.'

That's it?

'You don't understand,' says Window Face. 'Nobody's ever done it right. They're too rough. They leave a little and I'm left itchy. I just want to take control, just once, that's all.'

I don't know what to say, but lucky Window Face comes to the rescue with a question.

'Wanna continue?'

I tell them I'm not sure. I ask if they can give me a little time.

'Can't' says Window Face. 'Don't have long left.'

I ask what's the matter. Did their parents finally get the bill? I try and picture Window Face laying in a bed, face full of tubes as they're parents give a lecture on the evils of sex work.

I get a text back. It's just two words, 'Budget cuts.'

Funny how life can change the impact of words. See, never before would I have expected those two words to leave me feeling so goddamn sick.

I ask how long.

Window Face says they'd rather not say. It'll only ruin the mood.

<u>Two Years later</u>

The government's telling us how it's immoral to let people experience your body like that. Technological perversion. The futureman's prostitution.

Personally, I like it. I like to eat, to go to a sauna, why wouldn't I let someone pay for it? Hell, what's the problem with letting someone know, not guess, but really know how I feel?

The other day I heard about how we were creating a personality crisis. Making people gay, trans, and whatever else fits into their click-bait titles. Facts were less important than clicks.

Sure, they apologised when their opinions ruined lives. Still, what were they supposed to do? They've got to be the first to send out content. If anything, it's our fault for not being more obvious with our morality.

Personally, I don't think we were corrupting anyone. They were always that way. It's just now there are so many doors to help get you there. Before, we were all stuck in the basement, forced to make do with what little we got.

Funny, but, of all the people using interface technology, most of the clients are men. Yet, when it comes to the rude stuff, men say it's more gay to interface with a man. This includes sex.

You wouldn't believe the requests I get while fucking. Straight men desperate to be me. We don't talk about it, but they want to feel, to know what it's like to guide someone inside. It's an odd thought, them feeling as I do, while imagining that it's their dick making me, well, us, cum.

Could this be the new age wank?

It's a big hit, and Interface has played a big part in who I pick up. Now, my weeks are spent hunting the local hunks. Some guys aren't even my type, but the crowd gets what the crowd wants.

I don't tell the talent. Bad experience led me to keep it a secret. See, it's the new world version of finding out she used to have a dick, only it's a thousand dicks, all at once. Those dicks are now swimming around, turning my pussy into a kind of haunted house.

To mentally deal with the issue, I put it down as a cross between Polyamory and Financial Personality Disorder.

There's love and heartbreaks. Most of it is my own, and yes, I do keep some experiences personal. Way I see it, I'm no different than a blogger or influencer. It's just, I'm more honest.

Then things started to get weird when the company started offering advertisements.

This was money on top of money. They wanted me to do the usual stuff. Eat special cereal. Only cum with branded toys. Hell, I had one yet-to-be-named soda company offer a year's rent if I'd start everyday with their drink.

It was great, but the social side seeped into real life. Online groups were said to be harassing people.

I got let go from one of my office jobs when the boss found out what I did at home. Didn't stop him from trying to get me to do some nasty shit first. Fucker left that out of the company meeting.

It didn't matter. I was making money. Then the requests started to get weird.

One guy offered me enough to buy a car if I interfaced for a minute. Normally I do things my way. People are essentially guests in my body. They can't speak or do anything. Interfacing with a client is like going the other way. In the world of technological BDSM that would make me the Sub.

Still, I wanted a new car, so I clicked yes.

I feel the room melt like it did with poor old Window Face. When I hit the ground I find I'm sitting on a chair, rope bound tight over bloody wrists. The floor is concrete covered with plastic sheets. There's a man above me, face hidden beneath a neon mask.

He says, 'Welcome to my world.'

I look forward and see there's a woman. She's beautiful, naked, and tied to a chair. She's alive, but doesn't bother to scream or struggle. The only life I see is in her eyes. I watch as they dart back and forth. That's when I realise it's just a body, there's someone else inside, interfacing just like me.

The man then takes out a box of nails and an old rusted hammer. Ever so casually, he places a nail against the back of her hand and pushes it in. The hammer goes, 'Tat. Tat. Tat.'

The woman doesn't respond, and the three of us listen to the sound of violent silence. Up he goes, one nail at a time. When he gets to her face I can see the eyes have gone still. I don't know who it is, buried deep inside that body, but there was no struggle, only the cold stare as they looked into the distance.

He gets to me, hands all covered in blood. He says, 'Now, I want you to remember this, whore.'

Then, I feel it. The tug pulled me up through the black tunnel.

I'm spat back onto my bedroom floor. There, I take my first breath, and begin to scream.

A year later

The government referred to the abduction and torture of those women as, 'An unnecessary response to a breach of humanity.'

The local news were less sympathetic. 'Sell your body, what do you expect to happen?'

There was no love for me or those girls. Technically, the man in question didn't commit a crime. The bodies were willing participants. Friends and fellow psychos. None would press charges. But the women, the role models he'd convinced to interface. They weren't ok. The consensus was 'A psychological break brought on through technological abuse.'

The government's response wasn't to arrest the man but to criminalise interface technology.

The way they say it, 'You can't be hurt if you don't use it.'

The problem was the technology was widely available. People used it to make a living. But it was no use. The damage was done and we'd all suffer for it.

With no ads or active sites, it was getting tricky how to make money. Sure, there were options, but none were without their issues. A friend hooked me up to a new company on the dark web.

'It's customer driven, but it only lasts a minute.'

Customer driven was a result of military driven Interface. Why risk soldiers when you can puppet the enemy? I've learnt a lot through my time. I'm no fool, but customers are still creepy. Still, it's only a minute.

How bad can it be?

***

First customer slips in and I feel his hands rub over my body. I'm creeped out, but it doesn't go beyond a few squeezes and pokes.

The second guy's different. He comes in and heads straight to the front door. It takes me a minute to realise that he's looking for letters. I manage to take back control, but not before he sees my address.

After that it's the usual shit. I've got ten guys who think the best way to my heart is to drop the pants and masturbate. 10/10 for thought, but the delivery could use some work. Most don't know what they're doing and approach it like they're trying to start a fire.

At the end of the week I can barely walk. My clit's got friction burns and they're still asking for another go. I start screening out the horn balls and find a group of internet jokesters. They take over my body and have me slapped, walking into doors, and plunging my head into a bath of cold water.

I offered to sue when they threw me down the stairs. Their claim was, 'It's our material! We don't owe you shit!'

But it's my body. We could always take it up with the police. Both get done for engaging in illegal activity?

A week later

I get a parcel and before I can open it I'm offered a lot of money to interface. I accept and watch as I run down stairs. I open the box and take out a glass vial.

Before I can think, 'What the fuck?' I'm downing the contents. The session ends and that's when I check who the hell this guy is. Takes me a minute before, 'Oh, fuck me' it was the freak who wanted to know where I lived.

I tell myself it's going to be ok, but that night, I'm sat on the edge of the bed, watching my hand begin to shake.

A week later

I have to beg In between sessions. I don't use anyone else, that's part of the deal. First rule is: Don't tell anyone. He buys me, one minute at a time. Then, I walk up stairs, and head into the bedroom. Standing before the mirror, I strip completely naked, and then he has me watch.

I cannot move, or speak. The only freedom comes from the eyes. They can't do much, and so I take what control I stare deep into the mirror as I cry.

I don't know what he's done, but It's obvious something is very wrong. It's my skin, the way it's gone all dark and soft. The way it hangs loose around my joints. The hair is thin and breaks with a touch.

He has me stand there, before the mirror. His words come from my mouth. Always the same. 'Please,' he says, 'Please, don't let me die.'

I'm not sure if there really is a cure. Still, I like to hope, and so I wait and do as he says. I tell myself, 'Soon he will get bored. Soon I will live or I will die.'

Until then, I do as he says. The deliveries come often.

Vials filled with bitter juice. I think that's what keeps me going.

I tell myself, 'Be patient' and I weep as the flesh slips from my bones.

PHANTASY

Sometime in the Dark Ages

  Within the comforts of his own castle grounds, the king allows himself the pleasure of a walk. He did not walk alone, his Fool keeps him company, though, to tell the truth, it was Fool who suggested the walk, though none would be so foolish, not even a Fool as to suggest that a man could make the King do something he would rather not.
  The Fool was dressed in a tunic of gold and red. Upon his head was a cap-n-bells or Cockscomb, if you were so inclined. As he was the King's personal favourite, the bells upon the Fool's head were made of gold, and would 'a-Jingle-Bingle' wherever he went.
  It was there that the two walked under the shadow of the castle, staring up with eyes full of wonder and a nose pinched by finger and thumb.
  'Explain it again?' says the King.
  'There's nothing to explain, Sire. I ask only that you breathe through your nose.'
  The King allows himself a single sniff to which he regrets. 'The costs of Summer, dear Fool. It's as glorious as it is foul.'
  'But, Sire. What if we could remove the smell, and place it elsewhere?'
  The King regards his Fool with a playful look. 'I didn't know you were a magician? Don't tell me you wish to hang up

your motley and join the Alchemists?'

'If only, Sire, but I fear a life most foolish has left me bold. I do not think the Alchemists would much appreciate my questions, for they are most long and show no sign of stopping.'

A passing man at arms falls to one knee. To which, the King gives him a pat on the head. 'They may not appreciate it,' says the King, 'but that hasn't stopped you from your questions now, has it?'

The Fool smiles. 'I am the King's own pet. As loathsome as they find me, they cannot turn me away, for to reject the King's Fool is to reject the King himself.'

The King laughs at that. 'Fine, so tell me, why is it I'm out here, walking again?'

'The smell, Sire. How would you like to remove the smell?'

'Tell me, how does one rob Nightsoil of its stench?'

'You don't, Sire. You move it.'

The two watch a servant toss the contents of a chamberpot out of the castle window. There, it makes its way down to the bottom of the hill where, along with all the rest of the filth, it gathers by the homes of the poor.

Forty-five minutes later

In the far field of the Castle Ground, the King stares at a wooden box; it's as tall and wide as a single man.

'It's not very big,' says the king. 'Poor excuse for a house.'

'No, Sire. It's used for relief.'

'Ah,' says the king. 'So, you've got a woman inside have you?'

The Fool pinches the bridge of his nose. 'No, my King. This is where you lay your filth.'

The King looks back the way he came. The road is long and uphill. 'It's quite far, don't you think?'

'Indeed, Sire. That is the point. The distance is what will protect your people from the smell.'

The King did sniff and quickly regret it. 'Hardly much better here,' he says, 'This place is as foul as the stink by the castle.'

'Yes,' says the Fool, 'but that's because the folk still toss their mess in the street. Why, with your approval, they shall bring it here to be buried. Think of it, Sire. Soon your Kingdom will be a delight to the nose as well as the eye.'

Here, on the edge of the King's land, he watches his servants dig holes in which, at a nod from the Fool, is filled with the contents of chamber pots.

'What of it?' says the King. 'Stench is stench, every man with a soul does make it. Who are we to question the nature of the Almighty God?'

'Why, Sire. Have you heard much on the thoughts of John Preston?'

'Ah,' says the King, 'John Preston is one heathen remark away from jumping into bed with Satan himself. Why, if I had the good sense God gave a duck, I'd listen to the Bishops and have him arrested.'

'The man is as genius as he is rude, Sire. But tell me, have you heard of his latest thoughts? On those that link foul smells to the death of your people.'

'Yes,' The King, and then he folds his arms. 'I say this with love, but John Preston should count himself lucky he was born a man. For that wand between his legs is the only thing stopping him from being burnt as a witch.'

'Yes, yes,' says the Fool, 'but you must admit, Sire. It is odd how, of those who succumb to death and disease, it is those that live closest to the filth of your realm. Perhaps John Preston speaks true, there is some devilry that lives within the stink.'

The King does let out a sigh that is as long and it is tired. 'Surely, not even a Fool can be foolish?' He says. 'The Devil does not live in stink, Fool. No, the church has said as much. For it was God who gave us stench so that we may protect ourselves from the greasy eye of Satan.'

'Yes, Sire. But one can see wisdom in it. After all, like the Alchemist has said, there is a pattern between stink and death. Why, one has to only look at the royal household.'

The King did look at his Fool with a most unblinking stare. 'Oh,' he says, 'what of the royal stink?'

'Why, Sire. There isn't one. For you live within the castle atop the hill. All your stink is left to wander down to the poorest of your people.'

'And you think that is why I am of health?' says the King.

'Who knows, Sire. But one must admit, it's food for thought. That here you live, far from the stink, and possible demons within. Perhaps that is why you have yet to grow Ill?'

The King stands in silence, till all the mirth and joy did flee from the Fool's face.

'Who knows?' says the King. 'Why, I shall tell you, Fool; I know. If one is in doubt as to why I am not sick, you need not look to a chamberpot, steaming or otherwise. No, the answer is simple; I am strong and healthy for the same reasons that I am king: Tis the will of God, nothing more. Now, cast off this foolishness, that stink leads to Devilry. Stink is Godly. Stink is good. The Church has said as much, and who are we to argue with the word of God?'

With that, the King did begin to make his way back towards the castle. And there, the Fool did stand alone for a moment. Then, for a reason he did not fully understand, he did call out to his King.

'Would you care to make a wager then, Sire?'

And so it was that the two did wager. Though he would never admit to it publically, the King did agree that all manner of filth would be taken to the plot on the edge of the lands.There, it would be left, far from the noses of the castle and the people below.

This wager was carried out for a year, though, by the passing of the next Summer, there was no need to consult men of great wisdom and faith. The Winter had claimed its share of souls, but as the darkness did recede, and Spring gave way to Summer, the King found his days spent listening to his subject cheer of the lack of smell and death.

There, with each fresh compliment, the King found himself brooding a most dark thought: the Fool was right. More than that, he was a heretic. The man had gone against the Church, and God, and therefore against the King himself. To say that stink did lead to death was bad enough, to prove it was to invite damnation. There was only one thing that could be done: the Fool must die.

And so, the King did set about a plan. And there, upon a year to the day of their wager, he did add poison to the Fool's own cup and there did offer the man a toast, and the two did drink and jest, and laugh, and there, for the first time in many months, the King did find himself in possession of a most joyful disposition.

Twenty years later

All across the village, people were saying the same thing: this place is haunted.

Not all of it mind, mostly, the fingers pointed down to the spot at the bottom of the hill; the place where the townsfolk did bury their waste.

They say it had something to do with the old King, a man whose madness led him to poison many a good and God fearing soul; and while his castle may now lie in ruin, it appears the shadow of his dark craft lives on.

It's there that Father Sidion does make his way, bible in one hand, and silver crucifix in the other.

'Tell me again,' he says. 'What of this man?'

'It's not a man, Father. It's a ghost, a phantom, that which remains of the old King's evil.'

Father Sidion did pass a group of women, their smiles

were as large as they were buxom. In return, the Father did say, 'Have no fear, good ladies. For salvation is at hand.'

Father Sidion did watch the ladies go, and continued to do so until they vanished over the hill. All the while, his companion did continue his conversation, oblivious to the fact that the good Father was not the least bit interested.

'Your ghost,' says Father Sidion, 'does it have a name?'

'Not one it uses, Father. We just call it Fool due to how it's seen on motley and bell.'

'I'll keep it in mind,' says Father Sidion. Then, reaching the end of the grounds, he did stand before a single wooden box, as tall and wide as a single man. The man from the village did leave him there, and with a cross upon his head and shoulders, he did flee, hopping away on his left foot.

When Father Sidion did shout, 'Why do you hop so?'

The man did answer, 'It confuses the ghost, Father, and will stop it from attempting to follow.'

'Well, I don't know about ghosts,' says Father Sidion, 'but you've confused me.' He did this quietly so that the man does not hear and grow offended.

Then, with the man hopping off into the distance, Father Sidion did enter the wooden box, and there did light himself a candle and begin to read from his bible. He did not do this as a means of acquiring Godly courage, but more so out of boredom, and as a means to distract himself from the smell.

He read till the candle did lose a third of its height, and there with no visit from the supposed ghost, he did make his way back up the hill.

There, he met up with the man from the village. His face was fresh-bruised and blooded.

'What happened?' says Father Sidion. 'Did you cross swords with bandits?'

'No, Father. On the way back, I did stumble and fall upon a rock.'

'Ah,' says Father Sidion, 'yes, I forgot you like to hop.'

The man from the village did smile as the blood fell from

his nose. 'Better a few broken bones than have a ghost come visit.'

Then, the village folk did gather and ask how the Father about the ghost.

'I saw no spirit,' says Father Sidion, 'evil nor otherwise.'

What hope he had of putting their minds to rest was quickly dashed.

'Hellfire and brimstone,' says the man from the village. 'Seems not even the good Father can scare it off.'

Father Sidion did attempt to soothe their minds, to suggest that this 'ghost' was a figment of fancy and too much ale, and the village folk did fix him with a look most bitter.

So, Father Sidion, not liking the looks they gave him, offered to return to the place at the bottom of the hill, and there banish the ghost once and for all.

To that, the village did rejoice, and many a buxom beauty regarded him with a look, one that some would consider most improper. The smile left Father Sidion with a thought, one that, with care, could turn this opportunity to his advantage.

Three months later

The people of the village were not easily convinced. While none could agree on the proper amount of times it takes to exorcise a ghost, all agreed it was more than Father Sidion had attempted.

After a while, he came up with a plan. The place was foul, but It was also quiet. Here, Father Sidion did find himself a chance to read, which he did, out loud. In part, it was for show, so that any nosey villager would find him looking his most serious. The other reason he read aloud was because he did imagine himself an educator. He had tried to teach the village how to read, but soon he learnt that they considered the art of letters the first step on the road to Demonology.

So, Father Sidion did read aloud to an imaginary audience, one who sat silent as he not only read but explained the meaning of those words. He would point to each letter and there would talk of how it may change its sound when standing alone or in the company of other letters.

This was not the only thing that Father Sidion did down at the bottom of the hill. No, that came along with the blacksmith's wife, who did creep down the hill, pinching her nose between finger and thumb.

'Goodie Smith. How many I assist you on this fine morn?'

With her gaze fixed to the ground, she did sigh. 'Forgive me, Father. For I have sinned.'

'And how did you sin, good lady?'

Goodie Smith did then look up and bite her lip. 'Well,' she says, 'How's about we go in that privy there, and I'll show you?'

And the two did go into the privy, a place that was small as it was foul. And there, far from prying eyes, the two did kiss and feel, and there, with a hand upon the other's mouth, they did break the seventh commandment: thou shalt not commit adultery.

'Aren't you worried for your immortal soul?' asks Father Sidion.

Goodie Smith did wipe the sweat from her brow. 'That's why I do it, Father. For it's the sin that sweetens the act.'

And the two did return to their coupling, breaking the third commandment while they were at it, which they did, most loud and with excitement.

The two were enjoying themselves so much that they did not notice the figure appear beside them. Not even when the bells upon his head did jingle so.

He did clear his voice and say, 'Would you stop that please?'

The two did stop and stare at a man dressed in a motley of gold and red.

'Sorry about that,' says the Fool, 'it's just, I'd like to have a word.'

The blacksmith's wife was out the door before anyone could spit. For Father Sidion, things weren't as simple.

'What is the manner of this?' says Father Sidion. 'Watching another couple! Have you no shame?'

The Fool did smile at that. 'I wonder,' he says, 'what will the blacksmith think once he learns of this?'

Father Sidion did strike out against the Fool, only his hand did not hit cheek. No, instead, it did pass right through and there hit the wood behind.

By now, Father Sidion was pale with horror. 'Begon, demon! I am a man of faith, the Lord does walk with me!'

'Yes,' says the Fool, 'and I wonder, which one will they consider worse? You ploughing half the wives in the village, or betraying the oath you made to God?'

At this, Father Sidion did fall to his knees. 'Mercy!' He cried. 'What must I do?'

The Fool did wait and enjoy the Father's misery. Then, as the tear did border on medium. He did give the man a wave to stop.

'I wish for two things,' says the Fool. 'the first being, I have enjoyed your education, and I wish to see it furthered.'

Still on his knees, the good Father did blink several times. 'Education?'

The Fool did place his hand upon the Bible, and there his fingers did slip through. 'Letters,' says the Fool, 'parables. I wish to learn them all. Not just the stories, but the manner in which a man may read for himself.'

Father Sidion did stare at the Bible. 'You wish to learn His words? So, that you can finally pass on to His kingdom?'

'Perhaps,' says the Fool, 'but, in truth, I'm less concerned with passing on and more with the passing of time. Life in a box is bad enough, and with no end in sight, I wish to make the most of eternity: I wish to learn.

Father Sidion did get to his feet. 'And what is the second task?'

The Fool did gesture around the small confines of the

privy. 'This,' he says, 'is my prison, and I wish to see it extended.'

And with that, a deal was made. Father Sidion did honour his bargain, he would read through the Bible, teaching the meaning of stories and words, and how a letter may shift and change.

Then, Father Sidion convinced the village to extend the privy. There, over the month, they built a space big enough for two, a month later, a space for four. And so it went, till the village folk did find themselves brave enough to spill their waste down at the bottom of the hill.

Father Sidion found himself beloved by the village, the man who feared no ghost. And, for his part, the Fool did everything in his power to help promote the priest's reputation.

Those enemies who wished to harm Father Sidion would find themselves face to face with the ghost whenever down by the privy.

This was done to those enemies of a political and romantic nature, for Father Sidion did not stop his devotion to the wives of the village.

And so it went, little by little, that a priest did turn a small privy into a house, and there, he did educate a ghost in matters of letters and story, till at last, all he needed to do was turn the page and listen as the ghost did read for himself.

1865 AD

August Sinclair was of a line destined for greatness, his only problem was, he was sixteen years old, and, try as hard as he did, he could not distract his mind from the thought of women.

'By Job, does the boy has not an ounce of wit to call his own?' and with that, the chief scholar did collect up his things and there did return his advance, and leave Sinclair manner within the hour.

'We'll try again,' says August's mother, Rosemary, and she leaves August alone in a room filled with open books.

There, as August sits by the fire, trying to will the words into his mind, he did find himself in a manner of distraction, one that left him oblivious to the figure that had materialised behind him.

'There's an easier way,' says the Fool, and with it, August did drop his book

'Who are you, sir? And pray tell, what did possess you to dress in such garb?'

The Fool looks down at his motley of red and yellow. 'I had many a better outfit, but alas, these were the ones I died in.'

At that, dear August did go pale. 'So, it's true?' he says, 'that there is a ghost that haunts Sinclair manor?'

'It's all a matter of perspective,' says the Fool, 'see, if it wasn't for me, then your old Grandsire would have never amassed such a fortune.'

August puts the book away. 'Your saying my family have made a deal with the Devil?'

'Not Devil,' says the Fool, 'I am a phantom, sir. And besides, I haven't helped all of you. Your father, for one, is not a man who thinks too highly of ghosts.'

'What do you wish, sir?' says August. 'Do you wish to attempt to possess me? To turn my body to all manner most profane?'

The Fool laughs. 'My-My August, 'I do not think you need my help for that. No, what I wish is to make a deal.'

'What manner of deal would I wish to make with the dead?'

'How about the one where you find yourself free from study?'

August did smile. 'You could do that?'

'Bring your scholars back. Have them test you, I shall feed you the answers.'

And with that, the two did make a deal.

Two Years Later

August did lay upon his bed, planting one kiss after another upon the chambermaid.

'Careful, sir,' she says, 'for you are supposed to be a study.'

August waves across a room filled with open books. 'What does it look like I'm doing?'

The chambermaid does look in surprise. 'You can read it all from here?'

'A single glance,' says August. 'Didn't they tell you that I am a genius?'

'In truth,' says the chambermaid. 'I was more inclined to believe you were a drunken letcher, sir.'

August raises his glass. 'Can't a man be both?'

There's a single knock at the door, and several serious men, in both fashion and face enter. 'I thought you might return,' says August. 'Come to try another wager?'

'There's no way you learned it all,' says the man, and he glances around the room. 'The complete histories. Hundreds of volumes. I've seen you around town, sir. You're too busy in the fleshpits to learn anything of value.'

August waves at the books upon the floor. 'Give me an hour to write this essay of yours, and we shall see Basil, we shall see.'

With that, the man did leave, and August finds himself a spot on the desk that isn't covered with empty bottles. There, with parchment and ink, he tells the chambermaid, 'I think it's time for you to go now, my lady.'

With a kiss upon her neck, she leaves him to his work.

August stretches himself into action. 'Now then,' he says outloud, 'what was it we were learning again?'

The Fool appears behind him. 'The wager was to discuss the challenge of modern practices in dissection vs that of the Resurrectionists,'

'Ah,' says August, 'I take it were here to prove once and for all that the Resurrectionists are indeed correct?'

The Fool does smile. 'Repeat after me,' he says, 'and this time, I pray the drink will not affect your penmanship.'

Thirty years later

May Sinclair was nothing like his father, though, he was fairly sure nobody else knew it.

At the tender age of sixteen, he asks his father, 'Why does everyone think you're smart?' It was at that point that August knew it was time to introduce him to the family secret.

'You're a ghost?' says May.

'My name is Bog,' says the Fool. 'And I am what you may call the silent half of this business.'

'What business?'

The Fool gestures around the mansion. 'Your father is a sot. A womaniser, and a fool.'

'No he's not!'

'Trust me, a Fool knows a Fool. It's here that we welcome you into the club. See, I have been observing you for some time. You possess within you a most singular intellect, and together we do great things.'

'How are you still alive?' says May.

'The house. First, I was confined to the outhouse, there, upon many threats, and then a lucrative deal as a poltergeist, I did pursue a certain Arthur of Dod to become the first man in his village to connect a toilet to his home. After that, it was all a matter of finding the right person, someone who needed a little aid in reaching their dreams.'

May looks around the mansion. 'So, you're trapped here?'

''Tis both my prison and my salvation. My time is spent waiting for someone to help me extend, to grow the lands further.'

'Right,' says May, 'I understand.

Later that night, after much drink and trust from his fiercest friends, May did incite a riot. One that would bring fire and oil to Sinclair manor. He didn't even bother to allow his chair bound father a chance to escape. May simply raises a toast as the flames burnt away the last of the screams.

1982

The tour had been going on for fifteen minutes, and Luna was bored. It wasn't her real name, but then the only people who didn't call her Luna were people she'd rather avoid.

'I thought this was supposed to be a ghost tour?' she says.

'What do you want from me?' says Tourmaline. Her real name is Tracy, but ever since she found her purpose in the one true religion of Wicca, she refuses to acknowledge it outside of the police and the tax man.

The leader of the tour clears her throat. 'Is there a problem here?'

'No,' says Lana, who was currently going by Luna. 'I was just asking, isn't this place supposed to be haunted?'

The tour guide purses her lips. 'Ah, yes. Back in the eighteen hundreds, Sinclair house was said to be home to a ghost.'

'Not just any ghost,' says Tourmaline, 'I heard it was a jester or somethink, like David Bowie in Ashes to Ashes.'

'Well,' says the tour guide, 'I wouldn't know about all that. But, I do know that May Sinclair, in a bout of madness brought on no doubt by drinking leaded water decided to bring down this manner. And, it's taken many painstaking years to rebuild it, inch by authentic inch.'

The two follow the tour around, until Tourmaline catches sight of a red velvet rope. 'Ear,' she says, and she pulls Luna under the rope and into the section marked 'Staff only'

'What are you doing?' says Luna.

'Well, as a member of the Wiccan faith, I do feel it falls

upon me to not allow the patriarchy to control me. So, come on and let's have a laugh. God knows this place needs one.'

They head further in till they find a little spot. Just big enough for a person.

'What do you think it is?' says Luna.

'Looks like a torture room,' says Tourmaline.

Then, from the shadows, they hear a voice clear its throat. 'Actually,' it says, 'it's a toilet, but sometimes it's hard to tell.'

The two women flinch as a man steps from the shadows.

'What's with the getup?' says Tourmaline. 'Going to a fancy dress or something, mate?'

The man shakes the bells upon his head. 'Something like that.' Then he stares up at the small box. 'It's the only thing that survived the fire,' he says, 'luckily, it was built from stone and steel.'

'Odd thing to make a toilet out of?' says Tourmaline.

'Yes,' says the man, 'but, you have to keep in mind that there's a legend.'

'The legend of the ghost?' says Luna.

The man smiles. 'That's right. They believed that the ghost was good luck, but they had to protect the place of his death. See, if you were to look properly, you'd see that this is a very strange place to build a toilet: dead set in the middle of the mansion.'

'Why did they do it then?'

'Simple,' says the man, 'they believed that the ghost wanted access to the whole house.'

'Wait a minute,' says Tourmaline, 'I know who you are?'

'You do?'

'You're the ghost of the house.'

'Manor,' says the Fool. 'The Sinclair's may have been many things, but one thing they were not is understated.'

'What do you mean?' says Luna, 'how is he a ghost?'

'Use your head,' says Tourmaline, 'remember, all that stuff about the weird clown ghost. It's him. So, you're like a tour guide as well, or are you there to jump out at the end and scare everyone when they get their picture taken?'

'Not much of a guide,' says the Fool, 'But, I do have my moments.'

'Do you know any of the fun stuff?'

'Well, I can point you to where poor August spent his last dying moments, if you'd like?'

'Cool!' says Tourmaline. 'Nice one. Is he a ghost or something?'

'No,' says the Fool, 'he hung around for a while, but you need a purpose to stay.'

'Why did you stay then?'

'I'm a Fool,' he says, 'I'm too smart to give up.'

He shows them around, acting out in great detail the smells and images of the place. Then, refusing to accept a donation, the two wander back to the tour, just in time to be thrown out.

'Who cares?' says Tourmaline, 'place is naff.'

Luna hands them a tenner. 'Here,' she says, 'that other tour guide was really good.'

The woman took the money. 'Other?'

I'You know,' says Luna, 'the one you've got dressed up as a Medieval Jester?'

The tour guide sniffs. 'Well, I'm sure wherever you come from that passes for a joke.'

'What are you on about?' says Tourmaline.

'Oh yes,' says the tour guide, 'you're those ones. Yes, well, if I do see the ghost of Sinclair house, I will be sure to split the profits.'

'Manor,' says Luna.

'Pardon?'

'It's Sinclair Manor, not House.'

Two Weeks Later, Somewhere around Twelve-Twelve Thirty At Night

Luna didn't know what made her want to come back to the place. The fact she came in the middle of the night only furthered her confusion.

Perhaps, she was looking for a little trouble. Her plan to break into the place filled her with thoughts of excitement in which only breaking the law can manage.

Still, there was some part that wished she'd get caught. Now, it's not that Luna wishes to go to get a criminal record or anything like that. No, the answer was much more simple, Luna came back because, just maybe, that strange man might be there, the one wearing the motley.

She pries open the lock of the door, and then steps inside. The only sounds within are the clinking sounds of the bottles in her bag, and the heavy breathing of anxious lungs.

'Hello?' says Luna. 'Is anyone there?'

She walks through the entire place. There's no sign of people, ghosts, not even a rat.

She's about to leave when she hears the floor creak behind her.

There, standing in the shadows is the man in the motley.

'I knew it,' she says, 'I knew you'd be here.'

'And why's that?' says the man.

'Because you're like me,' says Luna. 'You're a right proper weirdo.'

They spend the night walking the length of the place. The man refused a drink, when asked why, he responded, 'Because I'm a ghost.'

It was weird as far as pick-up lines go, but Luna was no stranger to the strange.

She came back every night for a month. Each night, she'd talk, and the man would listen. He just sat there, in his strange little outfit.

'Why do you keep wearing that thing?'

The man shrugged. 'Because I'm a ghost.'

It was all magical. They didn't do much, not really. They held hands, they kissed. His touch was always cold, gentle, but cold.

Everything was going well, but Luna had a secret. Tomorrow, she's moving to London. She didn't know how to tell him. She didn't want to ruin their last night together, so she decided not to tell him, even though it broke her heart.

'I really like you,' she says, and then Luna begins to cry.

The man didn't say a word, he just kissed away her tears, and then, in the light of the moon, the two made love.

The next morning, Luna left. There was no note, no goodbye, and as she climbed upon the train, she wondered how on earth was she going to survive this heart ache.

Fifteen Minutes to the Year Two Thousand and Sixty Two

It had been eighty years since she had last been called Luna. Now, she went by Lana Mathews, though most were happy enough to call her Granny.

She didn't sleep at all that night. Thoughts of the past, of all the people who were now dead, and were unable to come and make sense of the world around her.

'Good morning,' says the orderly as they come in through the door. 'And how are we today, Granny?'

Lana Mathews fails to rub the ache from her wrist. 'Rotten.'

'Well, It's a big day today, so why don't I help you get dressed?'

'What's the point?' says Lana Mathews. 'I'll just spend it doing the same thing I do every day.'

The orderly began to take out several items of clothing. 'Someone doesn't remember what today is, do they?'

It was her birthday.

For Lana Mathews, birthdays were like a graveyard - all

thoughts went to the past, while the future loomed before her, a reminder of all the things she'd never get to do.

'I don't want a birthday,' says Lana Mathews. 'I'd rather spend it in bed.'

The orderly comes and strips away the covers. 'Well, unfortunately you can't. See, I need to wash these sheets, and I can't do that with you in the way now, can I?'

Lana Mathews shrugs. It's soft and bird-like. 'Wouldn't mind.'

'Plus,' says the orderly, 'you have to get dressed. Got to make a good impression on your little trip.'

Trip? What trip? The home didn't allow for that sort of thing. The only people who left were the residents who still had families. They'd come every few months, unable to shed that little bit of shame, they'd rescue their relative from the home, and there spend a few hours together until they grew bored, at which point they'd send them right back.

'Who's taking me on a trip?' says Lana Mathews.

'What do you mean 'who?' why, your family, of course.'

'Don't have any family. They're all dead.'

'Well, this one isn't,' says the orderly. 'Now, chop-chop. That limo has been waiting all morning for you.'

Lana Mathews was dressed, and after a light lunch consisting of an apple, and a spoonful of porridge, she was led outside. There, in the parking lot, she saw a white limousine.

'Here you are,' says the orderly. 'Just remember to bring her back before midnight or she'll turn it into a pumpkin.'

The driver didn't laugh. He didn't even bother to smile. Lana Mathews liked him immediately.

Fifteen Minutes Later And Stuck In Traffic

There was something odd about the driver. It took her a moment to put her finger on it. Then, she realised, Luna Mathews knew this man.

'We've met before?'

'That sounds like a question,' says the driver. 'I would have thought the clothes gave me away.'

Now that he mentioned it, there was something strange about his choice of clothes. Normally, drivers wear black suits. They look professional. This driver was not wearing a black suit, he wasn't wearing a suit of any kind. No, what he was wearing was some kind of fancy dress. Patches of yellow and red. Atop his head was a hat covered in bells.

'You like one of those things, mediaeval types. You know, likes to make jokes? What do you call them, idiots?'

'Fools?' suggests the driver.

Luna Mathews makes a non-committal sound. 'So, where do I know you from?'

The driver shakes his head, it causes the little bells to jingle. 'I'm a ghost,' he says. 'We met once, many years ago.'

Lana Mathews looks out of the window. 'There used to be a bakery there. Did the best donuts you've ever had.'

'Shame,' says the driver. 'But, as to the topic at hand?'

'What about it?'

'Well,' says the driver. 'I did just say that I am a ghost.'

'Yes,' says Lana Mathews, 'yes you did.'

'You're not surprised? Suppose you don't believe me?'

'It's not that, love. It's just, when you get to my age, you find it hard to care.'

The driver laughs. 'I suppose age is subjective when you're dead. In many ways, I am the same as I was when alive. I've the same temper, the same follies, it's just, now I know more, much-much more.'

'That's nice,' says Lana Mathews. 'So, how can a ghost be driving? I thought you lot were stuck inside houses?'

'It's a little more complicated than that,' says the driver. 'See, we can travel within the boundaries of our domain. Technically, a car is still our domain, so I can use it to get about.'

Lana Mathews continues to stare out of the window.

'What happens if a policeman asks you to step out of the vehicle?'

'Thankfully, it's never happened. But, let's just say, he'll get quite the shock when he finds the car sudden;y empty.'

'So, you're a ghost with a driving licence, is that why I'm here?'

'I'm a ghost with an opportunity,' says the driver. 'You see, I'm actually in the middle of expanding my territory.'

'You looking to get a jeep?'

'No, madame. 'I'm thinking of something a little bigger.'

'How big?' says Lana Mathews, and then she sees it.

Ahead, looming on the horizon, she sees a facility marked 'Sinclair Aeronautical Facility.'

Lana Mathews points at a huge object. 'Is that what I think it is?'

'Depends,' says the driver. 'Do you think it's a rocket ship?'

Lana Mathews makes a noise, it could have meant anything.

An Hour Later

They were leading her to a waiting area. Several people were fussing over her, touching her with stethoscopes, and testing her blood pressure. Beside her was the man in the clown suit.

'I don't get it,' says Lana Mathews. 'What's going on?'

'We have a facility on the moon,' says the Fool. 'It's been a project of mine. When one has nothing but time and resource, it tends to focus the perspective.'

'What does that mean?'

'It means I'm going. I've seen enough of this world, of its culture, of its people. There's no place for me here, so I've decided to leave.'

'So, this is goodbye, is it?'

'Well, I wouldn't say that. No doubt, I'll come back and visit. Afterall, this place is my first home - one can't expect me to grow up entirely.'

'So what's this got to do with me?'

Then, the Fool looks uncomfortable. 'Once upon a time, we had something, something special. You treated me with such kindness, and now, I want to offer you the chance to come with me.'

'To the moon?'

'And beyond,' says the Fool. 'See, I've figured out how to do it, to extend life. Say the word, and you'll never die. We can explore, the moon is just the beginning.'

Lana Mathews thinks for a moment. 'You're saying I can be like you?'

'Yes. Exactly. The two of us.'

"And tell me, love. Are you happy being a ghost?'

The Fool stops smiling. His face becomes pensive. 'I don't know what you mean?'

Lana Mathews places her hand on his. 'Yes, love. I think you do. Now, I'm grateful for the opportunity, but I've done my time. I've lived a life through the good days and the bad. I'm sure what we had was nice, but, if I'm honest, I can't really remember. I guess it was very long time ago.'

'But, what about me?' says the Fool. 'It gets so lonely sometimes.'

'You'll figure it, love. You're a smart boy.'

'Will you stay? Watch me leave?'

Lana gives his hand a squeeze. 'Yes, love. I can do that.'

Three Minutes to Launch

Lana Mathews was tired, so very tired. She'd come all this way, driven by a ghost in a onesie. They'd fed her some food from the canteen, and though she'd never admit it, compared to the stuff at the home, this really wasn't great.

Everyone's running around like a chicken without a head. They're so busy making sure everything is working that Lana Mathews is left by the window, staring up at the rocket ship.

She's never seen a rocket fly in real life before. She'd have thought it'd be more exciting, but in reality, it was just a lot of sitting around, waiting for something to happen. In a lot of ways, it reminds her of life.

Most of the time, you're just waiting for it to happen. You're so obsessed with the big explosion that you miss all the little things, all the stuff that really matters.

Lana Mathews has never seen a rocket fly for real before. She so desperately wants to watch it, but she can't, she's just so damn tired.

And as the ship begins to rumble, and everyone braces for a potential explosion, Lana Mathews begins to drift off to sleep.

She feels calm, safe, and secure. All feelings of doubt, and pain, and resentment, all of it is washed away.

'Sorry,' she says, and then Lana Mathews goes to sleep. A sleep so deep that she never wakes.

LOVE AT FIRST SIGHT

People always ask what it's like to be blind.

The worst part is, they talk to me as if I deaf or stupid. You know the kind, where someone talks in that 'YOU'RE . . . SO . . . BRAVE!' I'm not deaf, and I don't like when people keep touching me. Patting me on the back, or taking me by the wrist like I'm a wayward toddler in need of guidance.

The worst part is, It's been six days since my diagnosis, since I was labelled legally blind, and already, it's getting to me. That feeling like I'm not longer a person, and instead I've been reduced, like that little section in the supermarket, covered in little special offer stickers in the hopes that someone will come along, and against better judgement, they'll pick me before I pass the sell-by-date and they throw me in the bin.

First thing's first, yes I am legally blind, and yes, but no, my world isn't total darkness. In fact, my world doesn't have much darkness at all. I have this condition where everything around me is all fuzzy, like static on old TV. I can still see a small circle roughly about the width of my thumb.

That's my window into the world that you take for granted. A tiny hole through the fuzz and the static. Five years ago, that hole was the size of a football. The doctors didn't need to tell me that it was getting worse, all I had to do was watch as that football began to shrink down to an orange, an egg, and now the size of my thumb.

I know it sounds selfish, but the real reason I'm on these dating sites is because of my condition. It's not that I can't meet people in real life. Yes, the sticks do tend to put people off

- there's nothing more likely to kill someone's sex drive than the ever present thought of a life spent taking care of someone. Mostly, they're polite, they ask why I carry two sticks, and I tell them, 'So, then I have someone to fight with!'

Last time, I actually threw the stick. The lady mustn't have been expecting it, because, as I was told afterwards, she ducked, leaving the stick to go flying through the window. I didn't have to pay - one of the perks of people thinking being blind means you're less of a person.

I'm on the dating sites because I don't know how much time I have left. Who knows how long I will get to carry on seeing the world through a thumb-sized window. How long before it shrinks down to a knuckle, to a raisin?

I just want to find someone to love. Not because I'm needy and desperate, and scared to die alone. It's just, I want to know what she looks like. I want to take her in, one thumb-sized window at a time. Looking at people is like trying to piece together a jigsaw. I used to think it's annoying, but already, I've started seeing the edges of my window begin to shrink. Now, all I'm thinking is, 'Just give me long enough to find that jigsaw. Long enough to put together all those pieces.'

I can be happy then. Not that I think being unable to see someone makes you love them any less. It's just, I'd like to take a keepsake, a photo made one tiny scrap at a time. I'd like to take something with me, as I step forth into the dark, and forever close the door behind me.

So, here I am looking for love. I'd say I was back on the prowl, but in all honesty, it's more like a full on tactical assault. It's the sticks. I'm still getting used to them. So, if you catch me whacking you in the shins I'm really sorry. It's one of the reasons why I don't do chance encounters. It's hard to make someone fall for you after you've knocked them to the ground. So, if you see me coming your way, aggressively windshield wiping from left to right, do yourself a favour - just get out of the way.

I tell you what I miss about chance encounters, it's the

smell.

Now, I'd love to sit here and say that losing your sight heightens all the others, that I hop from room to room with my bat-like hearing. In truth, my hearing didn't get any better, nor did any of my other senses. What I will say is I've come to appreciate them a lot more.

It's like old music, like Pink Floyd. When I first started listening to them I was like, 'This is just noise!' but then, over time, I'd keep coming back, and I started developing this appreciation. It's like being stuck between two radio stations. They kinda just bleed into one another and you're left sat there in the middle, twitching in pain like that guy from Clockwork Orange. Then things began to change, ever so gently, and, as the radio twisted further to one station, the static lessened, the interference was gone, and I was left with deeper appreciation. Pink Floyd wasn't just noise, it was complex, it was complicated, and I loved it.

That's what it's like when you begin to rely on your other senses. See, all you people out there, you can smell and hear and touch, but it's like weird old music, sure you can experience it but you don't get it, and while I would never wish my condition on anyone, there's still a sadness to it, the fact that most people will never fine tune their senses. Then again, I don't think I ever bothered to really look, to pay attention, I took it all for granted, right up until I started noticing the fuzz and the static, creeping in at the corners of my world.

Smell is my favourite new sense.

People are always asking me, 'What's your favourite smell?' They want to hear something obvious like when I was six years old watching my Granny roast chestnuts. Fresh lavender or the chemical kind you get in skin products? Does Manuka Honey smell any different than the cheap economy kind you get at the shop?

I don't like lavender, it reminds me of a particularly cruel teacher from Primary School. Funny, I struggle to keep an image of the people in my life. When I close my eyes, I try and piece them together like a mosaic. But this teacher, Ms. Dunderhill. I don't have to piece her together. She's right there, waiting in the dark, like a monster looming out from a purple cardigan too sizes too big. She looked like a turtle coming out of its shell. She had these thick square glasses. I can still feel her standing there, an inch from my face, the itchy scratch of her whiskery chin.

No, I don't focus much on those smells. See, what I like most is the smell of people. It really bugs me that you all send so much money trying to smell like something else. See, everyone's got their own smell, it's like a fingerprint. Take my last girlfriend, my favourite smell of her was first thing in the morning, especially after she'd had some exciting dream. There'd be this mix in the sweat, like earth and red tea. When she'd get mad there was an edge of something bitter kinda like a lemon only darker like syrup in coffee.

My favourite thing is convincing the people around me to wear unscented deodorants. Yes, I am controlling, and yes, I feel terrible. I'm not going to change, though. I like the way people smell. It's not just one smell either. There's a base, a foundation, something unique to us all. But then there are the additions, the oil of grapefruit, orange peel, and hibiscus. Sometimes, when people are mad at me, they control the tone of their voice. Funny, I'm losing my sight and yet people still want to hide things from me. They can hide their voice, but not the smell. I don't tell anyone that - I don't want them taking that away as well.

You don't get smells when you use dating apps, and it really bugs me. I mean, how else are you supposed to find your soulmate?

So, I'm using all the sights. Everytime someone talks to me about it, and they're like, 'You can't use that one! That's for sex only!' I try and tell them the truth that they're all for sex, but they just sit there for a moment and then start offering suggestions as if I haven't already tried them.

'What about such-and-such? That's a site for people

looking to connect on an emotional level. That's where all the sapiosexuals go.'

First of all, I didn't know what a sapiosexual was. Apparently, it means someone who's attracted to your mind. You know what goes through my head when I hear someone say something like that? It's not 'Aww! How nice!' It's more like, 'This person's a psycho, and I need to get away.'

Attracted to your mind! As if anyone actually starts that way. I mena, I might be legally blind, but that doesn't mean I don't like to go down to the art gallery and stare at a few paintings. Might take me ten times longer than the next person, but I still like to look at beautiful things. Second, saying that you're different because you're attracted to someone's mind doesn't make you special, at least, not in the way you'd like to think. It isn't weird to like someone for who they are on the inside, though it is weird to think that you're one of the only people who actually does it.

Same with Empaths. Oh, you care about people's feelings, do you? Great, that means you're not a psycho. Though, if you keep bringing it up it might mean that you're a narcissist or at least desperate for attention.

I use all the apps. I use the ones where the woman speaks first. Funny that I had a worse time there then I did on the one which is supposed to be sex only. I also started signing up for activities, social meetups. I thought, one on one wasn't doing me any good, so why don't I jump in the deep end and see if I can't catch a winner.

Then things got bad when I signed up to Boardgames Night.

Don't ask me why I bothered to sign up for this. I mean, it's not like I play any board games. The last memory I have is watching my brother have a meltdown because he'd been caught cheating at Monopoly.

I thought, 'Well, as long as it's not that, I should be good.' Afterall, I'm pretty sure a room full of adults can't possibly be as bad as an eight year old throwing a temper tantrum.

Turns out I was wrong.

See, first night, I was introduced to the guy who ran the event. They do it every week, taking up several rooms in this big fancy pub.

So, I'm sitting at the table with the guy who runs the event, and we're trying to play this game. There were two problems with that: the first being, no one at the table had ever played the game before; and the second problem was that the guy in charge seemed completely unable to explain the rules to us.

The more he tried, the more confused we got. We must have sat there for two hours. Every turn would have the person pause and then the guy would explain the rules again. You could hear the edge in his voice getting sharper with every attempt.

I'm not sure why I did it. Maybe it's because we'd been here for two hours and only four of the six people had actually done something. Then again, maybe I just like to see the world burn. Whatever the case, it gets to my turn, lucky player number 5, and I turn to the take and ask, 'Does anyone want to play monopoly instead?'

Well, safe to say, he didn't like that. He didn't like that so much in fact, that he began to trash the table. He kept screaming, 'Who do you think you are? Who do you think you are?'

In the end, he asked if I'd like to step outside. So, I reached for my sticks, and said, 'Sure, but you have to show me the way.'

Now, I know I'm blind, but even I'm not scared of a bully who plays board games. Worst he could do is stink at me. Yes, I know that I said smells are my favourite, but that doesn't include a guy who smells like old burgers.

I'm thinking, 'Well, what a terrible evening' when I feel a hand touch my wrist.

'Sorry to bother. But, I am just wanting to say, what you did with that man and his meltdown? You make-a my night.'

It was a woman. She had this accent, vaguely european. I ask if it's Spanish or Italian maybe?

'It's Greek,' she tells me. 'I'm surprised you can even hear it. I thought I lost it many years ago.'

Like I said before, it's not that your ears get better, it's just, you learn how to really listen.

I recognised her voice from earlier. She was one of the other players. She sat on the opposite side of the table.

'Had too,' she says, 'that man makes me cry, both for my eyes and my nose.'

It was nice to hear her talk, taking each tired boring old word and transforming it into something that left me captivated.

She tells me her name is Medusa.

I tell her mine.

We spend the rest of the evening chatting at the bar. I offer to buy her a drink, and for the first time since I've carried these sticks, she doesn't give me the 'Friend Voice.'

'You may,' she tells me, 'but only if you tell me what it is like to be blind.'

Bold, most people don't ask, it's like they're scared they might catch it.

So, I tell her the truth. I talk about my thumb-sized world. I talk of the fuzz and the static. Then, because I'm drunk, I start talking about the future, about how I may be legally blind, but things are still getting worse. I tell her about seeing the world in mosaic, and how I want to find someone to look at, someone to take with me before it gets too dark.

For a moment, she doesn't respond. I'm left thinking I've ruined everything.

'Nobody looks at me,' she says. 'In all my years, I haven't sat and talked as I did tonight.'

All my years? I mean, I know it's rude to ask, but she can't be that old. I can hear it in her voice, like a stone wrapped in silk. She's been hurt before.

'I'm as old as my eyes,' she says, 'and a little older than my teeth.'

I tell her that I'm sure people look at her. I mean, I may only have a little thumb-sized window, and yet I've been spying on her all night.

She's got her head all wrapped up in a scarf. I ask if it's for religious reasons.

'No,' she says, 'It's just my hair, it upset people.'

I tell her maybe it's her shampoo.

She laughs. 'I don't use shampoo.'

I tell her maybe that's why people get so upset.

She laughs again. She tells me, 'This has been fun. But now, I must go.'

I feel her get up to leave. I've only just met her. It wasn't quite a date, not really, but still, I felt enough that I had to ask for her number.

There's another pause. She tells me, 'I don't think it's a good idea.'

I say if it's about the shampoo, don't worry. I can't smell anything, this nose is just to hold my glasses up.

I'm waiting for a laugh that never comes.

'You are fun,' she says, but I cut her off. I can hear it, that tone, that 'You're Really Nice' kinda tone.

I ask if she has a boyfriend.

She tells me, 'No.'

What about a husband? A wife maybe? A situationship, the kind that doesn't need a label, even though, deep down, you really want to give it one?

'I don't have a partner,' she tells me. 'And no, I am not married.'

A pet then? Is that it? She doesn't want to give me her number because she's scared what'll happen when she brings the blind guy around her puppy?

'I do not have a puppy. I have snakes.'

Snakes? Snakes as in plural?

'Yes. I have snakes. Many-many snakes.'

Hmm, I don't know how I feel about snakes. The most

experience I've had is watching Jake the Snake Roberts feed Macho Man Randy Savage to his python. It scared the living crap out of me.

She says, 'You don't like snakes, do you?'

I tell her I hadn't given it much thought until tonight. Then, I ask if it's a deal breaker.

She tells me, 'Yeah. You don't get me without the snakes.'

I ask if they bite.

'Yes,' she says, 'but only when I ask them.'

I ask for a date. I tell her, if I do good she can give me her number.

'And what if you do bad?' she asks, 'what if I don't like you?'

I tell her, the best thing about going on a date with a blind guy - if she doesn't like it, all she has to do is run. I won't even make it past the first wall.

She laughs at that. 'I give you one date. For you make me laugh.'

I tell her that I'd like nothing more than to make her life.

She tells me, 'You say this to get second date?'

I smile. I tell her of course.

'Is dirty trick, yes?'

I tell her that I'm blind, I can't be expected to play fair.

She gives me the address of her favourite restaurant.

'So, don't be psycho,' she says, 'because I do not wish to lose my favourite place.'

I tell her that I make no promises, and then, after she laughs for the final time, I sit there, listening as she walks away. I've got a smile so big it hurts, and I feel like life has stopped holding its breath and has finally allowed me to live again.

I head home that night, singing as I swing my sticks from side to side. I apologise as shins are smacked, and the people tell me, 'It's ok. It's ok.'

But, it's better than that. I feel like anything's possible. I spent the evening talking to a woman unlike any other that

I've met. We talked of movies, and stories. She knew so much about classical art. We talked of our family, and how I used my blindness to put distance between me and my family. She spoke of how people back home treat her like a monster.

I noticed that she always wore sunglasses, even in the night.

'I am like you,' she said, 'both of our eyes are bad.'

I told her that I didn't think my eyes were bad, in fact, I thought that my eyes were pretty special.

'But why?' she said, 'you can barely see, and soon you even that will be gone.'

Then I told her that, 'All of this is true, and yet, how can I say my eyes are bad when they waited so that I may get a chance to see you.'

She just smiled and told me, 'Tomorrow, Seven o Clock.'

I told her that I'd be there, and now I'm walking home with a smile on my face, singing Pink Floyd at the top of my lungs.

HELL OF A PLACE

1

Ambrose couldn't sleep.

He spent seven days and seven nights staring up at the ceiling, going over his life, one regret after another.

Things got really bad when the Drink stopped working. Years had given him a high tolerance for cheap spirit, but this was different. Last night, Ambrose finished three big bottles of economy vodka, and didn't feel a thing.

He waited in his bed, for the hangover that never came.

The next day, he went to the emergency room. They made him wait for four hours. By the time the doctor called him in, Ambrose was furious. No thank you, no apology, the doctor just smiled as if everything was A-Ok.

He told the doctor his issue, and then, after lots of prodding, and poking, 'Ums' and 'Ahs' The doctor lowered his stethoscope and smiled like he'd found a small fortune in his pocket

'Not to worry, Sir. I think it's fairly obvious what is wrong with you.'

By the sound of his voice, the doctor didn't think much of it. So, it was something common, like the cold, or light flu.

'Nothing to worry about, sir. Happens to us all.'

The doctor wrote Ambrose something on a strip of paper. The words were barely legible, like the half-hearted scribble of a child.

Ambrose frowned at the paper, hoping that his belligerent expression would will the scrawl into something he could understand. In the end, he had to ask what it said.

'It's Simple,' said the doctor, 'I've put you down for a casket.'

Ambrose chewed his lip. What's a casket then, like a code for one of those medical thingies?

'No, sir. It's more like one of those wooden box thingies.'

Wait, is he suggesting a coffin? Why would Ambrose want a coffin?

Then the doctor gave a look, it was the same look his Dad gave when Mum forced him to explain the Birds and the Bees.

'You're dead,' said the doctor. Then, he laughed. 'Surprised you didn't notice.'

2

Ambrose was dead, or so the doctor said. But, Ambrose didn't believe it.

He left the clinic in a fury. They made him wait all that time, and for what? Some bullshit diagnosis, and a doctor who thinks it's ok to laugh in your face. Ambrose was mad, so mad in fact that he stepped out into the road without looking.

Before you can say, 'This is gonna hurt' A car hit him with such force, that Ambrose was knocked ten feet up the road.

Everyone was in a panic, the driver who hit him, the mother with a child in each hand. People rushed over to see if he was alright, and Ambrose lay there, looking up at all those faces, thinking, 'There are more people here than all my birthdays combined.'

Ambrose told them that he was fine. He wasn't hurt. There was no pain.

The people stared in confusion till someone felt for a pulse. In a disappointed tone, they told the crowd, 'Don't worry, he's already dead.'

Just like that, everyone began to disperse. The driver let out a sigh of relief. 'Thank God,' he said, 'thought I'd killed someone.'

The mother sniffed in annoyance, 'Thanks for that. Now I'm going to be late for daycare.'

Ambrose continued to lay there, crumpled in the road, arms and legs twisted in all the wrong ways. After putting himself back together, he decided to accept the truth: He was dead, and there was nothing he could do about it.

Ambrose didn't work. He got benefits from the Government. He wondered whether being dead would count as a disability, which in turn would mean even more money. So, with that, he went down to his local benefit centre, and told them about his situation.

The smiley woman made changes to his documents, and Ambrose asked about how much money he'd be getting.

'I'm afraid we'll be cutting off your benefits,' said the woman. 'That is, the Government doesn't believe in supporting the dead.

Ambrose demanded to know what he was supposed to do now, to which the woman smiled and told, 'Have a nice death.'

3

He was told to get the bus, but he was warned not to pay until the end, it had something to do with public services or something (Ambrose wasn't listening). There was no shelter, no station, everyone stood by the stop, standing ankle deep in the same dirty water. Ambrose waited for hours in the long queue till the bus arrived, by then, everyone was cold and miserable.

The bus was a rickety, half-dead monster of a machine. A mess of electrical tape, bumps and screaming engines. It was already full, but the long line pushed inside regardless.

Ambrose could see the driver, so thin you could see the bones beneath his flesh. His face carried the expression of someone who hated their job. His hand extended outward to every person who got on the bus. Most ignored him, but the man in front paused and patted down his pockets.

'I'm sorry,' he said, 'but I don't have the money.'

The driver gestured an inviting finger and the old man stepped up to the glass. The driver's fingers rose up to the eyes of the man, and swiped across them, gentle and soft. It was as if he were reaching out to a lover. Just like that, the driver was holding up two pennies, both shined so bright it hurt Ambrose's eyes.

'Off,' said the driver, pocketing the pennies.

The old man glanced around in confusion. 'But, I have nowhere else to go?'

The driver reached out towards the man. His arm was long and unnatural. The driver pushed him out and into the puddle. The old man lay there, his sad expression trying to reach the eyes of those who passed him. None looked. None dared.

Now, it was Ambrose.

The driver held out his hand, but Ambrose shook his head.

The Driver ignored him, and moved onto the person behind, his thin hand extended outwards, pale, and thin, and waiting.

Ambrose was pushed down into the bus. All the seats were taken, most with more than one person. People sat in the foot spaces below, in the aisle, and draped over the baggage rail.

Ambrose shuffled and squirmed into a half-sitting position between a middle-aged man sitting on a suitcase and a mother clutching a baby that was blue, and stiff, and very dead. The woman wept bitterly, while the baby did its best to console her, stroking her cheek with a tiny cold hand.

The middle-aged man kept taking things from his suitcase: jackets, and leather shoes, watches, and precious stones.

'Please,' he told the people of the bus, 'I don't belong there. You must tell them.'

Ambrose watched people crawl out from under the seats. They sniffed at the opportunity, their milky eyes blind from years of crawling about in the dark.

'I don't belong there,' said the man. 'You mustn't let them take me.'

Ambrose watched one of those white eyed people place a dirty hand on the man's lap. 'You don't have to go,' they said in a soft voice. 'You can come with us. We know where to hide.'

The man got on his knees and followed them into the dark. He left the suitcase, which was soon divided amongst the more aggressive people of the bus. The other passengers watched, pretending like they didn't see anything till the man and the people were gone. But Ambrose could see those pale eyes shining in the dark, watching them as they watched him.

'It's safe in the dark,' they whispered, 'no one will find you here.'

Ambrose did his best to ignore them as the bus rocked and grunted, and made its way onwards.

4

The bus parked up in a run-down station. Everyone was told to get off, some walked, some were dragged. Ambrose went to hand his coins to the driver, but he just laughed.

'You already paid.'

Ambrose tried to assure him that there was a mistake, but the man just laughed again.

'You already paid,' said the driver. 'Every night, and every day. You paid your way down here, a long time ago, one penny at a time.'

Off the bus, Ambrose looked up at the brown stained sky. There were stars peering down at him, all the way from heaven. Hell did contain its own light, but it was the light of the depths, bubbling magma that stole the colours of the world, all but two - red and black.

There was a demon waiting for him. It was tall with two horns on its head. Its eyes were kind, which was strange as they burnt with pale fire.

Ambrose asked if the demon was going to hurt him.

'Yes,' said the demon, in a tone that was unmistakably sad.

The demon began to walk through Hell, and not knowing what else to do, Ambrose followed.

He saw people from the bus. In their grief, they wept, and blinded by their tears, they fell into the lake of fire. Some stumbled, while others were pushed. The heat was intense, Ambrose could feel it at such a distance, and yet, the fire didn't burn away their flesh. Even as the skin began to blacken and split, beneath he saw skin, fresh and new, and ready to burn.

Ambrose asked how he would be made to suffer?

'However you wish,' said the demon. 'Afterall, It is your afterlife.'

5

Ambrose was tasked with cleaning up the realms of Hell. It was the Devil's idea. The Devil, it turned out, wasn't some red guy with big horns and daddy issues, the Devil was another person, just like him.

'I got the job when the last guy decided he'd had enough,' said the Devil. 'I'm not like him, though. No, I know that once I sort things out, do things my way, then everything'll be A-ok, cushty.'

Ambrose didn't know what to make of the Devil, but he had to admit, it kinda felt nice having someone tell him what to do, someone to rebel against. So, if the Devil gave him a job, Ambrose made it his mission to do everything in his power to not go.

The Devil would send out demons to fetch him, drag him to work, kicking and screaming. There, under intense supervision, Ambrose would begin to clean.

Ambrose didn't think much of his new job, but it wasn't all bad. He liked cleaning the church of Hell. The windows were full of stained glass demons, living beings that would stand still till you looked away and then they'd move, disappear, or write things in the glass.

Sometimes, he'd stay in the church for hours, listening to the frosted tinkle as demonic shards tried to sneak up on him. He'd see the movement out of the corner of his eye and they'd freeze under his gaze. White eyes and sharp fangs. They were cool, in a 'whatever' kinda way.

One day, someone fresh off the bus threw a brick through the stained glass windows. The demons in the glass had nowhere to hide, and Ambrose watched them break into tiny shards.

Ambrose went to clean it up, but he was stopped by the new Devil. See, it turns out that the old Devil, the one who gave Ambrose the job, he decided that being in charge wasn't for him. 'Too political,' he said. 'No, victimhood, serfdom, slavery, that's where the real power is. Bring it down from within, that's what I say.'

The New Devil wasn't interested in making people suffer by doing things. His thing was to take away the stuff you liked. So, when Ambrose went to clean up the shards of broken demons, he was stopped.

'You know the rules,' said the New Devil, 'You don't do what you want down here.'

That lasted a week until the New Devil decided that he enjoyed his job so much that he dragged off never to return.

The moment Ambrose heard the news, he rushed over to the old Church. He'd feared the worst, that the shards of demons had been stolen, but in truth, they lay where they had fallen, a little pile of coloured glass and dust.

The little demon shards stared helplessly, grateful for every second that Ambrose spent glueing them back together. In the end, Ambrose told them that this was the best he could do.

The stained glass demons stared at him, all misshapen, bits of one demon were glued to the next. He looked away, but wasn't sure why? Perhaps he wanted to give them a moment to move, so that they could snarl, make rude gestures, or flee. But, when he looked back, he saw all the demons waiting, staring out at him, still damp from the drying glue. Each of them held out a glass flower, sparkling in the light.

6

Even though nobody made him, Ambrose continued his work. He always carries a tin of sardines when travelling through the sunken Hells.

He'd smile as the octopuses breached the slimy water, their old man faces twisting in a smile. He'd toss them each a fish, and they would wail in pleasure. He waved 'Mmm' and 'ahh'd' as they showed him what they had found at the bottom of their realms: treasure, sunken ships, and things best left unsaid. He told each and every one that he thought their gifts were, 'Very cool.' And the octopus men would beam with pride.

The silver monkey demons would shuffle over and go through his pockets. He had learnt to not carry anything important, as they would take everything they found. The amphibious creatures were happy with whatever, so he'd collect things for them to steal: mostly coins, and pens, and bits of coloured stone.

One day, a silver monkey fell, hitting the ground with a loud 'crack'. It lay there, holding its leg, screaming. Ambrose told it that he could take away the pain, but first, the monster would have to be very brave. The small creature nodded, and then its eyes widened as Ambrose raised the scraped knee to his lips and gave it a kiss.

Ambrose asked if the monster felt better. The silver monkey looked at its knee and then at Ambrose, its big eyes yellow and full of joy. The monster then joined its friends and scampered off to the next adventure.

The next time he arrived he was greeted by mobs of silver monkey creatures, each offering a hand, knee, or cheek to kiss. Most didn't have any wounds, and when this was brought up, they would begin to hit each other.

Ambrose didn't make the same mistake twice, and found himself going from monster to monster, one magic kiss at a time.

7

Ambrose wasn't a fan of music, but this was Hell, so he thought, 'Why not?'

So, he went to the little Jazz club known as The Pit. There, he listened as tall hairy spiders played trumpets and sang and wheezed about good days gone bad.

Occasionally the patron - Daddy Devil - would come and play. Armed with a $10 guitar, he'd sit on the stage before a crowd of crooners, damned, and demons, and Daddy would play.

He'd bring the greatest musicians of the world with him, all grey and dusty. It was always wild when Daddy played, you even found a few angels in the back, wings flapping in time with beat. Ambrose waved at one once, and they ran out of the fire exit before anyone could recognise them.

On his first night, Ambrose asked to play. He'd like to say he was forced, threatened with torture, but the truth was, he just wanted to see what would happen. It wasn't much, just a little blues, but when he finished he looked deep into Daddy's eyes and asked what he thought.

Daddy just smiled, and told him, 'Mighty Fine.'

For his performance, Daddy gave Ambrose the fedora from his skull. Ambrose put it on with pride, and has since refused to take it off.

8

It took him a moment to admit it, but Ambrose was happy: That's when things started to get bad.

He was shuffling down the streets of Hell, whistling a tune from the previous night, when a demon came up to him.

'Time to go.'

Go where? Ambrose knew Hell like the back of his hand. He'd worked with everyone, made more friends than he'd ever done while alive. So, where does the New Devil want him next?

'No,' said the demon. 'You've got to go.'

See, Hell has its rules. There aren't many, in fact, there's just one: You stay till you're happy.

There was no arguing with it. They gave him the rest of the day to say his goodbyes. When Ambrose asked how this was fair, they shrugged and told him, 'This is Hell, what did you expect?'

It was the final fuck you. Just when you thought it couldn't get any worse, just when you were starting to enjoy yourself, you had to go.

The hardest part of the job came with the demons that don't understand. Some monsters had once been gods, like Tialoc of the Aztecs. In the old days, he was so popular that mothers would drown their babies to win his favour. The bird headed god would squark with triumph and grant them boons and gifts.

Now, his religion was dead, and the god lived in Hell, tearing out his feathers in frustration, cursing in a language long since dead.

Ambrose brought a bag of baby dolls, and would pretend to drown them. The Aztec god would watch in fascination as the dolls were submerged, his expression silent, proud even, though it was hard to say so given how the god was covered in bald patches and bloody scabs.

Ambrose always remembered to carry a candle when visiting the Fox dens, home of the last of the Samurai. There he would sit with the ancient warriors, and each took a turn to tell a supernatural tale.

He hadn't quite managed to look scared, but they didn't seem to notice, Ambrose expected they were glad of the company. He remembered to drink some strong coffee before he came as last time he'd fallen asleep - this spurned the warriors to tell even more grotesque stories.

Most of the stories were about demon foxes, and sometimes, they'd talk about how they died. Once the story was complete they'd draw their sword and cut out the flame on their candle. This continued till the cavern was filled with darkness, and at which point the monsters from the story would come and scare everyone.

Ambrose liked to go for the atmosphere. To see so many strong killers jump because of words and punctuation thrilled him in a way stories had not when he was alive.

They had given him his own ceremonial armour, on the condition that he told a story. It wasn't very good, just the life of a drifter and a cheat, but they clapped when he finished, and then they ordered him to cut out the light.

The last time he came, there were no Samurai. So, Ambrose lit the candles himself, and spoke of the monsters of his own life. Each time, he would blow out the light, till at last the cave was darkness, and then the monsters came.

They didn't scream or moan or threaten to end his life, no, not this time. They just sat there with him, in the dark. Finally, one found the courage to ask, 'What are we going to do without you?'

Ambrose didn't have an answer.

On his last day, Ambrose listened to the Sirens as they sang in their rocky pools, waiting to lure Greek sailors to their deaths. This time, they didn't care, for each of those mermaids were staring at Ambrose, begging him, 'Please, don't go.'

He climbed the craggy peaks and sat with the Harpies, each a crude mix of vulture and crone. He would give them sweets, and cakes, and gossip magazines, and they'd give him shiny things they had stripped from the corpses of the damned. He took each item with a smile, and pretended to not cry.

He said goodbye to those demons who would understand, while those who didn't he simply gave them a hug and told them to be good.

At the very end, when the angels were ready to take him, he asked if they would give him a moment. They agreed, and Ambrose went to the little church to pray.

He didn't pray for himself, or for mankind, he prayed for the demons so that they might be ok. When he looked up he saw the stained glass demons were praying too, their little glassy faces full of tears.

He sat with the grey Cereberus, half-blind from age. It hadn't occurred to him that she was pregnant till the angels came and told him, 'Time to go.'

But he couldn't. The dog was pregnant. He couldn't just leave her there. What if something happened to her, or the pups? No, he can't leave, what if they need him?

The angels gave him a look, an equal mix of pride and sadness. 'That's why you have to go.'

And they took him up, out of hell, past the Earth, and into the Heavens above.

'How did you find it?' said the angel.

Ambrose looked down. He told them the truth: that it hurt.

'Yes,' said the angel. 'It really does, doesn't it?'

From time to time, people would come up, talking of the horrors of Hell, and Ambrose would sit, and listen.

They would cry, and curse, recounting it all in detail, and Ambrose smiled.

'Must be nice,' he said, 'must be nice.'

WHO'S A GOOD BOY?

England. 1991

I'm getting sick of it, getting pushed around, sent to bed, in the end, I thought 'Fuck it' and I call him a Shit-Burger.

Mum goes pale, voice all cracked like the walls in my bedroom. Must have upset her, it's not very often she uses her 'Parent Voice.' Mostly she just wants us to be friends, which, I mean, come on, is there anything more cringy?

Well, she wasn't playing mates, not tonight. 'What have I told you about using words like that?'

Remember, kids, parents are like the police, best to not say anything.

'Apologise,' says Mum. 'You know your Dad's not a . . . well, a you know what.'

I scream that he's not my Dad, he's just some old guy who likes to fuck young girls.

And that, ladies and germs, was that.

I head up to my room. Barely had time to touch my plate, and now I'm here, left to starve. Belly asks, 'Was it worth it?'

Doesn't matter, I found a Mars Bar in my jeans. It's only fun-size, and it's been through the wash. Tastes like chemicals and victory.

Normally, Mum doesn't care when I eat, barely notices when I'm in the house. Tonight's different. That tosser's 'round, and that means Mum wants to play pretend like we're all one big happy family.

Other week, I saw him in a car with Linda from the chippy. She's not much of a looker in the face department, but my god does that girl have the biggest chesticles I've ever seen. Shit-Burger was me looking at 'em, told me, 'I was just checking her pulse.' Was about to tell him that most go for the wrist not down the top, but then he handed me 20 quid and told me 'Shhhh.'

Told Mum about it, after I spent the money, of course. Didn't know what to expect, but I didn't think I'd get slapped for it.

She told me, 'Don't want to hear such filthy lies.'

Didn't say anything back, not even when Shit-Burger turned up and scolded me for making up something so horrible. Makes sense Mum would want to defend him, after all, he had the house, and the car, and the big pension.

Truth costs. Best to pretend - Mum's good at that.

Anyway, I went upstairs, blocked the door so no one could get in. Then, I peel back the mattress and smile at my buried treasure.

It's a porno mag: Bum Fun Warriors to be exact. The magazine's seen better days, but, then again, I did find it in the woods, all scrunched up under a bush.

With a glance at the door, I begin to unbutton my pants. A sudden noise has me jumping for cover like I'm in a bad Vietnam movie. I cry, 'I was just changing my clothes, when I realised what made the sound.

It was my dog. His name is Church, and he's the oldest German Shepherd that ever existed. He was old when I was a little kid, and now he just sits there, staring at nothing with those big white eyes.

Occasionally he'll cry, and if you're too slow, or forgetful, he'll piss himself. I tell Church to give me a minute. Then, I pick up the mag, apologise, and then flick back and forth.

I stop in the middle. The woman looks like our new English teacher, the young fit one with the cute face, not the old one with tits like runny eggs.

I begin to imagine the scene, I'm told to wait behind after class, there, Miss big bum tells me 'There's only one way you're getting a good grade.'

Then I hear the dog let out a whine.

I tell Church, 'Don't ruin this for me.'

But, the dog doesn't care, he just stares at me, those eyes, pale and vacant, and he whines again. It's tough to not feel bad, afterall, who could look at that face and not want to help?

So, I do the honourable thing, and I turn away and stare out of the window.

We live in a bungalow on the edge of the Moor, that means no neighbours for an hour in each direction, which means I don't bother to close the curtains.

The window stares out into the moorland hills. I see a night coloured in blue ink. I see stars and things that look like stars but are the wrong colour, or flash on and off. It really is beautiful, magnificent even, but it's not nothing on this mouldy old porn mag.

I go to grab my dick, but then I see something in the sky. It cuts through the dark, thick and pulsing. It moves through the night, zig-zagging as if it can't make up its mind.

A light begins to grow, and grow, till at last, I have to look away, close my eyes, but I can still see the light, growing as it bleeds through my eyelids.

There's a crash, and the whole house shakes like a ship in a storm. I don't know what it is, but it's up there, burning at the top of the hill.

I tell myself to ignore it. I tell myself what about your date with Miss. Centrefold? But it's no use, the boner's gone, and in its place is a question in need of an answer.

I slip on my jacket and head out through the window. I take Church with me, just in case I get caught. 'What? Can't take a dog for a piss?' That's the excuse anyway, but the truth is, I'm scared to go alone.

I make my way across the moor, guided by the fire. It's a long walk, and old Church isn't feeling up to it. Three times he lays down before I decide, 'Fuck it' and carry him up.

He smells like piss and old toys. With a grunt, I carry my very old dog up the hill, and we keep going till we reach the very top.

At the top of the hill, I find something - it's a hole - no - bigger than that - a crater. You could jump right down into it and you'd be lucky if you only broke your legs. It was deep and wide. All around it, things were burning. At first, I thought it was metal and wood, remains of a fighter jet or something that had crashed down. Then I looked at the things on fire, and thought 'What kind of wood squirms like that?'

I was about to turn back, when I caught sight of something moving down at the bottom of the hole.

It swayed back and forth, oh so slowly. It looked like it was dancing to a song that I couldn't hear.

It reached about half way up the hole. Thick as a tree, but made of meat. It looked like an arm, all long and boneless. I must have sat there for an hour watching it twitch and thrash down at the bottom of that hole.

I don't know what to do. I'm just staring till Church turns to me and make a noise.

Just like that, the thing in the hole stops moving. Ever so slowly, it turns those long spindly fingers towards us, and it gestures for me to come down.

I panic. I'm slipping on the dirt, kicking stones and burning things, and in the chaos, Church steps towards the crumbling edge, and falls down into the dark.

Without thinking, I drop the leash, and I run away.

I don't stop till I get home. There, I beat at the front door. I'm screaming how It's got him. That long drippy arm thingy, it got Church. We need to go, and we need to go now.

The door opens and out comes Mum and her new boyfriend. 'Thought I sent you to bed?'

I try to speak, but my body refuses to make sense, it's all tears and panic breaths. I didn't mean to run, but I was scared, so scared that I didn't think twice about leaving my dog out there, all alone in the dark.

That's when the boyfriend steps in, chest puffed out like Superman with a bad combover. 'Don't you even think about it, buster. You're not crying your way out of it this time.'

I ignore Shit-Burger, and turn all my attention on Mum. Stare her right in the eye, laser focus. I tell her please, don't let him die out there because of me.

Mum's face goes from angry marble into something soft and understanding. She's about to say something, but Shit-Burger grabs my arm and twists it till I yelp like Church when he fell down that hole.

'I told you. No more bullshit. Not in my house.'

I tell him to fuck off, then turn back to Mum. I tell her how mad it all sounds, but she's got to be believe me because -

The rest of the sentence is knocked out along with all the breath in my body. I double over, gasping, not quite understanding what's going on. Then I realise, it's him, he's just hit me.

This wasn't a slap on the wrist for saying something naughty. This wasn't me getting a red arse for stealing from the shop. This wasn't even getting punched by Rocky Tibbs, the school bully and world class dick-cheese. No, this was the punch of a full-grown man. Someone with a ring on each finger, someone who didn't think anything of hitting a kid with all his strength.

I manage to look at Mum. She's just standing there, mouth slowly opening like a flower in the spring. I can't speak, so I try and say it with my eyes, the look tells her 'See what I mean?'

Then he hits me again, right across the face. Everything goes wobbly, like a ship in a storm, and I'm going down into the mud.

Mum's screaming, 'Baby, my Baby.'

Then Shit-Burger kicks me in the ribs. 'You're right,' he says, 'what a fucking baby.'

He screams for Mum to go inside, and then, without

waiting, he begins to kick me, again and again. Hard as he can. I'm just lay there, staring up at Mum, thinking, 'Are you really gonna let me die?'

She doesn't go inside. She doesn't stop him. She just stands there, watching as he hits me over and over.

Thirty Five Years Later

Every night, the dream is the same.

Shit-Burger has gone inside. Mum too. It's just me, laying there in the rain, my face all broken like a mushed-up strawberry.

It took weeks for me to walk again, but in the dream, it was different. In the dream, I get right back up and run to the top of that Hill.

All around the top was covered with this yellow glowing snot. It smelt like old books, and crunched like ice. All those burning wiggly things weren't moving anymore. They were solid like yellow stone. It was the same as the thing in the hole. One long boneless arm, yellow and stiff, and glittering in the light of the rising sun.

I screamed for Church till I could feel the blood in my throat.

I was scared of the thing in the hole, but worse, I was scared of leaving Church for a second time. So, I went down, slow and steady, making sure to touch none of those yellow stones, each still steaming from the night before.

There, in the bottom, sticking to one of those yellow stones, I find a big pile of fur and meat. I scream, and I cry, and I curse myself for being a coward. Then, as I'm clawing at myself, I hear a noise coming from inside that fur.

Inside, I find a puppy, a little baby German Shepherd.

I don't know what's going on. but I'm sore, and I'm crying, and I've got this question that needs an answer. So, I turn to the little puppy and say it.

'Church?'

Then, that little German Shepherd opens his eyes, and looks up, right at me.

***

I'm standing at the podium, thinking wow. So, this is what it's like to win a Nobel prize? Funny, I thought I'd be happier. Instead, I'm standing in front of all these people, trying to not focus on how these suit pants are making my thighs itch.

I tell the crowd, You can tell things are getting bad when they give one of 'These' to the Moisturiser Guy.

People laugh, and clap, and roll their eyes. But they know the truth, my product is found in every house. Proven to not only stop the ageing process, we guarantee to take off a few years.

People ask, 'What's your secret? What do you put in that stuff?'

I tell them the truth - It's alien technology. Fell from the sky and into my pocket.

The crowd laughs and someone asks, 'Why do you call it Church? We thought you were an atheist?'

That's an easy one. None of this would have been possible without my Dog. Could say he was the inspiration. Then, I look down at Church, and I tell the crowd that it's his birthday.

They ask, 'How old is he? Five, Ten, older?'

I tell them the truth - much older. Though, you wouldn't tell by looking at him.

'So, what's the secret? Do you moisturise him too?'

I'd tell you the secret, but then I'd have to kill you.

A Day Later

I'm sitting at the table, waiting for my first breakfast as a retired man. I ask if there's any coffee?

'Sure,' says the wife, 'Pot's over there. Why don't you go and fill it?'

It's the first day of the rest of my life. Start as you mean to go on, that's what they say, so, I get up and make my own first coffee as a retired man.

I look through the cupboards and find a couple of bags, they've all got names like Pumpkin Spice and Birthday Cake.

I ask if we have any normal coffee? I'm not big on all that foo-foo stuff.

The wife makes a face. She's on the phone to her best friend 'Ten minutes into retirement,' she says, 'and he's already being a diva.'

Then, my son comes down, all hair, and groans as he stomps down the stairs. I tell him, morning, Jules.

Julian glares at me, a single eye staring out from beneath a blue fringe. 'Whatever.'

I ask if he's busy. Be good to start my retirement the right way. What does he think about a little father son adventure?

Julian looks at his Mum. 'Can you make him stop?'

'Don't worry,' says the wife. 'It's just a phase. He'll grow out of it.'

Julian takes some toast and then, with a dirty glance in my direction, he heads back upstairs.

I tell him, Nice talk, but he doesn't respond, he just makes his way back up, all moans and stomping.

I glance at the wife, but she just rolls her eyes. 'Don't even think about it.'

Then, before I can suggest anything else, she leaves me alone in the kitchen, nursing a mug of the world's worst coffee.

Happy retirement.

Two Days Later

I decide to stop by the facility. My excuse is I'm only here to say my goodbyes, but Norm just laughs.

'Sick of retirement already?'

I try and argue, but Norm's my oldest friend. Might as well lie to a mirror.

I tell him there's more to life than money and skin care.

'Yeah,' says Norm, 'like bio weapons for starters. Speaking of which. A certain country that shall-not-be-named is interested in buying some of our yellow stone.'

Apparently, they're putting on a demonstration today, so having me there would be good PR.

Norm takes me into the lift. There, he presses the button for the basement. He presses it several times in a specific order, and we go down, way down, way down beyond what most people would assume is our basement.

The air grows cold, it makes me cough till my chest hurts. The door opens and I can see ice on the walls, thick and glassy.

We're each given a hazmat suit, and then guided along to the 'Performance Area.'

We pass other people wearing hazmat suits. I say hello to Rachel, and I tell Mindy how the clinical lights really bring out the green in her eyes. Then, I pass Eddie and remind him how he still owes me that tenner.

Then we reach the 'Performance Area.' It's like one of those indoor enclosures at the zoo. You stare in through the glass only instead of seeing Tigers and Apes, and big scary lizards, you see people.

'We brought in a whole family,' says Norm. 'What with the investors coming to watch, we thought we'd do something special.'

The family didn't do much. They just sat in the centre of the white clinical room, huddled together, as if waiting for a bomb to drop.

On the far end of the room, I could see the yellow stone. Years of production had reduced its size, but still, it stood tall,

all twisted round, those boneless fingers grasping for a victim.

Norm takes out his walkie talkie and calls in. 'This is Papa Smurf, it's time to open Day-Care. Repeat. It's time to open Day-Care.'

In comes several men in hazmat suits, all armed with machine guns. One heads to the yellow stone, and chips off a tiny piece.

There, he grabs the child, and places the stone inside his mouth.

The rest of the family cry and try and fight, but the Hazmat suits are ready for this, and they beat the Dad till he goes very-very still.

After it's clear that the child has swallowed the stone, the hazmat suits get out of the room, and everyone watches as the little boy goes back to his family. They cuddle up once more, safe and sound.

For a few minutes anyway.

It doesn't take long before the rest of the family start gasping, clawing at their throats.

The Mum makes her way over to the glass. There, I watch as her body begins to bubble and swell.

She hits the glass over and over, till at last, she strikes out with that balloon hand, and I watch it burst an inch from my face, all bone, and blood, and puss.

Norm turns to me. 'You fancy doing anything after this?'

The Mum behind the glass begs for us to kill her.

'Feel free to say no,' says Norm. 'It's just, our Julie's got me on that Intermittent fasting, and I've got to say, matey, I-am-famished!'

I watch the Mum begin to melt like the Wicked Witch. The same thing happens to the rest of the family. They all screech and whine as they shrink down into a pile of bubbling clothes - all but the little boy.

There, we wait, till at long last, we see something get up out of the clothes. It was the little boy, several of him, each one identical to the last.

Norm listens to someone bark, sputter, and cough through the walkie-talkie. Then, when they were finished, he takes out a box of cigars, and offers me first pick. 'Good news, Boyo. They want three million units.'

A Year Later

Last week I found Julian in my bed with some random girl. The boy didn't have the decency to look embarrassed. I covered for him all the same, distracted the Wife, giving him enough time to sneak out round the back.

Hoped it would win me some brownie points, but then, a few days later I caught him sneaking my credit card.

There was a tussle, and then Julian looks me right in the eye and screams, 'You know Mum's fucking Richard, right?'

That caught me off guard long enough for Julian to knee me in the balls. Down I go, gasping on the carpet.

I wait till the Wife comes home. She's drunk, smoking, and smelling of man's cologne.

I ask where she was. She just ignores me and begins to head upstairs. She does the same thing the next night, and the whole week after. Every night, it's the same, drunk, smoking, and smelling of other men.

So, in the end, I just ask, Who's Richard?

That stopped her, but when she turns around, she doesn't look sad, or shocked, no, if anything, she looks relieved.

'Great,' she says, 'Now I don't have to hide it.'

I do the honourable thing, and throw all her shit out of the house. No screaming, no fighting, no 'Let's try and work it out' I just find everything I can, and I bin it right in the middle of the road.

The Wife tries to apologise, and when that doesn't work she switches to victim mode.

Up and down the street, she goes screaming for help, when no one bothers, so switches back and forth between anger and tears, all while she goes through the house, breaking everything I love.

The front door is swinging back and forth more times than a western saloon. The Wife's desperate to hurt me, so I send Church out the front so he doesn't get caught in the crossfire.

She's ringing anyone who'll listen, and before long some old geezer turns up in a brand new electric motor.

She hops in, cracks up the radio, and gives a big, 'Wooo!' before she off, racing into the sunset.

I'm so glad of the quiet, I don't realise that Church isn't in the house, not till someone comes knocking asking if I own a German Shepherd.

They can tell by the look on my face.

'Sorry, but he's hit by a car.'

***

There, in the vet clinic, they give it to me straight.

'It's a miracle he's lasted this long, but it'd be best to put him down.'

I ask for a minute with my dog. Then, with everyone out the room, I lay my head on his body, it's stiff with blood. I can hear his breath, all ragged and wet.

I tell him, Don't worry, I'll make it better.

Then, I put on a pair of latex gloves, and then take out a box full of yellow stone, and make him swallow.

The nurse comes in asks, 'Are you ready?'

I tell her that Church is making a strange noise, and could she check it out.

She leans over and presses her head to his chest. 'It's very normal,' she says, and then, right before she gives him the injection, Church lets out a final gasp and goes still.

'I won't charge for the shot,' she says.

I think to myself, even now, he's such a good boy.

Then, the nurse begins to cough. The cough becomes a

gag. The gag becomes a plea. I watch her skin begin to stretch and split, and beneath I see something that makes me smile:
long golden fur.

Five Years Later

Norm had given the girls access to his sound system, so my ears are ringing with the latest in shit-tasting music.

Really should go to the doctor about this constant earache, only, right now it's a blessing. You see, it's the only thing protecting me from the crap music, and the sounds of Norm fucking in the front garden.

I'm inside, listening to a girl tell me how she's over her ex, how she's independent, how she's never been happier.

I tell her about the divorce, how the wife took everything.

'Me and Mark were supposed to get married,' says the girl, and then she starts crying.

She takes out her phone, and I think, She's gonna call a cab, but instead she calls Mark. He picks up and she says, 'Look, I've been thinking-'

She gets cut off by the response. It was hard to tell at first, it sounds like he's running, all gasps and grunts. Then, I hear the sound of a woman crying in pleasure.

The girl's face takes on a look of horror. 'Mark?'

'Oh, he's here,' says the girl on the other end of the line, 'Only he can't speak right now as I'm sitting on his face.'

The sound continues for some time. The grunts of Norm in the front garden, the moans coming from the phone. The girl's in too much shock to hang up, so I reach over and end the call.

Then, the girl begins to sob. I get up and ask, 'Do you want anything? Water, tissue maybe?'

The girl's face is damp with tears. She looks me dead in the eye and says, 'Take off your pants.'

I don't know what to say, but the girl comes over and begins to yank at my belt. 'Whatever,' she says, 'I'll just suck it through the zip.'

I do the honourable thing, I tell her to stop, I tell her to think. I tell that this isn't what she really wants, and even if she did, this would be the wrong way to do it. Best thing would be to go home, get some sleep, and start focusing on a little 'Me Time.'

The girl stares at me for a moment, and then takes out her phone.

The girl tells the phone, 'Think your fucking funny, do you, Mark? Well, let's see how funny you think it is watching me suck off some old disgusting grandad.'

I'm just standing there, shocked. I'm not some old grandad, and I'm certainly not disgusting. But, she doesn't listen. She's too busy pulling my cock through the jeans. I feel the teeth of the zipper scratch back and forth, back and forth. I'm standing there, gritting my teeth, watching her ugly cry the name 'Mark! Over and over, as she sucks on my cock.

<u>A Few Years From Now</u>

Have to admit it, I'm getting old. The face in the mirror wasn't what it used to be, neck's all loose like a turkey's ballsack.

Get a call to come down to the clinic. Doctor tells me I've got cancer. Goes on for a while, but the words come and go, all I remember is him saying, 'Weeks not months.'

No one to talk to. Wife's shacked up, happily married. Julian won't return my calls. There's Norm, but he'd kept some yellow stone so he could go back and be a baby again. Last time I saw him, he was with his adopted mother sucking on her twenty-something tits - lucky bastard.

There's no one else, just me and Church.

Thing about the yellow stone is, it does different things

depending on how you use it. See, back at the start, you'd touch it and you'd go back to being a baby. Me, I was lucky, I saw what it did to Church and made sure not to touch it.

Then if you eat it, it turns you into a kinda clone maker. For several minutes, anyone who touches you will turn into a copy. It's gruesome, and it's grizzly, but it was a fun way to make a friend or two for Church.

Then, much later in life, I learned that, if you treat the stone with radiation, it'll never lose its potency. You could swallow that thing a year ago, and you'd be as contagious as ever.

So, when we were finished with our walk along the Moor, I gave Church a piece of radioactively charged stone, and I took him around every dog park, every field, and shop, anywhere you'd find people.

He's a really cute dog, and wherever we go, people want to pet him.

We travelled for weeks, from the top of the country to the bottom. Then, When we reached the very end, we went right back up. On the way, he saw Church, hundreds of him, all running in these massive packs, all excited to see me.

The news tells me to stay inside. 'Pandemic. Lethal. End of Days' They tell me to avoid the dogs, and then, after a few weeks, the news stopped altogether.

At the very end, I take him for a trip back home to the Moor. We cover the same trails we did back when I was kid. Church had been slow back then, always lagging behind, forcing me to go back and fetch him. Now it was my turn.

Every now and then, Church would look back with a worried look. I just wave him on and enjoy himself.

There, at the top of the hill, I stand there, exhausted and very sick. That's when I see the pack, millions of them, all waiting for me.

So, I raise my hands and call for them to come.

Churchy runs to greet me in a great wave of barks and blonde fur. Before I know it, they're on me, licking my face, whining in my ear.

I can't help but smile.

Throat's starting to hurt. But, I have just enough time to say something. It rings true now just as much as it did then. So, I look out at all those dogs. I look them right in the eye, and as one I ask them,

'So, who's a good boy?'

FOND FAREWELLS

The air outside was harsh and biting, but that didn't matter - it was Christmas!

A time for smiles, kisses, and woolly jumpers. It was a time of gift giving, fatty foods, and whatever passed for the rapid rise of yule-tide Veganism. Everyone was there, in one way or another, even those that had left us could be felt, brushing past, trailing their cobwebbed memories throughout this old creaky house.

Grandparents, friends, and animals were remembered with such a fondness you could still smell them in the hall. You'd see them flicker and move just on the edge of sight. Tonight would be the night that quarrels were laid to rest. Hugs would be given whether welcomed or not. Tears would be shed, and then kissed away, all while Doctor Who played on the telly, saving us from Darleks, and Cybermen, and social awkwardness.

Christmas is a time of magic, old and powerful magic. Its origins stretch all the way back into the hot drippy-egg-yolk of creation itself. Christmas is a time of wishes, promise, and pacts.

Dad was finishing off his second glass of wine when heard a knock at the door. His head felt fuzzy like it was stuffed with old cotton wool.

'Who the bloody hell is that then?' said Dad. He didn't get up, instead, he just sat there, picking bits of mashed potato out of his beard. Looked like a wild bush full of snow.

'It's Christmas,' said Mum. 'It's probably the carollers.'

Her face was worn from the day. It took her seventeen hours to make sure this Christmas would do as it was told. Everything from Turkey to decorations. From organising the playlist of songs, not too boring, not too modern, not too crazy. When coming to our house, you soon learn that there's very little room for doing Christmas any other way. It's like she exuded this forcefield, nothing would get in.

A few months ago, Mum fell pregnant. Mum called it her 'Early Christmas present.'

'Call it what you want,' said Dad. 'I just don't want to find out it's from a Secret Santa.'

Mum asked my little brother which he'd prefer, A boy or a Girl.

My little brother thought for a moment. 'Can I have a pony instead?'

Everyone laughed, well, everyone except him. He was six years old, and for the life of him, he couldn't understand what was so funny about his response, afterall, it said with complete and total sincerity.

'I'll go and get it then,' said Mum.

She waited for Dad to start shouting, 'Not in your condition, love.' Only he didn't say that. In fact, he didn't say anything at all. No, Dad carried on as he did before, sat in his chair, picking dinner from his beard.

'Thanks for all the help, Richard.'

Dad looked up from his pickings. 'You what?'

'Nothing, dear. Nothing at all.'

Mum shuffled and groaned her way to the door. No doubt, she was looking for a little sympathy, though she'd settle for a dash of shame. Instead, Dad let out a belch.

'Who'd be me?' said Mum.

She opened the door, and was greeted by a man. He was so tall that he had to kneel down on one knee just so he could look through the door. He wore a robe made from fur. Fox, and badger. Three kinds of bears, and a little snow leopard round the collar. Atop his head was a helm, the kind you get in cheesy

Viking cartoons. The horns on the helm were made of rough cut amethyst, and all through them, Mum watched as runes pulsed and throbbed like living gold.

It was clear that the man was not of this world. Normally, Mum would react just like any other sane person. She'd scream. She'd shout. She'd demand Dad fetch his cricket bat while she called the police. Normally, she'd react like that, but this wasn't a normal day. No, this was Christmas. And on Christmas, everything has to be perfect.

So, Mum did the best she could under these tense circumstances. She took all those signs of the strange and unusual, and she pushed them all the way to the back of her mind. There, those feelings would stay until she would let them out at a more appropriate time.

'One minute,' said Mum. Then, she went back into the house to fetch her purse. 'How much change do you need for the Shelter, love?'

Dad grumbled and cursed under his breath. 'If he wants any money, then he should go out and get a job like the rest of us.'

'Don't mind him,' said Mum, and she gave Dad's leg a smack. 'Please, love. Do come in.'

In came the man. His leather boots were heavy, you could tell by the way the wooden floor cracked beneath them. His face was covered in blue spirals. Like Dad, he too had a beard, but whereas Dad's beard was thick and scratchy, the stranger's was soft like moss on an old log.

Mum could feel some part of her brain begin to panic. She could feel it scratch up against the skull, looking for a way out, for somewhere to hide. She was confused. She was scared. But, she was also aware of what day it was, and though the laws of nature were crumbling around her, Christmas was Christmas. So, with a deep swallow, Mum smiled and asked, 'Would you like a drink, love?'

'Fermented Yak's milk,' said the man. 'Don't worry if you don't have it. Yak's milk will suffice.'

Mum knew there wasn't any Yak's milk in the house. There had never been any Yak's milk in the house. Truth be told, she wasn't sure what a Yak even was. Yet, under the harsh judging gaze of Christmas hospitality, Mum went to check anyway.

'We don't seem to have any, love. Would tea be ok instead?'

My Father didn't seem to notice the strangeness of the man beside him. Whether out of spite or as some kind of mental defence mechanism, I'm not really sure. All I knew was, Dad didn't give the man much thought. Instead, he focused all of his attention on the television in the corner.

The stranger pointed at the television. 'What is this visage I see before me?

Dad let out a sigh of disappointment. 'It's the Muppets Christmas Carol,' said Dad.

'And pray tell,' said the stranger. 'What exactly is this Muppet of which you speak?'

'You don't know the Muppets?' said Dad. 'Where've you been living, under a rock?'

The man considered the question. 'Yes, I have.'

'That explains a lot,' said Dad. Then, he stuck his hand down his pants and gave himself a good scratch.

Mum returned with a tray of red cups.

She offered one to the stranger, and then one to Dad. Dad took the second cup with a look that suggested he was far from happy. Afterall, he was the man of the house. He shouldn't be accepting the second of anything.

'Would you like something to eat?' asked my Mum.

'I'm not made of money!' said Dad, but Mum was already waddling back to the kitchen.

'That is all very gracious,' said the stranger, 'but you must understand. I come tonight, not to take but to give.'

'Here we go,' said Dad. 'That's how they rope you in. A few seashells, and a weekend in Zante, and next thing you know they've got you in one of them rectangle schemes.'

'No tricks,' said the stranger. 'I wish only to share my gifts.'

'Why are you doing that then?' said Dad.

'Today is Yule,' said the stranger. 'Is it not a time for charity?'

Dad's smile took on a sickly edge. 'Oh, now I get it!'

'Get what?' said Mum, as she came back in carrying a tray full of food.

'Him,' said Dad. 'He's with the charity lot. We'll, we don't want to join a new religion. We've done our bit for charity, so why don't you go and bother someone else, eh?'

Mum gave Dad another smack. 'Don't mind him, love. Go on, tell me, what's this charity then?'

'No charity,' said the stranger. 'Your family have helped me and my people through the year with offerings of goat. We've seen you put out riced pudding and the saucers of cream for the fairies, they're most grateful, by the way.'

'My Mum taught me that,' said Mum. 'She was only reminding to follow the old ways.'

'Yes,' said the stranger. 'You feed the foxes, the squirrels, and the crows. You wave at the moon, and bless the sun. You show love and compassion to your tended gardens, while leaving spots for little animals to come and nest. You're a family that celebrates the old and the new, and in that I've come to reward you.'

Dad was looking at the stranger now. 'So you're a stalker then?' said Dad. 'Tell me, where do you get off watching my family, eh?'

The stranger stood up. He continued to stand up all the way up until his horns scratched at the high ceiling above. 'Listen,' he said.

Dad opened his mouth, but the angry look from Mum made him shut it just as fast.

'I've come to give you a gift,' said the man. 'One for each of you.' His hand vanished inside a bag made from Polar Bear. There, he produced a small hat. 'This,' said the stranger. 'This is for the little man.'

My brother looked up at the gift. Then, because his parents were watching, he said, 'I'm not a-sposed to take things from strangers.' Each word spoken as miserably as the last.

Mother looked proud.

'Most wise,' said the stranger. Then, he placed the hat on the dining table. Mum sniffed, and then placed a coaster underneath it.

The hat was just big enough for my little brother. It looked like a motorcycle helm, only it was made from straw.

'What's that for then?' said Dad.

'That,' said the stranger. 'That's to keep him safe.'

'From what?' said Dad. Then, as if in answer, he heard a sound.

It was a distinct clop, and there, coming in through the front door, Mum, Dad, and my little brother all watched as something vaguely horse like, clicked and clacked its way in. Its hooves were made of straw, as were its legs, and its body, and his head. In fact, odd as it sounds, the entire horse was made out of straw.

Dad let out a wistful sigh. 'Would you look at that.'

'Yes,' said Mum. Her sigh was a lost less wistful. Maybe it had something to do with the way the straw horse trotted, leaving bits of dried grass all on the floor.

'Excuse me one moment,' said Mum, and she went off to fetch a dustpan and brush.

My brother let out a squeal of delight. The moment he saw the horse, he forgot all about the lessons on stranger-danger. 'Fank you,' said my brother. Then, he proceeded to plant several kisses all over his new straw pony.

'Do not thank me,' said the stranger. 'Thank Lughnasadh, for this is the last of his children.'

My little brother frowned. 'Thank who?'

'Lughnasadh,' said the stranger. Then he spelled it out. 'Loo-Nas-er.'

My little brother nodded. 'Fank you, Loo-Nas-er.' Then he turned to Mum. 'You see my new pony?'

'Yes,' said Mum. 'I see it.' And with that, she began to follow the pony around, sweeping up the straw as it moved.

'The steed must have a name,' said the stranger. Something bold. Something daring. Something to shake the foundations of the earth.'

My little brother thought for a second, and then gave the straw pony the biggest hug of its life. 'I'm gonna call him Denis.'

The horse stuck out a tongue of dried flowers and licked his face.

'It appears the steed is in agreement,' said the stranger. 'Denis it is.'

With that, the horse licked him again. It filled the room with the smell of spring rai, fresh flowers, and hope.

My little brother giggled, and then, after running his fingers through the pony's grass mane, he said, 'Come on, Denis. Let me show you my stuff.'

Off went my brother with Denis the straw horse following behind.

'How are we expected to pay for a horse then?' said Dad.

'It is a gift from the harvest god,' said the stranger.

'Some gift,' said Dad. 'Least he could do is send us a manual.'

'You don't understand,' said the stranger. 'This is the last foal of Lughnasadh. Upon its mane grows the First Fruit, that which is beyond all flavours and forever delicious. Why, wherever the horse will step, flowers shall bloom, and he who rides upon its back shall travel safely from here to the ends of time.'

Dad let out a grunt. 'What if we don't want fruit?'

The stranger blinked several times. 'I'm sorry?'

'I could be allergic for all you know. Did you ever think of that?'

'I can assure you,' said the stranger, 'this, the pony, will bring nothing but prosperity, for Lughnasadh was once the lord of the harvest.'

'Was?' said Dad. 'As in, not any longer? Why's that then?'

'Because nobody wants him to,' said the stranger. 'Spirits and gods are fickle, they need to be wanted. They must have faith if magic is to remain.'

'Sounds like someone's trying too hard,' said Dad. 'Might I suggest a different vocation?'

'Lughnasadh is leaving,' said the stranger. 'Along with all the rest. All he asks is that whenever you climb a hill, or enjoy a bilberry, he asks that you think of him, that's all. Do you think you could do that?'

Dad rolled his eyes. 'I'll think about it. So, go on, what else have you got? Let me guess, a squirrel that farts chocolate, or maybe a pair of magic trousers that'll help put up a shelf?'

The stranger removed a candle from his pocket. It was the colour of abalone, strands of rainbow trapped in cloudy white. He handed the candles to my Father.

'Go on then,' said Dad, 'what's this supposed to do?'

'Go to the window,' said the stranger. 'Light the wick, and the candle will allow you to speak to those you love, even those that have since passed on.'

Dad's face became all strange. He went to the window, and there, after lighting the candle, he smiled, and laughed, and eventually, he began to cry.

Dad called my name, and so I went to sit with him, and the two of us spoke. We spoke like we did a long time ago. Before things got all awkward and sad.

Then, the stranger went to Mum.

He looked at my Mum with a look, the kind of look you'd get between two childhood sweethearts.

'You raised your children to believe in fairies. You taught them to respect the animals, not just the pets, but all of them, even the strange and most unusual. Most of all, you taught them stories, and in that you gave them power. Power to weather the storm. Power to stand in the darkness, while the monster howls about them. In this, we are forever grateful.'

'You're very sweet,' said my Mum. 'So, what do I get then? Something shiny, I hope.'

'No, it's not shiny,' said the stranger. 'I'm come to take away the pain.'

'Pain, love? There's no pain here.' Every bit of Mum's word said she didn't understand. You could tell she wanted to believe it, but her face knew the truth.

'You work so very hard,' said the stranger. 'Every Christmas, you're up before dawn. You make sure that every little thing is perfect.'

'Thank you,' said Mum. 'I do try my best, love.'

'And every year, you cook for your family, and your friends, and every year, you leave one space on the table, a seat never to be used.'

As he spoke the words, I felt myself go funny all over. I tell Dad to wait for me.

'Please don't go,' said Dad, but the flame of the candle went out, and Dad sat there, wiping the tears from his face.

I head over to my mother. She doesn't see me, even as I wave in her face, telling her, 'Make the man leave.'

But the man doesn't leave. Though now, he's looking right at me.

'He's still here,' said the stranger. 'You know that, right?'

Mum looked down at her feet. 'Of course he is,' said Mum. 'It's not Christmas without him.'

'He shouldn't stay,' said the stranger. 'As much as it hurts to say goodbye, it is a mercy. To stay is to linger. It brings nothing but dust and bad memories.' He placed a huge hand on my mother's. 'You must let him go.'

She looked up at the man, staring up into his impossible size.

'That's why you're here, isn't it? All those gifts. You're just here to take him away.'

She began to cry then. The stranger wiped them away, one by one. 'No,' he said. 'They've already taken him away. I'm here to tell you that you've done enough. I'm here to take away the pain.'

With that, he reached down, and gave Mum a kiss upon her head.

I watched as all the sadness and the pain began to wash away. Then, when the stranger finished, I saw Mum give a look. I can't remember the last time I saw that look, but I remember when they stopped, it was the day she'd heard of the accident. It was the day I came home and never left.

She looked happy. The first time since she realised that she'd have to bury her son.

'Now go,' said the stranger. 'Finally, you can live your life.'

Mum gave the stranger a hug, and then went back in to see her family.

I wanted to follow, but my legs refused to follow.

'I know you're scared,' the stranger told me. 'But, this isn't the end.'

I had so many questions to ask, but I didn't know where to begin.

'Easy,' said the stranger, and he held out his hand. 'We start at the beginning.'

I took his hand, and the stranger led me out into the night. It wasn't cold. No, this was different, this was new. And with a wave at my family, I followed the stranger on, into the night, into a world of possibility.

FIRE IN BLOOM

I

The crick-crack of my knee tells me I'm too old for this. But there isn't much time. They're only in season for a short time.

Anyone with the sense God granted a duck is prepared. The hustle and bustle of the market. Vendors holding up the bones of old cats screaming, 'Get your dead things! Don't be scared, I've got enough for the whole family!'

I'm not interested in pets, or dried up trees burnt by lightning and choked with ivy. A man comes at me shaking the rusted frame of an old bike.

'Bike, madam? Oldest in town. Dredged it just the other second!'

I tell him to mind where he shakes that thing. I've just had my hair done and the effeminate hairdresser told me to avoid crabs and canal water.

I walk on. Passing apple cores, grape pips and a tin full of apricot stones.

A man flashes a toothless smile and holds out a carrier bag filled with bits of cloth.

'Finest dresses, madam. From the old country. What's that? Can't picture it? Nae bother. That's how you tell it's old!'

I head across the market till I reach a little bench at the end of town. Around this time you get a nice breeze. Perfect for a picnic.

There, I sit until I'm blinded by the shadow of an old woman.

I say, 'Hello, Winnie. Find any junk?'

The old woman sits next to me. 'Funny you should say that.' She empties the contents on the floor. 'Got the usual lamb bones, a headless broom, some candy wrappers for the boys.'

Winnie was always spoiling people. But I notice something else in the bag, so I give her a look and slowly Winnie folds.

'Had to,' she says, and Winnie takes out a human skull.

'What are you doing with that?'

'It's my Uncle Frank. Lads have been digging him up over the years. Done a good job. Just waiting for them to find that last Fibula.'

'How do you know that's Uncle Frank? People around these parts aren't rich enough to afford separate graves. No, the council just puts us all in a pit and has done with it.'

'It's the boys,' says Winnie. 'They're ever so smart. With their internet's and their Tubes. They saw a how-to video and, well, no we've got Uncle Frank back.'

I shrug and take out a cloth filled with wrinkled tomatoes.

'Thanks,' says Winnie. 'You're ever so kind.'

She takes a tomato, munches on it, and then begins to ponder a question. With a series of side glances, I can see her working up the courage to ask me something.

Naturally, Winnie's my best friend. So, I do the honest thing and leave her to struggle.

'I was thinking.'

'Bad time to start, Winnie Love.'

'We're having the party at your place, right?'

'Of course. It's always at my place. This time every year.'

'And I was thinking how we are really good mates and all.'

'Here it comes.'

'Well, is there any way I could get out of the admission

fee?'

I spit out a tomato, staining the sandy floor with a glob of wet red.

'Not indefinitely. I'd pay, naturally. It's just, well, with this being the season. Things are tough. Belts are tight as they can be, so to speak. I'd pay once the season was over. That's double, not bad seeing as the season only lasts forty five minutes.'

I sit there, munching on the pulp of my tomato. I tell her, 'Rules are rules. You pay before the season.'

'But we're friends! That's got to mean something!'

'Does. Season's short. Tricky too. Do right and you could make quite the harvest this time of year. Though, saying that, there's no guarantee.'

I didn't get here by being a fool. And the surest way to become a fool is to start giving handouts. Sure, I'd make friends. Sure as word got out I'd be the talk of the town. Only, I don't need any friends, I need assurances.

I tell her, 'Get them kids of yours to get digging. Fossils, old stuff. Heard Julie Ranston's daughter found a dinosaur bone. I'd be happy with that.'

Winnie makes a face. 'You know I've got nothing that old. I'm not a rich woman. Hell, everything I own is a month old at best. Look into your heart.'

I think for a moment. 'You still got bird bones? The one that likes to spend the day singing?'

'Sure,' says Winnie. 'You want I'll grab 'em for you.'

I tell her not to bother. 'Just crush the bones into a fine powder and cast it into the sea.'

'But,' says Winnie. 'I do that and I'll never see Mr Parrot again?'

I nod. That's the idea. 'That's a deal for you, Winnie. And I'm only doing it because of how much I hate that silly old bird.'

'You can't be serious?'

But I was. After all, when have I known to play? Go around acting like that and people will start to treat you like a joke. Almost as bad as making friends.

I leave Winnie and head back to my home. People try to stop me along the way, but it's no use. They've got nothing but junk. Might as well face it, there's not much old left in the world.

II

The great thing about where I live? The view. My house sits at the bottom of the hill. Well, when I say hill, it's more of a giant shell.

The kind that twists up and up. Back in my younger days, boys would come from all around to take me dancing up those twists.

I could move then, bend in all kinds of ways. Not now, not with this old hip. The bottom of the shell opens up, where the crab or snail or whatever it was used to live.

Took a hundred men on a hundred shoulders to try and reach from top to bottom of that hole, and a hundred men still couldn't do it.

All along the way, the people were preparing. They'd heard the news about how I wasn't taking anyone who didn't have a gift of something a hundred years or older.

Most did good, offering the second hand of grandfather clocks, the rusted crown of old king such-and-such.

Still, like always, there were chancers. One man offers me a pocket watch. 'Genuine stuff, missus. Won't find a better antique.'

Looked old enough, but a few taps and a wipe of my cloth showed the thing to be barely a day of twenty five.

Before you can spit, I've got the boys on him and off they take him, with them liar's boots scraping up the mud as he screams, 'Can't do this! People need a chance! Can't keep the season all to yourself!'

Oh well, there's plenty of work to do. People have been

waiting for days. Inspections are always slow, but steady as they come, people are welcomed in and the festivities are about to begin.

***

Inside, musicians are playing on antique violins. Singers slap on their thighs as they jig in tights made from patched cloth.
People were sharing the last of their vintage wine, While the rich traded crispy leaves for a glass of hundred year old red.
The name was on everyone's lips, 'Fire Angel.'
I try to maintain my stony expression. It's good for business. But, all the same, I fail to contain my excitement.
I pass a group of people older than me. I ask, 'What's the plan this year?'
'Same as always, Little Miss. We're gonna put on a show. Have so much damn fun the whole world will notice.'
Same as always. Dreamers are the worst, and for the old that goes double.
I move on, watching the staff explain the rules.
'Now, as you know, there isn't much time. They come slow at first, small and solo. But if we do good just like we practise then we might get to see a big one.'
One of the kids raises his hands. 'What's the biggest you've ever seen?'
'Why, when I was young, I saw one as big as a dog. But that was more of a fluke than anything.'
That's when I clear my throat and step in. The kids hush and stare in amazement. The name 'Granny' makes its way around in gentle waves.
I tell them, 'They come as big as needed. As big as we want. Why ever since I started hosting the party here they've gotten bigger every year. Last year, one was as big as a car. Year before, we had three, as fat as ponies they were.'
The kid raises his hand. 'How big are you looking for this

year?'

I point at the shell in the distance and try not to smile as the children gasp.

I leave them to chat amongst themselves, but the teacher grabs me by the arm. 'Sorry to bother you, Granny. But I have to ask, all that stuff about being big as a shell, that's a joke right?'

'What makes you think I'd do such a thing as a joke?'

'It's just that shell, Granny. It's enormous. A mountain. Something that big could very well get us all.'

I listen to the woman as she explains her worries. Then, with a spit in the sand, I tell her, 'Deal with it' and I head off into the distance.

***

There, we wait, me at the centre of my land looking out at a thousand or so people.

We all watch our watches and clocks, waiting till, at long last, the clock strikes 12 past 1.

It starts off as a hum. A mumble on the breeze. The sky grows a little brighter, and we see it, those little wings, glowing like a sunrise.

A kid points and yells, 'Fire Angel!'

It came alone. Slow and unsure. It was the size of a butterfly but wore a robe of shimmering fabric. Its face was human, eyes closed in deep and relaxing thought.

It heads through the camp, those present holding their breath. It circles this way and that, making its way through the dead trees and mouldy fruits.

The place was silent, until a child let out a sound.

It was a fart, the kind that squeaks long into the silence of the crowd.

There's a pause, as mother looks at son. Then, she looks to her husband, who, against better judgement, begins to smile.

She tells him, 'Don't.' But it's too late. The smile becomes a grin, and the mum and child smile back.

The dad hunches over, shoulders shaking up and down.

It's no use, the kid begins to laugh. The Fire Angel stops and stares. Its calm face goes still.

Then the dad begins to laugh. Then the mother. People watching sniggers and giggles. Soon, the whole crowd is laughing.

The Fire Angel looks around, its beady little eyes opening up. All around, the laughter booms.

The angel then smiles. It lets out the smallest of laughs.

All around, the people cheer. The angel laughs again, its voice ringing out, high above all others.

The crowd falls into silence as the angel flies up into the air, its body glowing brighter and brighter, till all had to look away.

The angel then shot down, fast as you can. The dad yells, 'Hold out your stuff, son.'

And the little boy holds up a handful of bones. The angel hits the bones, knocking them to the floor. There, the crowd watched as the angel and the bones burst into fire. Even for such a small thing, the fire was hot. The people step back, listening to the pop and crackle of the heat.

Then, they heard it, it was a meow. And out of the fire steps a ginger and white cat. The fire goes away and the boy scoops up the cat.

The crowd looked up to the sky. And then down at the little blackened spot on the ground. They watch the steam rise up, till. At last, they hear a call.

Down from the clouds they came, two fire angels. These were bigger than the first. Both the size of rats.

The crowd cheers and begins to break out into merriment.

Jokes, games, and lots of drinking.

The angels float around, smiling as they go. Eventually they broke apart. One went to investigate a joke about grandmothers, while the other watched a man make jokes with a variety of suggestively shaped vegetables.

The angels went up with a pop, and the performers rushed with their things. Out from the fire they plucked their precious things. Once old and broken, they were brand new. Old brown vines became heavy with red grapes. Shells became eggs. Wisen hands became young.

The fires were small and only lasted for a second. But, as expected, more came. Fatter than before.

These were the size of cats and swam through the air in a group of four.

The people created, performing and playing. The angels soon burned up, giving bigger fires for bigger problems.

Then they came as big as dogs, and the people worked, but the people had bigger problems. Then they came as big as people, and the people cheered. But the people weren't happy. They had bigger problems.

So they came, bigger and bigger than the last. Soon they came big as horses, cows, and elephants. Their fires made cars, and homes, and all the while the people complained and worked harder.

The fire angels continued to come, each bigger than the last. Till, they saw one so big it darkened the sky.

With a great pop, it burst into flames there. It burnt atop the mountain. A hundred foot fire that burned on and on.

The people looked at one another and stepped into the fire.

There they stayed, till the fire burned away leaving nothing but small children.

On and on they came, but the children didn't want to play games or make jokes. They were happy. So, they went to one adult they saw left.

I was there, sitting in my chair, rubbing the ache from my neck. They come buzzing around in all their shapes and sizes. I tell them, 'Go away.'

And they do, fire angels like fun.

So, they left me, surrounded by children.

Then, they played, till long into the night they started to get hungry. So, they came to the one adult in town.

They ask, 'What's for dinner, Grandma?'

I tell them they can have whatever they want, and the children cheer. Then I say, 'Because you'll be making it yourself.' Then they start to cry. They moan and kick and curse, but I don't care. This isn't my first time dealing with children.

So, I wander off the hill, feeling a chill in the air.

Then, I see them. Small at first, they were like teeny tiny people made of ice.

The children ran over to the snow angels and began to cry.

The angels were attracted to sadness, and so they burst into cold blue fire. There the children would poke at the cold, feeling their fingers and faces grow old.

They cried and the snow angels came, some bigger than those before.

And so it went, into the night.

Best get to sleep. It'll be morning soon. Got to prepare for the next problem and the angels that come with it.

CAST NO SHADOW

There are places in the world which are shaped by the changing of industry, altered by the whims of humanity, but Manchester is not one of these places.

It is, on the surface, an English city unlike no other. Its people are strange and socially awkward, and yet it is a city built on thievery. Its street names stolen from Mother London herself. While older ways carry Saxon heritage, of Wodin and his children back before they were Norse, back when they were simply Germanic. Even the name of the city is stolen, taken from the Romans. Mamucium or the hill of breasts.

It's all stolen, you see, but then that's how they like it - the people who built Manchester. Not the English, or the Saxon, but the original builders, the ones who existed back when Rome was but a child.

Manchester is a place of two worlds.

One is reserved for those travelling tourists that snap, point and drink. But the night, the night belongs to those few that live within the city. It is those who notice that something is strange. It is those that may listen to the call of its builders, of its thieves.

Manchester belongs to no-one, it seeps up creativity and culture like a sponge, though be wary or it'll spit you straight out. The city belongs to no single group. No culture can claim its ownership for long.

There are places where dangerous people come to work. Places where bailiffs fear to tread. This is a story of such a place, down a strip of canals known as the Cotton Fields. It is here, in the dead of winter, when all sane folk have gone elsewhere, it is here that the builders of this place begin to stir and look for prey.

***

Chaise wasn't a difficult child, she just refused to be a slave.

This world in which she belonged to was a cold place. It could be the middle of Summer, with sweat on her back, but still she felt it, that niggling chill, that reminder that she was far from safe.

Winter was good. It's bleak hours reminded her of the true nature of people. That for all their smiles and kindness, they were a vile bunch, one and all.

She lived on the street. Her dream was to live a life beyond survival. A world where the desperate need not steal to survive, nor be hanged for doing so.

Chaise watches two men bandy words with a local Copper, that police to you lot from across the pond. We call them Coppers. Common as pennies they are and as cheap to buy.

The Copper was listening to two men make their excuses. They were behind on their rent, and the local councillor had decided to make an example .

The Copper snaps his cudgel across the neck of the first man. The second got in the teeth. Both were Samson's men; a gang of Irish immigrants. In the old days, the councillors worked with men like that. Now they did as they pleased, and left Samson and his men in the gutter trying to pick up all those teeth.

If the councillor could come down on Samson what hope was there for Chaise and her lot?

She was skilled with her hands, but she was still a urchin. How long could being a child protect her from the eyes of vile men? Every day, The Pigeon tells her, 'My-My, you're going to be quite the beauty, aren't ya?'

The Pigeon is known all around the city, not just in the immigrant quarter known as Little Italy. He is known for two reasons: his 'children' are everywhere; and through them he saw everything.

Chaise ventures down the canal, her eyes making sure to check every corner, every shadow, all the places she could be pinched. She might still be a child, but some men don't mind. Some call it love. Some just want to make you cry, or make you dead.

'A beasts in man's clobber,' that's what Pigeon calls them. 'Not like me though, eh? Not sweet like dear old Pidge.'

That's why Chaise carries a razor, just in case.

She wasn't scared of men or beasts. Not tonight. No, what she was looking for were the Moonrakers.

They were thieves, everyone knew that. But no one could agree on what it is they stole.

Some said it was children. They'd nab you out your cot, just they could hear you laugh and cry. Then, when you got boring, they'd leave you out in the cold to die.

Some said it was skin they took. They'd wear your life like it were a nice new jacket.

Pigeon spoke of them. He was said to be a regular thief once. Stealing what he could with a band of outlaws. He was loved as well, stealing from nobles and giving to the beggars. People used to toast to his health back then. Now things have changed, and folk live in fear of Pigeon and his little birds.

His birds littered the streets. Some were clean enough, but most shared a mark or two. See, he liked to cut people. 'Tough love is all,' said the Pigeon. 'I do it cos I loves ya.'

Some say he does it as a warning to others. But Chaise knew the truth, he hurt because he wanted to, because nobody was coming to stop him.

The moon shines up from the blackened waters, and Chaise looks at her own reflection.

She was pretty. Why did she have to be pretty? Even the

ugliest flowers could still be snatched up, but the pretty daisies would always go first. One day, she knew that Pigeon would call, and she'd be taken in. He'd put her in a cage, and only let her out when someone wanted to play with his new little birdie.

That's why she was out tonight. That's why she sought the company of the Moonrakers. They may be monsters, but surely they were better than Pigeon. Surely they were better than a life in a cage.

***

Chaise makes her way down the canals. She walks as if she doesn't have a care in the world. This is difficult as the man following her makes no effort to be quiet.

Chaise removes the razor from her skirt, ready to strike but it was already too late. The large man snatches her hand, his other grabs her neck.

'Easy now, love. Drop the razor.'

She drops the blade, and gets a look at the guy.

He's one of the mill workers. Just another drunk.

The man's mouth split into a wide, blackened-toothed grin.

'How old are you, love?'

'Old enough to be one of the Pigeon's birds!'

If she could convince him she was the Pigeons property then he'd leave her be. Pigeon's known to pluck the feathers off those who upset him.

'Let me go,' she says, 'and the Pigeon won't hear of this.'

The man grabs her by the hair, and pulls out a tuft.

'Shut it, Bitch'

He knocks head against the sweaty stones under the bridge. Everything goes flat. The world hums like a whistle in the ear.

Chaise looks at the man, ready to defend himself. Only, he's looking up at something. It's a hook on a wire. Looks like a fishing line, only it's dangling in the air. There's one, and two, and on and on. They're all just floating there, making their way to the man.

'What's going on?' he says.

Then Chaise watches as the hooks bury themselves in the man.

They go in his hands, and his arms. They go in his shoulders. Up and down his legs. They're in his back, and all along his giant belly. They even go in his face, his eyes, and the top of his head.

The man stands there for a moment, grunting and panting. Then, Chaise watches all those wires begin to pull, causing the man to float a few inches off the ground.

'Hello,' says the man.

It speaks with the same voice, but it's clearly not the same man.

The man floats his way over to Chaise. The hooks pull on his features causing him to smile.

'Hope I didn't scare you?'

'What are you?' says Chaise.

The hooks pull on the man's face causing an eyebrow to rise, ever so slowly. 'You know the answer to that.'

'Moonraker?'

Chaise follows the hooks up to the strings. There, she stares up into the sky looking for the person who was holding up the man. All she saw was the moon, huge and full, it colours the world around her in silver and shadows.

'Why are you here?' asks the man with hooks in his face.

Chaise looks for the razor to defend herself.

'I got lost.'

'No,' says the man. 'That's a lie.'

'What's it to you if I lie?'

'You said you belonged to a pigeon. I know lots of pigeons, but none of them own anyone, certainly not you.'

'I said I work for The Pigeon. He's dangerous, you know, so you should let me go before anything bad happens to you.'

The man continues to float just off the ground, held up by all those wires and hooks. 'Why do you want to find the Moonrakers?'

'I don't know,' says Chaise. 'I thought you could help.'

'Do we look helpful?'

Chaise watches the blood run down his hooks. The constant drip-drap-dripping like the start of Summer rain.

He begins to float down the canal, pulled along by a series of hooks and strings. 'Come,' says the man, though it was obvious that he was no longer a man at all.

***

The walkways spiral and snake into various directions. It's as if the city likes to confuse its travels, leading them to various dead ends. The man on the strings does not get lost however. For him, every cobbled step is as familiar as the back of his hand.

Moonlight bleeds down through the gaps of the city. Chaise follows the man under the bridges through a world of iron and brick. The air is thick with sweat like a man caught with his pants down.

The man stops by the entrance to the black bridge. Chaise has never seen this bridge before, nor did she know what part of town they were in. The man stares at the entrance to the bridge.

'What are you looking at?' says Chaise.

Somewhere along their travels, the man had ceased to hold himself up correctly. It was as if he had forgotten how people move. For the last twenty minutes, his head lolled back as if he were staring up at the stars. When he speaks, his head continues to stare up. The hooks in his mouth move practically, they open and close to let out the sound, but they didn't move like the lips of a regular person. It was like a puppeteer who grown tired.

'I'm reading the words.'

'What words?' says Chaise. 'There are no words. It's just a bridge.'

The man points above the bridge. 'Cast no Shadow.'

Chaise looks but she sees no words. 'Is this a game?'

'It is a warning,' says the man. 'To travel across the bridge of black you must first give up your shadow.'

Chaise approaches the bridge. Up close, she can see the intricacies of its craft. It wasn't just a thing of flat metal. First, it wasn't built of metal at all, but some kind of polished black stone. Someone had carved it into shapes. Roses with thorns as big as fingers. Hedgehogs, foxes, owls. All stand watching, as lifelike as the real thing though carved and shaped from a stone so dark that even the shadows around it look pale in comparison.

'Are you ready?' says the man.

Chaise looks at the bridge. It rises up above her. She cannot see the other side. 'Will it keep me safe from the Pigeon?'

'Oh yes,' says the man. 'None are as far from harm as those who cast no shadow.'

Chaise watches the blood run down his face. 'Ok,' she says. 'What do I have do?'

Just like that, she watches a string fall from the air. Like the ones stuck in the man, it has a hook on the end. It comes down slowly and stops by Chaise's side.

'What do I do with this?'

'Shadows are loyal,' says the man. 'They won't stay unless you make them.'

Chaise knew how to make it stay. She takes the string with a hook on the end. The moment she feels the cold rope, she watches the shadow begin to move.

It waves its hands, pleading in silence.

'It doesn't want me to do it?'

'It,' says the man, 'is a he.'

'Shadows are boys?'

'Not all of them. But this one is. And yes, of course it

doesn't want to leave. It's been there your whole life.'

Chaise lifts the hook. It's heavy and so sharp that it cuts her finger. Then, she shoves the hook into her shadow. She watches it writhe and fight and scream its silent words. The rope begin to pull. Like the hooks in the man, it tugs at her shadow, pulling it away from Chaise.

'What do we do now?' says Chaise, but as the shadow is taken away, she feels herself begin to fall.

'I know,' says the man. 'But there is no other way.'

Chaise goes to speak, but the words are gone. It should scare her, but the feelings are gone as well. She just lies there on the floor, and then nothing ...

***

The shadow kicked and fought, but the man was used to such dramatic displays.

'Cry all you want,' says the man. 'But the deed is done.'

The shadow was not convinced.

'Enough. You've had your fun. You left us once, got yourself all tangled up with people. But now you're here. Now I have you, and it's time to come home.'

The shadow looks down at Chaise. She lies on the ground, ever so still.

'Yes,' says the man. 'She seemed very nice. But I need a body, one that's not guarded by a shadow. Yet, after the things this man has done, his shadow still decides to poison me.'

The man looks down at his own shadow. Unlike the body which is held by hooks and rope, the shadow moves of its own accord. It points and laughs.

The hooks release from the man's body. Then, they begin to make their way to Chaise. One by one, they sink into her flesh. There is no blood, no twisted parody of human movement. The hooks sink in gently, ever so soft. It's done so expertly that, once finished, one wouldn't be able to see the hooks at all.

It was the shadows, see. They once were separate, but now they're like dogs. Loyal, ready to follow you anywhere. They try and keep you safe, but they can't see well in the dark, they can't warn you from the things that move in the winter.

People think they're called Moonrakers because that's when they come. Truth is, they come all the time, well, whenever it's dark. The reason we call them Moonrakers is because that's the only time anyone's seen then, the only time anyone's got away.

It's light, see. Moonlight isn't much, but it's enough to make a shadow. It's enough for them to stare up at the Moonraker, to let them know that this one is protected. They can't fight, but they can stop them using you like a toy. They can poison your body making it so no one would ever think that thing was really a person.

Nobody remembers what we did to earn the trust of shadows, but whatever it was, it must have been good.

Once all the hooks had made their way into Chaise, she stands and inspects her body.

'Good,' she says. 'Not a mark.'

The shadow by her side struggles to free itself from a hook.

'Enough of that,' she says. 'We've got work to do.'

She turns to the other shadow, the one still latched onto the man full of holes and blood. The shadow pleads for her to sever the connection, to let it go.

'No,' she says. 'I think you should stay right here. That way, they can bury you with it, and as you lay there in the dark of the ground, I will come and see you, and I will laugh, and laugh, and laugh.'

With that, Chaise makes her way along the canals, following behind is her shadow. It doesn't move like it should, but then, nobody will notice. They never do.

Onwards she goes, with the moon at her front and the shadow at her back. Both trying to warn the world that something was terribly wrong.

Back in town, she runs into the Pigeon.

'What are you doing out so late, eh?'

'I was lost,' says Chaise.

'Lost? What do you mean lost? You're lucky you ain't dead.'

'It's ok,' says Chaise. 'I'm not lost now. Not anymore.'

The Pigeon didn't know what to say to that. 'Well, come inside. We'll soon get you warmed up.'

'Do you have any more stories to tell?' says Chaise.

'Oh yes, my dear. Lots of stories.'

'Do you have any about the Moonrakers?'

The Pigeon made an uncomfortable noise. 'Perhaps. But, It's best not to talk about such things on a night like this.'

Chaise looks at his shadow. She watches it silently tug on the Pigeon's jacket.

'I have a story about the Moonrakers, would you like to hear it?'

'You, a story? Didn't think you were the type?'

'I've changed,' says Chaise. 'People do it all the time.'

'Go on then,' says the Pigeon. 'Tell me this story.'

'Did you know, people call the Moonrakers thieves. But that's not true.'

'It isn't?'

'No,' she says. 'Truth is, it was the shadows that came stealing. They tricked the Moonrakers and stole their property.'

'And what did they steal?' says the pigeon.

Chaise gives one final look down at the shadow of the man. She watches it wave in a series of frantic gestures. Then, seeing it ignored, she begins to smile.

'They stole me. They stole you. But don't worry, that'll change.'

THE DEAD POLICE

'There's someone in the garden,' said Maude as she stared through the window.

When her husband refused to look up from his newspaper, she gave him a kick.

'Ow!' said Lionel. 'What's that for?'

'You're not listening. There's someone in the garden.'

'It's probably just a couple of kids fetching a ball or something.'

Maude looked again. 'There's only one of them, and it definitely isn't a child.'

'What do you want ?' said Lionel. 'I'm sure they'll go away.'

'It's just standing there.'

'What do you mean, it?' Lionel, rose to his feet. 'I thought you said someone, not something?'

'I don't know,' said Maude. 'Do you think we should call someone?'

Lionel looked out of the window. He saw the figure in the back, and then, just as quickly, he closed the curtains.

'Yeah,' he said. 'It's definitely an It.'

'We should call the police. Get someone to take it away.'

'Not the police,' said Lionel. 'It'll only make things worse.'

'But there's a thing in the garden!'

'Yes,' said Lionel, 'but the moment the police come round it'll affect the property value. We'll never sell the place then.'

Maude didn't say anything. She just gave him 'The Look' and while yes, they did have a thing in their garden, and yes,

Lionel was in fact a man in his forties, but still, in over twelve years of marriage, he'd not figured out how to survive 'The Look.'

'Fine,' he said. 'I'll ring the police if that makes you happy?'

'And safe,' said Maude.

He removed the phone from the wall mount and dialled the emergency services.

'State the service you require,' said a voice on the other end of the line.

'Erm, Police, please.'

'Has there been a crime you wish to report?'

'No,' said Lionel with a sigh. 'Not that kind of police. I, er, want the other kind, please.'

'One moment,' said the voice and there was a pause.

Finally, a new voice on the other end started to speak.

'Hello there, me old mucker. How can I help you today?'

'Hi,' said Lionel. 'Is this the err police?'

'Yes,' said the voice. 'This is, as you say, the police.'

'Look,' said Lionel, 'we've got one of them, you know, one of your lot. It's in the garden.'

'Oh? Lucky you.'

'Lucky me? I'll have you know, my wife and I moved out of the city to avoid this sort of thing. So, we'd appreciate you taking this seriously.'

'Rest assured, this issue is of utmost seriousness. Now, can I have your name, sir?'

'Fletcher, Lionel Fletcher.'

'Well, Mr Fletcher, make sure your exits are locked, the windows are closed, and all manner of cat-flaps and pet entrances are bolted firmly shut. Would you be so kind as to tell me whether the person is in one piece?'

'What sort of question is that?'

'I'll tell you what sort of question it is, Mr Fletcher. It's the kind of question that could mean the difference between a bad evening and something much-much worse.'

'Right,' said Lionel. 'When you put it like that.'

He looked through the window. 'It seems fine, well except for the whole ... disgustingness of it.'

'All of its limbs, Mr Fletcher? Arms, feet? Hands, fingers, knees and toes knees and toes?'

'I thought you said this was serious?'

'Apologies, Mr Fletcher. Just trying to keep up morale.'

'It's got both of its feet,' said Lionel. 'Both arms too, but it's too dark to see the hands.'

'That's right, Mr Fletcher. We do sometimes forget how different you lot really are.'

'What does that mean?'

'It means we'll be with you shortly, Mr Fletcher.'

'Right,' said Lionel. 'So, what should I do now?'

'Keep safe,' said the voice on the other end of the line. 'And make sure to not let it touch you. A single scratch is all it takes.'

'All it takes for what?' said Lionel, but the line was already dead.

'So,' said Maude. 'What did they say?'

'Lock all the doors. Can't let that thing in.'

'Well the doors are locked,' said Maude. 'Might be the country, but we're not mad.'

'Windows too, and the cat-flap?'

Maude said nothing for a moment.

'Well,' she said. 'I haven't locked the cat flap.'

'WHAT?'

'How could I?' said Maude. 'My little Twitchy-kins is still out there.'

'That bloody cat!' said Lionel.

He ran over to the front door. Lionel locked the flap, but saw it was encrusted with mud.

'That cat of yours? Does he like getting dirty?'

'He's our cat, love. And no, my little Twitchy-bobs is a good boy. He keeps nice and clean for his mummy-wummy.'

There were dirty smears on the carpet he swallowed

hard. Something had crawled into the house.

'What is it?' said Maude. 'You look like you've seen a ghost.'

'Try not to panic, love, but I think we've got a hand in the house.'

Maude frowned in confusion. 'You mean like a helper?'

'No, you idiot. I mean like a hand, like a human hand. Well, not human, not anymore.'

'Lionel, you're not making any sense.'

'There's a hand crawling about somewhere.'

Lionel followed the trail into the kitchen.

'Is that bad?'

'The guy on the phone said all it takes is one scratch.'

'Then what?'

Lionel didn't know, but he could imagine. So, to keep the image from his mind, he continued on, following the dirty trail along the floor and into the kitchen.

'You know,' said Maude. 'I heard they're not so bad.'

'Who?'

Maude pointed to the garden.

'Are you crazy? It's a thing, of course it's bad! They say so on the news.'

'I know,' said Maude, 'but have you actually seen one do anything? I mean, except bother people?'

'It's a dead thing, love. It being alive is bad enough.'

In the kitchen, Lionel crawled on the floor. He pushed aside the bins. He looked into the corners. Maude opened the cupboards, and pushed aside the tins.

'What are you doing?' said Lionel.

'What does it look like? I'm searching for the hand.'

'In the pasta cupboard?'

'Well, why not? It might be hungry.'

They heard a bang from upstairs.

'What should we do?' said Maude.

'We need some protection.'

So, the two went up the stairs. Lionel led the way armed

with a lamp, while Maude came up behind with a colander.

'What are you holding there?'

'Thought we might use it to trap the thing.'

'It's a hand,' said Lionel, 'not a spider.'

Outside the bedroom, they heard a sound. It was wet, like someone stepping in paint. The door groans its way open, and there, on the bed, Lionel sees their cat Twitch gnawing on a severed hand.

'Oh look,' said Maude, 'has my little ickle soldier caught himself some din-dins? Who's a big scary hunter, eh? Yes you are. Yes you are.'

Lionel raised his lamp. 'Get it off him. Now!'

'No thanks. I tried last time, remember?'

'That was a bird,' said Lionel. 'This is different. Who knows what that hand's doing to him.'

Twitch bites off a strip of mouldy green skin. The hand twitched and tried desperately to drag itself away.

'Well,' said Maude. 'It does look to be suffering.'

She went over to the bed. 'Come now, my little Twitchy-Tits, let go of the hand. Look, you're hurting it.'

Twitch did not wish to give up his prize so easily. With a hiss, he swiped at Maude, who in turn swatted him with the colander.

'Enough of your cheek. I said scram.'

Twitch gave the hand a look, one that said 'You wait till next time' then, quick as a flash, he was out of the room and down the stairs.

Maude picked up the hand with tender care.

'What do you think you're doing?'

'Look. He's shaking.'

'First of all,' said Lionel. 'It's not a he! It is an 'It.'

Maude looked at him. 'And second?'

'You what?'

'You said 'First of all' that normally means you have more to say.'

'Yes,' said Lionel. 'Second, they told me to stay away from

it. 'One scratch' they said, that's all it takes.'

Maude gave the hand a stroke. 'Look, he's shaking.'

'Put it down.'

'Do you think he's scared?'

'Hands don't get scared,' said Lionel, 'especially the hands of dead things.'

With his lamp raised high, Lionel approached the hand.

'Drop it, love. I'll do the rest.'

'No,' said Maude. 'Don't you hurt it.'

'Better it than us.'

Then, as he went to snatch the hand away, it raised a yellow fingernail, and quick as thought, it scratched them. It wasn't hard or painful. There was a little blood on each of their hands.

'Now look what you've done,' said Maude. 'You've scared it.'

Lionel didn't respond. He was too busy listening to the sound.

It came from the garden. It was quiet at first, almost so that you weren't sure you actually heard it. Then, as the seconds became minutes, Lionel could hear the sound, it was as clear as day.

'What is it?' said Maude. 'What's going on? Is someone shouting?'

Lionel put down the lamp. 'No,' he said. 'It's not that.'

'What then?'

'Someone's crying.'

There was a knock at the front door, loud and professional.

Lionel felt his stomach begin to twist.

'Who's that?' said Maude.

'Who else is it going to be at this time? It's the police.'

They left the hand trapped under the colander. They put a few books on top to make sure it couldn't get out.

'Don't worry,' said Maude. 'We'll be back.'

'Stop talking to it like that.'

'Like what?'

'Like it's a pet.'

'It's not so bad. A lot less mess. Plus, I don't think it needs to eat.'

Lionel went down the stairs and opened the door.

He did his best to smile, and pretend that the person on the other side was human.

'Here is,' said the man. 'Mr Fletcher, I presume?'

'Uhm,' said Lionel.

The man leaned in and sniffed. 'Yes, I thought I recognised your smell from our earlier conversation.'

'Smell?' said Lionel. 'How could you smell me? We were on the phone?'

The man tapped the stub of his nose. 'It's not just for decoration, Mr Fletcher. Now, may I come in?'

He was tall, much taller than any man had right to be, and then there were the eyes. They filled most of the face, like a frog, they were all damp and sticky. The skin was grey and dripped all over the floor.

Lionel had no choice to but let the man inside.

'Now, don't want you to worry, Mr Fletcher. I'll soon be out your hair, have everything all nice and tickety boo.'

Maude came downstairs, and after Lionel invited the man inside, the three of them walked to the window facing the back garden.

Lionel could hear the sound so very clearly. It was the thing in the garden, and it was crying.

'Frightful noise,' said the man. 'Heard some folk say it sounds like nails on a chalkboard.'

It didn't sound like that to Lionel.

No, the sound he heard filled him with pity. The thing in the garden may have looked like a monster, all rotten and falling to pieces, but it didn't sound like one. It sounded like something young, something scared.

'Are you alright, Mr Fletcher? Got a strange look to you.'

'Sorry,' said Lionel. 'I just don't like having things in my garden.'

'It's not a thing,' said Maude.

Lionel told her to shh.

'But it's not,' said Maude. 'It's a girl.'

The man gave her a big confused look. 'Very good, Mrs Fletcher. Most people don't have an ear for it. Most people hear only groans and moans.'

'Sounds clear enough to me,' said Maude. 'She's a girl, and she sounds in pain.'

The man gave Maude a funny look, and before she could say anything else, Lionel told her, 'Why don't you make us drink, love.'

'Alright,' said Maude. 'Fancy a tea? Coffee?'

'No thank you, Mrs Fletcher. I don't tend to go in for that sort of thing. But, if you wouldn't mind, I'll pop into the garden and do my job.'

Lionel gave the man a nod, and watched him head into the garden.

He left the door open, and Lionel could hear them both.

The thing was indeed a she, and over and over, she spoke.

'Please, help me. Please, help me!'

Lionel didn't realise at first, but she'd been saying it all night. That groaning he heard from the garden. He knew what the words meant now. It was the scratch from the hand. It made him understand, though he wished with all his heart that he didn't.

'Please, help me.'

When the man spoke, he did so in the same language as the girl. To anyone listening, it would sound like a grumbling moan, nonsensical and strange. But, Lionel could hear the truth. The news say that thing is a mindless monster, and yet here he was listening to them talk in its language.

'Please, help me.'

'Don't worry,' said the man. 'Help is here.'

The woman regarded him as if she were a child deciding

whether or not to trust a stranger.

'Please, help me?'

'Yes,' said the man. 'But first, you must help me.'

With that, he leapt upon her, and tearing her apart, bit by bit, the man, the thing began to feast.

Lionel couldn't watch for long. He went back into the kitchen, to join his wife. They both stood by the kettle not saying a word.

Once finished, the man came in licking his lips. He asked for a bag to collect the rest. When asked what for, the man simply stated, 'Boys are hungry.'

He collected the hand from upstairs, and was nibbling the meat off the fingers as he came down the stairs and went out the front door.

'So, that's it then?' said Lionel.

'As I said, Mr Fletcher. There's no need to worry. You can rest easy, we are here for your protection.'

Lionel could see the hand of the girl. The man had stripped away most of the meat, yet still it moved, twitching in pain.

'Right,' said Lionel. 'If you say so.'

That night, they got into bed. They didn't say a word, and Lionel held his wife and listened as she cried herself to sleep.

Then, in early hours of the morning, the house phone began to ring.

Lionel did his best to ignore it, but the phone continued to ring for over an hour.

'What time do you call this?'

'Good evening, Mr Fletcher.'

'You?'

'Yes, Mr Fletcher. Me.'

'What's the meaning of this? Why are you calling me so late?'

'Just wanted to ask if it touched you, Mr Fletcher.'

'You what?'

'The thing in your garden, sir. Though, your wife preferred to call it |'Her' Just wanted to make sure it didn't touch you.'

Lionel looked at the scratch upon his hand.

'No?'

He could hear the thing sniff down the phone.

'You wouldn't be lying to me, would you, Mr Fletcher? Telling me porkie pies?'

'No,' said Lionel. 'It didn't touch us.'

'That's good. Very good. I like you, Mr Fletcher, and I'd like to think you feel the same. So, it'd be a shame for something to come between us.'

'What do you mean?'

'It's a defence of there's, Mr Fletcher. One scratch.'

'Then what happens?'

'Then you become like them,' said the voice. 'But you already know that. Don't you, Mr Fletcher.'

Lionel heard someone knock at the front door. It was loud and professional.

'Now, don't want you to worry, Mr Fletcher. I'll soon have everything all nice and tickety boo.'

Printed in Great Britain
by Amazon